Dééd Yázhí

Little Girl Warrior
Who Came Home

Book Two

By Evangeline Parsons Yazzie

SALINABOOKSHELFINC
MULTICULTURAL PUBLISHING

Designed by Corey Begay

ISBN 978-1-893354-27-2
First Edition, Second Printing
Printed in the United States of America

Salina Bookshelf, Inc.
Flagstaff, Arizona 86001
www.salinabookshelf.com
www.facebook.com/salinabookshelf

Dedication

To my Lord and Savior Jesus Christ who has blessed me with storytellers throughout my life. He brought stories to mind to make this novel a reality.

To my mother and father, the late Etta Yazzie and Rev. Bruce Yazzie, Sr. who told me my first stories and taught me the value of storytelling.

To my maternal-grandmother, the one who safely deposited the stories in my mind and in my heart by saying, "Kwe'é shíighahgi dah nídaah, shitsóí yázhí, nił hashne'. Hwéeldi ..." Sit right here next to me, my little granddaughter, let me tell you a story. At Fort Sumner...

To my four wonderful children who were my first audience to hear my stories and who listened anxiously. In listening to my stories, they kept the stories alive within me.

To Navajo girls and women who are and continue to be the strength of the matriarchal society of the Navajo people.

To our precious Navajo elders who when called upon to speak, always begin their speech with, "Hwéeldidę́ę́' nináda'iisdee' yę́ędą́ą́'..." When they came back from Fort Sumner... Navajo elders refer to the time when our Navajo ancestors came back from Fort Sumner (after surviving four long years of prisoner of war status) as if that was when time began for the Navajo people.

To my many friends who have voiced words of encouragement in this endeavor.

Table of Contents

"Háshinee', háshinee', háshinee', háshinee'! Ayóó
'ánihíínísh'ní! Nihilahkéí kǫ́ǫ́ siké 'ałdó'." *Dear ones, dear
ones, dear ones, dear ones! I love you. Your older brothers are
sitting here too.* Dééd Yázhí and her younger sister covered
their mouths to keep their sobs from escaping their mouths.
Looking across the river, they saw lights flickering around the
place where a picket fort was situated. Several soldiers were
assigned to each picket fort that surrounded the reservation set
aside for the Naabeehó *Navajo* people. Dééd Yázhí knew one or
two soldiers were always assigned to guard their picket fort at
night, so she and her younger sister did not allow themselves to
breathe. Dééd Yázhí figured her father had also become aware
of the flickering lights, and so silence was all that greeted them.
No singing could be heard.

Once the flickering lights became stationary, Dééd Yázhí
and her younger sister listened intently for more singing. Only
silence met them. After a long stretch of time, the sisters heard
sounds coming from the water. There was the sound of the
running water being disturbed. There was the quiet sound of
voices. Fear gripped Dééd Yázhí's heart. She asked herself, what
if the soldiers have kidnapped a Naabeehó man to lure us?
What if they have come to kidnap us and take us to the other
side, away from our families? Her head began to ache from the
various scary scenarios that marched in a determined manner
through her mind.

Dééd Yázhí and her younger sister grabbed one another and
clung to each other when they heard soft Navajo words being
spoken. The soft familiar words reassured Dééd Yázhí and her
younger sister as they peered into the darkness. Dééd Yázhí was

startled by a man who had silently approached her. She heard the young man speaking to her and her younger sister. It was her younger brother speaking to them. In excitement, Dééd Yázhí and her younger sister hugged and cried with their brother who came to rescue them.

Their brother told his sisters about the urgency for them to move fast because of the young warriors who were standing in the swirling waters ready to help them cross the river. Dééd Yázhí and her younger sister heard the song being sung again which sent fountains of bravery and strength through the veins of the two sisters.

Their brother announced,

"Nihizhé'é díí tó nílínígíí tsé'naají nihiba' sizį," *Our father is standing on the opposite side of this river, waiting for you.* The two sisters hugged each other and asked,

"Nihimá shą'?" *Where is our mother?*

"Níléí kéédahwiit'įįdi nihiba' sidá. T'áá hazhó'ó shik'is dóó nihizhé'é dóó binaabaahii danilínígíí t'éiyá díí tó nílínígíí tsé'naa nidanihidii'ish biniiyé kwe'é neiikai." *She is waiting for you at the place where we make our home. Only my brother and our father and his warriors are here to take you to the other side of this river.*

Dééd Yázhí told her younger brother of her young sons and Kiizhóní *Pretty Boy* then told of their sister's husband who is a member of the Naashgálí dine'é *Mescalero people* and their child. The information caused their younger brother to spring into action when he realized the young warriors would have to stand in the water longer than they had planned to bring his sisters and their children across the river.

8

Dééd Yázhí's younger brother whistled several low whistles then he listened for a response. They heard a low whistle coming from the eastern direction. Once again, Dééd Yázhí's younger brother heard a low whistle, only this time the responding low whistle sounded like it came from a closer distance. He whistled another low whistle and soon they heard the rustling of young cottonwood tree branches. Soon Dééd Yázhí and her younger sister were reunited with their little sons and Kiizhóní and the Mescalero man. The group quickly hugged one another in gratitude of their reunion.

To prepare to cross the river, Dééd Yázhí bravely handed her moccasins to Kiizhóní, the young man who had cared for her and her son as they had been forced to walk the many hundreds of miles to Fort Sumner in eastern New Mexico Territory.

Fort Sumner was established for the Naabeehó *Navajo* people who were being held as prisoners of war because they were wrongly accused of raiding and stealing from the Mexicans and the New Mexicans by a greedy general and a governor who wanted to mine the land the Naabeehó people occupied. The Navajo-United States war was a smokescreen for their greed. Dééd Yázhí's mind flew back to the time when the hateful soldiers rode on their horses, pushing Dééd Yázhí and her people to walk eastward, covering twelve to fifteen miles a day regardless of how tired and weary the Naabeehó people were. Dééd Yázhí and her Naabeehó people were forced to cross too many angry rivers that claimed the lives of many of her Naabeehó children and women and men.

Facing the swift running river, Dééd Yázhí remembered how she greeted each angry river that she and her Naabeehó people crossed by telling it her clan, saying that she was a member of the Water Flows Together People *Tó 'Aheedlíinii dine'é*. Once I greeted the river as I stood on the bank of each river, I made the river my relative and I asked it to allow me to cross in safety, she thought. This river, the Pecos River was no different, except for one important aspect. What was different was that her father was standing on the other side of the river. He was singing the song he used to sing to her and her younger sister throughout their young lives.

Dééd Yázhí felt a hand reach out to her in the dark. She heard a voice and recognized the sound of her younger brother's voice, who said,

"Tsjįłgo 'ádeiit'įįgo t'éí. Nihizhé'é binaabaahii nihíká'iijeeh. Tó nílínígíí tsé'naa nidanihidoo'ish. Nihí, shí dóó shitsilí, 'éí nihííníitą'go tsé'naa nidiikah. Nihizhé'é tó nílínígíí tsé'naadi nihiba' sizį. Txį'. Shiiłtsóód, shádí, ni 'áłtsé dooleeł. Niyáázh, nihida', bíká tsé'naa ninádiit'ash." *We need to hurry. Our father's warriors are going to help us. They will help us get across the river. We, me and my younger brother, will take you across by holding on to you. Our father is waiting for us on the other side of the river. Let's go. Take hold of me, my older sister, you will be first. Our brother and I will come back across for your son, our nephew.* With those words, Dééd Yázhí held the strong hand of her younger brother and walked to the river's edge.

As she bravely placed one foot into the cold, churning water, she took a moment to greet the water as she held the hand of her younger brother. Behind her, she could hear her younger sister as she also sang the song her father was singing. The bank of the river dropped away but Dééd Yázhí was picked up by the strong arms of her younger brother. She held on to him as he allowed her father's young warriors to hold him up as they handed them over to the next warrior. Tears mingled with the thick waters that splashed on the two siblings as they held tightly on to each other as they were handed over to a tall warrior who picked them up and said,

"Yá'át'ééh, shilah," *Hello, my sister,* before he handed them to the next warrior, who also greeted her with words that established their relationship. To each greeting, Dééd Yázhí breathed,

"Aoo', yá'át'ééh," *Yes, greetings,* through chattering teeth, due to the cold water. The same cold water caused each warrior to sway slightly as he handed her and her younger brother onto the next strong warrior, as they all braved the strong current with their arms locked.

The water was very cold and threatened to pull Dééd Yázhí out of the arms of her younger brother and the young warriors, but the strength of the warriors kept them safe. The swirling waters no longer frightened Dééd Yázhí as they were being carried from one strong warrior to the next.

Moving westward, Dééd Yázhí knew she was moving away from her son, Kiizhóní *Pretty Boy,* and her younger sister and her family, but on the western side of the river was her father bravely waiting for his firstborn child — his daughter to be placed in his arms.

Dééd Yázhí heard her father singing the same song that united their minds and emotions a few days ago, and now the song was physically bringing them together. As she and her younger brother were handed over to the next warrior, Dééd

Yázhí could hear the song her father sang become louder. Behind her, she could hear the young men greet her younger sister, whose teeth also chattered with a greeting. She also heard her little one whimpering in the arms of Kiizhóní. Dééd Yázhí looked back toward the eastern bank of the river but all she could see were the tall, faint figures of each warrior as they braved the cold churning water to bring their leader's children to safety.

Dééd Yázhí looked toward the western bank of the river to make sure her father was still standing there. She could hear the beautiful song he was singing, but at times, she could not see him because of the way the warriors preferred to hold up her and her younger brother to place them in the arms of the next strong warrior. Finally, she felt her younger brother lowering her to her feet and her cold numbed feet touched the sandy bottom of the river.

The next few moments were a blur. Dééd Yázhí turned toward the open arms of her father and collapsed into his arms. For an instant, she wanted to bite herself to see if this was no longer a dream but reality, but she was so overcome with emotion that she could not think or talk. All Dééd Yázhí was capable of was to just lean into her father's body. As she leaned her head against her father's warm dry chest, she listened for the sound of his voice. She leaned in even closer, aware that she was crushing his chest. Her father spoke. The memories of her childhood came charging into her mind, forcing dry sobs to loudly begin to exit her body. In between her dry sobs, Dééd Yázhí heard her father softly say,

"Ních'aad, shiyázhí. Nikáa'jį' hazlįį́. Yisdéíníyá. Yáa, yáa, yáa, ha'át'íí da shą' bii' tádííníyá. Ha'át'ííshį́į bii' tádííníyáhígíí k'ad bits'ą́ąjį' dah didíínáál. K'ad shaa néínídzá. Háshinee', shiyázhí. Ních'aad, shiyázhí. Nizhé'é nishłį́. Tó 'Aheedlíinii dine'é nílį́ dóó Ma'ii Deeshgiizhnii dine'é bá shínílchíín. Táchii'nii dine'é danicheii 'áádóó Tó Díchʼíiʼnii dine'é 'éí daninálí. 'Ákót'éego shiyázhí nílį́. Nikáa'jį' hazlįį́, shiyázhí, ních'aad." *Don't cry, my little one. You have survived. You have been spared. I can only wonder what you have been through. Whatever you have been through, you can now walk away from. You have come back to me. My dear little one. Don't cry, my little one. I am your father. You belong to the Water Flows Together People and you are born for the Coyote Pass People. The Red Running into the Water People are your maternal grandfathers and the Bitter Water People are your paternal grandfathers. In that way, you are my little one. You have survived, my little one, don't cry.*

Dééd Yázhí was oblivious to all that was happening around her. She could only concentrate on her father's soothing words and his strong arms that held her. At her father's soothing words that she had yearned to hear for the past few years, Dééd Yázhí turned her head toward her father's chest and forced her sobs to subside for an instant to allow herself to breathe in the scent of her father. In the silence, she breathed in a deep breath that hurt her lungs as she forced them to open to their fullest capacity so she could permeate her mind with her father's scent.

Once again the scent of her father caused memories of her childhood that represented safety, happiness, and contentment to rush into her mind. Dééd Yázhí's weak arms clung onto her father, not only to hold him close to her but also to keep the memories of her childhood from fading. Her dry, sad sobs would not subside. She could not hold onto her father any longer, so she allowed herself to be held by her father's strong arms. His words were now muffled by his chest, and his strong arms and the scent of him kept her father close and kept the memories racing back into her mind.

Dééd Yázhí shook her head to chase the doubt that surfaced, which told her it was only a dream. With all her strength, she leaned into her father's chest once again. The parent she loved so dearly was the one who was holding her now. It was the memories of her father whose songs and gentle words that had helped her survive such horrendous experiences since her and her younger sister's capture. During her capture, it was the memory of her father that held her and kept her safe. Now, her father was holding her in his arms as her wet clothes saturated his warm, soft clothing. She had kept the promise she made to herself—that of not allowing herself to cry until she saw her father again. Her frail thin body just shook from the many waves of tears that were forced to the surface.

Slowly, the memories of the last few years were being swept into one corner of her mind, allowing the safe, sweet memories of her childhood to begin racing back into her mind.

In the safety of her father's strong arms, Dééd Yázhí's mind left the river banks of the swift-running Pecos River and settled gently on her childhood to the times when her father was home. Being a respected War Leader, her father was away from home many days, but when he was home, he would easily scoop her up in his arms and carry her around. Dééd Yázhí remembered it was when she was in her father's arms and through her father's gentle words that she began to become aware of her environment outside of the hooghan nímazí *round hogan*.

Her father showed her many things, and when he did, he named the many plants, trees, bugs, reptiles, and insects as he took her on walks to explore around their home. Dééd Yázhí thought her father was the one who gave the many plants, trees, bugs, reptiles, and insects their name because it was in his arms that she first heard their names.

"Díí gad át'é." *This is a juniper tree.*

"Díí dibé 'át'é. Dibé." *This is a sheep. Sheep.*

"Díí tł'ízí yázhí 'át'é." *This is a kid goat.*

"Díí béhí 'át'é." *This is a little lamb.*

"Díí ts'ah át'é." *This is a sage brush.*

"Díí łį́į́' át'é. " *This is a horse.* And,

"Níléí yá 'át'é," *That is the sky,* were the many words Dééd Yázhí heard her father say.

Dééd Yázhí remembered how her father's deep voice carried across the valley when he spoke to his warriors, but when he spoke to her, his voice was deep and soft and very comforting. She noticed her father's voice was also very soft when he spoke to her mother and her younger sister. It was through her mother's and her father's kind voices that Dééd Yázhí felt the deep love her parents had for her and her siblings.

The soft whimpers of her young son brought her mind back to the Pecos River bank. Reluctantly, Dééd Yázhí released her hold on her father. She noticed her sister had safely crossed the river and was being carried to their father. Dééd Yázhí looked around for her younger brothers, but they had returned to the eastern side of the river to help bring her baby and Kiizhóní across the river. Her baby was tied to the back of Kiizhóní. The soft sobs of her younger sister and her father were deafening. The only sounds were of her father greeting her younger sister as they both cried.

As Dééd Yázhí stood patiently waiting for her baby and Kiizhóní, her father's and her younger sister's cries released more memories of her own childhood. In the darkness, Dééd Yázhí looked at her father holding her younger sister. Not wanting to alert the soldiers, father and daughter quieted and held one another as they softly cried.

Dééd Yázhí remembered that her younger sister had been her constant playmate and the environment around their home had been their playground. Even as little children, she and her siblings were being trained for warfare. Her younger brothers were being trained to become War Leaders just like their father, while Dééd Yázhí and her younger sister, Dzáníbaa', were being trained to become the wives of War Leaders for the Naabeehó people of Dziłíjiin *Black Mesa.*

To her siblings, Dééd Yázhí was known as Dédii and to her relatives she was called Dééd Yázhí. She grew up among many maternal relatives. Her maternal grandparents doted on her and her younger brothers and her younger sister.

Dééd Yázhí's thoughts were interrupted when she heard the frightened cries of her little one as he was handed over to her father. Soon, the cries of her younger sister's baby joined the sounds of the cries of her own little one. Cries of the little ones mingled with the low cries of her father. Dééd Yázhí thought the river ran deep but her tears on this night seemed to run even deeper as her tears refused to stop making their way down her face.

Once everyone had crossed the river and the warriors had all been accounted for, Hashké Yił Naabaah led the procession of his loved ones as he proudly carried his grandsons to his people's camping spot.

****

Dééd Yázhí and her sister were carried by their brothers to their mother and father's camping spot. By the light of the fires within her father's people's camping spot, Dééd Yázhí saw her father's face for the first time in five years. She remembered him as a strong leader and not the man with the frail body who stood near her mother. She was further shocked to see her mother's hair which had many streaks of gray that mingled with her black hair.

Hugging her mother brought a deep sense of peace to Dééd Yázhí's heart. It also brought worrisome thoughts to her mind. In her mind, her mother was a slender graceful and elegant woman, but the woman standing before her was very frail and needed help standing. Dééd Yázhí's worrisome thoughts were scattered when she heard her mother give out orders for water to be warmed up over the fire and coals to be drawn out to feed her beautiful daughters and their families. Dééd Yázhí could not help but giggle when she heard her mother loudly say,

"Haalá danoht'éé dó'? Haa da'iildahgo lá hááhgóóshįį ch'índa jiisiłgo, 'ádízhdílchidgo nikizhdilwo'. Bíighahí hajiiłtł'iidgo naníjoolwoł łeh!" *What is wrong with all of you? When someone comes to visit you, you begin running around grabbing things,*

17

you run around and feel on your person for something to give to your visitors. You even begin throwing things out of their place as you run around! At their mother's words, Dééd Yázhí's younger brothers and her adopted brothers and sisters began to run around doing exactly what their mother told them to do. Dééd Yázhí heard her younger sister giggle, causing the two sisters to begin laughing. Dééd Yázhí thought, yes, we are back in our mother's home! Tears mingled with her laughter as she watched her mother ordering people around.

Dééd Yázhí's mother brought corn kernels out of a tattered bag and began grinding the corn between two flat rocks. Dééd Yázhí closed her eyes and allowed her mind to listen to the grinding of the corn. The sound was cathartic to her bruised mind and thoughts. Her mother quickly made a beautiful stack of blue corn crepes for her daughters while her sister-in-law warmed long, fat strips of jerky over the open coals. While the jerky was cooking, Dééd Yázhí's mother gave each of her daughters a beautiful woven rug dress that welcomed the two sisters.

After their meal, Dééd Yázhí's mother asked her daughters to bathe in water and yucca soap. Hidden behind the women who surrounded them, Dééd Yázhí stepped out of the crumpled dress that lay on the ground. Her nostrils flared from the scent of the yucca soap with which she washed her body. Such sweet memories began to flow into her mind and began to crush the hurtful memories of the past five years. The sweet scent of the water-saturated yucca soap caused her mind to fly back to her childhood and revived her earliest memories of her mother.

Dééd Yázhí closed her eyes. Her mind focused on the time when she was an infant. She knew she loved listening to her mother's soft voice speaking to her when she was nuzzled up against her mother's breast as she lazily sucked the sweet nutritious milk her mother provided her. She also knew she loved to lie nestled in her cradleboard which her mother held safely in her lap. Dééd Yázhí also remembered how her mother played with her little locks of hair and sang soft beautiful songs to her, which always put her into a deep restful and peaceful sleep.

The sound of the crackling fire brought Dééd Yázhí's mind back to her father's people's camp. With the women still surrounding her, she picked up her rug dress and allowed her new soft rug dress to slowly slip over her shoulders, her breasts, her waist, her hips, and finally to softly settle on her body. As her dress slipped over her head, Dééd Yázhí noticed the scent of her mother's sheep was still attached to each woolen fiber that her dress was made of, which flooded her mind with even more memories.

****

When the faint light of dawn stretched its dainty plumes of light into the eastern sky, Dééd Yázhí and her family settled down for the night. As Dééd Yázhí and her little one rested on her mother's worn sheep skin, she lay still, looking into the beautiful predawn sky. The stars seemed brighter and twinkled even sweeter as the eastern sky began to relinquish its hold on the smaller fainter stars in the sky. Dééd Yázhí allowed her mind to wander back into her childhood, to the time when she felt safe in her mother's hooghan *hogan.*

19

Déd Yázhí's reminiscing mind then settled on one of her earliest memories, which usually happened at the end of the day when the sun was completely hidden by the western horizon, and when the sky was covered with a thick black rug blanket, and when she was securely wrapped up in the cradleboard her father made for her. She recalled the many times she wondered why her mother and her father did not have their own cradleboard in which to sleep. Instead, her mother and her father slept on the thick soft yaateł *skins of sheep.* Déd Yázhí giggled to herself when she remembered how she thought her mother and father slept on a sheep that was still alive. She remembered thinking that it was because her mother slept on the same sheep every night that the sheep became flat and spread out. She knew her father also slept on the same sheep he slept on the night before, and that was how the skin of his sheep became so wide and flat. Déd Yázhí allowed her mind to meander back to the many nights when she waited for the sheep her mother and father slept on to begin bleating, but she never heard the sheep make a sound. She felt sorry for the poor sheep that had to hold the bodies of her mother and her father. Once again, Déd Yázhí heard a giggle that she had not heard in a long time, and it was her own giggle. She hugged herself then hugged her little one, who was soundly sleeping.

With her mind in a relaxed mode, Déd Yázhí allowed her thoughts to wander further back into her childhood. Her thoughts settled on the nights when she slept in the safety of her cradleboard near her mother. She thought about the nights when she heard her mother and father whispering to one another. She remembered that it was when the fire went out that one of her favorite memories would begin to unwind when she could hear her father saying to her mother,

"Hágo, shiyázhí." *Come here, my little one.* Dééd Yázhí always wondered who her father was talking to because her father called her "Shiyázhí" *My little one.* She loved the way the word "Shiyázhí" easily slid off of her father's tongue and into her ears, making her warm inside. She remembered wondering if the word "Shiyázhí" easily slid into her mother's ears and also made her mother warm inside just as the word did to her.

Dééd Yázhí watched the stars fade as she listened to the sounds of the early dawn. Her father's people began to stir. The men cleaned the campsite, and the women prepared a meager breakfast of corn crepes left over from the night before. Dééd Yázhí fed her little one before her father came and gathered his grandson in his arms and left to gather his second grandson in his arms to explore their new environment. Dééd Yázhí took a deep breath, got up, and walked to where her mother sat on the ground. Without a word, she sat down and placed her head in her mother's lap.

Her mother began to sing a beautiful song as she patted Dééd Yázhí's hair into place. Dééd Yázhí began to tell her mother of the day when she and her younger sister were kidnapped by a mean anaa'í *enemy.* Slowly, her thoughts began to spill out as if they were on a page. Page by page, her thoughts organized themselves to inform her mother of the memories she planned to forget.

Chapter Two
Footprints of the Enemy!

At'ééd Yázhí Naazbaa' *Little Girl Warrior Who Came Home* was the oldest child and daughter of Nínááníbaa' and Hashké Yił Naabaah. At'ééd Yázhí Naazbaa' felt so much love in her mother's home. Her mother and father called her Dééd Yázhí for short because her name, At'ééd Yázhí Naazbaa', was sacred and it was used only at special times.

Dééd Yázhí had a loving mother and an adoring father. She also had two younger brothers and one younger sister.

First there was her brother who was just younger than she, and who was named Nahat'á Yinaabaah *One who Surrounds War with Plans.* He was so named because he was born when their father was still training to become a War Leader. Well-laid plans were of the utmost importance for the survival of their Naabeehó people so their father was required to attend all Leadership gatherings.

Dééd Yázhí's youngest brother was named Tł'ée'go Naabaah *One who Goes to War at Night.* He was given his name because he was born at night and because his father refused to leave their home while their mother was having labor pains, even if the labor pains proved to be false pains that visited her body at night. Their father was chided by the War Leaders and was severely chided by the women who were in attendance at the delivery of his youngest son.

Her sister Dzání Yázhí Naazbaa' *Little Woman Warrior Who Came Home* was the youngest child and youngest daughter of her mother and father. Just like her older sister, she was given a name of strength. Although Naabeehó *Navajo* women were not allowed to participate in warfare activities, it was important that their names were a representation of strength because the Naabeehó people were constantly facing warfare. Naabeehó women were treasured in Navajo society in that they represented life because they were the bearers of babies, a belief that caused Naabeehó men to want to become even fiercer warriors.

Dééd Yázhí and her siblings were favored by their many relatives. First of all, they were the grandchildren of the great War Leader Hastiin Naabaahii *Man Who Goes to War*, who lived at the base of Black Mesa. Secondly, Dééd Yázhí and her siblings were the children of the new and respected War Leader whom the Naabeehó people looked up to and whose name was Hashké Yił Naabaah. Dééd Yázhí knew her father greatly respected her maternal grandfather and the elder leader placed most of the leadership responsibilities upon the shoulders of her father. Dééd Yázhí was very proud of her father.

****

Dééd Yázhí was glad her father was very strict with his children. She remembered the abrupt way her father woke her

23

brothers from their deep sleep, then stood them up before they were fully awake and told his sons to follow him out the door to run toward the east while the dark eastern horizon was still covered with a dark slumber. Many dawn mornings, Dééd Yázhí heard one of her brothers say,

"Shizhé'é, t'ah tł'éé', doo hoot'į́į da!" *My father, it is still night, it is too dark to see!*

Her father would answer,

"Nihe'anaa'í hanii jį́į́go t'éiyá nidaabaah. Tł'ée'go 'áłdó' nidaabaah. Tł'ée'go nihąąh nidaa'na'." *Our enemies do not only conduct warfare during the day. They also conduct warfare at night. They sneak up on us at night.* Her father's voice trailed off as he said,

"Tsxį́į́łgo shikéé' ahi'noołchééł!" *Hurry and run after me!*

Dééd Yázhí's mother would pull the rug blanket off of Dééd Yázhí and her younger sister and tell them to get up and comb and fix their hair and begin their morning chores. Not long after the sun had come up, their mother would tell Dééd Yázhí and her younger sister to run toward the east.

"Nihí dó', dighá'ahi'noołchééh. Na'ídínółtaah. Ahi'noołchéełgo sodołzin doo. Baa 'ahééh nohsinígíí Diyin bee bił hołne'go 'ahi'noołchééł doo," *The two of you also, run. Test yourselves. Pray as you run. As you run, tell the Creator of the things you are thankful for,* their mother would tell them. Dééd Yázhí and her younger sister would join the other young women and girls to run toward the east. No one spoke. Everyone seemed to be praying to their Creator to thank Him for their bounties.

Dééd Yázhí heard Naabeehó *Navajo* parents constantly warning their children about the strangers that frequently came near the base of Dził́ijiin *Black Mesa* looking for a lone Naabeehó *Navajo* herding sheep. The enemy knew the person herding sheep would lead him to the homes of Naabeehó families. Dééd Yázhí and her siblings were told never to come back home when they saw a stranger lurking near. They were told to make the forest and the rocky hills their ally. They were also taught how to use their environment to hide from their enemy. Many times, young men who were being trained to become warriors were sent out with the children so they could pass on to the children the survival skills they had been taught by the War Leaders and older Naabeehó men.

****

Dééd Yázhí's mother was also very strict in teaching her daughters the culture and traditions of the Naabeehó *Navajo* people. When Dééd Yázhí became a young woman, her mother reminded her she had to be strong physically and mentally and know the values of her people so she would be prepared when she became a wife of a War Leader.

Daily, Dééd Yázhí was told,

"Nidine'é bi'í'ool'įįł bik'ehgo ne'iina' naniłt'i'. Ts'ídá t'áá'ákwííji̇́ nidine'é bi'í'ool'įįł bik'ehgo ne'iina' naniłt'i'go 'éí doo háadi da naa yáhodoosjįł da. Nidine'é bi'í'ool'įįł t'óó bik'i nanilne'go 'éí háadi da léi' naa yáhodoosjįł. Nimá dóó nizhé'é dóó nicheii baa yádahodoosjįł. T'áá'ałtsoní nił niłįįgo baa nitsíníkees. Bínani'di'neeztą́ą́' yę́ę bi'íł'įįgo'éí doo tsístł'ah díínáał da. Diné t'áá'ałtsoh nił danilįįgo baa nitsíníkees. Bíla' ashdla'ii t'áá'ałtsoh nił danilįįgo baa nitsíníkees." *Live your life according*

to your people's (the Navajo people) culture. If you abide by
your people's cultural teachings on a daily basis, you will never
feel ashamed. If you ignore your people's cultural teachings, you
will bring shame to yourself and you will bring shame upon your
mother and your father and your maternal grandfather. Have
respect for all things. If you abide by the things you were taught,
you will never find yourself in a place where you cannot escape.
Respect all Navajo people. Respect all human beings.

Dééd Yázhí trusted her mother's teaching because her
mother was considered one of the prominent caretakers of
the Navajo culture, traditions, and teachings for the people of
Dziłíjiin *Black Mesa.* She was also the wife of a respected War
Leader, and Dééd Yázhí wanted to be prepared to carry on her
mother's teachings when a young War Leader asked for her in
marriage.

To solidify the teachings of her mother, Dééd Yázhí was
told to teach her younger sister to be a strong and respected
woman. She taught her younger sister everything she was
taught. She was told that in doing this,

"Nina'nitin hólǫ́ǫ doo. Na'áłchíní bínabidíníítįįłígíí nee hólǫ́ǫ
doo. Na'áłchíní doo dichin yiih dínóodah da." *You will have*
things to teach. You will have things to teach your children. Your
children will not fall into hunger.

Dééd Yázhí and her younger sister were reminded daily of
the status of their mother and their father and they were told
not to do anything to bring shame to their name. Dééd Yázhí
did not mind carrying the burden of upholding the name her
mother and her father had worked very hard to maintain.

****

Before Dééd Yázhí's father took on his role as a War Leader
once again for the coming fall and winter seasons, he went
hunting so his people of Dziłíjiin *Black Mesa* would have meat to
make into jerky for the upcoming long cold winter months. He
also wanted to teach the young warriors the full art of hunting
so they could care for their own families as they grew older.

 Dééd Yázhí's father promised her mother he and a few of
his young warriors would be gone for just a few days, which they
would devote to hunting, but her mother was not convinced
their family was completely safe. Her father reassured his wife
and his daughters he was leaving them in safe hands. Dééd
Yázhí's younger brothers and her maternal grandfather as well
as a few warriors were asked to stay behind to protect the
women and children and the families who lived at the base of
Dziłíjiin *Black Mesa.*

Two days after Dééd Yázhí's father and his warriors left
for their hunting trip, two young warriors told Dééd Yázhí's
maternal grandfather they had seen a set of footprints they
had not seen before. The footprints belonged to intruders and
to horses whose horseshoe prints were strange. The warriors
further reported the footprints were one day old.

The elder War Leader, Dééd Yázhí's maternal grandfather,
gathered the young warriors together and they began to
strategize in anticipation for the approach of the 'anaa'í *enemy.*
The young warriors were divided into groups based upon their
training, their knowledge, and their warfare skills. Those who
were skilled at tracking were sent out to track the prints of the
enemy; another group was sent out to find Dééd Yázhí's father

to deliver the message about the strange intruders. A third group was sent to distract the 'anaa'í by riding in the high hills of Dziłíjiin *Black Mesa* to keep the enemy away from the Naabeehó *Navajo* settlements. Still another group of fierce warriors was sent to follow in the footsteps of the trackers to maim and kill the 'anaa'í *enemy.* The warriors knew the 'anaa'í were looking for Naabeehó women and young children to sell at the Indian slave markets. The last group of warriors was kept near the home of Dééd Yázhí's family and extended family members for protection.

Dééd Yázhí stood outside and watched the young warriors and her brothers leave in haste to carry out the orders of the elder War Leader. She was amazed. I blinked my eyes only four times and the young warriors have all left in an orderly fashion in obedience to my maternal grandfather, she thought as pride filled her heart.

"Shizhé'é dóó shicheii binaabaahii nizhónígo neineeztą́ą́'. T'áadoo kót'é 'ílíní t'óó dah a'diilyiz lágo baa 'ákoniizį́į́'," *My father and my maternal grandfather have trained their warriors very well. I realized they all left in an extreme hurry without hesitation,* she breathed in amazement. She was extremely proud of her maternal grandfather's and her father's leadership skills.

Dééd Yázhí's maternal grandfather called all of his relatives to his home to let them know about the closeness of the 'anaa'í *enemy.* Although the elder leader spoke in a subdued tone, the people could hear him clearly as he spoke words of warning and protection as he said,

"Áłtsé 'éiyá, niha'áłchíní t'áadoo t'áá sáhí nida'niłkaadgo 'ádeiyínóhsingo bééda'diyoołnihí. Ch'ikę́ę́h dóó 'asdzání dóó sáanii danohłínígíí t'áadoo nida'nołkaadí. Bini'dii nihitsíłkéí dóó nihidinééh dóó nihinaabaahii danilínígíí nihá nida'niłkaad." *For one thing, do not allow the children to herd sheep alone. You who are teenage girls and young women and women are not to herd your sheep. Let the ones who are our teenage boys and our young men and our young warriors herd sheep for you.*

All of the women and girls were not happy with the demands of their elder War Leader. The protective nature of the women rose up within all the women as they voiced that they were not at all happy about having to comply with the wishes of their elder leader and explained their apprehension by saying,

"'Ei yee' nihí danihilį́į́'. Bee nihaa dahojoozba'ígíí 'át'é. 'Ashiiké danihidibé dóó danihitł'ízí ła' nihits'ą́ą́' yóó 'adeidoonił. 'Éí doodai' da tsį́įłgo baa deyíjeehgo danihidibéhę́ę dabits'iiní dadooleeł. K'ad yee' aak'eed biih yiikai. Kojį' ahalzhishgo yee' nihidibé hazhóó'ígo nidaniilkaadgo yinahjį' danilk'ah. Ei 'ashiiké danihilį́į́' doo yaa hą́ą́h danízin da dooleeł. Ei dibé dóó tł'ízí k'ad danilk'ahgo t'éí hai bii' ahalzhishgo doo tsį́įłgo dabits'iiní da dadooleeł. Ei tsį́įłgo bidi'noolkałgo biniinaa dabits'iiní daazlį́į́'go haijį' ahoolzhiizhgo danihilį́į́' ałtsoh dadoodlóół." *These are our livestock. We have been blessed with them. The boys will lose some of our sheep and goats. As they herd our sheep in a hurried manner, our sheep will become skinny. We have come into the fall season. Sheep and goats are to be allowed to become fatter now, and as we go into the winter season, they will become skinny. They will become skinny because when they were herded they were made to run fast and when it becomes winter, all of our herd will freeze to death.*

29

The women who could not imagine themselves without the daily responsibility of herding their sheep defended themselves by stating that they know their sheep and their sheep know them. The women did not have the confidence in the sheepherding skills of the young warriors. To remain in contact with their sheep and goats, the women agreed to keep only a few of their large herds and allow sheepherders to care for the larger number of their herds. The women also agreed not to take their reduced number of sheep very far from their settlements and agreed to accept the presence and the protection of young warriors throughout their sheepherding day. The final concession the women agreed to was to keep the children safe by not allowing the children to herd sheep at all.

While the older women stayed home and cared for their grandchildren, the young women took their sheep out to the nearby pasture and then on to the nearby shallow watering spring. Many young brave warriors could be seen throughout the hills of Dził íjiin *Black Mesa*.

Dééd Yázhí and her younger sister, Dzáníbaa', kept their herd of sheep and goats as well as their mother's herd together. Herding sheep and goats without the help of the children was more difficult than they had imagined.

On the way home from herding sheep late in the afternoon, Dééd Yázhí saw a beautiful new thick, green patch of ch'il ahwéhé *Navajo tea* nearby and stopped to pick a few stalks for her mother. Dééd Yázhí felt her mouth watering as she looked at the many new tender, light green stalks that gently waved their little yellow flowers at her. Cupping the new stalks, leaves, and dainty flowers in her hand, Dééd Yázhí called out to her younger sister and said,

"Shideezhí, 'áłtsé, nihimá ch'il ahwéhé ła' bá 'áshłééh." *My younger sister, wait, I am going to gather some Navajo tea for our mother.* Her younger sister, Dzáníbaa', spoke back and said,

"Dooda, shádí, bíni'dii dinééh naabaahii danilínígíí nihá 'ádeilééh, ni 'éí dooda. Shą́ą́' nihe'anaa'í ką́ą́ nihinaagóó nidaakai, jiní; ła' t'áadoo hooyání nihik'ídoogááł. Txį'. Tsxį́įłgo, shádí. K'ad shį́į. Txį'! K'adí, shádí, k'adí! Txį'," *No, my older sister, let the young men who are the warriors gather them for us, not you. It is said that there are enemies among us; one may unexpectedly come up upon us. Let's go. Hurry, my older sister. That's probably enough. Let's go! That is enough, my older sister, that's enough! Let's go,* Dzáníbaa' pleaded, as she kept looking back to watch her older sister lovingly pick Navajo tea for their mother.

Dééd Yázhí was so excited about the late fall harvest of ch'il ahwéhé *Navajo tea,* she forgot they were to remain on guard at all times. She did not stop to think that her actions were placing her and her younger sister's lives at risk as she happily picked the Navajo tea. Her actions were also placing the young warriors in a perilous situation, that of making sure all the young women and their sheep and goats arrived at home safely, and that of looking for the two sisters whose herd of sheep and goats that had already begun to wander back into their corral without their caretakers.

To hurry Dééd Yázhí along, Dzáníbaa' ran back and began wildly picking the ch'il ahwéhé *Navajo tea* alongside her older sister. Once they had each obtained a handful of the tender plants, the sisters tied each handful with a loose tea stalk and reached out to grab another handful. Both young women knew their mother treasured the taste of Navajo tea, and the young women did not know when they would be allowed to herd their sheep in this direction again. Their maternal grandfather had ordered his warriors to make sure the women herded their sheep in a different direction every day so as to keep the enemy from easily tracking their path. They were also told to allow a few sheep to follow them so as to cover their tracks so the enemy would have more trouble tracking the young women.

****

Dééd Yázhí heard the sound of a man's voice. She smiled when she thought she heard her younger brothers' voices. She looked up and suddenly looked into the eyes of two strangers, a big tall man and a shorter man who were one of their anaa'í *enemies!* She frantically looked around for her sister and saw that her younger sister had been picked up by the shorter anaa'í *enemy* and was being held under the arm of their anaa'í as if she were a large bag of wool. Her younger sister's breath was being squeezed out of her so she could not cry out. Dééd Yázhí screamed a threatening scream, threw down the bundle of fresh tea stalks, and began running toward home but the big anaa'í *enemy* wrapped his arm around her waist and lifted her off of her feet and began running toward an arroyo.

Dééd Yázhí quickly looked back and saw her younger brothers chasing them from a far distance. "Where are their horses?" she frantically wondered. She filled her lungs to scream again when the big anaa'í threw her down onto the sandy floor of the arroyo, then turned toward her younger sister and pushed her younger sister out of the hands of the second kidnapper before the big anaa'í threw his heavy body on top of them.

Dééd Yázhí could not breathe! She could hear her younger sister also struggling for breath. She and her younger sister hit the ground so hard that the air was forced out of their lungs, and the weight of the big anaa'í further kept their lungs from filling with air.

Dééd Yázhí heard the sound of horses' hooves pounding on the ground above them. Hoping and praying it was her younger brothers and her maternal grandfather coming to their aid, she tried in vain to fill her lungs to scream, but the big enemy's heavy body was crushing her and her younger sister's bodies. She looked up hoping to see the faces of her brothers. Instead, she noticed strange horses galloping above the steep bank of the arroyo above them. In an instant, the big anaa'í *enemy* wrapped his arms around her and her younger sister and while still holding them, he jumped to his feet and tightly held them close to his chest, crushing the air out of their lungs with his big muscular arms.

In horror, Dééd Yázhí realized this was the war tactic the big enemy used to keep women and children from screaming to alert any Naabeehó *Navajo* warrior of the danger. She was horrified when she thought back to the times when she judged Naabeehó women and girls for not putting up a fight or not screaming.

The worst had happened. What Dééd Yázhí and her younger sister had been warned about since they were children happened. As her thoughts raced, the air was being crushed out of her chest, causing her to lose focus and become unable to think about a way out of their predicament. All she wanted to do was free her younger sister. Dééd Yázhí was afraid for her younger sister.

In silence, the big anaa'í began running through the sandy arroyo as his strong arms held the two sisters, crushing them as he ran. With all her strength, Dééd Yázhí lifted her head to see the 'anaa'í *enemy* riding their horses down the bank of the arroyo to catch up with their leader, the big anaa'í.

Every once in a while, Dééd Yázhí could feel her feet brush against the soft sand on the floor of the arroyo bed. No matter how hard she squirmed, she could not release herself from the big enemy's strong grip. Her only thought was the safety of her younger sister from whom she could hear strained whimpering as her sister's head bobbed up and down. Although her younger sister's face was so near to hers by the way they were being held within the strong arms of the big anaa'í, Dééd Yázhí felt as if her younger sister was far away.

In the bed of the arroyo, the horses sped up and began galloping ahead of the big enemy. Dééd Yázhí could not see because of the thick dust in the air that was kicked up by the galloping horses. All she could see was the ground rising and falling as the foul-smelling big anaa'í held them and ran with them. The big anaa'í was deliberately holding his captives so tight so that the two sisters could not get their lungs full enough of air to scream for help. Dééd Yázhí quickly looked across and saw her red-faced younger sister once again struggling for air as they were being hauled toward the horses.

The horses slowed down and the big anaa'í *enemy* threw each sister onto a horse in front of a rider. After many hours of riding through the arroyo, the big anaa'í yelled at the riders up ahead and told them to run the horses up out of the arroyo. The horses ahead immediately began running up the steep bank of

34

the arroyo. The big anaa'í stopped the two horses upon which Dééd Yázhí and her younger sister were being held. He dragged the two sisters off of their horses with the help of the riders, then stuffed the two sisters under his arms and began running up the steep side of the arroyo so fast that Dééd Yázhí thought she was going to bang her head on the side of the steep hill. The horses came running back down the steep bank of the arroyo nearly crashing into them. Surprised, the big anaa'í stumbled, and nearly dropped Dééd Yázhí and her sister, but his steps caught up with his body and he continued running.

One of the big anaa'í's accomplices slowed down and slid his arm around Dééd Yázhí's younger sister and threw her body across a horse in front of a rider. The rider slapped the younger sister in the face because she tried to scream when her breath re-entered her body. A horse being led by another enemy slowed down long enough for the man to grab Dééd Yázhí as the big anaa'í jumped on another horse. Air began to fill Dééd Yázhí's lungs as she prepared herself to scream as loud as she could. Instead, a dull pain flashed across her face and the sun began to fade. She found herself lying crosswise in front of the big anaa'í. Filthy, foul-smelling rags had been shoved into the two sisters' mouths, making them gag, while the raggedy ends of the old rags were tied around their heads. Just before a thick, filthy rug was thrown over her body to hide her body, Dééd Yázhí saw her younger sister's body draped over a horse as she lay crosswise in front of another member of the enemy. Back in the winding arroyo, off they went, riding as fast as their horses could carry them.

Lying face down and crosswise on the horse, Dééd Yázhí could not see how many men were riding with their kidnapper. She found her wrists and ankles were tied together as she was held on the horse by a thick, dirty, heavy hand, and all she could see was the ground as it rose and fell away with the horse's fast stride. Raising her head as high as she could so she could lift the filthy rug to see her surroundings, all she could see were the legs of the men who kidnapped them and the legs of the horses that were carrying their anaa'í *enemies.* She had never seen a horse from this vantage point.

Dééd Yázhí was quickly becoming dizzy from looking at the fast-moving legs of the horses. She could hear the men carelessly kick the sides of their horses to force them to run faster. The horse that carried her and the anaa'í was struggling. She knew the horse that carried the second kidnapper and her younger sister was struggling as well. The horses were not used to running with so much weight on their backs, nevertheless, the horses increased their speed causing Dééd Yázhí to recklessly bounce up and down even more.

Her hair that was tightly tied in a tsiiyééł *hair knot* at the back of her head was heavy because her hair was very thick and long and her hair knot was now pounding on the back of her head. Dééd Yázhí was dizzy, the back of her head hurt, and her neck hurt from the weight of her head being bounced up and down.

Dééd Yázhí bit down on the foul-smelling dirty rag that was stuffed in her mouth because she did not want her kidnappers to know the rag had loosened due to the bouncing up and down of her head. She was afraid the ends of the rag were hanging loose.

36

To add to her misery, the man who held Dééd Yázhí captive upon his horse was becoming bold in his actions, possibly because they rode under the cover of flight. Her captor kept the heel of his palm on the small of her back, but every once in a while he allowed his hand to slide further down her back as she lay crosswise in front of him as he rode on his horse. My thick rug dress will protect me from his dirty hands, Dééd Yázhí thought as her captor pushed down hard on the small of her back. Her captor giggled as she struggled to turn when she felt his hand moving toward the top of her buttocks, causing her to feel as if she was sliding head first off of his horse. She looked at the ground rising toward her. Her captor grabbed her thick dress and yanked her back onto his horse. The strange man once again held her down by pressing down on the small of her back with the palm of his hand. He was crushing her. In this manner they rode for miles.

Dééd Yázhí strained and lifted her head and looked toward the right. She caught glimpses of her younger sister in the bright sunlight, riding in front of an old dirty man who held her by wrapping his right arm around her waist as she rode with both of her legs draped over the right side of the horse. Dééd Yázhí could see her younger sister's breasts rise and fall as they rode which only made the evil old man smile and hold her younger sister closer. She caught glimpses of the dirty man's hand moving to explore more of her sister's body. With another glance at her sister, she saw her sister breathing deeply in anger as she gritted her teeth. The big anaa'í *enemy* rode on his horse at the front of the pack while keeping an eye on the two men who held their captives.

"I warn you, do not hurt the muchachas!" he growled. "We can take them to market and get the most pesos for them. Healthy Navajo girls and ladies make a kidnapper rich. We can sell them for two hundred pesos at the Trade Fair in Taos. Taos is a long way from here, but your desires are close! These girls have been well cared for and can bring us a lot of pesos, comprende? Think of the pesos! If it would serve you, we will look for an old Navajo woman you men can satisfy yourselves with. For now, leave them alone!" the big anaa'í *enemy* hoarsely bellowed at the two men who held their prized captives. A young man translated the message into Spanish. The two dirty men nodded in submission.

Dééd Yázhí felt a sickening feeling of helplessness enter her body. She was horrified! Her body was threatening to vomit the tortilla and jerky she had eaten earlier in the day. Without warning, her mouth flew open and out spilled her meal, spraying on the horses' legs. Some of her lunch that continued to spew out of her mouth was lifted by the wind and flew back toward the horses and riders who were following their big anaa'í *enemy* kidnapper.

One of the men who rode with the big anaa'í *enemy*, lifted his right arm high in the air and used his horse whip to begin whipping Dééd Yázhí, causing her to muffle her scream and writhe under the heavy hand of her kidnapper. The big anaa'í *enemy* swung back at his accomplice and snarled in a loud low whisper,

"If you hurt her bad, we can't sell her for many pesos! Comprende?"

The big anaa'í sneered at his accomplice as he continued to growl,

"Think of the pesos, my friend."

Lifting and turning her head, Dééd Yázhí saw that her kidnapper's accomplice was wiping his pants with a dirty rag. She was glad she opened her mouth really wide to get rid of her meal. She knew her younger sister was feeling nauseated as well. Fear replaced Dééd Yázhí's nausea; she did not want her younger sister to be whipped by one of their enemy kidnappers.

To distract herself, Dééd Yázhí looked toward the ground. Watching the vegetation disappear underneath them, she could see the horses had taken them out of tall pine and juniper country, which only meant their kidnappers were taking them southward toward Kin Yis'áanii *Hopi* country. The terrain toward the southern and western directions were rocky as the elevation lowered while the northern direction held a sheer cliff that left a person breathless, Dééd Yázhí reasoned as she tried to determine where they were.

Dééd Yázhí's attention was brought back to her younger sister when she heard the muffled sounds of her sister crying. She could hardly make out the words but she thought she heard her sister say,

"Dédii, násdzid! Dédii, doo chohoo'į́į́góó násdzid!" Dédii, *I am scared! I am extremely scared!* With those words, Dééd Yázhí heard her younger sister begin to gag and wail uncontrollably. All of a sudden there was silence.

Once again, the big anaa'í was shouting at one of his men. The horses slightly slowed their pace which gave Dééd Yázhí a chance to look for her sister. Her younger sister's kidnapper had stopped his horse to shove the dirty rag deeper into her mouth. Although she could only see glimpses of her younger sister's limp body, Dééd Yázhí could not believe what she saw. One of the violent men had hit her sister across the face so hard that the place where she was hit had turned a deep red color and was already swelling at the point of impact. The big anaa'í *enemy* shouted at the man, then whipped at him with his horsewhip. The man who was whipped told the big anaa'í in Spanish that he saw Naabeehó warriors and that was why he silenced the young woman. The big anaa'í told the man who hit Dééd Yázhí's younger sister that he would have no pesos to take home, but he could eat and have safety with the group as they traveled.

Tears began to drop out of Dééd Yázhí's eyes. She shut her eyes tight when she remembered the voice of her younger sister when she begged to wait until another time to gather ch'il ahwéhé *Navajo tea.* She felt so guilty. She wished she were the only one who was kidnapped but felt even worse when she remembered her younger sister did not leave her behind when she continued to pick stalks of ch'il ahwéhé. Instead of leaving to return to the safety of their home, her younger sister stayed to help her gather the tender stalks of Navajo tea, and now her sister had also been kidnapped and was being abused.

Dééd Yázhí's mind snapped back to their present situation. To console her helpless younger sister, she forced herself to speak, although her words were badly muffled, and said,

"T'áadoo náníldzidí, shideezhí. Nihicheii shį́į́ 'aadę́ę́' nihikéé' oołkah. Nihilahkéí shį́į́ 'ałdó' naabaahii yił nihikéé' deiyíbááh. Nihik'ídadoobah, ních'aad, shideezhí." *Don't be afraid, my*

40

younger sister. Our maternal grandfather is probably tracking us. Our brothers are probably with the warriors following us in warfare. They will come up upon us, don't cry, my younger sister. Dééd Yázhí wanted to believe her words but with the old filthy rugs concealing her and her younger sister, she doubted her own words. Talking caused the foul-smelling rag to become saturated with her saliva, bringing an overpowering acrid taste to her mouth. She began heaving.

Dééd Yázhí waited for her younger sister's response. Her stomach had been emptied earlier but it kept trying to drain out the contents of her stomach. In between her heaving, she listened for her younger sister's response, but her sister did not respond. Dééd Yázhí was worried. She was very upset with herself. Their kidnapping was her fault! When her heaving began again, the big anaa'í slapped her on the back to stop her uncontrollable body movement.

Chapter Three
Moving with the Enemy

After riding for a while, their kidnappers slowed their horses. Dééd Yázhí lifted her head to notice a group of strange men waiting in an arroyo. Hope filled her heart. She could not see clearly. She looked for signs of Naabeehó warriors. As they approached the men, she realized with fear that the men were additional anaa'í *enemy* with fresh horses.

Dééd Yázhí and her sister were carelessly pulled off of the horses, untied then tied up again, blindfolded, gagged with another filthy rag, and thrown onto another horse with a different rider. The big anaa'í *enemy* spoke a different language and ordered the riders who had helped to kidnap the sisters to ride off further toward the south.

Dééd Yázhí and her younger sister remained with the big anaa'í *enemy* and several men who had been waiting for them. With her hands tied behind her back and her ankles tied together, she raised her head as high as she could. She looked for the sun through the thick dark rag that covered her eyes. She could barely see. The sun was orange and setting and they were now riding toward the early sunset.

42

Dééd Yázhí did not want the sun to dip below the horizon. There was no way to know what would happen to her and her younger sister once darkness had crept across the landscape. Through the dirty rag that covered her eyes, she tried many times in vain to lock eyes with the sun when her blindfold was lifted by the wind. She was desperate to plead with the sun to stay in place but the dirty rag and the bouncing motion of the horse's steps kept her from focusing on the face of the sun.

Dééd Yázhí was relieved when she heard her sister's faint muffled wailing as she said,

"Dédii, nihizhé'é shą'? Nihi'disnáhígíí daats'í bił bééhózin? Násdzid! Shitsiits'iin neezgai dóó shiwos neezgai dóó shibid neezgai. 'Abínídą́ą́' shimá shitsiiyéél yéigo ye'astł'ǫ́, 'áko shitsiiyéél dah naalts'idgo biniinaa shitsiits'iin neezgai. Shináá' dóó shichį́į́h shį́į́ haidzaago neezgai." *Where is our father? Does he know we have been kidnapped? I am afraid! My head hurts and my shoulders hurt and my stomach hurts. My mother tied my hair real tight this morning and my head hurts from my hair bun bouncing up and down. I don't know what happened to my eye and my nose, but they hurt.* Dééd Yázhí thought about the words she thought she heard her sister speak through muffled tones. After a little bit, she responded,

"T'áadoo yáníłti'í, shideezhí. Nihe'anaa'í 'atínáádanidoodlííł." *Don't talk, my younger sister. Our enemies will hurt you again.*

The men hit the two sisters on the back of the head with the handle of their whips to warn them not to talk to one another. Dééd Yázhí's younger sister cried out in pain. Dééd Yázhí wanted so much to hold her younger sister and comfort her.

43

When Dééd Yázhí stretched her neck upwards whenever the filthy rug was lifted by the wind, she saw through the dark dirty rag covering her eyes that the setting sun kept bobbing up and down with each galloping step of her rider's horse. She voiced a prayer to the Creator and asked the Creator to allow the sun to remain above the horizon. It seemed that as long as they rode toward the western direction, the sun remained in the sky, even if it appeared as a sliver. There was light and that was what she wanted.

As their kidnappers recklessly rode on, the landscape changed again to rocks dotting the landscape and the sand that the wind had deposited in between the rocks had turned from a soft light tannish brown color to a slightly reddish tan color. After stopping to change horses once again, the kidnappers frantically pulled the sisters off of the horses in a rough manner then stood them up on the ground, but since Dééd Yázhí and her younger sister had their hands tied behind their backs and their ankles tied together, Dééd Yázhí and her younger sister could not hold their balance and they fell to the ground with one loud thud followed by another. Making a heap of two bodies, the two sisters did not try to get up, they were satisfied to feel the other so close. They leaned into one another, allowing their weakened bodies to communicate with the other.

Dééd Yázhí felt her body shaking out of fear and anger. How could these filthy dirty men treat her younger sister like this? she thought. We are the daughters of the great War Leader Hashké Yił Naabaah. We are above this! Dééd Yázhí began to cry when she saw a puddle of water forming around her sister.

44

Once again, Dééd Yázhí and her younger sister were thrown across a horse, covered by the filthy rugs after which they felt the heavy hand of their kidnappers holding them down. Their kidnapper, the big anaa'í, kept his eye on his men, barking at them whenever their hands began to wander. The man who held Dééd Yázhí's younger sister, winced when he coaxed his horse to a gallop. He swore and yanked a dirty multicolored rag out of his pocket and shoved a part of the rag up his nostrils. Dééd Yázhí figured he objected to the smell of urine that came from her younger sister's thick rug dress.

Dééd Yázhí sensed they had changed direction, she guessed they were traveling in a northwestern direction, toward their anaa'í *enemy* who lived in Nóoda'í bikéyah *Ute country.* They had traveled in a large half circle only to be traveling west of her beautiful Dził́íjiin *Black Mesa.* Dééd Yázhí felt her heart sink. The Nóoda'í *Ute* people were not known for their kindness toward Naabeehó women and children. She worried if their brothers and their maternal grandfather would be able to track them. They had ridden on flat rocky surfaces for many miles. Dééd Yázhí watched the rocky terrain rise and fall as the color of the rocks changed.

The riders stopped. Dééd Yázhí and her younger sister were pulled off of the horses again and were helped to a sitting position. The dirty rags were untied and removed from the two sisters' mouths. Their blindfolds were tightened, after which a thick slab of rotten smelling jerky was shoved into their faces. The jerky smelled like their kidnappers! No wonder their kidnappers smelled so badly, they eat rotten meat, thought Dééd Yázhí as her younger sister began to gag, saying,

"We'! We'! We'!" *Yuck! Yuck! Yuck!* followed by the sound of a fist hitting skin. Dééd Yázhí was not prepared to hear her younger sister immediately cry out in a shrill painful cry. She heard the big anaa'í *enemy* whip at the air with his horse whip to warn the evil men. He told the men to stay away from the two sisters. He then threw a rock and told his men to go where they heard the rock fall and rest there.

Around a small clearing near a hill covered with sagebrush, the men fed the girls dried corn. The corn was stale. The men displayed a sense of safety as they rested.

Dééd Yázhí heard soft whimpers coming from the direction of her sister. She told her sister to be brave, whispering,

"Ha'íínílní, shideezhí. Nihizhé'é shįį nihikéé' oołkah. Doo shįį t'áá díítł'ée' da, yiskáągo daats'í 'índa bilįį' ayóo dilwo'ígíí yee nihídoołááł." *Have faith, my younger sister. Our father is probably following us by tracking us. It may not be tonight, it may not be until tomorrow that he will catch up with us on his horse that runs very fast.*

Dééd Yázhí's comforting whispers only brought sniffles and tears to her younger sister's eyes. As the huge tears rolled down her younger sister's cheeks, Dééd Yázhí vowed not to cry until she saw her father again as she said quietly,

"Shí 'éí shizhé'é néiłtsą́ą́go 'índa deeshchah, *I will not cry until I see my father again.* Dééd Yázhí repeated the words to herself and to the darkness of dusk, hoping to strengthen herself.

"Ni dó', nihimá bił ná'ahiiniłtsą́ą́go 'índa dííchah. K'ad éí dooda. Nihe'anaa'í bináałgo 'éí dooda. Yéigo ha'íínílníh, shideezhí, shiyázhí. Ayóó'áníínish'ní." *You too, you can cry when*

46

you see our mother again. Now is not the time. Not in front of our enemy. Have hope, my younger sister, my little one. I love you.

With those words, Dééd Yázhí could hear her younger sister beginning to cry soft dry sobs.

"T'áadoo 'ádíníní, shiyázhí, nihimá nénáznii'go 'índa dííchah. K'ad éí 'adziil t'éí bich'į' nitsíníkees. Doo 'éí nihik'eh hodeesdlį́į' da. Naabeehó ch'ikę́ę́h niidlį́. Nizhónígo nihiyaahoo'a'. Nihimá nizhónígo nanihineeztą́ą́'. Nihizhé'é naabaahii 'ayóó 'át'éi nilį́. Naat'áanii 'ayóó 'át'éi nilį́. Nihicheii 'ałdó' naabaahii dóó naat'áanii 'ayóó 'át'éi nilį́. Nihilahkéí 'ałdó' naabaahii yéigo nabidi'neestą́'ígíí nilį́." *Don't say that, my little one, don't cry until our mother is hugging you. For now, only think thoughts of strength. We have not been defeated. We are young Navajo women. We were raised very well. Our mother taught us well. Our father is a great warrior. He is a great leader. Our maternal grandfather is also a great warrior and leader. Our brothers are also warriors who have been taught very well.*

There was enough late dusk light for Dééd Yázhí to clearly see her younger sister's face. She could see pain and fear on her sister's face. Her facial bruises were noticeable. Dééd Yázhí's heart hurt for her younger sister and she found herself near tears. She closed her eyes and shook her head in frustration. She thought back to her mother and softly spoke the first thoughts that came to her mind, those of her mother's words of comfort she heard her mother speak to her. She said,

"Ních'aad, shiyázhí, t'óó naa hojoobá'ígo nichah. T'áadoo nichaaí. Nik'éí 'ádin nahalingo nichah. Hooghandi nániit'áazhgo nihimá 'azee' ła' ná 'íidoolííł. Ninii' azee' ná yą́ąh íidoolííł,

shideezhí." *Don't cry, my little one, I feel so much sympathy for you as you are crying. Don't cry. You are crying as if you do not have any relatives. When we get home, our mother will gather herbs for you. She will apply the herbal medicine to your face, my younger sister.*

The two sisters' kidnappers and the men who joined them declared they were tired. They decided to find a place to hide so they could get some rest. From under the low branches of mature juniper trees, the big anaa'í *enemy* motioned to Dééd Yázhí and her younger sister to tell them to sleep under one blanket. Dééd Yázhí missed the soft sheepskin her maternal grandmother so lovingly tanned for her.

The big anaa'í tied his wrist to the ankles of the sisters with a long rope then laid down to rest at their feet. Throughout the early night, Dééd Yázhí spoke to her younger sister in a gentle voice, asking her to stay near her. Several times she heard her sister cry out whenever her sister moved. Their hands were still tied behind their backs and their ankles were tied together. Dééd Yázhí prayed to the Creator for the light of a bright moon once the sun settled in its resting place in the west. She knew she would feel better when the pale light of the moon cast light around her and her younger sister. She hoped their blindfolds would come loose by then.

The full branches of the juniper trees hid the faint light of the moon that had risen above the rock formation in the east some time ago. Dééd Yázhí heard her younger sister whimper every time she moved. As they both lay on the ground, their pelvic bones clashed against the hard rocky ground. The sisters held hands even though it meant they had to turn their bodies in an awkward position to do so.

Sleep was kind to the sisters, it helped them forget they were captives, but their sleep came and went in waves. During the early night, Dééd Yázhí heard the whimpers of her younger sister. All she could do was hold her sister's hand tightly and whisper,

"Ních'aad, shideezhí. 'Ayóó 'áho'dó'níigo doo jichah da. Ních'aad." *Don't cry, my younger sister. When a person is loved, they should not cry. Don't cry.*

In the emerging pale moonlight, Dééd Yázhí could see only a sliver of the faint outline of the rock formation that rose high into the air to the east of their crude campsite. Their 'anaa'í kidnappers decided to rest longer in the safety of the early night darkness. They rested near the place the Naabeehó call Tsé 'Awé'é *Baby Rocks.* Dééd Yázhí was very sad. The area northwest of their campsite was where her maternal grandfather was from. The two sisters took shallow breaths, not wanting to wake the sleeping 'anaa'í. Dééd Yázhí and her younger sister drew comfort knowing they were breathing the same air their maternal grandfather had breathed when he was young.

Dééd Yázhí woke to a strange but familiar sound. The big anaa'í was sharpening a long dangerous-looking knife. Dééd Yázhí could hear the deadly sound of the knife sliding across the rock the man used to sharpen each side of the long blade of his knife.

Unexpectedly, Dééd Yázhí's eyes filled with tears. She felt responsible for the mistreatment of her younger sister as she quietly whispered,

"Nihicheii bité'ázíní bikéyah biih yiikai." *We entered the land of our maternal grandfather's relatives.* Her younger sister answered in a quivering whisper,

49

"Háadi da shą' nidaakai?" *I wonder where they are?*

"Hóla. Tsé ní'áhígíí shį́į́ yitsį́įgi kéédahat'į́," *I don't know. They probably live at the base of the rock mesa,* whispered Dééd Yázhí as she raised her head to search the rocky mesa for signs of life by looking out from under her dirty blindfold.

It seemed as if the big anaa'í *enemy* heard and understood Dééd Yázhí's words and read her thoughts. Without warning, the big anaa'í jumped up, kicked the two sisters' feet, and loosened the rope he had used to tie himself to the girls. While keeping an eye on the two sisters, he ran to where the men were sleeping, then kicked them awake and told them they needed to be on their way.

Dééd Yázhí felt tears slowly making their way down her face. In their dangerous surroundings, she wished she was at home, sitting down to a late evening meal of soft tortillas and mutton jerky. She wanted to be sleeping on her soft sheepskin while she listened to the sounds of the night—the sound of a lazy cricket announcing his whereabouts, a coyote howling for its mate, the wind quietly shuffling the pinon tree branches and the short stalks of the many sagebrush bushes that dotted the nearby landscape, as well as hearing the gentle breeze moving the small granules of sand outside their hooghan *hogan.*

Dééd Yázhí was oblivious to the tears that wetted the dirty rag that covered her eyes as she remembered how as a child she used to hear her father whisper to her mother in the nocturnal darkness, when he would say,

"Hágo, shiyázhí." *Come here, my little one.* Dééd Yázhí remembered her father's voice was always gentle and loving, but when he spoke to their mother in the still of darkness, his voice was even more tender. Reluctant tears followed on the tail of the memory of her father and his voice.

"Nihizhé'é shą'?" *Where is our father?* Dééd Yázhí whispered without allowing her whispering voice to falter.

"Ha'íínílní, shádí," *Have hope, my older sister,* Dééd Yázhí heard her younger sister whisper to her.

Dééd Yázhí lifted her face toward the sky to keep her tears under her eyelids so her tears would not run out and saturate the dirty rag that covered her eyes, causing her eyes to sting from the filthy rag. She begged her tears to stay near her eyes and begged them not to run down her face to show her kidnappers she was afraid. Instead, more tears came to her eyes and saturated the filthy rag causing it to renew its foul smell.

After a meal of stale water, the men tightened the blindfolds over Dééd Yázhí and her younger sister's eyes. The ropes tying their ankles together and their wrists together were tied even tighter. Then the two sisters were plopped on a horse so that they were lying crosswise on the horses again. The filthy rug blankets were thrown over Dééd Yázhí and her younger sister to appear as if they were bedding that the 'anaa'í *enemy* were hauling. To make matters even worse, the filthy rags were once again pushed even farther into the sisters' mouths making them gag. The raggedy ends of the old rags were once again tied around their head. With every breath Dééd Yázhí and her younger sister took, they smelled or tasted filth.

The silent procession of horses, kidnappers, and captives stealthily made their way along the base of the rocky mesa. The big anaa'í *enemy* told his group of grubby, dirty, mean men that they had a few hours of riding before they would stop again.

51

Dééd Yázhí knew her father and her younger brothers would have trouble tracking them because of the route they had taken, traveling in a large semicircle and because their enemies had changed horses along the way.

Lifting her head to look at the faint moonlit shadows of the feet of their kidnappers, Dééd Yázhí knew they were riding in a northern direction toward Nóoda'í bikéyah *Ute territory*. Even the Nóoda'í *Ute* women disliked the Naabeehó women, Dééd Yázhí reminded herself as she feared for her younger sister.

After riding to the point where Dééd Yázhí was falling asleep, although her body ached from the position she was placed in, she noticed the sound of the horses' hooves was different. Soon, the horses stopped. She heard strange voices. Her heart began to beat faster.

The kidnappers were met once again with another group of strange men who had fresh horses. Dééd Yázhí was relieved to see the man who had hit her younger sister join the ones who met them. Two older men who met them, possibly Naakai *Mexican*, joined the kidnappers and were assigned to care for the two sisters.

Dééd Yázhí's wrists were untied but held behind her back by a strong enemy's hand. The rag was left in her mouth. Her nostrils flared. She heard the sound of a rope being pulled and then being pulled tight around her younger sister's ankles and wrists. The same was done for Dééd Yázhí. In spite of the foul-smelling rag, she noticed the rope smelled different.

Dééd Yázhí smelled yucca leaves! She became dizzy with homesickness and an acute sense of fear. The scent was overwhelming! She wondered where they were.

She tried moving her legs. The rope felt different. She heard her younger sister being pulled off of the horse. A loud thud was all Dééd Yázhí heard. Quietly, she said in a muffled whisper,

"Shideezhí,..." *My younger sister,...*

All of a sudden Dééd Yázhí felt herself being pulled off of the horse too. Their captors forgot her knees and ankles were stiff from being tied. She could not catch herself because her wrists were tied behind her. She also landed with a thud on the ground. The wind was knocked out of her and she had a difficult time catching her breath. She gagged, but once again, she determinedly whispered,

"Shideezhí,..." *My younger sister,...*

Dééd Yázhí began to panic because she did not hear an answer from her younger sister. She took a deep breath through her nose, became nauseated from the filthy rag tied over her mouth but tried concentrating on the scent of the yucca leaves and once again she muffled a whisper, a little louder this time, "Shideezhí,..." *My younger sister,...*

There was no answer. Dééd Yázhí felt an incredible sense of sadness come over her. She allowed tears to freely flow down her face, only to wet the filthy foul-smelling rag covering her eyes, causing the smell to become even more pronounced. Her breaths were finally becoming even again. Her throat hurt. Her shoulders hurt. Her ankles hurt. Her wrists hurt. Her stomach hurt from bouncing on the fast running horse. Dééd Yázhí's heart hurt the most because she could smell the scent of freshly picked and cut yucca leaves.

The scent of yucca leaves sent Dééd Yázhí's memory to the forefront of her mind. She lovingly remembered her mother's newly washed hair, which always carried the scent of yucca root. She remembered her father and her brothers and her maternal grandfather making ropes of yucca leaves. The scent overwhelmed her with homesickness.

Her thoughts came crashing to a halt! She could not even hear herself breathing. A deep sense of sadness flowed through her veins when she realized her ankles and her wrists were tied with ropes made of yucca leaves! The yucca leaves had become an ally to her enemy!

Gentle, keen thoughts of home began crashing into one another in her mind. Dééd Yázhí could feel the hot tears surface in her eyes and then escape the foul rag and make delicate patterns on her face as they rushed down her face, onto her chest, and then rushed to the ground to mix with the footprints of her enemies' moccasins.

Dééd Yázhí did not allow herself to rest, instead, she tortured and chided herself during the time her enemies rested. She had ignored the pleas of her younger sister and now they were captives of some of the most notorious anaa'í *enemies* the Naabeehó have. The sound of her younger sister whimpering brought Dééd Yázhí back to the present. She had to concentrate upon the survival of her younger sister. In a muffled whisper, she softly said,

"Shideezhí, díní'įį'ísh? Díí nihich'į' áhóót'įįdígíí doo chohoo'įįgóó baa shíni'. Shí shiniinaa yisnááh ánihi'diilyaa. Baa shíni', shideezhí." *My younger sister, are you awake? What has happened to us, I am very sorry for. It is because of me that we have been kidnapped. I feel very sorry, my younger sister.* Dééd Yázhí listened for an answer. She did not hear one.

54

A while after, she heard her younger sister's shaky reply in a soft whisper.

"Dédii, shił hodiniih. Yishchago biniinaa nihe'anaa'í 'atídashiilaa. Nihe'anaa'í ła' bíla' neeshjołgo yee shiniitsj'gi náshidíiłts'in. Shináá' kojígo 'ayóo neezgai. Shináá' ąą' ánéiish'įįhgo doo chohoo'įįgóó diniih biih nágoh nahalin. Nihizhé'é dóó nihicheii shą'? Naat'áanii dóó naabaahii 'ayóó 'át'éi nilį. Hadanihinitáa daats'í. Shimá 'ayóo bíhásááh, Dédii. Ni shįį nihizhé'é 'ayóo bíhósááh. Shí dó', yisnááh ánihi'diilyaaígíí baa shíni'. T'áá'íídą́ą́' yee' hooghangóó dah yiideeshtxeeł nít'ę́ę́' lá nisin. T'áá shǫǫ da, t'áá hái da bił hweeshne' doo nít'ę́ę́'." *Dédii, I am in pain. Our enemy tortured me because I was crying. One of our enemies made a fist and hit my cheek with his fist. My eye on this side really hurts. When I open my eyes, it feels as if pain is poured into my eye. Where are our father and our maternal grandfather? They are great leaders and great warriors. Maybe they are looking for us. I really miss my mother, Dedii. You probably really miss our father. Me too, I feel very bad that we have been kidnapped. I keep thinking I should have taken off running to our home. It is possible that I could have alerted someone.*

"Ha'íínílní, shideezhí. Nihizhé'é dóó nihicheii níhídoołkah. Aadę́ę́' shįį nihikéé' oołkahgo 'át'é. Ha'ííníilníigo t'éí nihikáa'jį' hodooleeł. K'adę́ę shįį hayoołkááł bich'į' hoolzhish. Íłhosh, shideezhí. Shí 'éí t'áá dínísh'įį doo. Ni 'áłtsé 'iidííłhosh, shideezhí. T'áá shǫǫh háínílyįį'go shí t'áá kónígháníjį' iideeshhosh. Iilghaazhgo t'éí náásgóó bíighah dooleeł. Díí yee' nizhónígo nihimá dóó nihizhé'é nanihineeztą́ą́'. Bínanihidi'neeztą́'ígíí bénéiilniihgo 'éí nihikáa'jį' hodooleeł."

Be strong, my younger sister. Our father and our maternal grandfather will catch up with us by tracking us. They are probably tracking us right now. If we remain strong, we will survive. It is probably predawn now. Sleep, my younger sister. I will remain awake. You go to sleep first, my younger sister. At least, when you have received a little rest, I will sleep for a little while. We can make it further if we get some sleep. We have received very good training from our mother and our father. If we remember what we were taught then we will survive.

Dééd Yázhí heard her younger sister whisper in agreement when she replied,

"Hágoshį́į́, shádí. Hodíínáá'ígo ch'ééshidíísił." *O.K., my older sister. Wake me up in a little while.*

"Hágoshį́į́, shideezhí," *O.K., my younger sister,* Dééd Yázhí replied.

Dééd Yázhí lightly squirmed, being careful not to wake her enemies. She wanted to bruise the yucca rope with which she was tied up, hoping the scent of yucca would be lifted by the light breeze and the scent sent her to senses. She wanted to be reminded of the safety of her home where she could smell her mother's newly washed hair that smelled of yucca soap. She knew if she smelled the gentle scent of the yucca plant, her mind would become stronger.

Dééd Yázhí listened as her younger sister's breathing became more pronounced. She knew her younger sister was sleeping due to fatigue. She was thankful her younger sister could sleep through the pain she felt.

Dééd Yázhí turned her face toward the eastern sky but something covered the sky and hid the moon. Complete darkness covered the ground. The scent of the yucca leaves brought gentle dreams of home.

Chapter Four
Separation!

Dééd Yázhí smiled as she heard her mother's voice calling her. She mumbled that it was too early to get up, saying,

"Shimá, t'ah nidii yee' tł'éé'. Áłtsé 'ashhosh." *My mother, it is still night. Let me sleep.*

Dééd Yázhí began to fall back asleep when she heard her name being called again, only this time it, was not her mother's sweet voice. It was her younger sister's pained pitiful voice!

In the faint light of dawn, Dééd Yázhí saw her younger sister being dragged away from the camp that had been set up for the night! Dééd Yázhí rolled toward her sister and lunged for her, but the man to whose ankle she was tied, jerked his leg in the opposite direction, sending her sprawling on the hard ground. Their captors laughed. They were looking at some shiny objects in their dirty hands. Dééd Yázhí saw that a filthy rag was stuffed in her younger sister's mouth and her hands and feet were tied even tighter. Her rug dress her mother had woven was being ripped from her sister's body as she was dragged along by some 'anaa'í *enemy*, possibly a Naakai *Mexican*.

"Dédii! Dédii! Kodi! Shíká 'anilyeed! Díí hastiin binásdzid! Dédii! Kodi! Dédii, kodi!" *Dédii! Dédii! Over here! Help me! I am afraid of this man! Dédii! Over here! Dédii, over here!*

Dééd Yázhí was helpless as she heard the muffled screams of her younger sister being tortured into submission. Dééd Yázhí was made helpless from the yucca straps that held her down, and helpless from the disbelief that this was happening to them again! Although her mind did not want to watch her sister being hauled off, she forced her eyes to remain open. She did not want to forget what her younger sister looked like. She watched as her sister's tsiiyééł *hair bun* and long white tsiitł'óół *hair string* hung down to the side of her shoulder. She cried hot tears as she watched the man tear the top of her younger sister's rug dress as he bent down and bit her soft skin, leaving a red mark on her right breast.

Dééd Yázhí heard her younger sister scream from the pain! She tried reaching out for her younger sister but the yucca rope held tight and cut into her wrists. Dééd Yázhí's younger sister screamed again out of fear, but could not shield her body from the 'anaa'í *enemy*. Dééd Yázhí screamed at the big anaa'í *enemy,* saying,

"Shígo!" Shígo! Shideezhí 'éí dooda! T'áá shǫǫdí, shideezhí 'éí dooda!" *Me instead! Me instead! Not my younger sister! Please, not my younger sister!* Dééd Yázhí's captors looked at her in confusion. Her captors did not speak her language. They just jerked the yucca rope that was tied to her ankles, causing her to fall and roll over onto her face. Her captors laughed evil laughter and pointed to the shiny objects in their hands. Dééd Yázhí felt a heavy sickness in her stomach. Her younger sister had just been sold to a tall 'anaa'í *enemy!*

Dééd Yázhí opened her mouth only to swallow the sand and dust she had rolled in. She again began to beg that she be taken instead of her sister when the thought that if she was taken, her younger sister would be left to these men and be alone. Dééd Yázhí felt incredibly helpless. She searched for the familiarity of the sun. She knew if the sun were fully up, this would not be happening. Her wild-looking eyes would not close!

In all the confusion, all Dééd Yázhí could say was,

"Ha'íínílní, shideezhí yázhí. Nitah hółdzilgo 'í'dílnééh. Nihimá bizaad béénílniih, shideezhí. Ná'ahiidiiltséełgo 'át'é. 'Ayóó'áníínísh'ní." *Have hope, my younger little sister. Make yourself strong. Remember the words of our mother, my younger sister. We will see one another again. I love you.* Dééd Yázhí only hoped her younger sister heard her words. She wished she had spoken more encouraging words to her sister when they were still together. She felt a desperate loneliness that made her heart hurt. She gripped the part of her rug dress that covered her heart and clenched it in her fists. Silent tears ran freely down her face.

The dust stung her eyes. She tried desperately not to blink, but as she watched, her younger sister and the tall anaa'í disappeared behind the horses, then behind the trees. She could hear her sister's desperate screams for help. Her sister's wild screams for help haunted her that night and the many nights following. Time never erased the sounds of the screams of her younger sister.

Once again, the big anaa'í who had kidnapped Dééd Yázhí and her sister warned his men to stay away from Dééd Yázhí.

"Look at how many pesos we got for the screaming one!" he yelled as he poked at some shiny coins in his hand.

The group holding Dééd Yázhí remained in the same spot for the rest of the day. Although Dééd Yázhí was exhausted, she did not want sleep to visit her because she knew her sister would not be getting any sleep. She hugged herself and cried herself into a troubled sleep.

A dirty man poked Dééd Yázhí with a stick and woke her out of her troubled sleep. It was very dark. There was no light from the moon. One of her captors dragged her out from under the tree then picked her up and carelessly sat her on a horse. Untying her ankles, the man forced her to straddle the horse. To her horror, her rug dress rose up high on her thighs exposing her legs! She could almost hear the evil smile of her captors. The big anaa'í threw a thin blanket at her then jumped off of his horse and covered her legs, then tucked the sides under her.

Before the men began their journey, the big anaa'í *enemy* changed his clothes. It was the third time since he had kidnapped Dééd Yázhí and her younger sister. After riding for a long time, the first dim white light of dawn began to peek over the eastern horizon. In the faint light, Dééd Yázhí could see the big anaa'í was wearing funny clothes. He was wearing a shirt that was blue and had many shiny round objects placed down the front. The same material covered his arms and his legs. She thought, he is wearing a small, funny war bonnet. She kept looking back at the big enemy's war bonnet. The war bonnet was round, tight around the head then rose up and it seemed to her that someone had put too much weight on top of the war bonnet so it just fell down onto the bonnet, flattening it like the waste of a cow. A hard-looking piece of material stuck straight out from the big enemy's head that looked like the beak of a bird, which was actually the visor of the hat. Brown moccasins that did not look soft completed his outfit.

The men the big anaa'í was riding with also changed their clothes. They were dressed the same as her kidnapper. In fear, Dééd Yázhí searched the appearance of the men for signs of the ones who had kidnapped her and her younger sister from their home in Dziłíjiin *Black Mesa.*

The men who changed their clothes seemed to sit straighter on their horses in these new clothes, and they paid less attention to her and paid more attention to their surroundings. Each man carried a "stick" that had a metal rod attached to it which they carried with them wherever they went. Even when they slept, they had this long gun next to them.

The group turned toward the eastern direction. Dééd Yázhí was pulled off of the horse she had been riding on and was lifted onto another horse.

"Your desires and greed for young Navajo women are too close!" the big anaa'í *enemy* shouted to the man she rode in front of. Although her captors allowed Dééd Yázhí to sit on her own horse, they did not allow her to hold the reins. Instead, a short, brown-haired man kept her reins and smiled greedily out of lust as he watched her ride bareback while she held onto the horse's mane. The thin blanket covering her legs kept coming loose. Not wanting to be slowed down, the big anaa'í tied the blanket tight around her waist so it would stay in place.

As they rode, Dééd Yázhí remained alert and observant of her surroundings. There may come a time when I will be left alone long enough to run away, and the direction I run to will mean life or death, she told herself in silent thoughts.

Dééd Yázhí and her captors rode past the mesa she knew from the times when they followed their father to the leadership gatherings. Thoughts of her father brought tears to her eyes but she scolded herself and the tears disappeared. Soon, they were riding toward the northeast, far away from her high mesa into an area that was sandy. The sand beneath her horse's hooves was of a reddish color instead of the light brown landscape they had traveled through.

Behind them were mesa walls, while to the north of them was a long valley, where they could see for miles. Strange looking hills made of stone rose from the ground. To the east, the valley continued with sagebrush turning the entire valley a pale blue green, while here and there the red ground appeared. In the southern direction, the mesa curled back and forth like the pattern of a snake's crawl. The shape of the mesa walls created shadows and showed areas where the sand dunes were piled so high they nearly reached the top of the mesa. It was on one of these sand dunes that they made their way off of a tall mesa. Behind them, the western sky was hidden by the mesa that rose high into the sky. The rocks seemed soft enough to be carried away by the wind.

The landscape had completely changed and Dééd Yázhí was not used to seeing red hills made of one big solid rock. Homesickness set in. The sagebrush reminded her of the safety of home, but not being able to see juniper trees spreading out and up, and not being able to see her tall pine trees rise toward the sky made her afraid. She desperately wanted to go home! Dééd Yázhí wanted to see her younger sister again! She wanted to hear her father's voice booming in the valley. There was a sense of intense fear she felt as she observed her surroundings.

Toward evening, they moved slowly since Dééd Yázhí's captors were looking for small game to kill. Without success, the big anaa'í jumped off of his horse, threw down his blanket, and spread it out. He put his round, gray pouch to his mouth and turned it up and gulped its contents. Without warning, he threw the gray pouch at Dééd Yázhí, spraying her with water. Dééd Yázhí was so thirsty. With her hands tied she could not lift the pouch to her mouth. One of the men jumped up, picked up the pouch and put it to her mouth. She tasted the contents. The water was salty and stale tasting. Not caring how hungry or thirsty she was, she turned her head away from the pouch and water spilled out onto the ground. The man slapped her face for wasting water. Her cheek stung from the pain and tears rose to the surface of her eyes.

"Doo deeshchah da!" *I am not going to cry!* she said with determination as pain kept threatening her tears to appear. She blinked, closing her eyes as tight as she could and forced the tears back into their place while the face of her father flashed before her eyes.

The big anaa'í told the men they were going to settle down to spend the night near the tall mesa wall. Dééd Yázhí watched as the men dropped their exhausted bodies on the ground and stared up into the sky. Soon all light from the sun dropped behind the mesa wall and darkness began to visit the sky. When the light from the bright moon shone upon them, Dééd Yázhí could not sleep because her mind kept asking how the moon could shine. She asked in accusing thoughts of how could the moon not know that I am suffering, or that my sister is suffering? How could the sky look so normal?

These questions marched through her mind until they made a well-worn path and her head began to hurt.

Dééd Yázhí sat up and began to observe her surroundings in the moonlight, but only found her heart beginning to beat fast. To the north of their temporary camp, she looked at the rock formations that rose menacingly from the ground. Staring at the formations, she felt her heart and mind fill with fear! The formations were actually marching! The moonlight shadows filled her heart with fear when she saw that the formations loomed larger at night. She shut her eyes but found her heart began beating even faster. As long as her eyes were open, the formations seemed to stay away, but with her eyes closed, the formations marched faster toward her.

Dééd Yázhí wished she had been more observant earlier in the day. At least I would have taken a better look at my surroundings, she thought as her head began to pound along with every beat of her heart. She was near tears. She remembered her ankle was tied to the dirty man who wore his boots even when he slept. She moved her feet away from his leg to make him stir so he could wake up and keep her company as the formations marched toward her. Instead, the man rolled over and in doing so, his arm fell across her lap. Once again, she jerked her leg and watched as the man stirred and moved his arm. She desperately wanted him to wake up because she believed the formations were coming closer! She jerked her leg again only to watch the man roll over pulling her blanket off of her. Feeling weak, cold, and vulnerable, she began to yell,

"Nihe'anaa'í 'aadę́ę́' nihich'į' yinééł!" *Our enemies are moving toward us!* In unison, the men sat up and began

65

grabbing for rocks to throw at the approaching enemy. The big anaa'í reached for his gun and swung it back and forth in front of him. Her kidnappers wildly searched the immediate area without getting up. When they did not notice danger, they looked at her in disgust. Dééd Yázhí pointed toward the north, toward the formation that was marching toward her. They looked but did not seem concerned.

Soon, Dééd Yázhí could feel the ground begin to shake along with the pounding of her heart. She began to panic and tried pulling on the blanket to cover herself. The man to whom she was tied, stirred and yelled at her, then slumped back in his blanket and fell asleep once again. As she kept her eye on the formation, it seemed not to move as fast, but when she turned away from it, it came closer with every beat of her heart.

The early dawn was very slow in coming, and soon Dééd Yázhí sat shivering from fear, cold, and fatigue. When the darkness began to disappear and the eastern sky began to turn a pale white, she finally fell asleep from fatigue. It seemed she was asleep for just minutes when the men began kicking her, wanting her to get up. She sat up and looked to the north and saw the large rock formation that put so much fear in her heart during the night. It remained in the same spot as when she had first seen it.

Somehow this rock formation moves at night, Dééd Yázhí thought, as fear once again caused her heart to beat faster. If only I were at home, on my soft sheepskin, with my mother near me and my father keeping the fire going all night, and with my brothers and my younger sister sleeping near me, I would not be so afraid, she thought as tears slowly made their way down her cheeks, dripping off her chin. It was painful to think of home, but she forced herself to remember her home to keep herself company and to keep herself strong. In anger, Dééd Yázhí pushed her tears into her skin so they would not fall where her enemies walked.

Quietly, she whispered to herself,

"Nizhé'é néiniltsą́ą́go 'índa díichah. Ních'aad, shiyázhí. Ha'íínílníh. Naabeehó 'asdzání nílį́, 'éí bee ha'íínílní." *You can cry when you see your father again. Don't cry, my little one. Be comforted. Comfort yourself in knowing that you are a Navajo woman.* She pretended it was her mother who was telling her these words of strength. Her tears were forcing themselves to the surface of her eyes again as she blinked to keep them in her eyes.

The kidnappers and Dééd Yázhí moved on, still riding in an easterly direction. Soon, they were riding past a deep canyon. As they rode past the canyon, her captors decided to wait until nightfall to ride again. The big anaa'í tied her arms together and forced her mouth open to stuff in dirty rags that smelled like dead animals. With each breath, she gagged. Each time she gagged, the men poked her with their long sticks that had the metal rod attached to them. With each poke of their gun, Dééd Yázhí became more weak. The big anaa'í *enemy* warned the men not to poke her so hard, that they had to keep her in good condition so they could get their pesos. Nonetheless, the sharp pokes continued.

The kidnappers waited until the blackness of night had claimed the sky to decide to continue their eastern ride. Dééd Yázhí kept her head near the horse's mane to keep from falling off and clung to the horse's mane because her hands were tied. She appreciated the fact that her wrists were tied with ropes made of yucca leaves. With each rise and fall of her horse, she caught scents of the yucca plant. As she clung to her horse's mane, she unexpectedly whispered,

"Yisnááh áshi'diilyaaígíí biniinaa t'áá hazhó'ó díí t'éiyá shik'éí danilį," *Because I am held captive, these are my only relatives,"* she said as she breathed in deeply to catch the scent of the yucca rope. Dééd Yázhí surprised herself when she heard herself greet the ropes made of yucca by saying,

"Yá'át'ééh, shidine'é." *Greetings, my people.*

Dééd Yázhí's captors continued riding in an easterly direction and soon they reached higher ground, where the sagebrush were taller and were beginning to brush the bottoms of her moccasins as she rode. Juniper trees began to appear again. Once again, rock formations appeared, only this time they were gray instead of red. As the formations loomed in the dark, she was not as afraid as she was the first night when they rested among the mesas.

A faint, sad smile crossed Dééd Yázhí's face when she felt the sharp needles of the tall sagebrush plants playfully pull at the gray blanket that covered her legs. She looked down and said,

"Dooda. Háni'dii shik'ésti'. Ahéhéé', shik'éí." *No. Allow it (the blanket) to cover me. Thank you, my relatives.*

Continuing eastward, Dééd Yázhí could see in the faint light of the moon that the sagebrush became sparse and the ground turned to a dark color. The sheen that reflected from the sand had disappeared. Through this land the men hurried themselves along. The dust kicked up by the horses in front of Dééd Yázhí's horse loosely hung in the night air, blurring her vision and causing her eyes to tear up. It was very difficult to for her to wipe her eyes when she had to hang on to her horse's mane to maintain her balance. Dééd Yázhí welcomed the "dust tears" because they seemed to keep the memories of her family close. She thought of the way her father stood tall and strong, the way her beautiful mother looked, the way her brothers and sister laughed, and the way her father looked at their mother, and the way he looked at his children. A sob threatened to surface, but Dééd Yázhí caught it in time and swallowed it and chided herself because she had made a promise to herself not to cry until she saw her father again. She vowed to remain strong to get through this ordeal. Besides, she could not let the anaa'í *enemy* see that she loved her family because they would make sure she never sees her family again.

Dééd Yázhí had lost track of time. How long had it been since she and her younger sister had been kidnapped? Her mind lost track of the mornings that marked the days. She was well aware that it had been two days since she had last eaten. Her stomach hurt, her heart hurt, and her head hurt. Each hurt resulted from a hunger of a different kind.

Dééd Yázhí could see tall pine trees in the distance. She cautiously looked up into the sky to look for the constellations that would give her a clue regarding the direction they were traveling. Eastward, they were traveling eastward. Soon black canyon walls came into view, and they were still traveling toward the east. As they rode, she noticed the ground was sparsely covered with sagebrush and small weeds once again.

The canyon walls, which rose high and in even more strange formations were now north of them. They camped in the folds of the canyon walls. The men were careful not to make a fire.

Dééd Yázhí was given a round tortilla that was yellow in color and had round blue dots of mold on it. She thought about the times when her mother's bread sat too long, round blue dots would appear on her bread too. She remembered that her mother used to place the bread that had mold on them out in the sun to dry, saying,

"Bááh dláád bąąh daazlį́'ígíí sháą'jį' nidanohnííł. Hání'dii bááh yéigo yigan. Dláád bik'i'diidíingo 'éí dó' doogą́ą́ł. Dláád yigą́ąhgo doo halniih da łeh. Haigo 'ayóo deesk'aazgo 'ei bááhígíí 'atoo' biih jitihgo t'áá shǫǫ bee názhniicha'. *Place the bread that have mold on them in the sun. Let the bread dry out. When the sun shines on the mold, it will dry out too. In the winter when it is real cold you can break the bread into your stew and you will get full. Once dried, the mold does not have a taste to it.* Dééd Yázhí shut her eyes and strained to remember her father's voice intermingled with the voices of her siblings and her mother.

Dééd Yázhí woke and felt moistness under her. In horror, she realized it was the sacred time of the month for her. She had been told many times that the blood that flowed from her body was sacred and that it represented life. These men must not have been taught well by their mothers, she thought, as she tried searching her surroundings for the soft branches of the 'awééts'áál" (a bush whose soft branches were placed under a baby to absorb the baby's urine). The only bush she could see for a distance was the sagebrush. Whenever her captors stopped to rest, Dééd Yázhí was allowed to relieve herself behind a short bush. She peered into the distance under the faint light of dawn that was hidden by the large formations off in the eastern direction. She saw sumac bushes and many small sagebrush plants. After relieving herself, she pulled off a few of the newer branches of a young sagebrush and wiped between her legs and then tried placing the thin branches between her legs, but the branches had an occasional thorn, which cut into her delicate skin.

Followed by a short man, she returned to her captors. She noticed her monthly blood flow had already settled in the thin blanket that covered her legs and her blood had matted with the coarse rug she slept on. Embarrassed because a Naabeehó woman was not to allow anyone to see a women's menstrual flow, Dééd Yázhí wrapped the lower part of her body with the thin blanket and stood waiting for one of her kidnappers to place her on her horse.

As her body rose and fell in time with the horse's gallop, she could feel her flow freely run to mat with her previously semidried blood. She wished she was at home where she could care for herself the way Naabeehó women were supposed to. She shut her eyes tight and shook her head to keep herself from thinking of her predicament, but her thoughts of home were very strong and they pulled her close to tears.

Dééd Yázhí wondered how her younger sister was doing. Had she experienced her time of the month among her enemies too? she wondered. A lone, large tear sat on the edge of her eyelid, then slid slowly down her face as she lifted her head to pray to the Creator to ask Him to protect her younger sister.

The procession continued as Dééd Yázhí's kidnappers searched the landscapes and rock formations around them looking for their enemies. In the warmth of the day, Dééd Yázhí felt like her skin was stuck to the gray blanket, which was most likely glued to her horse from the blood that flowed from her. She kept her head down so as to avoid looking at her kidnappers' faces.

Late in the day Dééd Yázhí and her captors arrived at a large gathering, where there were many men with white skin. There were so many of them and they all seemed to look alike. They also wore the same type of clothes Dééd Yázhí's kidnappers had changed into. The men stared at the seven riders in wonder. The white men spoke in a language Dééd Yázhí did not understand. While the men talked, she looked around. A quick thought raced through her mind. Shizhé'é daats'í kodi shik'ídínóotaał? *Will my father be able to find me here?* Tears began to make their way down her face. In her mind, she saw her mother, then she saw her brothers, and she could still see her sister being carried away by the tall anaa'í *enemy*. Dééd Yázhí felt an incredible sense of homesickness. She was afraid. She was alone. Shizhé'é shą'? *Where is my father?* was all she could think about.

A tall, gray-haired man became angry as Dééd Yázhí's six kidnappers argued with him. The big anaa'í *enemy* pointed at Dééd Yázhí. Her heart raced with fear. The tall, gray-haired man pointed to all the dried blood under her, and her short kidnapper reached up and recklessly pulled her off of the horse. When he did, Dééd Yázhí felt a sudden flow of blood that she could not control, and the dusty moccasins her maternal grandfather made for her became wet inside. Her torn rug dress did not hide her blood-stained legs.

I cannot let these men see my blood during this sacred time, Dééd Yázhí told herself as she backed away from the men and moved closer to the horse she rode. One of her captors grabbed her and pushed her toward the white haired men, causing her to stumble.

"Dooda, t'áá shǫǫdí! Dooda!" *No, please. No!* Dééd Yázhí pleaded but no one listened. She watched helplessly as she saw the tall, gray-haired man gave the big anaa'í two shiny objects. The big anaa'í stared at the two objects in the palm of his hand. In anger, he threw the shiny objects on the ground and kicked at the ground. The big anaa'í and his men began to argue. One short man picked up the two shiny objects and began grinning as he looked at the shiny objects. The big anaa'í *enemy* snatched the two shiny objects out of the short man's hand, then turned and walked toward his horse. Before he got on his horse, he took out his gun and shot the horse Dééd Yázhí had been riding, an action that sent the white men running in different directions, hiding behind anything that would provide protection. The white men regained their wits and aimed their long guns at the big anaa'í.

Dééd Yázhí noticed the only man who stood his ground was the tall, gray-haired white man. She later realized he had a pronounced limp, which could have been the reason he did not move when the big anaa'í *enemy* shot the horse.

Dééd Yázhí did not see what happened next because a white man threw a blanket over her and two white men carried her as she kicked and silently screamed.

Not again, screamed Dééd Yázhí in her thoughts. When she finally found her voice, she screamed,

"Shizhé'é! Shimá! Kodi! Kodi! 'Ayóo násdzid! Nihe'anaa'í binásdzid! Doo daats'íid da!" *My father! My mother! Help! Help! I am really scared! I am afraid of our enemy! They are not kind!*

She thought of her younger sister who begged and begged to be released by the enemy to no avail. She tried covering her ears to shut out the sound of her sister screaming. To comfort herself, she was grateful her younger sister only had to worry about one man carrying her off. Here she had to worry about a dozen men surrounding her as the two men dropped her on the ground. Dééd Yázhí forced her thoughts to come to a screeching halt. Here she was feeling sorry for herself when her younger sister was in an unknown place, most likely being tortured by the man who took her away.

Dééd Yázhí forced her mind back to the present. Her body hurt from hitting the ground so hard. The white men laughed at her rug dress that was stained with urine and blood and began kicking her with strange looking moccasins. She was embarrassed! This was her sacred time of the month. She was not supposed to be treated like this. People, especially men, were not to see her like this! The light faded from her eyes, and she did not see what happened after being kicked by the men.

Chapter Five

Among the 'Anaa'í *Enemy*

Dééd Yázhí's womanhood did not prepare her for the following two months. A dirty little square shed was where she was forced into and became the place where she was kept. It was in the dirty shed that she had to fight off dirty, hairy white men. Men who were as tall and as strong as her father, men who were hairier than the lambs she had so lovingly cared for at the base of Dziłíjiin *Black Mesa*. Men who were ravenous and who, at the end of the day, would begin fighting among themselves over "having their turn" with the Indian prisoner who was just brought in. Men who forgot Dééd Yázhí was human and could feel pain and embarrassment and instead showed their hatred for her as she crouched in pain and fear in the shadows.

The shed Dééd Yázhí was kept in was square and small. It had a hard floor that was covered with mud and straw. The walls of the shed were made of logs that were stacked as high as the height of the tallest dirty white enemy. The doorway of the shed faced the southern direction, which caused

Dééd Yázhí much concern. The door was thick and made of logs that were tied together and not anything like the soft rug blanket that her mother covered the entrance to her hooghan *hogan* in the spring and summer months or the thick hide that covered the entrance in the cold months. Before she was shoved into the shed, she noticed the roof of the shed was slanted instead of shaped in a gentle dome like her mother's home. There was a square hole in the roof to allow smoke to escape. The hole for the smoke was her only connection to the outside.

Dééd Yázhí's heart was filled with fear because she could not see outside except through little holes between the logs. At night, her sleep was interrupted by the sharp sticks of straw covering the floor, which poked her body whenever she moved. She had not been allowed to clean herself since she was sold to the soldiers at Fort Canby (present day Fort Defiance). In the darkness of the shed, she tried rubbing off the dried blood that still covered her legs. Her rug dress was torn, torn by the dirty, hairy white men who forced themselves on her. At first, Dééd Yázhí tried to fight off the dirty, hairy white men but after a few days, she became more and more weakened by the pain and fear that was inflicted upon her several times a day.

There was only one man who did not want to hurt her. The tall, gray-haired man who gave the big anaa'í *enemy* two shiny objects offered Dééd Yázhí protection. He was quiet and communicated with her through hand signals. The tall, gray-haired man was thin and his skin appeared whiter than the mean men with whom he worked. He walked with a slight limp. Dééd Yázhí was afraid of him. Peering through the little holes in between the logs that made the wall of the shed, she watched as he yelled with a loud voice that bellowed across the green valley several times a day when he yelled at the mean dirty hairy white men.

He brought her white broth every morning. The broth was as white as his skin. Dééd Yázhí knew she should not be taking in the food of the enemy because by noon the white broth made her stomach feel extended and very full. The broth was similar in appearance to goat's milk. It was not as thick as goat's milk and the broth was a lighter shade of white. Dééd Yázhí loved goat's milk. It was sweet and tasted even better with her mother's soft blue-corn crepes.

One morning, Dééd Yázhí softly declared to herself,

"Tł'ízí bibe' ayóo 'aajooba'. Díí shį́į́ ha'á'tíí 'át'ée, sha'shin. Ayóo na'nisol dóó ts'ídá doo łikan da, 'ako nidi díí t'éí shaa néíkááh. Shizhe'é t'áá'aaníí 'áníí lá. Nihe'anaa'í bich'iiyą' doo nihí nihá 'át'ée da." *Goat's milk is very kind. It is uncertain what this is. It causes one to bloat and it just does not taste good at all but this is all he gives me. What my father said is very true, our enemy's food is not for us.*

The broth was all Dééd Yázhí was given. It did not have a taste to it, but once she drank it, the broth would cause her as much pain as the men who forced themselves upon her. By evening, when one of the dirty, hairy white men would force himself on top of her, her stomach pains would be excruciating. She could not help but cry out in pain, fear, and embarrassment.

During those painful times, Dééd Yázhí reminded herself of the vow she had made to herself, that of not crying until she saw her father. Soon, her vow made her stronger. Tears frequently flowed but no voice was heard to accompany the tears.

After a few days, when the tall, gray-haired man brought her the white broth, he greeted her by nodding at her when he left the bowlful of broth near the entrance. After many mornings of leaving the broth, he did not leave as he usually did. He waited for her to take the bowl of broth from his hand. After many mornings of waiting for her to take the white broth, Dééd Yázhí reached out and accepted the bowl in her shaking hand. She was immediately regretful of her actions because the tall, gray-haired man stayed to watch her drink the broth.

She did not know how to tell the man she did not like the white broth he gave her. She was afraid not to take the broth for fear that he would begin to treat her the way the other dirty, hairy white men treated her. Instead, she fought with her body so as not to gag on the broth. Every morning, she obediently drank the broth, gagging on every sip she swallowed.

By the appearance of the moon, although she could not see the entire moon through the smoke hole, she believed the moon told her she had been held captive at the fort for a month. When it was time for her sacred time of the month to come around again, she became very worried. Her breasts were becoming tender to the touch. She became afraid.

She held her stomach and said in a voice she did not recognize.

"Haashą' nisht'é? T'áadoo lé'é shaa néíkáhígíí da shą' ha'át'íí yił ádeił'į? 'Ayóo la' shiiłkóóh." *I wonder what it is. I wonder what they put into the broth they give me. It is making me very nauseated.* She listened for an answer but none was to be heard.

78

Dééd Yázhí looked into the night sky through the smoke hole, although as a child she was told never to look through it. She needed to see the shape of the moon. Staying awake late one night, she was finally rewarded with the sight of only a sliver of the moon in the clear night. The beautiful sight of the moon was soon replaced with a black sky. She sat quietly dreading the morning when she would feel sick again.

Late one evening, one of the dirty, white hairy men interrupted her thoughts when he kicked in her door. The dirty, hairy man looked at her, frowned, then smiled an evil smile. He tore at her ragged rug dress, kicked at her moccasins, bit her neck, bit her shoulders and her breasts, and recklessly touched her in places where she hurt the most. Dééd Yázhí cried out in pain. She fought against the man with all her might, but the more she fought with him, the harder he bit at her skin.

All of a sudden she felt the dirty man's weight that held her down being lifted off of her body. The dirty, hairy man had an angry confused look on his face. Dééd Yázhí could hear the distinct sound of the anger of one man against another.

She realized the tall, gray-haired man who fed her in the morning dragged the foul-smelling hairy man off of her. She became very afraid because the tall, gray-haired man who fed her broth was beating the dirty, hairy man who was on top of her. He continued to beat the dirty, hairy man until he was not moving anymore. The tall, gray-haired one turned from the man and looked in Dééd Yázhí's direction. He then grabbed the dirty, torn blanket on the floor and gently draped it around her and helped her up and led her to the corner of the shed, to the place he usually found her sitting in the morning.

He helped her lower herself to the ground and draped the blanket around her shoulders again before he left and came back and had the hairy man removed from the shed.

Dééd Yázhí sat on the floor shivering with blood flowing freely from between her legs. All she could do was try to wrap her arms around her stomach to make the bleeding stop, but it was useless. The tall, gray-haired one disappeared out the door. Not long after, she lost consciousness.

When she awoke, she noticed the sun was setting. She looked around to find the tall, gray-haired one who fed her broth sitting in the corner with his head resting against the wall. He must have heard her. With some difficulty, he got up as fast as he could and ran to her side and touched her arm. At his touch, Dééd Yázhí's breathing became uneven out of fear.

Dééd Yázhí had dreamed her mother had rolled out her soft sheepskin and had asked her to lie down on it. It felt so soft, but she could not determine where she was. She wanted to go back into a deep sleep to visit her family again.

Upon fully waking, she found she was sleeping on softer blankets, not quite clean, but definitely soft. The tall, gray-haired one held out another cup of warm white broth, but Dééd Yázhí immediately became nauseated at the thought of drinking it.

"Don't you want some warm milk?" he said with a concerned look on his face. "You have always liked it." Dééd Yázhí shut her eyes real tight so she would not have to see the awful warm white liquid. This was the first time she had heard the tall, gray-haired one speaking to her. His voice was rather gentle. It was not the voice that he used when he barked at her kidnappers or at the men he worked with (volunteer soldiers).

After offering her the white broth that she refused, the tall, gray-haired one stopped visiting as often as he used to. Dééd Yázhí was afraid that without his presence, the dirty, hairy white men would come back to attack her again. For some reason, the attacks stopped. She did not understand why the attacks stopped but she was grateful.

One day while thinking about her mother and her father and her sister and her brothers, Dééd Yázhí found that having to exist without fear, she could concentrate on her situation. She wondered where it was that she was being held captive. She knew she was a captive of the tall, gray-haired one because she was unable to open the door to the shed from the inside.

Dééd Yázhí wanted to see her father and hear his beautiful words of strength, and she wanted to hear her mother's quiet words of comfort, but she did not know where she was being held. If I do not know where I am, how can my father and my brothers know where I am? How can they find me if I can't even find myself? she silently questioned herself. She felt even more helpless. She comforted herself in her belief that her home was toward the western direction.

One day as she was thinking about her family, Dééd Yázhí jumped up to look between the boards that made the walls of her shed. She desperately wanted to see the path of the sun in the sky. From the light that was cast upon the high walls of the shed, she could tell the sun was going down. Hoping the sky would hear her, she asked the sky to ask the sun to tell her father where she was being held captive.

"Shizhé'é kwe'é shi'dótą shá bidiní. Kwe'é atah ąąhéeshjéé'
nishłį́, shá bidiní. Baa nánooshkąąh. Shimá 'ałdó shá bił hodíilnih.
Shizhé'é dóó shimá shá bił hwíínílne'go doo ts'íí 'át'éégóó baa
'ahééh nisin dooleeł." *Tell my father I am being held here. Tell
him I am a captive here. I am pleading with you. Tell my mother
too. If you tell them, I will be ever so thankful.* Tears slid down
her face and made their way into the side of her mouth. Her
tears were hot and bitter. She did not bother to wipe the tears
away. They dried on her face and made a lacy pattern of white
dried tears on her face.

I have to be strong for my younger sister. She is also being
held captive somewhere, she thought. Dééd Yázhí looked
toward the small patch of sky through the smoke hole in the
roof and asked the Creator to watch over her precious younger
sister.

"Shideezhí shá baa 'áhólyą́ą dooleeł. Shá bik'i díní'į́į'
dooleeł. T'ááshǫǫdí..." *Take care of my younger sister for me.
Look out for her for me. Please...* her voice trailed off into
sadness. Looking down at her hands, she told herself,

"Nideezhí bił ná'ahiidííltséełgo 'át'é." *You will see your
younger sister again.* Her voice trailed off into sadness.

****

It was at Fort Canby (later named Fort Defiance) Dééd Yázhí
was held captive. The dirty, hairy white men were soldiers.
Dééd Yázhí remembered back to the time when she was left at
the fort by her kidnappers. At the time, she was shocked when
she noticed the dirty, hairy white men did not have the same
colored hair. Her people all had black hair and the older ones
had gray hair, but these dirty men had yellow hair, brown hair,

82

red hair, gray hair, dark hair, and tan colored hair. Dééd Yázhí wondered if the dirty, hairy white men dipped their hair in the natural dyes she and her mother used for dying wool. A sad little snicker escaped her lips, which surprised her. She quickly looked around her to see who witnessed her snicker. There was no one around. She was alone in the little shed. She wondered how long she had been held captive by the dirty, white hairy men.

Dééd Yázhí still had to worry about survival although the white hairy men were kept away from her, but her heart ached with loneliness and hurt deeply with homesickness. She wondered when her thoughts would drift to other things instead of dwelling only upon survival.

All of a sudden, she looked up. She stopped thinking to listen to the sounds that came from outside. Someone's footsteps were approaching the shed. Her heart began to beat fast making her dizzy. Fear was getting the best of her. Someone from the outside slipped the lock off of her door. Dééd Yázhí held her breath. The door opened and sunshine from the early evening poured in from the outside, blinding her.

The tall, gray-haired one stood in the doorway. Dééd Yázhí did not want to admit it, but it was under his care the attacks against her stopped. Under his care, her bleeding slowed, then stopped. Under his care, she was slowly regaining strength. Still, she was afraid of him. Like the others, he had white skin.

He walked to where she sat on the floor and handed her a plate of food. Dééd Yázhí looked up, but her glance was blocked by the tall, gray-haired one's face. She was shocked when she saw his eyes. He had light turquoise colored eyes! This was the first time she looked into his eyes. She immediately shut her eyes very tight because she had never seen a five-fingered one with turquoise-colored eyes. The only time she had seen eyes that color was when she saw a fat horned toad that had turquoise-colored eyes, but never a person!

She was sure she glimpsed signs of kindness on his face. The wrinkles near his eyes were not as deep as she imagined they would be. His face looked young but his hair was that of an older man. She wondered if his short, curly hair was soft like that of her newborn goats. She noticed his beard was also gray and long, reminding her of the tł'ízí chǫǫh *billy goat* her mother kept near the herd of goats. His moustache curled at the ends, making his face appear as if he was smiling all the time. Maybe that is why he appears to be kind, Dééd Yázhí thought, immediately becoming embarrassed about thinking of the appearance of her people's enemy.

Although she was afraid of the tall, gray-haired man, he alone took care of her more often as she began to regain her strength.

****

Dééd Yázhí was glad she did not feel nauseated anymore nor did her breasts feel tender. Although she was held captive by her people's enemies, she was relieved to feel better. It was not until she had time to think and reason that she realized she had had a miscarriage.

Had I carried my 'awéé' *baby* to full term, I would not have known who the father was, she thought in sadness. Upon realizing she had miscarried her little one, she wanted to cry, but she did not know whom to cry for—her unborn baby or for herself having been raped by so many dirty, hairy white men.

She noticed her body had become taller, her breasts grew larger, her abdomen became thinner, and her hips seemed to have drifted apart. Just from the way her body had changed, Dééd Yázhí presumed she had been held captive for nearly one fall and winter season. She wondered several times where the winter went. She did not remember feeling the cold air of winter.

"Da' niheeísh yíhai?" *Did we have a winter?* she would ask herself, but her mind became a blur at the thought.

"Shizhé'é dóó shicheii daats'í haigo baa dahané'ígíí yaa nahasne'?" *Did my father and my maternal grandfather tell winter stories?* she quietly asked herself. She allowed her thoughts to revisit her happy childhood as she remembered her maternal grandfather telling his winter stories during the long, cold winter nights.

She loved spending time with her maternal grandparents. Her maternal grandfather told the funniest and the best stories, and her maternal grandmother made the softest and tastiest bááh dootł'izhí *blue corn bread.*

Dééd Yázhí remembered many of her maternal grandfather's stories were for the children, but everyone, including the adults, listened when he told his stories. Although her grandfather told many of the same stories every year, she never grew tired of the stories. All the grandchildren took turns sitting in her grandfather's lap when he told stories.

When Dééd Yázhí sat in her maternal grandfather's lap as he told a story, she loved to watch his turquoise earrings swing back and forth as he talked. She also loved to touch his smooth, slightly wrinkled cheeks. His eyes sparkled with kindness. Dééd Yázhí loved her maternal grandfather. He was a thoughtful and generous man.

Dééd Yázhí allowed her thoughts to wander into the memories of her maternal grandmother who was a little woman but she was strong. Many times, Dééd Yázhí watched her grandmother single-handedly push over a full-grown sheep, tie it up, hold it down, and begin to shear the sheep using a flat stone with a very sharp edge. Other women needed the help of another person, but not her grandmother. Dééd Yázhí was so proud of her maternal grandmother. After all the day's work, her grandmother would make the smoothest, roundest, tastiest, and most beautiful bááh dootł'izhí *blue bread* with her little hands that had just sheared several sheep. As Dééd Yázhí watched her grandmother make bread, she promised herself she would be just as strong as her maternal grandmother. Dééd Yázhí loved her maternal grandmother. Her grandmother was a loving and kind woman.

At the memories, tears slid from her eyes and warmed her hand. Trauma had cast a blur on the seasons that came and went. The present nights were warmer.

The dirty, hairy white men must be afraid of the tall, gray-haired one, she thought. They did not bust in the door anymore, yet she was very afraid of them. One evening, Dééd Yázhí heard a familiar sound that caused her heart to beat fast. She tried in vain to peer between the logs that made the walls of the shed to determine the direction the sound was coming from. She cautiously walked to the heavy door and pushed on it. It moved but would not open. The sound become a little louder when she pushed on the door. The sound made her so homesick and lonely. Tears flowed freely. She chided herself for allowing her memories to cause her to become less alert.

She jumped back from the door. Someone was walking and talking. She listened. She could no longer hear the sound that made her so lonesome. In between footsteps, she listened for the familiar sound. The footsteps did not sound familiar. They were not the footsteps of the tall, gray-haired one where one foot stepped heavier than the other.

Dééd Yázhí took quick quiet steps back to fall on the blankets on the floor. She could feel her breath becoming louder due to fear. She tried to control her breath so she could prepare herself to fight with a dirty, hairy soldier.

The lock on the door was slowly slid out of its place. Dééd Yázhí fought her desire to look toward the door. She heard someone enter her shed. Her heart was beating faster out of fear. The person who entered spoke. She could not believe her ears! She looked up to see to whom the voice belonged. It was a young boy who spoke Naabeehó *Navajo!*

"Shádí," *My older sister*, he said.

Dééd Yázhí just sat on the floor and stared at the outline of the young boy. This visit was so unexpected.

Was he an 'anaa'í *enemy* sent to her by the dirty, hairy soldiers? she thought as her mind raced. She did not dare to respond to the young boy.

Once again, she heard the familiar sounds of sheep bleating coming from beyond the open door. Although the sun was setting, she had not seen so much sun.

Quietly, she said,

"Dibé shạ' háadi naakai?" *Where are the sheep?* Without waiting for an answer, she softly asked, "Háíshạ' bidibé?" *Whom do the sheep belong to?*

"Naabeehó dine'é bidibé nanishkaad. Ákǫ́ǫ́sh níni'?" *I am herding the Navajo people's sheep. Do you want to go over there?*

As if in a trance, Dééd Yázhí slowly got up, looked past the young boy, straightened her tattered rug dress, shook her tangled hair, and took one step toward the sound of the sheep. She knew she was not allowed to leave the shed. Without answering, she boldly walked out of the shed. She looked around, then cast her eyes upward and saw the fort was surrounded by tall rock walls and hills, bearing tall trees on the southern, western, and northern sides. On the side that faced the east, she saw a beautiful green meadow.

The sound of the sheep bleating forced Dééd Yázhí to bravely take more steps forward. The young Naabeehó *Navajo* boy ran after her saying,

"Áłtsé. Ch'iiyáán ła' naa deeshkááł biniiyé naa níyáá nít'ę́ę́'. Díí nihe'anaa'í nich'į' bádahodoochxįįł. Áłtsé. Nił da da'di'doołdǫǫł!" *Wait. I came to see you to bring you some food. Our enemies will get mad at you. Wait. They may shoot you!*

Nothing else mattered. Dééd Yázhí heard the beautiful familiar sound of sheep once again. She was determined to go to the sheep. She felt alive! She heard sheep bleating for the first time since her capture. Tears danced in her eyes. She wanted to smell the sheep and feel their wool. She wanted the scent of the sheep to fill her nostrils and from there fill her whole body. She wanted to feel the sheep nuzzle against her legs. Dééd Yázhí felt a strong urge to keep walking. The sheep were in the meadow. Her feet began to carry her even faster toward them. She had no strength to stop her feet. She just put one foot in front of the other and half-walked and half-ran toward the herd of sheep in the meadow.

Maybe the sheep could tell me where I am, she thought. As the bleating of the sheep grew louder in her ears and the scent of the sheep filled her nostrils, Dééd Yázhí felt a knot in her stomach that rose to her throat. She watched as the flock of sheep was being herded closer. She wanted to run toward the sheep but her legs would not move any faster. She moved as if she was in a trance.

"Hey, there is a nice shooting target!" one of the soldiers yelled as he aimed his rifle toward Dééd Yázhí's back. Startled, the tall, gray-haired one jumped up from the table where he sat with four soldiers as they talked loudly.

"Hey, shoot at that target! She's moving pretty fast!" one of the soldiers yelled.

"Put your arms down! That's an order! If you shoot her, you will start another Indian war!" the tall, gray-haired one scolded.

Afraid one of his soldiers would shoot at Dééd Yázhí thinking she was trying to run away, the tall, gray-haired one ran with a pronounced limp toward her to stop her from going further. She walked with a determined wild look in her eyes, saying,

"Dibé naakaiígóó yisháał." *I am going to the sheep.*

The tall, gray-haired one could not catch up with her. He yelled at the young Naabeehó 'ashkii *Navajo boy,* saying,

89

"Tell her to stop! She will start another Navajo war. If her people see her here, they will attack the fort. Our soldiers are in the canyon looking for raiders. We do not have enough soldiers here to hold off many Navajo warriors! Tell her to stop!"

The young Naabeehó 'ashkii *Navajo boy* stood in one place paralyzed. He could not speak.

"Tell her, you can't be walking around here. It is too dangerous for you. Let me take you back to your home," the gray-haired one said in a subdued tone. He heard a sound to which Dééd Yázhí spun around. Not far from where they stood, the tall, gray-haired one saw a little lamb. He ran, limping, to pick up the lamb.

Watching the tall, gray-haired one limping as he ran, Dééd Yázhí's mind quickly wondered what had happened to his leg. The tall, gray-haired one bent down and picked up the lamb. The lamb squirmed in his arms. The tall, gray-haired one turned around and came limping back with the little lamb in his arms. He brought the lamb to Dééd Yázhí and held it out for her to touch.

Dééd Yázhí reached out and began to pull the lamb into her arms. Before she knew, a raw, loud sob escaped from her throat as tears slid easily down her face. The feel and smell of the lamb's wool brought back memories of home, memories of her younger sister, memories of her mother and her father, and other memories she dared not recall.

Although the lamb was suspended between the tall, gray-haired one and Dééd Yázhí, the lamb seemed to know Dééd Yázhí was hurting. The lamb lifted its little head and leaned into her chest. Dééd Yázhí began to tell a story.

"Hádą́ą́ léiyá … (sob!) Hádą́ą́ léiyá shizhé'é … (sob!) Hádą́ą́ léiyá shizhé'é náshidiiłtį́ … (sob!) Hádą́ą́ léiyá shizhé'é náshidiiłtį́í dóó dibé yázhí léi' yik'i dah shineesdá … (sob!) 'áádóó shí 'éí (sob!) dibé yázhí bik'i dah sédáago dibé bighan bii' dibé yázhí shił naashdloozh ne' (sob!), *There was the time … (sob!) There was the time when my father … (sob!) There was the time when my father picked me up … (sob!) There was the time when my father picked me up and set me down on a lamb … (sob!) and I … (sob!), and I rode around in the corral on the lamb's back* (sob!), she whispered in between sobs.

It was with all her might that Dééd Yázhí tried to hold back her tears, but the lamb brought her father so close to her that she could not fight the bitter sweet tears anymore. She buried her head in the lamb's neck and cried. Her body shook with each sob. The lamb sensed her weakness and remained content in her embrace as he nuzzled her.

The tall, gray-haired one did not have the heart to take the lamb away from Dééd Yázhí. He turned her around to walk her back toward the old shed where she stayed. Once there, he walked her in and left her and the little lamb inside then locked the door from the outside.

Having witnessed the act of kindness, the officers who sat at a table called the tall, gray-haired soldier over to where they sat. Words of explanation were exchanged between the tall, gray-haired one and his superiors. The tall, gray-haired one knew the sheep were confiscated from the notorious Navajo people who were to be forced to walk to Fort Sumner, New Mexico.

"Colonel, I am giving the lamb to the girl in the shed," the tall, gray-haired man said assertively. "I request to be made responsible for her welfare as well as the welfare of the lamb, sir," he further stated.

"Don't allow yourself to become attached to *her*. She is the enemy. We cannot always look the other way," replied the Colonel.

"It was our own men who took advantage of the fact that she is an enemy, sir. I could not go along with that. Someone needs to take care of her. No one has come looking for her. Wasn't that our plan of attack? Kill the men and kidnap the women and children. We were confident her male relatives would come looking for her. Our scouts have not heard one word. She is all alone here, sir," the tall, gray-haired man said in a gentle voice as he responded to his superior officer.

"Be reminded she is the enemy and must be treated as a prisoner. She will be sent to Fort Sumner with all the other lawless Navajo Indians! You cannot be accountable for her daily activities when you are on duty. She will remain locked up in the shed, is that clear?" the superior officer demanded.

"Yes sir," was the final response, and the gathering at the table dispersed for the remainder of the evening.

That evening, the little lamb carried Dééd Yázhí's mind back to her homeland. She was reminded of every aspect of home. She remembered how once while still at home in the early spring, when there was much snow, she and her younger sister were told the sheep could not be taken out. Instead, with their mother and aunts' help, they gathered sagebrush leaves and brought them back to the corral to feed the sheep. The newborn lambs were kept in their mother's hooghan *hogan* to be kept warm.

Dééd Yázhí remembered it was fun having the lambs in their home to play with. She also remembered back to the time when two of the newborn lambs froze to death. Dééd Yázhí and her younger sister Dzáníbaa' were told to butcher the lambs.

"Dibé yázhí nidahadlóhígíí nínáoł'ahgo ná'á'ah bíhwiidooł'ááł dóó bídínóołdįįł." *When you butcher the lambs that have frozen to death, you will learn how to butcher and you will get used to butchering,* they were told by their mother. Dééd Yázhí remembered it took her and her younger sister a long time to butcher the lambs because their tears were blinding them. Their mother and their maternal aunts watched and gave them directions as they butchered the lambs. After cooking the meat, they found it to be so tender. The sisters cried again as they ate the delicious lamb stew.

Dééd Yázhí was very grateful for her little lamb and she was grateful to the little lamb. The lamb brought clear memories of her family back to her mind. She had begun to forget how her mother's voice sounded, but the lamb brought the sound of her mother's voice back to her. The little lamb also brought the sound of her younger sister's laughter back to her mind.

Dééd Yázhí hugged her little lamb. The lamb gave her strength. The lamb brought her the young Naabeehó 'ashkii *Navajo boy.* The lamb also let the tall, gray-haired one know that although she was a captive, she had a heart. Although she did not want to, Dééd Yázhí was beginning to see the tall, gray-haired man's heart. At that thought, she chided herself by saying,

"Yíiyá! 'Ei yee' nihe'anaa'í nilį́! Nichxǫ', t'áadoo baa nitsíníkeesí. Doo nihígi 'át'éego bitsį' yishtłizh da. Doo nihígi 'át'éego bitsii' łizhin da. Doo nihígi 'át'éego bináá' łizhin da. Doo nihígi 'át'éego nitsékees da. Doo nidi bił ahidinits'a' da. Yíiyá! Yíiyá! T'óó nichxǫ'!" *Scary! He is our enemy! Don't, don't think about him. His skin is not brown like ours. His hair is not black like ours. His eyes are not black like ours. He does not think like us. You do not even understand him (his words). Scary! Scary! Just don't!*

The tall, gray-haired one and the young Naabeehó 'ashkii *Navajo boy* stepped in the door of the shed where Dééd Yázhí was kept. The Navajo boy told Dééd Yázhí they needed to take the lamb back to its mother. The boy further told her he would bring the lamb back in the morning. Reluctantly, and in deep sadness, Dééd Yázhí released her hold on the lamb. She knew the lamb needed its mother.

Dééd Yázhí cried most of the night as one memory after another filtered through her mind and filled every crevice of her mind.

Chapter Six
The Soldier

Dééd Yázhí treasured the memories the lamb was bringing to her. Earlier in the day, the lamb had sent her memory back to the time when she was a toddler and when she had become sturdy on her feet. She remembered she would follow her mother to the sheep corral. There was a song her mother sang to her when they walked to the sheep corral. Dééd Yázhí wanted to learn the song because her mother told her she would not get tired walking to the sheep corral when she sang. Her short legs could only take her so fast, and she kept falling behind and she would have to grab the hem of her mother's rug dress to keep up. Upon hearing her mother's song, the sheep and goats would rush toward the sound of the song, then crowd near the side of the corral.

Dééd Yázhí remembered she watched the birds flying above her to see if they would stop to listen to her mother singing. At the time, she wondered if the birds knew what her mother was going to do next because of the song she sang. The birds seemed to fly ahead of them as if they knew where

Dééd Yázhí and her mother were going. Her mother called the birds, "Tsídii," *bird*. Dééd Yázhí remembered how she wondered if her father also knew the bird was named "tsídii." She had many questions to ask, but her Navajo vocabulary was limited to the names of things her father and mother taught her. She was also learning words as she listened to her mother and her father sing to her. She loved the sounds around her.

As her little lamb bleated, Dééd Yázhí found the sound comforting. She quieted the lamb by offering her finger, allowing the lamb to suck on it. She heard herself make an unfamiliar sound. She looked around to see if anyone else was in the room who could have made the unfamiliar sound. What she heard was the sound of laughter. This was the first time she had laughed since she had been kidnapped. She laughed again and soon she felt tears making their way down her young face. She thought she had forgotten how to laugh. Dééd Yázhí slept soundly that night knowing the lamb was bringing her memories back. She missed the lamb, but it also needed its mother just as she needed her own mother.

Dééd Yázhí appreciated the tall, gray-haired one for giving her the little lamb. As if her thoughts called to him, he came into the shed carrying a plate of food for her. He was talking to someone. Dééd Yázhí heard someone speaking her language. It was the young Naabeehó 'ashkii *Navajo boy*. The young boy greeted her by referring to her as his older sister saying,

"Shádí," *My older sister*, to which she replied,

"Shitsilí," *My little brother*. With her acknowledgement of him, the young boy explained to her who the tall, gray-haired one was, as he said,

"Díí hastiin doo ła'ííyígíí nahalingo hashkée da. Kwe'é atah bóhólnííh. Nihidine'é yik'ijį' nidaabaahígíí biniinaa kwe'é bił haz'á. Ni 'éí nik'é hastiin léi', Nóoda'í nilį́įgo, yáál ła' beiyí'nil. Nihe'anaa'í Naabeehó sáanii dóó Naabeehó 'at'ééké 'ayóo nidaalnishígíí bił béédahózin. Éí biniinaa Naabeehó sáanii dóó 'at'ééké hadeinitá 'áádóó yisnááh ádeidoolííł yiniiyé nihidine'é yitahgóó tánídadibah. Naabeehó sáanii dóó 'at'ééké Naakai yich'į' baa nidahaniihgo yik'é yáál t'óó'ahayóí bich'į' nidahalyé. Díí hastiin Nóoda'í yisnááh ániilaaígíí yáál nik'é yeinínil. *This man does not scold like the others. He along with others has authority here. This place is here because they are at war against our people. You are being held here because a Ute man was given money in exchange for you. Our enemies know Navajo women and children are hard workers, and for that reason they use warfare to kidnap Navajo women and children. They sell the Navajo women and girls to the Mexicans and they get a lot of money for them. This man (the gray-haired soldier) gave the Ute who kidnapped you money in exchange for you.*

K'ad éí nizhé'é níkanitáago kodi níkanootáałgo bí dó' bi'di'dooltsoł biniiyé kwe'é ni'dótą. Díí hastói kwe'é nidaalnishígíí nihidine'é yik'ijį' nidaabaahgo nihidine'é yisnááh ádeile'go, nihidine'é níléí ha'a'aahjigo yił adahakááh. Áadi 'ą́ą́héeshjéé' dadooleeł yiniiyé 'ákǫ́ǫ́ yił adahakááh. Naabeehó dine'é binaabaahii 'ayóo da'ni'įįh daaníigo yaa dahalne'. Áko nidi, Naabeehó binaabaahii kodi yah adayii'éshígíí 'ádaaníigo 'éí nihí doo da'niit'įįh da daaní. Danihizáanii dóó nihada'áłchíní hadaniitáago biniiyé nihe'anaa'í bitah tánídadiibah daaní."

Now, they are keeping you here hoping your father comes looking for you. When he does, they will catch him and hold him prisoner here. The men who work here are making war against our people and when they do, they kidnap our people and then take our people toward the eastern direction. They are taking them there to make them prisoners of war. They tell about how the Navajo warriors are thieves. But the Navajo men they are bringing here say they are not the ones who are stealing. They say they raid their enemy's settlements to look for their wives and their children who have been kidnapped.

Dééd Yázhí was overwhelmed by the information she received. She could not believe what she heard. According to the young boy, the lives of her father and her brothers and her maternal grandfather were in jeopardy, and she was the one to blame if her father and brothers and maternal grandfather are brought in as captives. She could not imagine her father as a captive. He was too strong. But on the other hand, she knew her father would be looking for her. He would do all he could to get his daughters back. Dééd Yázhí realized she had a new fear.

Just when she thought she could trust the tall, gray-haired one, she found he was looking to kill her father and her brothers, as well as her maternal grandfather and their warriors. Dééd Yázhí felt sick to her stomach because of fear. Now she was conflicted; she did not want her father to come looking for her. The people she loved were in jeopardy because of her.

****

As the days of the fall season grew shorter because of the shortened path of the sun, the air became cooler by the day and the leaves on the trees began to lose their vibrant color and turn yellow. One day, the tall, gray-haired man came to the shed with a bundle under his arm. Unfolding the bundle, he said,

"I cannot allow you to exit your living quarters with your Navajo dress. If you want to see your lamb, you will need to wear this. It is dangerous out there for you and your relatives. It is better that you wear this," as he held up a blouse made of a thin material. The tall, gray-haired one also produced a long, full skirt made of the same thin material. The background color of the material was white and many little purple flowers created a colorful pattern on the material. Dééd Yázhí wondered how a thin piece of material could protect a person.

She was feeling confusion and fear. Using the young boy as an interpreter, Dééd Yázhí was horrified when the tall, gray-haired one told her she could no longer wear her rug dress when she left the shed. Her thoughts crashed into one another in her mind. With her eyes snapping with hurt and anger, she boldly responded.

"Díí biil éé' yee' shimá shá yistł'ǫ́! Díí biil éé' bii' sétįįgo 'éí shimá shik'i déez'įį' nahalin łeh." *My mother wove this rug dress for me! When I wear this rug dress, I feel as if my mother is protecting me*, she spoke with conviction.

She spit out another worry she had,

"Díí biil éé' bii' sétįįgo 'éí shizhé'é dóó shilahkéí shéédahodoosįįł. Shíká danootáałgo shibiil éé' doo bii' sétįįgóó 'éí doo shéédahodoosįįł da. Shimá shibiil éé' yitł'óogo t'áá sahdii naashch'ąą́go yitł'óo łeh. Nááná ła' doo kót'éego biil éé' neich'ąąh da, t'áá hazhó'ó shimá dóó shideezhí t'éiyá. 'Ayóo bee béého'dílzin." *If I am wearing my rug dress, my father and my brothers will recognize me. If they come looking for me, they will not recognize me without my rug dress. When my mother weaves rug dresses, they have a distinct design. There is no one*

*else who weaves these designs into their rug dresses, only my
mother and my younger sister do. They are well-known for their
design.*

With her eyes still snapping with anger, she continued by
saying,

"Díí shibiil ééʼ biiʼ sétįįgo ʼéí Naabeehó ʼasdzání nishłínígíí
yééshiyiiłnííh. Shibiil ééʼ biiʼ sétįįgo ʼéí Naabeehó ʼasdzání
nishłínígíí bee shééhoʼdílzin. Díí shibiil ééʼ biiʼ sétínígíí ʼéí
Naabeehó binaatʼáanii dóó Naabeehó binaabaahii binaatʼáanii
bitsiʼ nishłínígíí yaa halneʼ." *When I wear my rug dress, it reminds
me that I am a young Navajo woman. When I wear my rug
dress, it lets others know that I am a young Navajo woman.
When I wear my rug dress, it lets others know that I am the
daughter of a Navajo leader and a leader of Navajo warriors.*

Looking at the clothes given to her by the tall, gray-haired
one, Dééd Yázhí said, "Eidí ʼééʼ biiʼ sétįįgo ʼéí niheʼanaaʼí
háádadiitʼįįh nahalingo hadínishtʼee dooleeł. Eidí ʼééʼ biiʼ sétįįgo
ʼéí niheʼanaaʼí nahonishłin dooleeł. Shizheʼé yikʼijiʼ nidaabaahígíí
nahonishłin doo. Yówéé ʼázhdoonííł! Yówéé ʼátʼéego hazhéʼé doo
hoł nilįį da dooleeł! Doo ʼíinisin da! ʼEi ʼééʼ doo biih yíyáágóó
shąʼ haa dashidoolííł?" *If I wear those clothes, I will be dressed
like our enemy. If I wear those clothes, I will look like our enemy.
I will look like our enemy, who fight against my father. What a
horrible thing to do! What a horrible way to show your father
that you do not respect him! I do not want to! If I do not wear
those clothes, what will they do to me?*

Without waiting for an answer, Dééd Yázhí boldly continued
by saying,

"Dooda. Shí doo ʼei biih deeshʼnah da."
No. I will not put that on.

The tall, gray-haired one reasoned,

"Tell her if she wants to see her lamb again, she will have to wear these clothes. We could take walks to the sheep corral or ride horses up to this beautiful clearing I visit every now and then."

The young Naabeehó 'ashkii *Navajo boy* pleaded,

"Dibé yázhí bich'į' níni'go 'éí díí ni'éé' ádííłíił. Dibé naakaiígóó diikah niłní, áádóó hózhóní léi'góó łį́į́' bee 'ałnánéiikah doo, ní díí hastiin." *If you want to see the lamb, you will need to make this your dress. We could go to where the sheep are and we will go to a beautiful place on horseback, this man said.*

After a while, the young Naabeehó 'ashkii turned to Dééd Yázhí once again and said, "Díí 'éé' át'é. Díí nihe'anaa'í bi'éé' át'é." *These are clothes. These are the clothes of the enemy.*

Dééd Yázhí's mouth flew open. The young boy continued by saying,

"Díí 'éé' biih yíníyáago 'índa dibé bighangóó diikah, niłní. 'Ei biil éé' ni'ée'go 'éí nihe'anaa'í ła' atínidoolíiłgo da 'át'é." *He said to you, we will not go to the sheep corral until you put these clothes on. If you have that rug dress on, one of our enemies might torture you.*

Dééd Yázhí frowned. She could not believe her ears as she clearly said,

"Dooda!"

The tall, gray-haired one frowned. He knew what "dooda" meant.

Dééd Yázhí still could not believe she was hearing the Naabeehó language and speaking it to another person.
For months, since she had been kidnapped, the only way she

101

had known her language was through her thoughts. She thought in Navajo and dreamed in Navajo. Her thoughts and her dreams brought her father and her mother and her family and her sheep closer to her. They visited often.

The tall, gray-haired one offered to show Dééd Yázhí how to put on her new clothes. She refused. She would not bring shame to her people by making her appearance as one of the enemy. However, her loneliness for her lamb forced her to put on the clothes the tall, gray-haired one had given her. She slipped the blouse over her head to cover her rug dress. The skirt she tied in place at her waist over her rug dress. Once dressed, she sat and waited for the tall, gray-haired man and the young Naabeehó 'ashkii to come for their daily visit. The tall, gray-haired one placed a colorful bonnet on her head which made Dééd Yázhí cringe, but her desire to see the sheep was stronger than her obstinacy.

Pleased with his negotiating and communication skills, the tall, gray-haired one led her out the door and toward the sheep corral. Dééd Yázhí called to her lamb and watched it jump up and wobble among the lambs on its spindly legs until it found her and leaned against her legs. She wanted to be left alone with the sheep, but the tall, gray-haired one remained close by her side. She was allowed to wander among the sheep as long as the tall, gray-haired one followed. Dééd Yázhí was used to the man watching her. Since she had put on the clothes of the enemy, she noticed his gaze felt even more kind. She did not mind the boy because he reminded her of her younger brothers.

The young boy began teaching Dééd Yázhí the few English words he knew, then would laugh when she could not say a word right. Saying an English word aloud sounded strange, as if it was forbidden by the earth and the sky.

****

The days of the late fall season grew even shorter, and the air became cooler by the day. Dééd Yázhí knew from an occasional leaf that the wind carried and dropped into the smoke hole that the leaves on the trees had begun to lose their vibrant color and had turned yellow. She was becoming worried about the shed she was kept in. Her little lamb started the healing process where she could once again feel the cold and be concerned about it. There were thin spaces between the logs that made the wall. It was through the thin spaces that the cold air rushed in to get away from the source of the cold. The thin slivers of sunshine sneaking in between the logs brought a little light during the day, and at night the faded light of the moon brought sinister dark shadows. Dééd Yázhí had been aware of the bold stare of strangers on several nights as they peered through the cracks. She was afraid, but the lamb brought her bravery back to the surface. Dééd Yázhí began to dare to think she would survive and see her mother and father and sister and brothers again.

She remembered the first year she was held captive at the fort, she was oblivious to the cold winter air, the warm sunshine, the shadows at night, and the bold stares. The familiar and strange elements made her feel she was alive only on the outside of her body. The inside of her body did not have feeling, so when it was cold she did not know it. She recalled those horrible days when she felt she had died, but some mean aspect of life kept her alive only to torture her more each day. It was

103

not until the time when the tall, gray-haired one gave her the little lamb and she cried bitter tears that she began to notice the warm sunshine, the cold breezes, the shadows, and the stares of strange men.

One day when the leaves of the trees turned a deep copper color, the tall, gray-haired one came to the shed. He held the reins of two horses. The young Naabeehó 'ashkii *Navajo boy* stayed close by to relay to Dééd Yázhí the wishes of the tall, gray-haired one. A ridiculous bonnet was placed on her head after she put on the clothes of the enemy.

The tall, gray-haired one led Dééd Yázhí outside and held out the reins of a black horse and asked her to get on the horse. It had been so long since she had been on a horse. Her mind stumbled on the memory of the last time she had ridden a horse, which was when she was kidnapped and sold to the soldiers. Her mind paused. Thoughts were crashing into one another in her mind. Her father taught her and her younger sister to ride a horse like a warrior.

"Nihi'disnááhdą́ą́', łį́į́' nihił dah yiidootxeeł, éí biniinaa nanihinishtin," *In the event, you are kidnapped, you can ride your horse well, that is why I am teaching you,* her father said to his daughters. Dééd Yázhí remembered she did not want to do anything to make her kidnappers angry because she did not want her younger sister to be mistreated.

She thought, if I had told my sister to ride fast, maybe we could have escaped. But her troubled mind reminded her that they were not allowed to ride on a horse alone. Instead, they were held by mean men who were their 'anaa'í *enemies.*

Now, she had her chance. She knew she could get away from the tall, gray-haired one because of the way he limped when he walked.

"Ch'ééh nídídáhí nilį. Ch'ééh nídídáhí nahalingo naaghá. Bich'į' anáhóót'i'." *He is an old, tired sheep. He walks around like an old sheep. He is handicapped,* she told herself, then smiled at her silent words.

Dééd Yázhí saw a strange, heavy saddle on the horse. The tall, gray-haired one turned and got on his horse and waited for her to do the same. He was unaware that she wore her rug dress underneath the enemy's clothing, which made getting on the horse awkward. The tall, gray-haired one got down from his horse and touched his boot, then pointed to the stirrup and conducted the same gestures several times. After long silent moments, Dééd Yázhí pulled the material off of the horse, then draped the material around her waist. The material was the long piece of fabric the soldier gave her to drape around her body because her skirt was so thin and it would not allow her to straddle the horse without it riding up high on her legs, exposing them. The gray-haired one smiled a big smile and nodded his head.

"That's it, girl," he said.

Dééd Yázhí stepped weakly into the stirrup and tried pulling herself up, but she did not have the strength. The tall, gray-haired one reached gently under her arms to help her up, but she shrieked in panic and backed away from the horse, nearly falling.

The tall, gray-haired one mumbled,

"I'm sorry. I was only trying to help you. I'm sorry,"

105

and called the young Naabeehó 'ashkii. The young boy came
running and stood in front of the tall, gray-haired one.

"Tell her I was just trying to help her. I do not want to hurt
her. Tell her to try getting on the horse again." The boy came to
her and said,

"Níká'iilyeed yiniiyé nigaan yiyiiłstood nít'ę́ę́'. Nááná shą',
bínáánítááh, niłní. Shooh." *He got a hold of your arm because he
wanted to help you. Again, he told you to try it again. Watch.*
The boy got on the horse with ease, got back down, and said,

"Shooh." The young boy gently nudged her shoulder and
said,

"Ni shą'?" *What about you?* Once again, Dééd Yázhí tried,
but she did not have the strength to get on the horse. The young
Naabeehó 'ashkii ran to the other side of the horse and caught
her hand and said,

"Aoo', shíla yiiłtsóód." *Yes, get a hold of my hand.*
Embarrassed, she reached out to the young Naabeehó 'ashkii
who grabbed hold of her hand and pulled her up. Once she
was on the horse, she immediately became dizzy and put her
head down close to the mane of the horse. She remained in
this position for a few minutes, then sat up and wobbled some
more. The tall, gray-haired one barked a few words at the young
boy, and with one leap the boy was sitting behind her. The boy
held her steady as the horse began to walk gently with them.
Trembling, Dééd Yázhí held on to the horse's mane while the
boy held the horse's reins and followed the tall, gray-haired one
out of the fort. Once out, the tall, gray-haired one slowed his
horse to ride side by side with them.

Many memories slid slowly into Dééd Yázhí's mind. She thought of the last time she had ridden a horse, which was during her sacred time of the month, when she bled; the terrified screams of her sister as she was being torn away from her early one morning; the way her sister bounced up and down on the horse as she was being held from behind by a short dirty man; the way she lay crosswise on the ugly man's horse as they rode fast through familiar territory, which later became unfamiliar; and then the thought of her father teaching his sons and young warriors how to leap onto a horse from behind and instantaneously urge the horse into a fast gallop.

Dééd Yázhí could hear her father's words. She had not forgotten how handsome her father was. At the thoughts of her father, tears began flowing down her face, but she did not dare let go of the horse's mane to wipe her face. The tall, gray-haired one looked at her and stopped his horse and asked the boy to do the same. Then without warning, the tall, gray-haired one leaned close to her, then reached out and gently wiped a tear from her chin.

This was the first time she saw him up close again. Dééd Yázhí cringed and moved away from him. His eyes were still as turquoise as the fat horned toad's eyes. In the sunlight, she saw that he had deeper wrinkles on the sides of his eyes and his graying eyelashes curled slightly up. His eyebrows were long and gray like the clouds that gather in the sky just before the summer rain. She noticed his neck. It was wrinkled just like the neck of the fat horned toad she had seen at home at the base of Dziłíjiin *Black Mesa*. To make it worse, his neck looked chapped just like the fat horned toad's neck.

Quickly as she observed him, she shut her eyes tightly so as to erase what she saw. Then she began to wipe her eyes with the back of her hands in a confused fashion. What would my father say, she thought frantically, I have looked into the eyes of an anaa'í *enemy!* Immediately, she felt ashamed, yet triumphant. She had looked into the eyes of the enemy and she did not back away nor did she see hate or dislike. The rest of the ride was a blur. It was her first time out of the fort, but she could not remember what she had seen. All she could remember were the big turquoise eyes of the tall, gray-haired one, which reminded her of the fat horned toad she had seen near her home.

A few days later, the tall, gray-haired man entered the shed and placed a plate of food on the floor, then cussed, seized Dééd Yázhí's arms, and jerked her up off of the floor and pulled her toward the door. As he did, he put his arms around her waist and felt her hollow stomach and remembered how healthy she looked when she was brought in over a year ago, in spite of the fact that she then wore a dirty rug dress matted with blood, weeds, and dirt. At the time, her hair was tangled and hanging in her face, and her ankles and wrists were swollen from the tightness of the yucca rope that bound her. Her appearance had not improved much over the year except that she was extremely thin.

The tall, gray-haired one broke the silent struggle.

"I know you see me as your enemy. I only want to take care of you and take away the pain I see in your beautiful eyes. I want to see you smile. I want to hear you laugh. I want to hear your voice," As he spoke, his voice lowered to a whisper.

"All I see is a lost child," he said in a hoarse voice, but it did not dawn on the gray-haired man that she was indeed lost and one who had been kidnapped from her home and taken far away from her family.

Dééd Yázhí came alive. She scratched at his arms, kicked at his legs, and held her arms out straight so the tall, gray-haired one could not carry her past the door. But his strength overpowered her. He carried her toward another shed as she continued to kick, scratch, and bite at him. He carried her into the small shed and set her down on the floor then turned and walked out, locking the door behind him. Dééd Yázhí sat in the darkness without a sound.

"Shidibé yázhí shạ'?" *Where is my little lamb?* she asked.

As her eyes became accustomed to the dark, she saw a wide board attached to legs (a table). There was a large bowl with a pot, like the water jugs her mother wove and covered with pitch to hold water. Near the pot were some thin rugs that were neatly folded. Behind her on the floor there was a soft rug that was spread out. On the other side of the square room was a large gaping hole (a fireplace). Seeing the hole made her afraid and tired. She missed her lamb. Exhausted, hungry, and weak she leaned back and fell asleep.

She did not dream at all. She wanted to see her family in her dreams. Hot tears ran down her face, into her hair, and onto the soft rug underneath her. She missed her lamb. The presence of her lamb brought her dreams of her family. Her lamb brought her family close to her. She missed her father. She missed her mother. She missed her younger sister. She missed her brothers. She just missed …

Chapter Seven
The Scent of Yucca Root

Dééd Yázhí heard the door open. The evening sun stung her eyes, and for a minute, she could not see who the person was who was entering her shed, but her ears told her it was the tall, gray-haired one.

The tall, gray-haired one had brought food to Dééd Yázhí, along with a large jug of fresh water. With great difficulty, he set the large jug of water on the floor near Dééd Yázhí. He then set the plate of food down on the floor in front of her and motioned to her to eat. He took a piece of meat out of his pocket and began eating it.

Dééd Yázhí was afraid to look at him but she was puzzled by his action of taking food out of his clothes. The gray-haired one sat and stared at her and did not allow her to look at him to inspect him. She did not want to eat her food because she wondered where on his clothes he had kept her food before offering it to her. She wondered if he had kept her food in his clothes, and then just before entering her shed he had placed it on a plate. She did not even want to look at her food.

The tall, gray-haired one ate the piece of meat he had taken out of his pocket as if it had come freshly from the grate above the hot coals. When he had eaten the meat, he poured water in the bowl he brought earlier. He slid the bowl along the floor and let it rest near Dééd Yázhí. Out of his back pocket he produced a rag and began to soak the rag in the water.

Dééd Yázhí could not believe what the tall, gray-haired one was producing from his clothes. First it was a piece of meat and now a rag? She wondered if he was going to eat the rag. She was puzzled even more when her ears heard a beautiful sound.

The sound of fresh water spilling back down upon itself sounded as beautiful as listening to her mother singing. Dééd Yázhí closed her eyes and listened to the water dripping off of the rag. She listened as the tall, gray-haired one was wringing out the rag.

In her thoughts, Dééd Yázhí began to greet the water. Before she knew it, words began to softly drift out of her lips as she said,

"Yá'át'ééh shik'éí. Tó 'aheedlíinii nishłį́. Ma'ii deeshgiizhnii bá shíshchíín nááná ... *Hello, my relatives. I am of the Water Flows Together People. I am born for the Coyote Pass people and...* The tall, gray-haired one interrupted her greeting as she declared the water as her relative. Shrieking out of excitement he said,

"You are speaking! Are you speaking to me? What do you want me to know? I want to know! What are you trying to tell me! Oh, your voice is so beautiful! It is so sensuous and so beautiful!" The tall, gray-haired one regretted that he had just interrupted her speech. She stopped talking and now she was silent. He was instantly sorry that he had interrupted her.

His thoughts were crashing into one another. What did she want to tell me? What did she want me to know? He kept asking himself. He could not believe he was brought to helplessness by the voice of a beautiful young woman.

He remembered his actions that brought about speech within Dééd Yázhí. He reached into the bowl of water and lifted the wet rag and gently wrung out the rag as he watched her face intently. She had her eyes closed and her lips were not moving. He wanted to hear her voice again. He was in love with her voice. He was in love with this young Navajo woman!

The tall, gray-haired one lifted the wet rag and cautiously brought it close to Dééd Yázhí's face. He hesitated then without warning, began to gently wipe her face. Her eyes flew open. She began to back away. He reached around her waist and brought her close then gently said,

"Shhh, shhh." Too scared to fight, Dééd Yázhí allowed him to wipe off her forehead as he continued to say,

"Shhh shhh." He was jubilant as he tenderly wiped her entire face.

Earlier, Dééd Yázhí noticed the scent of the yucca plant but with the tall, gray-haired one producing a piece of meat and a rag from his clothes, her mind had been distracted and she did not think about the beautiful scent. As she leaned back away from the man, she once again noticed the gentle scent of the yucca plant.

She looked around her and noticed he had brought yucca roots that were wrapped in a towel. She timidly reached out toward the root, which the tall, gray-haired one had forgotten about.

Earlier in the day, the young Naabeehó 'ashkii *Navajo boy* had given him the yucca root to bring to Dééd Yázhí. The tall, gray-haired one picked up the bundle of yucca roots and laid it on the floor before her. He then backed away from her a little to sit back and watch to see what she would do with the yucca root. His nostrils were picking up the gentle fragrance, making him more aware of the woman before him. When the night air enclosed Dééd Yázhí's shed in darkness, the tall, gray-haired one finally decided to leave to return to his quarters.

Dééd Yázhí waited until he left and locked the door to the shed from the outside before she picked up a piece of firewood and began pounding the yucca root. The scent of the pounded root delicately rose into the air, making her tilt her head back to slowly breathe in the sweet fragrance. Tears flowing down her face cleaned a path from her eyes to her cheeks and onto her chin then down to her neck. She took another deep breath to smell the fragrance of the yucca root and felt a slight moan escape from her body, which started from her abdomen and left her lips and gently hung in the air.

Shaking her head, she instinctively pulled her hair forward and watched it fall in one lump into the bowl of cool fresh water. Slowly and ceremoniously, she washed her hair, all the while breathing in the therapeutic fragrance. Not wanting the scent of the yucca plant to leave her hair, she gently rinsed the soap out of her hair, then slid off her tattered rug dress and dipped the wet rag in the lightly soapy water and began wiping her body with the wet rag. Her skin was not used to the cool water and she noticed goose bumps all over her body. It felt good to wash her body.

After her bath, she used the rag to vigorously wipe her dress. She then rinsed off the rag with the remaining water in the large jug, then stretched out her rug dress. With a thin blanket wrapped around her, she dug a shallow, wide hole in the soft dirt floor until she found wet earth. Laying her rug dress on the wet earth, she placed a layer of wet sand on her dress as she stretched out her rug dress. This was what her mother taught her. It would keep her rug dress from shrinking her mother told her as a child.

Dééd Yázhí closed her eyes and remembered her mother's words of instruction. Kót'éego séí ditłé'ígíí habiil 'éé' bik'i nijiłka', áko ha'éé' doo 'aháąh niigháah da, háálá ha'éé' dibé bighaa' bee ályaa. Dibé bikágí nálshohgo bighaa'ígíí t'óó nizhónígo yishch'ilgo 'áyiił'įįh. *It is so one's dress will not shrink that a person spreads wet sand on the rug dress because the dress is made of wool. When the sheep's wool becomes damp, the wool just curls up.* Dééd Yázhí did as her mother's words told her to do. Her mother made her dress so she wanted to preserve her rug dress.

Feeling refreshed from the bath, she did not have the strength to stay awake. She lay down on her soft blankets and fell fast asleep. In the full light of morning, she felt a soft moist nose nuzzling against her side. She woke to find her lamb nudging her. She reached out and held the lamb close. She wanted to revisit her beautiful dreams of home. She was grateful for the bath in that it brought the words of her mother close, and further it brought vivid dreams of home as she slept. In her sleepy state, she did not hear the footsteps of the person approaching her shed.

Without warning, the tall, gray-haired one walked in carrying a dish of jerky. Dééd Yázhí was horrified. She did not have the protection of her thick rug dress, instead she was still wrapped in the thin blanket. Her rug dress was not dry.

As the lamb moved nearer to her to settle into a more comfortable position, it lay down on the blanket Dééd Yázhí had wrapped around her while she waited for her dress to dry. The lamb's weight pulled the blanket off of her right shoulder exposing her right breast. She quickly covered herself with her long hair then quickly pulled the blanket up around her, but not before the soldier noticed her bare skin. She heard the tall, gray-haired one gasp and utter a soft moan when he saw her bare breast.

Dééd Yázhí became immediately afraid. No man had hurt her since she had the miscarriage. The memories of the attacks stalked her mind and put fear into her heart. Sensing her fear, the tall, gray-haired one mumbled,

"I'm so sorry. I didn't mean to burst right in. Usually I slide the lock slowly and wait a bit." With a few more inaudible words, he left her shed, sliding the lock back into its place. Dééd Yázhí heard his footsteps carrying him away from her shed.

The cool fall air was not allowing her rug dress to dry as quickly as she wanted. She sat in her shed separated from the sheep she enjoyed visiting. She wondered if the sheep missed her. The sand holding her dress to its original size was slowly drying.

After a few days, Dééd Yázhí pulled her dress out of its sandy storage and shook it. Clean sand rained down on the lamb which lay comfortably on the floor. When her lamb shook its head, its ears made a comical sound as its ears beat against its head with every shake. Dééd Yázhí shook her dress again and smiled as the clean sand rained down on her lamb causing it to gently beat its head with its ears as it shook its head from side to side. She laughed when she saw that he shook his head first, then shook his tail afterward. She fell on the floor and hugged her lamb lovingly, saying,

"Ahéhee', anáshdlohgo 'ánáshiinidlaa." *Thank you, you have made me laugh again.*

The tall, gray-haired one came to deliver his plate of food but did not stay because Dééd Yázhí still wore the thin blanket as a dress. Once she had shaken most of the sand off of her rug dress, she put her dress on. The faint scent of the sheep had returned to her dress, making her dress even more precious to her.

The tall, gray-haired one visited once a day, bringing her food, water, yucca roots, or pieces of meat. One day, he brought her several yards of fabric that reminded her of the enemy's clothes she had to wear when she visited the sheep corral or when she rode a horse. The material also reminded her of the shirt her dirty kidnappers wore. When the tall, gray-haired man held the fabric out to her, Dééd Yázhí retreated into a corner of the shed. Painful, fearful memories began to slide back into her mind. She shut her eyes and said,

"No," in a timid voice.

The tall, gray-haired one jumped up and in a loud excited voice said,

"Did you say something?" He realized he must have scared her, then lowered his voice and asked again,

"Did you tell me no? Was that you speaking?" He was elated. He had a little conversation with her. He ran his hand through his graying hair and sat back down. He sat and beamed at the woman he secretly named Sunflower.

He left with a skip in his step, which caused his limp to become more pronounced as he returned to his quarters. Back in his quarters that night, the tall, gray-haired one happily dreamed of his Sunflower. He dreamed of her soft sensuous voice. He dreamed of her soft round breast. He dreamed of her smooth lightly browned skin.

The tall, gray-haired one began to stay with her longer in the evenings after he and Dééd Yázhí took their daily walk to the sheep corral. He loved watching her tenderness unfold before him when she was among the sheep. He loved the way she touched the top of the head of each lamb as she moved gracefully from one to the other. He loved how she seemed to greet each animal differently and they seemed to accept her presence for they too enjoyed her company. On their way back to her shed he watched as she cupped her hands up to her face and took long breaths of air as if she was memorizing the scent of the sheep left on her hands.

One evening, while making their way back to her shed, the tall, gray-haired one picked a dainty yellow flower and instinctively held it out to Dééd Yázhí. She looked at the flower then looked the other way and faintly smiled. Once again, he held the dainty flower out to her and she accepted the flower. She turned and murmured something to her lamb who followed her closely. The tall, gray-haired one sadly watched her offer the flower to her lamb. The lamb bit the flower off, then opened its mouth for the stem. The tall, gray-haired one was disappointed and wondered if they would ever speak the same language.

When they entered the shed where Dééd Yázhí was kept, the tall, gray-haired one lit the crude kerosene lamp, then sat down in the corner to watch Dééd Yázhí play with her lamb. He loved to hear her making cooing noises to the lamb. The lamb responded by lying down by her and nuzzling against her side.

The tall, gray-haired one stood up with some difficulty and then got ready to leave.

"I am going now," he said and waited.

Dééd Yázhí sat on the floor and stopped playing with the lamb. He took the opportunity to walk to where she sat on the floor and knelt down near her. He put his head down and ran his hand through his hair and said,

"I have been given orders to join the rest of the officers who have been sent to the South where a war is raging between the northern and southern states. I did not expect to fall in love with you, but I have. I do not want to leave from here without placing you under someone's protection, otherwise the savage soldiers will harm you with only one thought in mind. I have put much thought into my decision and my request, and that is to ask you to marry me. If the soldiers know you are my wife, you will have more protection than if I just left from here. As my wife, they will be obligated to protect you and you will be free to remain here until I return. The time of my return is uncertain. Knowing you are here waiting for me will cause me to fight more valiantly so that I may return to you, my beautiful Sunflower."

Dééd Yázhí was surprised by the many words the tall, gray-haired man spoke but she kept her head down as he spoke. She had listened to her father tell stories after supper.

Is he telling me a story? she wondered. Fear began to stir in her heart when she looked up to see the tall, gray-haired one looking intently at her. Why does he keep looking at me? she questioned her mind rhetorically. Maybe he is scolding me for spending too much time at the sheep corral, she reasoned.

When the tall, gray-haired one finished talking, he touched her shoulder and rested his hand on her shoulder. As he did, she flinched, but did not move away. Earlier, he did give me a flower to feed to my lamb, she thought so she decided to return the kindness by not moving away.

With the back of his hand, the tall, gray-haired one ran his hand from her earlobe down under her chin and back up to her other ear. Dééd Yázhí was too embarrassed to move. She just sat and with her index finger, she followed the design in the thin material he gave her earlier.

"I never thought I would find love in these parts. I just came here to do my duty and that was to subdue the Navajo Indians, your people, at any cost. You have a quiet beauty that calms me just like this lamb calms you. We all need one another," he said quietly. With those words he stood up and started walking with heavy steps toward the door.

Dééd Yázhí lifted her head and said,

"No," and after a long pause she said,

"Sit." These were the only two words she had learned from the young Naabeehó 'ashkii *Navajo boy.* One would have thought she had just yanked on a string that was tied to the man. The tall, gray-haired one turned around as if in a trance and took two long steps toward Dééd Yázhí and sank down on the blanket beside her, wanting to touch her but afraid to.

Her two words of English confused Dééd Yázhí. She was trying hard to remember the words of her mother, who had warned her about getting close to the enemy. If only I had spent more time with my mother, I would know what to do, she thought, as she looked at the tall, gray-haired one's boots. She watched as he cautiously reached out and put his hand on hers. When she did not move her hand away, he reached under her hand, slowly lifted it to his lips and kissed the back of her hand.

Dééd Yázhí instantly became aware of the moistness of his lips on her hand. He further cooled the wet spot on her hand when she felt his breath on the moist spot. She was confused. Her skin tingled at his touch, and yet, he was an anaa'í *enemy!*

Dééd Yázhí turned her head away and shut her eyes very tight. All she could think about was that his eyes resembled the eyes of the fat horned toad. Her mind traveled over the tall, gray-haired one's face and saw the wrinkles in the corner of his eyes, which appeared and accompanied his easy laughter and his soft smiles. Her mind could not stop. It continued to trace the many wrinkles on his neck that brought the image of the wrinkly neck of the fat horned toad. She had to force herself to think about how the tall, gray-haired one had protected her from the dirty, hairy white men. She forced herself to sit still and sit close to the enemy of her people.

In silence, the tall, gray-haired one pulled her hand to him and placed her hand on his chest. Dééd Yázhí noticed he closed his eyes. She thought, I am his enemy! He should keep his eyes open! Who taught him about being a warrior? She wondered what he was saying when he said softly,

"I did not want my clothing separating my skin from your hand but I have to proceed with caution because I am well aware of how much abuse you have suffered before I intervened on your behalf." Looking at her, he continued,

"This can be dangerous." As he spoke, the tall, gray-haired man put her hand down and prepared to leave. Her brown skin and her pretty dark brown eyes were tempting him. After a little difficulty, the tall, gray-haired one stood, leaned down, and placed a kiss on the top of Dééd Yázhí's head. As his kiss lingered on her soft hair, he breathed in the scent of the wild yucca roots in her hair, the roots he had brought to her earlier. Dééd Yázhí heard the tall, gray-haired one breathe in deeply.

The tall, gray-haired one remembered her long black silky hair that she had used to cover her soft round breast. He wanted to feel her silky, long black hair fall across his face, his chest, his arms, and his abdomen. Without another look back, he walked out the door and placed the lock loosely on the door from the outside.

"Goodnight, my sweet Sunflower," he whispered hoarsely as he turned toward his quarters.

Dééd Yázhí was confused once again. She wondered what she did to make the tall, gray-haired one leave. Her thoughts went back to when she said, "No" and "Sit." Apprehension began to fill her mind. Did I learn the words correctly? she thought. Did I say the words correctly? Did the young Naabeehó 'ashkii teach me the wrong words?

She blew out the flame in the crude kerosene lamp and sat in the dark repeating the words, "No" and "Sit." These were the

121

words she would say to ask the young Naabeehó 'ashkii *Navajo boy* what the words meant the next time she saw him.

"Sháhanii, dooda dóó sínídá bidííniid ni. Ha'át'íí lá bidííniid?" *I thought I told him "no" and "to sit". What did I say to him?* she whispered.

Dééd Yázhí kissed the back of her hand, then softly breathed on her hand to commit to her memory the sense she felt when the tall, gray-haired one kissed the back of her hand.

Chapter Eight

A Set of Watchful Eyes

The tall, gray-haired one's orders to leave came much earlier than he had expected. At the top of the neatly folded paper was the name Lt. Charles Arnold Folton. As he read the orders, he could not help but feel apprehension for Sunflower. He went to see his commanding officer to discuss the plans for the woman he called Sunflower. After telling his commanding officer about his love for his Sunflower, the tall, gray-haired man stood taller.

"Do you think this is wise, Charles?" he was asked. "I knew you were concerned about her survival and I was aware that you protected her from the savage volunteer soldiers, but I did not know you had feelings for her. You *are* aware she is the enemy!" the officer barked.

Looking at the face of the tall, gray-haired man, the officer shook his head and continued,

"I did not realize your feelings were that strong. Granted, you do want to protect her, but you can't go running around trying to save all the savage women you feel sorry for."

The tall, gray-haired one responded by saying,

"This is different, sir, my request remains unchanged. I do want permission to marry her. In all respect, sir, the savages who are around us are not the Navajo Indians, they have been guardedly friendly. The savages among us are our own soldiers who repeatedly raped her before I intervened. I love her and I want to protect her. I have found love in a place of so much hatred, hatred for a people who just want to live on their land," the gray-haired one said bravely.

"How old is she? You are old enough to be her father! Or her uncle! I will have to take my time in making a decision. We are well aware, as you are, that she *is* the enemy we came here to fight. You are a good soldier. You have represented the United States Army well, Charles," his commanding officer said as he resumed smoking his cigar. At the words of the officer, the tall, gray-haired one winced.

"Sir, with all respect, may I add that at times, I am not proud to be a soldier. We are not soldiers! We have declared war against the Navajo women and the children," the tall, gray-haired one said sadly.

His commanding officer spun around to face the tall, gray-haired one and stated,

"She is being held here to lure her father and his warriors to the fort! No one has come searching for her. It is possible she is not who the Indian scouts thought she was. As I said before, I will carefully consider your request, Charles," the officer said as he dismissed the tall, gray-haired one.

The tall, gray-haired one saluted his commanding officer and turned to leave.

"Thank you, sir. I will eagerly await your decision," he said as he stepped out into the bright sunshine.

Two days later the tall, gray-haired one was told of the decision his superior officer made. He was nervous as he faced his superior officer who said pensively,

"I have discussed this matter with the other officers. We all agree that this young Navajo woman who is at the center of our discussion does need protection from the soldiers who will remain here when most of the regiment has been sent to join the Union troops in the South. We have to provide some protection for the young woman. So far, she is the only female prisoner we have. I think our Ute scouts have kept a majority of the young women for themselves as slaves or to sell on the Indian slavery market in Santa Fe or Taos."

The officer shook his head as if to shake off his thoughts and turned back to the conversation by saying,

"We have agreed to allow you to marry her, but you will *not* be allowed to remain here at this fort. You will accompany the volunteer troops who are being sent to join the Union troops in the South who are fighting in the Civil War. The savage Navajo Indians are our enemy and we cannot have our soldiers marrying the enemy, but we acknowledged the fact that you cared for her and brought her back to health. Without your intervention, she would have died. We need her to bring her father in. You are aware she is the daughter of one of the prominent leaders for the western Navajos. It's puzzling ...."

"What is puzzling, sir?" the tall, gray-haired one asked.

"Well, her father has not come to the fort searching for her. She has been here over a year. It is possible that he was killed by our troops or maybe our Indian scouts have killed him. It is also possible that our Indian scouts made an error in identifying him as a prominent leader. We believe she does not have family, otherwise they would have come looking for her."

The tall, gray-haired one only wanted to hear the information regarding his commanding officer's decision as he said,

"Sir, will there be someone here to marry us? Possibly the chaplain?"

The older officer once again shook his head and answered by saying,

"Charles, a secret wedding ceremony will be conducted by the chaplain, which will be sparsely attended. The chaplain will conduct this three days from now, and you will leave three days after that. You deserve a little happiness before we offer up your life in the war between the states," the commanding officer said with a sarcastic laugh.

"You *will* be expected to stay in the officer's quarters even after you are married to her. Is that clear?"

"Yes, sir. Thank you, sir," the tall, gray-haired one replied with his voice void of any excitement for the time being.

It was difficult for the gray-haired one to maintain his composure throughout the remainder of the day. That evening, he went to the shed Dééd Yázhí was kept in.

"Today's visit will be different," he said quietly as he unlocked the door from the outside and stepped inside. As he walked into the shed, he wanted to gather Dééd Yázhí in his arms and kiss her face, kiss her neck, her breasts. He wanted to bury his face in her soft skin and breathe in her scent until it permeated his mind because her scent would have to sustain him for many months. Instead, he pulled up the one chair in the room and sat down heavily upon it and sat in silence.

Dééd Yázhí sat in the corner lacing yucca plant leaves, fashioning them into a tightly laced rope. It was only the Naabeehó *Navajo* men whom she had seen braiding yucca ropes as a child. The one she had been braiding resembled the ones her father and brothers made. Once she taught herself how to braid the yucca leaves, the rope grew quickly in length.

The tall, gray-haired one moved his chair so he could sit closer to the young woman he called Sunflower. He reached out and touched her hair and asked her to join him.

"Háágo," *Come here*, he said timidly. Dééd Yázhí was surprised to hear a Naabeehó *Navajo* word coming from the man. She looked at him. She remembered the way her father said the word, "Hágo" *Come here*. My father said it with such power in his voice, but this man sounded like a woman when he said, "Hágo" to me, she thought.

Although he mispronounced the Navajo word for "Come here," the tall, gray-haired one was pleased that the word he spoke did not bring out fear in her. "Háágo" was one of the words the young Naabeehó 'ashkii *Navajo boy* had painstakingly taught him.

Dééd Yázhí became afraid. The last time the young Naabeehó 'ashkii had said "Hágo" to her, she ended up on a horse with a thin blanket covering her legs. Her mind returned to the first time she rode a horse with the tall, gray-haired one and the young boy. She remembered she enjoyed the horse ride. He did not hurt me, she reasoned in her thoughts.

127

As the tall, gray-haired one stood to leave, Dééd Yázhí set her yucca leaves aside as she allowed her gaze to follow him out the door. Slowly she got up and followed him to the door. He waited for her. The tall, gray-haired one had never felt self-conscious before, but now it seemed like everyone was looking at them, but when he became more observant of the others around them, he found they conducted their usual chores oblivious to him and Dééd Yázhí.

"Dibé bighangóó daats'í deeyá. Shí dó' ákǫ́ǫ́ deeshááł nisin. Dibé bitah tádideeshaał nisin." *Maybe he is going to the sheep corral. I also want to go there. I want to walk among the sheep,* she quietly said.

That evening was to be different. The tall, gray-haired one pointed to the clothing of the enemy and told the young Naabeehó 'ashkii to tell Dééd Yázhí to put the clothes on. She obeyed because she wanted to visit the sheep. Instead of going to the sheep corral, the tall, gray-haired one cautiously led her to the horse corral where he had two horses saddled. The young Naabeehó 'ashkii was holding the reins of the horses. He smiled at Dééd Yázhí. She looked back at the young Navajo boy and he answered her inquisitive look.

"Shí 'éí dooda. Shí t'áá kǫ́ǫ́ naashá." *Not me. I am staying here.* Dééd Yázhí looked back at the young Navajo boy saying,

"Dooda, niłgo t'éiyá. T'áá sáhígo 'éí dooda." *No, I will only go if you go. I will not go alone.* The Navajo boy interpreted her words with the same adamant tone she spoke.

The tall, gray-haired one led the horses out of the corral and offered Dééd Yázhí the reins of one horse. After helping her wrap a long piece of fabric around her waist, he stood by and

watched her get on her horse with some difficulty. He wanted
to help her but he knew she would not allow him to help her,
so he watched as she struggled to get on her horse. The tall,
gray-haired one made sure her legs were covered with the
fabric before he got on his own horse. Dééd Yázhí appeared
uncomfortable. The tall, gray-haired one needed an ally.

He yelled at the young boy and told him to get on the horse
with her. The young boy happily jumped up on the horse and
settled behind Dééd Yázhí.

The riders rode off slowly toward the rocky hill on the west
side of the military fort, the area that was restricted to military
personnel. They continued to ride a rather steep rocky incline
until they reached the top of the hill. Dééd Yázhí caught her
breath when she saw tall pine trees. In a beautiful clearing
where the grass was thinning, they stopped. The tall, gray-haired
one got off of his horse, then tied his horse to the branch of a
tree that was hidden among the taller trees.

Dééd Yázhí glanced around her, noticing that her
surroundings resembled the area her family called home
in Dziłíjiin *Black Mesa*. She was confused. She felt intense
homesickness and felt sharp pains of loneliness. Her eyes
changed from being fearful to being wild.

From which direction was I led here when my kidnappers
brought me here? she thought as she became aware of the
power in her knees to urge the animal forward at a fast run.
The tall, gray-haired one sensed her thoughts and in one quick
move, quickly placed a firm hand on her horse's bridle. He then
reached up and clumsily pulled Dééd Yázhí off of her horse,
then led her to a soft, sandy spot near some tall pine trees.

He then ordered the young boy to take Dééd Yázhí's horse's reins and tie the horse to a tree nearby.

The tall, gray-haired one led Dééd Yázhí by taking her hand saying,

"Háágo." Dééd Yázhí followed the Navajo word. It was comforting. She looked around for the young boy. He had taken the horse a short distance away and held the reins as he watched billowing clouds slide easily through the western sky.

The tall gray-haired one felt the wild sense of urgency begin to leave her body. After laying a blanket down, he motioned to her, asking her to sit on it. Dééd Yázhí once again observed her surroundings, began to tremble, covered her eyes with the back of her hands, and began softly crying. Seeing her heart breaking, the tall, gray-haired one moved closer to where she was standing and slowly reached out to her. She turned away from him and whimpered mournfully. The tall, gray-haired one had no idea that the landscape before them brought sorrowful memories to her.

Her tears continued to silently flow out of her eyes. The place where they were standing was very similar to the area where her kidnappers camped for the night before her younger sister, Dzáníbaa', was sold to the tall 'anaa'í *enemy*. Dééd Yázhí remembered back to that one sad early morning when the 'anaa'í *enemy* rode off with her younger sister. Her sister's calls for help came back so vividly. Dééd Yázhí's heart was breaking. The memories of her younger sister screaming her name were too painful, and she needed strength for her own survival. Now, she felt she had been defeated once again. Questions regarding her younger sister just kept marching through her mind.

Shideezhí da shą' háadi naaghá? T'ah daats'í hiná? Bił daats'í
ná'ahiideestsééł? *I wonder where my younger sister is? Is she
still alive? Will I ever see her again?* After thinking about her
younger sister, Dééd Yázhí's thoughts became accusatory as
she pondered the actions of her father by thinking, Ha'át'íishą'
biniinaa shizhé'é t'ahdoo shíká nanitáago kodi yígháah da? Da'
shizhé'éésh t'óó shaa yooznah? Shicheii shą'? Éí nidi daats'í
doo shíhásáah da. Shideezhí daats'í yik'ídeineeztą́ą́'. Shí daats'í
t'áá sáhí yisnááh áshi'diilyaa? *Why hasn't my father come to
find me? Has my father forgotten about me? What about my
maternal grandfather? Maybe they do not even miss me. Maybe
they have found my younger sister. Maybe I am the only one
who is being kept as a prisoner.* Questions like these burned
into her mind one after another. She desperately wanted to be
comforted in Navajo.

The tall, gray-haired one sensed her need and gathered her
in his arms and gently held her. Although Dééd Yázhí did not
have the strength to push him away, she tried, but collapsed in
his arms. The tall, gray-haired one tenderly lowered her down
onto the blanket then sat near her, stroking her hair and her
face, saying,

"Shhhh, my beautiful little Sunflower."

Dééd Yázhí listened to his gentle voice. His voice was
not the voice of the man she had seen at the fort, where
he barked orders at the soldiers expecting them to heed his
orders immediately. She covered her eyes with her hands to
block out the fact that he was her anaa'í *enemy*, but she was
always surprised to hear him use this soft language when he
spoke to her.

This one who is my people's enemy uses a soft language that almost sounds like my father's soft language, she thought. His voice almost sounds kind like my father's voice ..., she thought, then winced. Only, I can hardly remember how my father's voice sounds, she thought. At this thought, she began to cry again, this time allowing her sobs to find the sorrow she felt. The memories were burning her mind, and it hurt so intensely that she curled up in a fetal position on the blanket and wanted to remain there always. The tall, gray-haired one gathered her in his arms once again and rocked her. He murmured soft, soothing words into her ear as he said,

"Shhhh, please don't cry. I love you, my beautiful Sunflower. Shhhh."

During the times when she was sad, she turned to her lamb for comfort but now she was allowing her source of comfort to be the tall, gray-haired one whose company she was becoming used to. She was surprised that she momentarily forgot he was her anaa'í *enemy*.

The tall, gray-haired one followed his natural instinct to kiss her hurt away.

"I am going to kiss you," he announced softly.

Cautiously he began to kiss first her forehead, then her eyes with their hot tears that were slowly washing away her painful memories, her cheeks, her ears, and finally her lips. He slowly kissed her lips, gently pressing her lips apart with his tongue.

At that instant, the tall, gray-haired man felt a chill run up and down his spine! He sensed a set of wild watchful eyes on him. Distracted, he quickly opened his eyes to look around, but

132

instead, he looked directly into Dééd Yázhí's wild, wide-open, surprised eyes. Her eyes were wide open and were just a couple of inches from his face.

Her white bonnet did not match her face. Instantly, the tall, gray-haired one felt sympathy for her. She was obeying him by wearing the ridiculous bonnet.

The tall, gray-haired one became self-conscious and asked Dééd Yázhí to close her eyes. He demonstrated by closing his eyes, then reached up and gently placed his hand over her wild, wide-open eyes and resumed his embrace. He once again began kissing her gently on the mouth. His hungry tongue began to press her lips apart at which he heard her squeal a high-pitched squeal.

Dééd Yázhí pushed him away and spat in the grass. She wiped her mouth with the back of her hand and kept spitting. By the sound she was making the tall, gray-haired one thought she was nauseated. All he heard was Dééd Yázhí spitting out the words,

"Nídinilgą́ą́zhgo hanii 'ánít'į́!" *Are you doing this because you are having a nightmare?* The tall, gray-haired one had forgotten the young Naabeehó 'ashkii *Navajo boy* but was reminded of his presence when he heard him chuckle at Dééd Yázhí's chiding words. The tall, gray-haired one jerked his head up when he heard Dééd Yázhí saying,

"We'! We'! We'! We'! Wéee'!" *Yuck! Yuck! Yuck! Yuck! Yuck!* The tall, gray-haired one noticed that her voice became softer each time she voiced the word, "We'!" *Yuck!*

He was becoming addicted to the presence of Dééd Yázhí. He wanted to let her know the effect she had on him.

He cautiously took the opportunity to ready his lips to place another kiss on her sweet mouth when he became distracted once again. He felt the intense gaze of another person once again, and upon opening his eyes, he saw that Dééd Yázhí's wild eyes were crossed because she was studying his face from such a close distance.

At the beginning of a laugh, the tall, gray-haired one reached up and gently put his hand on her eyelids and pressed her eyelids closed. She shook her head and softly said,

"No, sit."

He loved the sound of her velvet voice, and he loved the taste of her soft lips and her mouth and wanted to kiss her more, but her wildly opened, crossed eyes did not lend intimacy to the moment. Neither did the bonnet and her ill-fitting blouse and skirt lend intimacy to the moment. The tall, gray-haired one wanted to focus upon her beautiful eyes, but her clothes were a distraction. Instead he placed several soft kisses on her lips and kissed her eyes again. In his kisses, he noticed her tears were not as hot as they were before. Instead, her tears had a salty, sweet taste.

Dééd Yázhí moved away from him and smoothed her hair down. Then she got up and walked to the horses. She wanted to leave the place that brought vivid memories of her younger sister. She was aware that the tall, gray-haired one wanted her to close her eyes, but she could not close her eyes when her enemy was directly in front of her!

Acknowledging that she was bold in her actions, she took the reins of the horse she rode. With the long piece of fabric wrapped around her thighs and her legs, she got up on her horse with less difficulty as the young Naabeehó 'ashkii *Navajo boy* jumped up to sit on the horse behind her. Reluctantly, the tall, gray-haired one rolled up the blanket, tied it to his saddle, and got on his horse. They rode in silence back toward the fort. Dééd Yázhí committed to memory the sagebrush, the tall pine trees, and the tall yellowing grass. Several times, the tall, gray-haired one guided his horse to follow Dééd Yázhí's horse just so he could watch her appear from behind the young Navajo boy.

Every once in a while, the tall, gray-haired one would grin thinking of her crossed eyes as she studied him from up close when he was kissing her. He was very glad Sunflower had come into his life, but he was very sad because he was to leave her in a few short days.

The next day the tall, gray-haired one and Dééd Yázhí and the Naabeehó 'ashkii rode to the same spot. The tall, gray-haired one saw Dééd Yázhí's expression move from sadness to thoughtfulness and back to sadness again. This time she did not cry like she did the day before, instead her tears were silent tears. He moved in close to comfort her every time he saw tears visiting her eyes. He loved comforting her, it was his excuse to hold and attempt to kiss her.

As they came around a shallow hill, they saw a beautiful clearing containing the last stubborn flowers of the summer. The tall, gray-haired one spread his blanket down on the ground.

"Please sit," he said as he patted the blanket.

At his gesture, Dééd Yázhí sat down and picked a flower and gave it to the tall, gray-haired one after she said,

"Na', díí ch'il látah hózhóón naa nishłé." *Here, I am giving you this flower.* Her gesture brought back the memory of the first time he gave her a flower, whereupon accepting the flower she fed the flower to her lamb. He grinned at the thought. He took the flower from Dééd Yázhí then reached up and placed it in her hair, then kissed the flower and her hair.

The tall, gray-haired one took her hand and looked deep into her beautiful eyes and said,

"I want you to be married to me, and I want to be married to you. I want you to be my wife. I want to take care of you." He waited, but Dééd Yázhí responded to his serious words with eyes that were oblivious to his amorous emotions.

"Wife," he said awkwardly. "I always thought I would marry someone from my hometown. I thought it would be a woman who wore beautiful dresses and voiced beautiful words. I never thought I would fall in love with a Navajo woman who hardly spoke." His voice became nearly inaudible when he continued by saying,

"... and a woman who wore the same dress every day, one who smelled of sheep, and one who did not comb her hair too often."

At his last words, he jumped. He had never seen another rug dress on Dééd Yázhí except the one that she was wearing nor had he seen a comb or brush in her shed. He remembered back to the last time they were in the meadow, when Dééd Yázhí and the young Naabeehó 'ashkii the *Navajo boy* were collecting tall grass stalks and she painstakingly placed each stalk together so that the stalks were uniform in size and length. At the time, he did not know what she was doing but he had seen the brush she had made and thought she had made it to be used as a short broom. The tall, gray-haired one began to think about where he could find the items she would need for her daily care.

"I don't know the things a woman needs. I have never been married before. I do not have time to learn about you. I want more time with you. I promise you, my little Sunflower, I will come back to reclaim my love for you." The tall, gray-haired one felt tears forming in his eyes. In silence, they returned to the shed Dééd Yázhí was kept in.

Chapter Nine

Mrs. Charles Arnold Folton

The tall, gray-haired one was anxious. He and Dééd Yázhí's wedding ceremony was to take place later that evening. He cleared his throat, knocked on the door of the shed where Dééd Yázhí was kept, looked in, then entered the room. He noticed she had not moved from the place where she had been sitting the evening before when he left her. Disappointed, the tall, gray-haired one left and came back with the young Naabeehó 'ashkii *Navajo boy.*

The tall gray-haired one spoke slowly and deliberately to the young boy when he said,

"Tell her to wash her hair." Making sure Dééd Yázhí was watching him, he raised his hands and placed them in his hair and began messing up his hair. He then placed the palms of his hands against his nostrils and breathed in deeply with a smile on his face. The young Naabeehó 'ashkii *Navajo boy* and Dééd Yázhí just stared back at him as they held a hidden smile on their face.

Again, the tall, gray-haired one looked at the Naabeehó 'ashkii *Navajo boy* and made his demand.

"Wash. Tell her to wash her hair," he one told the young boy again. The young boy frowned, wanting to let the tall, gray-haired one know that it was not proper for a Navajo boy to tell a Navajo woman to wash her hair. The young boy said,

"No. Not me. Her mother tell her."

The tall, gray-haired one sat down heavily on the little chair. He ran his fingers through his hair with Dééd Yázhí and the boy watching his gesture. Quickly, he removed his hands and placed them in his lap.

"Tell her to change her clothes. Tell her to put this one on," he said, showing the boy a flowery white skirt with a pattern of blue flowers that was gathered at the waist and a blouse of the same fabric with flouncy sleeves.

"Tell her we got it from the commissary. I bought it for her," he said. The young Naabeehó 'ashkii *Navajo boy* began shaking his head.

"No," was all the Naabeehó boy could say.

"Tell her!" the tall, gray-haired one ordered.

Dééd Yázhí jumped at the booming voice the tall, gray-haired one used. Wanting to make sure the tall, gray-haired one understood what he was saying, the young Naabeehó 'ashkii *Navajo boy* showed discomfort and looked away from Dééd Yázhí as he gestured to her to demonstrate that she was to wash her hair then take off her rug dress and put on the new clothes as he said,

"Nitsii' táánígis áádóó díí 'éé' biih díí'nah niłní, díí hastiin."
This man said to wash your hair and put this dress on.

Dééd Yázhí did not respond because she was so embarrassed and offended. It was not the place of a man or a

139

boy to tell her to wash her hair and change her dress. The boy looked away and with great difficulty due to his limited English-speaking skills, asked the tall, gray-haired one if he had some yucca roots with which Dééd Yázhí could wash her hair. It was one way that they could possibly get her to understand that the tall, gray-haired one wanted her to change out of her rug dress.

Excited, the tall, gray-haired one slowly got up from the chair and said,

"Yes, it worked the last time. I should have thought of that." Without another word, away he went, nearly skipping toward the officers' quarters. After bringing in some warm water in a large jug along with a few yucca roots rolled up in some colorful material, the tall, gray-haired one and the Naabeehó 'ashkii *Navajo boy* left the shed after gesturing to Dééd Yázhí to wash her hair and change her dress.

The tall, gray-haired one and the young Navajo boy came back after what seemed like an endless amount of time and found that Dééd Yázhí had washed her hair, possibly had bathed, and had placed the blouse and skirt over her rug dress. Her hair had been brushed and pulled back then knotted in the back. She had secured the knot in place with strips of the colorful material the yucca roots had been carried in.

"Oh she's beautiful, isn't she?" the tall, gray-haired one asked softly, not expecting a response. He saw a crude brush made of the long stalks of grass that he had seen Dééd Yázhí pick and lay carefully in little even groups. He thought she was a genius to think of using the tied stalks of grass as a brush. He did not know this was what her people called the bé'ázhóó' *hair brush* and that the grass she had picked was known by the same name.

Looking around, the tall, gray-haired one noticed Dééd Yázhí had put the skirt and blouse on over her rug dress. He studied the scene for a minute. Without another thought, he softly said,

"Háágo," *Come here,* and held out his hand to her. Dééd Yázhí ignored his extended hand and got up and walked out after him thinking they were going for a ride on their horses. Instead, the tall, gray-haired one grabbed her around the waist. As he did, he noticed her waist was much thicker than he remembered. He also noticed she smelled of sheep. Feeling uncomfortable that they were going to face his officers smelling like sheep, the tall, gray-haired one led her into one of the buildings she had seen him disappear into many evenings after their visit when he left her shed. Dééd Yázhí did not know they were walking into the officers' quarters, nor did she know very few people had been allowed to enter into any one of the buildings called the officers' quarters.

Once inside, Dééd Yázhí and the tall, gray-haired one were greeted by the chaplain who stood at attention and stared at Dééd Yázhí. The tall, gray-haired one cleared his throat then introduced Dééd Yázhí to the chaplain. The chaplain did not greet her, leaving an uncomfortable silence drifting about in the room. Without another word, the chaplain picked up his black book, opened it, and took a long deep breath as a frown deeply creased his forehead.

"It is unusual to conduct such a ceremony in a place so full of turmoil ..." the chaplain began. After more talk about what his thoughts were concerning the importance of a marriage, the chaplain turned to the tall, gray-haired one and asked,

"Charles Arnold Folton, are you of sound mind?"

The tall, gray-haired one cleared his throat and muttered in a low voice,

"Yes, I am of a sound mind." The chaplain then looked at the couple and asked,

"Is this woman of a sound mind?" At the question, no one answered. Instead, the ones who were in the room, who included the gray-haired one, the chaplain, and two officers, and the young Naabeehó 'ashkii *Navajo boy* looked at one another in surprise. The young Navajo boy looked at Dééd Yázhí and quietly said,

"Aoo', diní." *Say yes.*

Dééd Yázhí looked at him with a puzzled look on her face and softly whispered,

"Ha'át'ííshą' biniiyé?" *What for?*

"Jó t'óó..." *Just because* ... the young boy answered.

"Aoo' shįį," *Probably yes*, Dééd Yázhí whispered.

"She said yes," the young boy told the gray-haired man. The chaplain nodded and continued by asking,

"Charles Arnold Folton, do you take this, this woman ..." and leaning closer to the tall, gray-haired one asked,

"Uh, what is her name?"

"Sunflower, sir. Her name is Sunflower," the tall, gray-haired one answered, smiling.

"Oh, what a relief!" stated the chaplain.

"I thought she would have a ridiculously difficult Indian name, but that one will sure do!" He began again by asking,

"Charles Arnold Folton, do you take Sunflower to be your wife in sickness and in health ...?"

"I do," replied the tall, gray-haired one.

The scene at the officers' quarters was a confused blur to Dééd Yázhí. In the room were the tall, gray-haired one, an older man who had a wrinkled face (the chaplain), the young Naabeehó 'ashkii *Navajo boy* who stood next to her, and two officers who appeared to be angry. Dééd Yázhí did not know what the meeting was about.

Are they talking about me? Have I done something wrong? she wondered. She stole a look at the tall, gray-haired one, but the semi-happy face of the tall, gray-haired one did not match her assumption, she reasoned. Peeking once again at the two officers' faces told her she had done something wrong. They seemed very unhappy, maybe even mad.

Her thoughts were interrupted when the chaplain announced,

"With great misgivings, I pronounce you husband and Indian wife."

With a yellowed handkerchief, the chaplain wiped the sweat that congregated in beads on his deeply creased brow, then nervously looked in the direction of the two angry officers and announced,

"I don't think it would be appropriate for me to say you may kiss the bride."

As soon as he spoke the words, the air in the room took on a different tone. A tone of uneasiness. Everyone in the room anxiously waited. The tall, gray-haired one leaned forward and softly said,

"No, with all due respect, sir, I will not be kissing my bride."

Dééd Yázhí understood the word "No," but nothing else. The tall, gray-haired one shook hands with the chaplain, then looked in her direction and said,

"Háágo," *Come here,* and led her outside. Once outside, the tall, gray-haired one shook hands with the Naabeehó 'ashkii *Navajo boy* and then gave Dééd Yázhí's hand a quick squeeze, which was something he had never done before outside of the shed. So I must not have done anything wrong, Dééd Yázhí wondered as she sorted out her confused thoughts.

The moon was coming up in the pale, late-evening sky as the tall, gray-haired one led Dééd Yázhí back to the shed. After they entered the shed and closed the door, the tall, gray-haired one gathered her in his arms, picked her up, and carried her to the blankets, then set her on her feet and began kissing her passionately, not caring about her open, confused, crossed eyes.

Dééd Yázhí kept looking at the hungry man who was trying in vain to swallow her lips. She had not liked the way his mustache tickled her nose nor did she like the way his mustache burned her lips as he passionately tried to swallow her.

He tastes salty, but what is wrong with him? she thought. Weakly, she pulled her face away from him. She felt so uncomfortable. Didn't he eat? she wondered as he reached out and gently pressed himself against her and began to push her lips apart with his soft tongue. Dééd Yázhí's thoughts flew from one thought to the next as her mind settled on the thought that she had no food in the shed. The tall, gray-haired one had been the one who brought her food.

"Haash nit'į?" *What are you trying to do?* she demanded as she pushed him away with the palms of her hand. Instantly,

144

she was sorry she pushed him away. The tall, gray-haired one stumbled backward, making his limp even more pronounced.

She was horrified when the tall, gray-haired one began to unbutton his shirt! She was afraid she had made him mad and now he would begin to treat her the way the dirty, hairy white men had treated her. In growing anger, she asked,

"Nídinilgą́ą́zhgo hanii 'ánít'į́?" *Are you acting like this because you are having a nightmare?* That was all that she could muster up to say. The tall, gray-haired one just looked into her face and smiled a crooked smile at her.

"Your words are so sensuous. I love your language," he said as he began to unbuckle his belt. Dééd Yázhí was flustered and could not think of the word she had learned from the young Navajo boy. Finally, closing her eyes so she would not see the tall, gray-haired one in front of her, her thoughts began to return.

"No," she softly said, hugging herself as she stood before the tall, hungry gray-haired man. Still confused, she looked around her for something to do so she would not have to watch him act like he was having a nightmare.

All of a sudden, she remembered her lamb.

"Shidibé yázhí shą'?" *Where is my lamb?* she asked.

"Mmmm, come here, my Sunflower, I love you too," the tall, gray-haired man said as he reached out to gather her in his arms.

"No," she said. "Mééee', mééee', mééee'," she added hoping he would understand she was missing her lamb.

"Not tonight. I will be your lamb tonight, my darling," the tall, gray-haired one softly said, as he began to nuzzle against her neck, saying,

145

"Méeee', méeee', méeee'." He grinned at their means of communication, then shrugged his shoulders.

The conversation and the actions of the tall, gray-haired one were so ridiculous to Dééd Yázhí that she began to giggle. He took her giggle as an invitation to resume his amorous reach for her. He had his eyes closed as he reached for her. Dééd Yázhí did not dare to close her eyes. She kept them wide open as she saw his mouth come closer to her face. The tall, gray-haired one opened his eyes and saw her eyes crossed and a frown on her forehead. He smiled, then gently reached up and placed his hand over her eyes to close them. Dééd Yázhí did not want to close her eyes.

"Dooda!" She'anaa'í nílį́!" *No! You are my enemy!* she announced. She figured the tall, gray-haired one had heard her because he stopped trying to kiss her. Instead, he limped to the chair, sat down heavily upon it and began taking his boots off. Dééd Yázhí felt helpless. She did not know what to think!

Shą́ą́' ániidí k'ad ni' ashijiłneeh ne'. K'ad shą' haash jit'į? *Just a while ago, he was trying to swallow me. What is he doing now?* she thought, as she quickly looked away from him.

"Naabaahii doo bi'éé' t'áágééd nidaakai da. Hwe'anaa'í da ła' t'áadoo hooyání hak'élwo'!" *Warriors are not supposed to be walking around without their clothes on. All of a sudden, an enemy may come up upon you without warning!* she scolded, remembering the words of her father when he was teaching his young warriors.

As if the tall, gray-haired one had understood her chiding, he stopped. Instead, he stood up and took off his shirt and his undershirt. Dééd Yázhí was horrified! This man who was kind to her was just as white and hairy as the dirty men who raped her when she first arrived at the fort!

She closed her eyes very tight, trying to separate the tall, gray-haired one from the mean, dirty, hairy white men who raped her repeatedly. She associated the tall, gray-haired one with her lamb by whispering,

"Shidibé yázhí nahalingo jiditł'oh. Éí shį́į́ biniinaa dibé yázhí 'ánínígíí k'ehgo hó dó' 'Mééee'', jiní. *He is hairy just like my lamb! No wonder he was making the sounds of a lamb.*

As the tall, gray-haired man came closer, all she could do was close her eyes very tight. The tall, gray-haired man took the opportunity to begin kissing her once again with passion. Dééd Yázhí kept her fists clenched as she felt fear rising within her body. He held her head and pressed her head closer to him. She was not familiar with this, nor had she witnessed any of her people doing this to one another. But then again, maybe he is really hungry, she thought again.

Her mind was jolted back to the times when she was intensely hungry when her kidnappers would not allow her to eat. The thought of her kidnappers' tongues made her nauseated and she had to get away from this man. Although she feared for her life, she placed both hands on his chest and pushed at him with all her might and watched him clumsily stagger away from her. He tried to regain his balance, but he was unsuccessful and fell back clumsily into a sitting position. Falling on his buttocks knocked the air out of his lungs. Dééd Yázhí watched helplessly as the tall, gray-haired one tried to regain his composure.

She was surprised she had that much strength. She went into a corner, quickly dug a hole, and began throwing up. The tall, gray-haired one got up with great difficulty then picked up the one chair in the room and sat down heavily upon it and ran his hands through his hair. Dééd Yázhí immediately became ashamed of reacting in this way, but how was she to communicate that it was not him who made her sick. It was the thought of her kidnappers that sickened her. She tenderly looked at him and said the first word that came to mind,

"No."

With sadness, he said,

"I am sorry. I did not mean to make you sick. How can I make you know that I love you. I do not want to hurt you. I just want to love you." He put his head down and softly said, "I want to make love to you. I will be leaving in a few days. I want to feel you. I want to yearn for you when I leave for the South. I want to yearn for you when I am far away from you. I need you to love me." With those words, he got up slowly and walked out the door, placing the lock on the door.

Dééd Yázhí felt bad, but she also felt very helpless. She so desperately wanted to tell the tall, gray-haired one it was not his fault. She knew from the way he spoke his words that the words were kind. All of a sudden, she felt a deep sense of loneliness. She wanted him to come back. She also wanted her lamb to be brought back to her.

She did not want to sleep in the strange clothes she wore so she took them off to wipe off any trace of the enemy she had faced earlier. Stretching and placing her tattered rug dress in the sand, she wrapped herself in a thin blanket and lay down. She missed her lamb. She needed to feel warmth near her.

Dééd Yázhí did not hear the lock on the door being slid out of its place. She gasped when she heard the sound of heavy footsteps entering the room. She reached around her and found nothing but sand at the end of her reach. Just when she was ready to fling the dirt into the air, she heard the voice of the tall, gray-haired one. She was puzzled.

Why couldn't I recognize his footsteps? she wondered. The tall, gray-haired one lit the crude kerosene lamp and smiled at her. Dééd Yázhí looked up and smiled back and said,

"Sit."

The tall, gray-haired one sat down hard on the floor. Dééd Yázhí noticed his boots. They were the tall boots he wore at times. The boots that he wore earlier sat on the floor. Earlier, he had run out of the shed so fast that he had left his boots. Dééd Yázhí smiled. The tall, gray-haired one moved closer to her and gently closed her eyes with his fingers.

"Mmmmm, mmmmm," was all she could hear him say. He moved away from her so he could take his shirt off. He picked up her hand and lifted it to his chest, then placed her palm against his chest. Dééd Yázhí could feel the hair on his chest. She was so surprised to find that the hair on his chest was very soft. She felt a little safer. She did not remove her hand from his chest. She forced herself to think of the times when he took care of her and protected her by keeping the men off of her. She kept her hand where he placed it. She thought of her lamb. Thoughts of her lamb calmed her.

The tall, gray-haired one reached out for her. He noticed she was wrapped in a blanket and that she did not have her rug dress on. He smiled and said,

"I love you." With those words, he began to leave soft kisses all over her face. With difficulty, he got up off of the floor and stepped forward to turn off the kerosene lamp.

Dééd Yázhí sat up still wrapped in the thin blanket. It was a slight struggle for the tall, gray-haired one to get down on the floor, but Dééd Yázhí felt herself being pulled down to the floor and onto the thin blankets she slept on. The tall, gray-haired one did not try to kiss her on the lips. Instead, he allowed his hand to slowly explore her soft supple body through the thin blanket.

Dééd Yázhí was afraid to stop him. She was afraid he would become mean and force her into actions that Naabeehó slaves who had escaped talked about. She was confused by her feelings. She wanted him near her. She needed his warmth. His hand was gentle. She silently wondered if a young Naabeehó warrior's hand would be as gentle as the tall, gray-haired one's hand.

Slowly, the tall, gray-haired one lifted the blanket off of her body and moaned a low soft moan into her ear as his hand caressed her soft skin. Dééd Yázhí felt her breathing speed up. The tall, gray-haired one's hand began to gently fondle her supple warm breast when she interrupted his actions by swiftly reaching out and slapping his hand, saying,

"Nóweh, ei 'awéé' bá. Ni 'éí dooda!" *Leave it alone, that is for the baby. It is not for you!* The tall, gray-haired one withdrew his hand from her breast and murmured,

"I am sorry, my beautiful Sunflower. Your thick Navajo dress hides the beauty of your bountiful body. I want to remember you with my eyes, my mind, and my hands. Let me touch your soft body, my beautiful one. Let me memorize every part of your body. You are beautiful," he whispered. Dééd Yázhí did not know what to say so she answered him by saying,

"Yááh?" *What?*

"Umhum. I have waited for you for the longest time. You are worth the wait, my beautiful Sunflower. I do not want to leave you. I want to love you and make sweet love with you. I want to stay and take care of you the way you should be cared for," he said in soft whispers.

Dééd Yázhí answered him by saying,

"Yááh?" *What?* He seems to talk more when I say that, she thought as she felt his hand gently lift her chin. She began to giggle. Something was tickling her ear. She lifted her hand and felt his face.

"Yíiyá!" *Scary!* was all she could say as she withdrew her hand from his face. His whiskers were ticklish to her ears but harsh to her hand. The tall, gray-haired one welcomed her giggle as his hand began to boldly claim her soft, supple body. In one swift motion, he lifted up his hips and pushed off his pants and underpants then settled back down beside her.

Dééd Yázhí gasped when his hand reached out to pull her close to him in the darkness. She could feel her body being moved closer to him. He felt for her hand and guided her hand as he silently encouraged her to explore his hairy body. She thought of her little lamb. His breathing became uneven. He knew what his Sunflower tasted like, but he wanted to know what she felt like and with that thought he became even more bold in his actions. He knew he would soon know the answer to that question, which up to now had just been a whisper in his mind.

In one motion, the tall, gray-haired one slid onto his back, rocked his body, and pulled her on top of him using his strong hands and knees to gently press her legs apart to straddle him. She tried voicing her discomfort and disapproval by saying,

"Áłtsé! 'Áłtsé! T'áadoo ..." *Wait! Wait! Don't ...* but he had no ears for her pleas. He lifted her to ease her into place, and when he did, he caught his breath and began his rhythmic movement as he firmly held her in place. Their bodies became one as Dééd Yázhí gently rode the tall, gray-haired one. In silence, the tall, gray-haired one made love to her, voicing only soft moans.

When his breathing became even again, he gently rocked Dééd Yázhí back off and onto her back to lay beside him. He kissed her neck that glistened in the silver moonlight that shone in from the smoke hole in the ceiling.

"You have fulfilled my dreams, my beautiful Sunflower," the tall, gray-haired one said as he held her close, leaving soft kisses on her smooth skin.

Dééd Yázhí covered her face with her hands. *My protection was not important to him,* she thought sadly. She shivered when she fully realized she had been with the 'anaa'í *enemy* without any clothing separating them. *I was his protector. I was the one who was shielding him from all things bad. What kind of a warrior does that?* she thought as deep sadness crept through her mind. Dééd Yázhí slept uneasily. She tried chasing away the thoughts that marched through her mind.

Shimá da shą' hait'éego shaa nitsékees dooleeł? T'ah náá yówohgo, nihe'anaa'í binák'ee góne' déé'íį'. T'áá 'éí náá bíláahdi nihe'anaa'í séljh. Hatíhíláane'ęę'! Nihe'anaa'í bíighah nétį́į dóó bił nétééžh. *What would my mother think of me? To make it worse, I have looked into the eyes of the enemy. Worse yet, I have tasted the enemy. What a terrible thing! I have laid down near the enemy, and I have laid down with the enemy!*

Dééd Yázhí had no trouble chasing the thoughts away when her mind stumbled upon the activities of earlier in the day. She began to realize that maybe the activity at the square building was an iigeh *wedding* that took place, only now she was really confused. Where was the corn mush she was supposed to carry into the hooghan *hogan?* Where was her maternal uncle who was to direct her through the motions of eating the mush and washing her man's hands? Who were the ones who were supposed to counsel them? Where was the food that her people gathered around to eat and tell stories over? In the past, her memories had been vivid in all aspects of the iigeh *wedding* that were held at her home at the base of Dziłíjiin *Black Mesa.* Other remembrances of home were vibrant in her mind, but the memories of the iigeh *wedding* were now becoming illusive.

One thought that was bothersome to Dééd Yázhí was, if we had an iigeh *wedding*, we did not observe the four days of not having any physical contact.

"Yáadilá baa niséyáá dó'? *What have I done?* she whispered. Her sadness increased as she thought, Shimá bina'nitin yę́ę t'óó shikéé' adíítąąd. *My mother's teachings are littered behind me. Hot tears began to form in her eyes.*

****

The thought that nagged at Dééd Yázhí's memory were the teachings her maternal grandmother gave to her older cousin whose marriage had been arranged. Her maternal aunt was visiting the neighbors looking for freshly ground blue corn, because her aunt had depleted her own supply of corn for her daughter and two nieces who had had their Kinaaldá *puberty observance* around the same time.

Dééd Yázhí remembered her maternal grandmother saying,

"Naadą́ą́' ak'áán dootł'izhígíí 'iigehgo choo'įį łeh. Asdzání bá 'iigehígíí dóó dinééh łį́į́' bá neelkaadígíí 'adoołts'ah biniiyé bá hasht'eel'įįh. Doo lá dó' dooda da! Doo naadą́ą́' ak'áán nishójoołt'eehgóó 'éí 'asdzání dóó dinééh bighan nizhónígo nidoolts'ił yéeni' dóó yee be'iina' ałhił íidoolííł yéeni' t'óó bits'ą́ą́' yiłgą́hígi 'áyiił'įįh. Dichin da yiih dínóodah. Tsołtį', naadą́ą́' ak'áán yee nihíká 'adoojahígíí bitah hootaikai dooleeł."

Blue corn flour is needed at the time of a wedding. Oh, what grief! If one does not obtain this flour, then the home that should fall into place for the young bride and groom and the life they will make together would experience deficiency; it would not be nurtured. They may fall into physical hunger. Come on, let us go visit the people who can give us blue corn flour.

At the time, Dééd Yázhí saw in her imagination images of a skinny marriage because of the words her grandmother chose to describe a wedding that is held when blue corn flour is not available. With these thoughts she remembered joining the group of women who were very concerned about the shortage of freshly ground corn.

Now, she did not have freshly ground blue corn flour. If it was an iigeh *wedding* that she and the tall, gray-haired one took part in, was her own marriage going to suffer due to the lack of essential ingredients? She closed her eyes and tried hard to concentrate on other things, but her mind lingered on the consequences of a nontraditional marriage because of the absence of the blue corn flour.

Her thoughts became even more troubling to her. If this was an iigeh *wedding,* then they were not to have had physical contact for four days and four nights because those days are sacred and it was the normal time of observance after an iigeh *wedding.* Once again, Dééd Yázhí was confused. She admitted she was afraid for her safety if she had not submitted to this man. She knew what crazed men were capable of.

Dééd Yázhí was relieved when the tall, gray-haired one left and when the hole in the ceiling told her the predawn morning was beginning to shed itself of the dark night sky and was pulling the white light of the sun into place in the eastern sky. She was left to sort out her thoughts. Her mind kept visiting the memory of the gray-haired one kissing her deeply. She was beginning to feel dizzy when she remembered he stuck his tongue in her mouth and had been moving it around for a long time as if his tongue was searching for something. Further, he was moaning like he had been hurt. Dééd Yázhí did not want to have any physical contact with him for the next three nights. Little did she know that within three day's time, the tall, gray-haired one would be sent to the South to fight in a war, the Civil War.

Through the small cracks in between the stacked logs that made the walls of the shed where she was kept, Dééd Yázhí saw the tall, gray-haired one during the day barking orders at the long line of men who were practicing how to carry a long glimmering piece of metal (rifles). The tall, gray-haired one stood straight like a warrior and looked strong in his clothes that were all one color, the color of łizhingo dootł'izh *dark blue,* like the color of the evening sky at dusk.

Toward evening, with the sun still bright, the tall, gray-haired one asked Dééd Yázhí to change her clothes and to put her bonnet on to visit the sheep. She did as she was told, but the embarrassment and the humiliation of wearing the clothes of the enemy had not worn off. The tall, gray-haired one accompanied her and the young Naabeehó 'ashkii *Navajo boy* to the sheep corral. Dééd Yázhí questioned in her mind how the tall, gray-haired one could think that covering her body with colorful material would hide the fact that she is Naabeehó *Navajo.* Through the crudely interpreted message of the young Naabeehó 'ashkii *Navajo boy,* she learned she had to cover her head to hide her identity as a Naabeehó captive. Early in her captivity, the tall, gray-haired one had told her that her presence would start a war between the Navajo and the U.S. military. He also told her she would not be allowed to leave the shed to visit the sheep anymore. Dééd Yázhí thought it was just the tall, gray-haired one whose jealousy kept her hidden, but the pointed guns of the dirty, hairy white men told her otherwise.

She decided she would be careful because she wanted so desperately to see the sheep. She wanted to see her lamb. It was the sheep that kept her mind strong even though she was held in captivity. It was the sheep that helped her to remain Naabeehó even though she wore clothes that brought shame to her. The sheep in the corral showed their delight in seeing her.

Shizhé'é shiká níyáago t'ah Naabeehó nishłínígíí yaa 'ákodínóozįįł. *When my father comes for me, he will know I am still Navajo,* she thought sadly. For a short time, she was apprehensive that she could even begin to walk back into her Navajo life and live it again. Now, she was sure she could. She wandered among the older sheep that had been kept in the corral because they were slow and the young boy did not want them to slow down the herd. She felt an understanding for the old ones. She too had been left behind by her people. They had not come for her. She knew her father and mother did not leave her behind. It was her people who had left her behind. Dééd Yázhí felt a sadness being draped over her.

She did not want to become sad, so she began to concentrate on regaining her language.

"Yá'át'ééh, dibé danohłínígíí. T'óó la' nizhónígo danihighan dóó nizhónígo nihaa 'ádahayą́," *Greetings, those of you who are sheep. You have a nice place to live and you are cared for in a good way,* she said aloud to the sheep, surprising herself at her ability to speak. She became even more surprised at the sound of her own voice. It was a mature voice, not the voice of the younger woman who had been kidnapped and sold. At hearing her voice, several of the sheep moved closer to her and nuzzled against her, and she felt she had been greeted once again by her people. Her people were here. Dééd Yázhí reached out and hugged the air. In her action, she had hugged her people. She breathed in the air and allowed it to settle deep in her lungs and felt the strength that flowed into her body.

After spending the evening talking with the sheep and thinking, Dééd Yázhí and the tall, gray-haired one returned to the shed. She found a sadness that surrounded the tall, gray-haired one. He had a sad look on his face. She glanced up at him and was reminded of their earlier contact that was a taboo in her Navajo eyes. He looked at her and smiled a weak smile.

"Are you O.K.?" he asked, and she wanted so much to communicate with him to let him know it was not he who had made her sick, so again she uttered some of the few words she was confident enough to voice.

"No, sit," she said. Without thinking she may not have understood his question, the tall, gray-haired one stood despondently by the door. He loved her so much and he wanted to let her know again in his manly way that he loved her.

After a short time of silence, she said,

"Sit."

So used to giving commands, the tall, gray-haired one was surprised to see himself sit down so quickly at her request. Dééd Yázhí was desperate to let him know that he had helped heal her and that he had brought her words and her life back to her by giving her a lamb which she so dearly loved. The words came spilling out of her mouth as she spoke the most words he had ever heard her say. It did not matter that she spoke in Navajo, she was communicating with him.

The tall, gray-haired one was overjoyed; yet dismayed, that he had not understood one word she spoke. He just threw his hands up in the air, and said,

"Háágo my beautiful Sunflower," as he motioned for her to come to him.

Dééd Yázhí remained seated on the floor and did not move. She thought, how could I tell him I cannot have any physical contact with him for the next three days and nights?

Ignoring the puzzled look on her face, the tall, gray-haired one continued to patiently say,

"Háágo, my beautiful Sunflower."

Out of fear and remembering his loud voice when he barked commands at his soldiers, Dééd Yázhí slowly moved closer to him, all the while keeping her distance.

"Fair enough, I will meet you halfway," he said smiling as he stepped closer to her. She backed away and he stopped. He did not want a replay of what happened the evening before when he had been overcome with wanting her.

He gently reached out and touched her hair. He slowly knelt in front of her and moaned,

"Sunflower, the name I gave you is appropriate. The sunflower is a hardy plant. It flourishes in the most difficult of places and is also very beautiful."

Dééd Yázhí noticed his breathing became more intense, and she in turn felt his excitement but her mother's words began ringing in her ears.

"T'óó 'índa há 'asgehgo, hastiin baa ho'deeltínígíí doo bił ałhaaníjít'įį da. Díį' yiłkááhdóó 'índa." *When you are first married, you and the man you were given to are not supposed to have physical contact with one another. Not for four days.*

She also heard her mother's warnings of the 'anaa'í the *enemy*. She was excited and yet afraid. With one swift movement, the tall, gray-haired one gathered her in his arms and began kissing her hair, voicing a soft moan. The night before, when he had to return to his quarters in confusion, he vowed to be gentle, cautious, kind, and loving to her. He gently placed kisses on her neck and began to allow his hands to softly touch her, very aware that she had been sexually abused by some of his own men. He decided not to kiss her so passionately on the mouth because his passionate kisses apparently made her sick, he rationalized.

He held her in a tender embrace. He kissed her face tenderly. Dééd Yázhí was afraid to push him away. She saw in her mind the image of her people who had strict cultural teachings. Her thoughts were interrupted when the tall, gray-haired one began talking to her. She found if she put her head against his chest, she could hear the strength of his voice vibrating in his chest. She thought of her mother's words, but her people had not come looking for her and this man was the one who saved her life by giving her a lamb and he was kind to her.

When the tall, gray-haired one sensed she was feeling more comfortable with their closeness, he held her even closer. He smiled cautiously. He felt her timidly pressing her breasts against him. He smiled again when he thought of how she slapped his hand and scolded him when he touched her soft, round breast. He desperately wanted to answer his longing by leading her to her blankets on the floor.

Instead, he let her go and walked out without a look back. A few minutes later, he came back carrying an armload of kindling. With some difficulty he knelt at the fireplace. With bark and little pieces of wood, he built a fire. Dééd Yázhí lifted her face and took a long, deep breath, letting the smell of the cedar wood cover her with a sweet scent. After adding more wood and satisfied that the fire was going to burn, the tall, gray-haired one moved closer to her and began to untie her long beautiful hair. She answered him by fully untying her hair and gently shook her head to allow her long hair to fall out of its tie.

Dééd Yázhí looked at him when he said,

"Háágo." *Come here*. She moved slightly closer. The tall, gray-haired one was happy with this gesture of acceptance. He felt rushed because he knew he was leaving the day after tomorrow at the first morning light. He told Dééd Yázhí,

"I feel sad. I am extremely sad that I will be leaving this place where I found an unexpected love. I am also sad that I will have to fight in a war I do not quite understand, but I am a soldier and I follow orders. I am proud to serve my country."

Dééd Yázhí sheepishly moved closer to the fire to remind the tall, gray-haired one of her presence. He reached out and gathered her in his arms as he lay down and gently pulled her down with him.

As he held her tightly, he said softly,

"I want to feel your Navajo body against mine again. I want you to hear me wanting you. I beg for satisfaction, my sweet Sunflower."

Dééd Yázhí seemed oblivious to his words as she played with the corner of her blanket. He continued,

"Respond to me. I want you to want me. I want you to feel me. I want you to hear me become breathless from my want of you. I want you to feel my gentle, yet demanding, impatience as I moan tender utterances of satisfaction," the tall, gray-haired one found himself saying.

He moved closer to Dééd Yázhí as he whispered,

"Love in Navajo is very sweet and intoxicating." He began to place soft kisses on the exposed parts of her body.

"My sweet Sunflower, how do I tell you to take your clothes off? I do not want anything separating us," he said softly.

Dééd Yázhí felt so vulnerable in the clothes of the enemy. Her rug dress was still drying in the sand. After visiting the sheep, she had placed it back in the dry sand to stretch out and dry, and she had put on the clothes of the enemy. She shivered. She felt every movement of the hand of the tall, gray-haired one as he caressed her body through the thin blouse and skirt of the enemy.

He is still the enemy! Her mind screamed.

The tall, gray-haired one became bold in his want for his beautiful Sunflower. He slowly began to coax her out of her clothes. Dééd Yázhí knew Naabeehó *Navajo* were not to be without their clothes when they are near an enemy.

How can I explain this to him? she desperately thought as one hand held her blouse close to her and in the other clenched hand, she held her thin skirt in place. The tall, gray-haired one expertly slipped his hand underneath her blouse and began caressing her body being careful not to touch her soft breast, although he wanted to touch her and taste her. He did not want his Sunflower to slap and scold him again although he did not know why she had done so. Dééd Yázhí was unaware the tall, gray-haired one was left confused as well.

With his strong body, the tall, gray-haired one tried in vain to lift Dééd Yázhí to help her get on top of him. She did not understand. She was confused. The kind man she knew the tall gray-haired one to be was not behaving like a warrior. Before, when he made his demands on her body, she was afraid so she did what he demanded of her.

Her thoughts were bringing the teachings of her father and her mother close. Without anyone's knowledge of her presence, she heard her father and maternal grandfather telling the young warriors never to allow a woman to be on top during the ceremonial act of making love to produce a baby. Her thoughts stumbled on their teachings she heard during one of the Winter Leadership gatherings.

A Naabeehó *Navajo* warrior is to always be protective of what is his—his wife. He is to be ready to jump up at an instant. Warfare is always near. A strong warrior cannot be in a defenseless position. If the woman is on top, how can you jump up and face the enemy in an instant? Do not expect your woman to protect you, absolutely not! She is already protecting your children by feeding them and caring for them.

Dééd Yázhí caught her breath. But this white warrior wants me to protect him, she thought as her mind began to accuse the tall, gray-haired one of betraying her. Out of fear of the 'anaa'í *enemy,* she reluctantly allowed the gray-haired one to hold her close as he rolled until she was on top of him.

Their lovemaking was awkward. Dééd Yázhí felt vulnerable and unprotected. She felt the urge to keep looking over her shoulder. She was in a place where there were many enemies around, enemies of her people. She felt a confusing mixture of fear, acceptance, guilt, and a budding love as she allowed her anaa'í *enemy* to make love to her.

As she lay close to him, Dééd Yázhí wondered why the tall, gray-haired man was sad. He appeared as if he was ready to cry. She thought it was because she had become nauseated at his kiss. She wanted to let him know it was not him who made her sick.

"Ních'aad," *Don't cry,* was all she could say. She wanted to comfort the man who spared her life when she was first brought to the place they call the fort.

In the faint light of the kerosene lamp, the tall, gray-haired one looked into her face. He wanted to memorize the color of her eyes, the shape of her lips, her beautifully shaped nose, and the scent of her hair. He knew he had to obtain some roots of the yucca plant to take with him when he left Fort Canby for the South. He loved the scent of the yucca root. The sweet scent of the yucca root would stir his memory to bring his beautiful Sunflower close.

With his eyes fixed upon her face, he allowed his thoughts and his heart to roam freely, without boundaries. His heart did not need to hover around the possibility of love with his beautiful Sunflower. He no longer needed to wonder what she felt like, what she tasted like, and what she sounded like when she was being satisfied with his love. She was all he had expected. Her sounds of love were soft utterances in her own Navajo language which he found very sensual as she met him and timidly allowed him to guide them through their expressions of love.

The tall, gray-haired one considered himself to be a strong man, but he found his weakness in the arms of his beautiful Sunflower. He fell asleep after being left satisfied again. He wanted to hear his Sunflower begging,

"Áłtsé. Kót'éego 'éí dooda. 'Áłtsé." *Wait. Not like this. Wait.* He assumed she was begging for satisfaction. He did not know he had allowed his beautiful Sunflower to feel vulnerable, unloved, and unprotected. As the rest of the fort slept in the early morning hours, the tall, gray-haired one returned to his quarters and fell into his bed to claim a couple of hours of sleep. Before he drifted off to sleep, his mind playfully drifted into the nearby hills, to the spot where he first kissed his beautiful Sunflower.

Chapter Ten
Where Did You Go?

On the tall, gray-haired one's last full day at Fort Canby, he ordered his soldiers to chop an extra amount of wood and had the wood taken and stacked beside his Sunflower's shed. He further collected cooking utensils, which would help her become self-sufficient. Other items were brought to the shed. Dééd Yázhí kept herself busy by inspecting each item that was brought in. Not even in her wildest dreams did she think her imagination would have to be her guide in the first few weeks of being on her own.

It was the tall, gray-haired one's and Dééd Yázhí's last night together. Dééd Yázhí worked quietly side by side with the gray-haired one while they prepared their simple meal of biscuits and lamb gravy. Although the food was familiar to her, she had never seen how it was prepared in the shiny pots and the flat pans. Is this something I will have to get used to? she questioned her thoughts in silence.

The young Naabeehó 'ashkii *Navajo boy* came to join them for supper and his limited understanding of English caused him to have difficulty in explaining to Dééd Yázhí the tall, gray-haired one would be leaving the fort for an unknown amount of time.

After the young boy left, the tall, gray-haired one felt extremely inadequate. He had many questions he wanted to ask of Dééd Yázhí but he forced them to remain a silent thought. He knew they had things they wanted to express to one another but could not.

The tall, gray-haired one brought back the young Navajo boy. It was through the young Navajo boy that he told Dééd Yázhí she would be well cared for at the fort. Dééd Yázhí was confused when the Navajo boy told her the money the tall, gray-haired one earned would be paid to her instead. She asked the young boy,

"Yáál shą' ha'át'íí 'óolyé?" *What is the meaning of coins (money)?*

She wondered what she would do if she were given the yáál *coins* the tall, gray-haired one promised would be given her. Her mind flew back to her home at the base of Dziłíjiin *Black Mesa* and to her father. She remembered her father kept a pouch of shiny coins, which was given to him by the Naakaiłbáhí *Spaniards* when he was a little boy. Her father called the coins yáál. Her father did not have a place to trade his shiny coins so he just collected them. Dééd Yázhí decided she would collect them as her father had done.

Thinking of her father made her very sad. Unwanted tears began to collect in her eyes. She became ashamed and fearful because she was sitting beside the 'anaa'í *enemy* who tried many times to kill her people, and in some instances, had succeeded. She shook her head to shed the deep sadness she felt.

The tall, gray-haired one stopped what he was doing and looked at her when he noticed her expression had changed to one of sadness.

"What's wrong?" he asked gently.

Dééd Yázhí did not understand his words but spoke what she knew.

"No. Sit." At her words, the tall, gray-haired one settled back down on the floor.

Dééd Yázhí and the tall, gray-haired one expressed their thoughts to each other in their own language. Their words drifted into the air above them, bounced off of the walls, then gently settled back down around them as they found common ground in the love and growing acceptance they felt for each other. Their expression of love was just as tender and as exhilarating as the night before.

The tall, gray-haired one was extremely sad that he would leave his new Navajo wife. He promised to keep himself safe and come back to her when the war in the South was over. Before he left, he tearfully told Dééd Yázhí,

"I am a soldier. I am told what to do. Amazingly, I healed you without being told to heal you. I fell in love with you without being told to love you. I chose to love you. No one told me to love you or how to love you. You have empowered me. Thank you, my beautiful Sunflower, for coming into my life. Caring for your lonely battered body made my own deeply felt loneliness leave. As your body grew stronger, I too, became stronger."

He looked into her face and continued, saying,

"I found you in a desert of destruction, destruction of your people. As a young tender sunflower in a dry desert, you turned

167

and leaned toward the source of the gentle rain, the care that I showered on you. I will never get enough of you, my beautiful Sunflower. My life now has meaning. My life has a purpose. I will come back when the war in the South is over. I love you, my darling. My love for you will bring me back to you."

Taking a folded paper out of his pocket, he said,

"Keep this paper in a safe spot." He demonstrated the value of the paper by folding it neatly and holding it over his heart and even kissed the paper gently. He then gave the paper to Dééd Yázhí. Pointing to it, he said,

"That paper is our marriage license. It says you are my wife. That paper will keep you safe until I return to you. Take care of it by keeping it in a safe spot."

He looked deep into the eyes of Dééd Yázhí. She looked back at him, not noticing his turquoise eyes and the wrinkles that bordered his eyes. Silent words danced on her lips. Gently and with deep emotion, the tall, gray-haired one whispered into her ear,

"I love you. My love will bring me back to you. Wait for me."

Somehow Dééd Yázhí knew the words "no" and "sit" would not stop him from leaving her warm blankets. Without another word, the tall, gray-haired one kissed her deeply and hungrily, then left before he could think another thought about her. His heart was breaking when he slid the lock back into its place. His tears flowed freely as he stumbled back to the officers' quarters to claim an hour of sleep.

****

Dééd Yázhí was relieved when she began to hear the sounds of the early morning. Fear usually kept her awake at night as she anxiously waited until the fan of light appeared on the ceiling of the shed to announce the early dawn. She wondered when the tall, gray-haired one was coming back. She allowed the sounds of the morning in the distance to comfort her. She turned toward the sound of the bugle that would wake up the soldiers who slept soundly. She heard the far away sound of a rooster announcing the morning sun's appearance. She smiled a faint smile when she heard the sound of the officers yelling at the young soldiers as they came running out of their barracks. She listened for the voice of the tall, gray-haired one. She did not hear his voice barking at the soldiers.

In the following predawn mornings when the air was kept still by the blanket of the heavy dawn, Dééd Yázhí woke up in anticipation of hearing the tall, gray-haired one yelling at the young soldiers. After several days of his absence, sadness and fear crept into her heart. She was sad because she had looked into his eyes and had seen kindness. She was fearful without his presence protecting her. She worried about how she was going to keep the mean, white, hairy soldiers from coming near her to claim her body.

****

With the disappearance of the tall, gray-haired one, Dééd Yázhí looked forward to the daily sporadic visits of the young Naabeehó 'ashkii *Navajo boy.* He was not to be away from the sheep without permission. Stealing away to visit Dééd Yázhí was dangerous for him. He hoped he found a reason for going to her shed by taking handfuls of hay to feed her lamb. In the safety of the shed, they fed the lamb, spoke to one another in Navajo, dreamed of a Navajo meal that is cooked over an open fire, talked about their families, and quietly spoke of the tall, gray-haired one. They both seemed to want to keep the memory of the tall, gray-haired one fresh in their minds as they spoke of him.

As promised, the officers at Fort Canby sent a supply of food every three days and kept a steady supply of firewood stacked outside Dééd Yázhí's shed. Dééd Yázhí had to wait until the young Naabeehó 'ashkii *Navajo boy* came to visit to go to the crude outhouse or have firewood brought in because the door was always locked from the outside.

When the young Naabeehó 'ashkii *Navajo boy* delivered her three-day supply of food, Dééd Yázhí looked through the items. There were several small pieces of fresh meat. These she made into jerky and hung them out to dry. Later in the day, she told the young boy she needed a grate to place over the open fire in the fireplace so they could cook the meat.

"Díí béésh ásaa' doo yá'áshǫǫ da. 'Atsį' t'óó yidiłid. Atoo' ádoolníiłgi t'éí choo'į, 'áko nidi 'áłahjį' atoo' ánéish'įįhgo t'óó shidiiłch'ee'. Ni shą', atoo'ísh nidiiłch'ee' ałdó'?" *This metal pot is not useful. It just burns the meat. It is only useful for making stew, but I am tired of eating stew. What about you, are you tired of eating stew too?* she asked the young boy.

"Nidaga', shí 'atoo' ayóo shił łikan. Atoo' yishch'algo 'ayóo shił łikan," *No, I really like stew. I like lapping up the stew,* he said with a sweet smile and with the last comment, both Dééd Yázhí and the young boy began laughing.

Dééd Yázhí could picture him lapping up his stew. The sound of their laughter hung gently in the air.

"Bikáá' at'eesí ła' nisin. Bikáá' at'eesí ła' shá yídííkił, ya'?" *I want a grate for cooking over an open fire. Ask for a cooking grate for me, O.K.?* she asked.

Not knowing where he would be able to obtain one, the young boy eagerly answered, saying,

"Hágoshį́į́." *O.K.*

Two days later the young Naabeehó 'ashkii *Navajo boy* came by for his visit carrying a round object. It was a makeshift small round grate for cooking over an open fire.

Excitedly, Dééd Yázhí grabbed the grate out of the young boy's hand and they rekindled the fire in the fireplace, then pulled out several strips of jerky. They talked softly about their Naabeehó people and how much they missed eating fresh corn. The grate was just what both Dééd Yázhí and the young boy needed. They ate the jerky they had cooked, then looked at the rest of the jerky that was hanging to dry. Dééd Yázhí jumped up and pulled the remaining jerky off of the rope and began roasting the meat without thinking they were about to consume her three-day supply of meat.

"Doo lá dó' ayóó 'áhálniihgo yishghal da," *That was so delicious as I ate it,* she said as she licked her fingers clean. All the young boy could say was,

"Eidí ga'," *I agree,* as he licked the stick they used to turn the jerky as it cooked over the hot coals. Watching the young boy, Dééd Yázhí wished she had asked for a grate much earlier. She was aware of how much the young Naabeehó 'ashkii *Navajo boy* missed his Naabeehó people too.

****

After many days had passed, Dééd Yázhí was still confused. She knew many soldiers had left, but she had no way of knowing where the tall, gray-haired one had gone or when he would come back. Nevertheless, she vowed to take care of the child he left within her. Finding herself pregnant again, Dééd Yázhí did not have the nauseating feeling she experienced the last time she became pregnant after having been raped by several dirty, mean, white soldiers. Even in giving me a child, he is tender and gentle, she thought as she massaged her flat stomach. This child will know about his father, she silently vowed.

****

Dééd Yázhí woke early one morning to a strange cold wind. The cold wind woke her out of her comforting dream. In her sleep, she dreamed she was back at the base of her mountain, the beautiful Dziłíjiin *Black Mesa*. The cold wind was happily playing with the hem of her rug dress as it lifted her rug dress so it could warm itself.

She reached out to pull her rug blanket around her to chase the cold away. Her rug blanket was the one her mother had woven for her. She could not pull her rug dress close enough to keep out the bitter cold. She heard one of her younger brothers chopping wood. The wind carried the sound of the sharp flint axe hitting the soft cedar wood.

All of a sudden she was fully awake. She was disappointed to find she was still in the shed at the fort. The wind was blowing the door open. With the next strong gust of wind, the door would open and close again.

Dééd Yázhí could not believe her eyes. The door was open. There was no lock on the door. She pulled the thin blanket close around her and cautiously walked to the door. She realized this was the first time she would actually be seeing the sun peek over the horizon before the wind yanked it up high into the eastern sky. She guardedly stepped outside and looked toward the sheep corral.

Her mind flew back to when she was a child. Her father would chase his two sons out the door, then come back for her and her younger sister. On cold mornings, their father would take them to the sheep corral and tell them to look for the warm steam that collected just above the heads of the sheep and goats where the steam was created by the warm breath of the sheep and goats on cold mornings.

Her father would say with excitement,

"Sha'áłchíní, siil nihilį́į́' bikáa'gi naanáaldohígíí hádadóh'į́į́'. Ei siil tó nídoodleełgo 'át'é. Nihilį́į́' ásdįįdgo 'éí doo nihee nínáhálṭįįh da dooleeł, háálá siil íidoolį́łígíí 'ádin doo. 'Ei siil binahjį' níłtsą́ naanáaldoh łeh. Éí biniinaa hadibé dóó hatł'ízí hólǫ́ǫgo 'ál'į́į́ dóó habéégashii dóó halį́į' hólǫ́ǫgo 'ál'į́. Nihilį́į́' ayóo nihaa dajooba'go 'át'é." *My children, look for the steam that hovers above our livestock. That steam will become water. If we no longer have livestock, it will not rain anymore because what created the steam, which led to rain, will be gone. The moisture that leads to rain drifts around as a result of the steam. That is the reason it is important to have sheep and goats and cows and horses. Our livestock are very kind to us.* Dééd Yázhí remembered how she looked for the steam on cold mornings when she was still at her mother's home and when she saw the steam, her worries were alleviated.

Standing just outside of the cold shed, Dééd Yázhí was glad she and her younger sister were taught to look for the steam as the sheep and goats breathed moisture into the crisp, cold morning air. In her mind, she could see what looked like a wide shallow band of steam rising into the early morning air each time the sheep and goats breathed the crisp cold air. Another band of steam would rise into the morning air as the sheep and goats began to stir.

Dééd Yázhí realized she missed seeing the steam that drifted up above the heads of the sheep and goats. As if in a trance, she went back inside, smoothed down her hair, adjusted her rug dress so it hung straight, and put on her white calico blouse and skirt over her rug dress and stepped outside.

Since her capture, this was the first predawn morning she was free to walk to the sheep corral to look for the steam that gently rose into the air as the sheep and goats began to stir. No one was outside. She felt relatively safe. Quietly and boldly she walked to the sheep corral. The eastern sun had not shed its heavy blanket of darkness, but she could hear the muffled bleats of the sheep and goats. As she slowly made her way toward the sound of the sheep and goats, Dééd Yázhí could see where she was going by the faint outline of the log buildings against the predawn sky.

When she approached the sheep corral, the sheep and goats began to stir. Dééd Yázhí could not see the steam, but she knew it hovered just above the sheep and goats.

"Méeeee'. Méeeee'. Me'e'e," was all she could hear.

Dééd Yázhí stood frozen in her tracks. She felt the presence of another person. She forced herself to turn to look to see who was standing near her.

"Shádí, da' niísh ánít'į?" *My older sister, is it you?* she heard a young voice ask. It was the voice of the Naabeehó 'ashkii *Navajo boy.*

"Dibé dóó tł'ízí bikáa'gi siil naanáaldohgo t'áá shiidą́ą́'dii t'éí yish'į́į́ nít'ę́ę́'. Dibé dóó tł'ízí nídahididziihgo bits'ą́ą́dóó siil nihwiileeh. Éí siilígíí yideestséél nisingo 'aadę́ę́' yóó 'aneesht'į́í'. Siil dah naaldogo yiistséehgo'ayóo baa shił hózhǫ́ǫ łeh. Txį', siil hádídíit'įįł," *It has been a long time since I have seen steam rising above the sheep and goats. The steam appears when the sheep and goats breathe out air. I snuck out because I wanted to see the steam. When I see steam rising in the air, it makes me very happy. Come on, let's go look for the steam,* Dééd Yázhí replied, still in her trance-like state.

Not wanting to interfere with the excitement Dééd Yázhí was displaying, the young Naabeehó 'ashkii *Navajo boy* followed in her footsteps, as he said,

"Txi'ínee', tsį́įłgo siil hádídíit'įįł. Hastóí 'ayóo bádahachxį. Kodi nanináago daniiłtsą́ągo haa da danidoolííł," *Let's go then, let's hurry and look for the steam. The men are real angry men. They may do something to you if they see you walking around here.* The young boy coaxed her to sit down on a low rising slab of rock.

Dééd Yázhí sat down and reached up to cover her hair with the bonnet, but she realized she had left it in the shed. Immediately, she became fearful. She had been told by the young Naabeehó 'ashkii *Navaho boy* the bonnet was what identified her as Lt. Charles Arnold Folton's wife. Without it, the soldiers could label her as a Naabeehó enemy and the mistreatment would begin.

She began to panic, but she told her heart she would not miss seeing the steam rising above the sheep and the goats. Dééd Yázhí and the young boy huddled together on the cold slab of rock with their eyes fixed on the air just above the sheep and goats.

When the delicate white light of the sun cast its light on the eastern horizon, Dééd Yázhí held her breath as she looked for the siil *steam*. Just as soft as a whisper, the steam appeared, as fragile as ever. Dééd Yázhí choked back a sob. It was this sacred event that her father wanted her and her younger siblings to witness when he took them out to the sheep corral each morning.

She batted tears away from her eyes. The faint white light of dawn grew brighter to shed a faint white light on the siil. Dééd Yázhí noticed a halo forming above the sheep and goats. She also noticed that the siil *steam* appeared as if it was alive and breathing. When the sheep and goats breathed out into the cold, the siil grew in size, which then slowly dissipated into the cold thin air. Once again, she watched as the siil appeared where the cold dawn air held the fragile siil ever so delicately in its cold pocket as the steam grew in size then slowly dissipated again.

Dééd Yázhí was mesmerized by the beautiful sight before her. She knew she had to return to the shed before the soldiers began spilling out of their barracks in a reckless manner but she could not pull herself away from the ceremonial moment of watching the delicate siil *steam* appear in the crisp cold air above the sheep and goats.

In a respectful whisper, she expressed gratitude by softly saying,

"Ahéhee', shiTaa'. Siil náánéiłtsą́. K'ad lą́ą́ nííłtsą́ nikídooldoh. *Thank you, my Divine Father. I saw steam once again. Now moisture will reach the earth.*

Tearfully, she added,

"Shik'i hojisdli'. T'áá 'óolyéego shik'i hojisdli'. *I have been blessed. I have been truly blessed.* With those reverent words, she reached up and gathered the cool, crisp dawn air and hugged it close.

Unable to maintain her composure, Dééd Yázhí freed her tears. One after another, her hot, restrained tears made their way down her face. She held out her hands to catch each tear so they would not spill onto the land of the 'anaa'í *enemy.* Looking back at the siil *steam,* she softly whispered,

"Shimá dóó shizhé'é t'ah shénálniih. Shideezhí bił, t'ah nihénálniih. T'ah ayóó'áshi'dó'ní. Shideezhí 'ałdó' ayóó'ábi'dó'ní." *My mother and my father still remember me. Along with my younger sister, they still remember us. I am still dearly loved. My younger sister is also dearly loved.*

She reached up to wipe tears off of her cheek, and when she did so, she realized there was an ever so thin coating of ice that protected her tears and kept them from rolling further down her face and onto the hard slab of rock she sat upon.

With her hands still slightly moist from her tears, Dééd Yázhí reached down and began rubbing her abdomen to wake the little life that grew within her. She wanted her little one to experience the sacred appearance of siil *steam* above the sheep corral. As if her little one heard her wishes, the little one softly bumped against the side of her yishch'id *womb.* Dééd Yázhí knew this morning was a gift from the Creator and her mother and her father. She held her abdomen to let her little one feel her love and to thank it for greeting her with its movement.

Déédyázhí was so overcome with emotion. Without realizing it, she asked,

"Háájíísh ííníyá?" *Where did you go?* The emotion of seeing the siil *steam* and feeling her little one greet her made her miss the tall, gray-haired one. She wanted him to be here standing behind her to witness the wonderment of the predawn morning. She wanted to feel his breath on her hair. She wanted to feel his warmth. She wanted to lean against his strong body. She wanted to hear his voice whispering soft words in her ear. She wanted to let the tall, gray-haired one know she missed him.

"Háájíísh ííníyá, shiyázhí bizhé'é nílíinii? *Where did you go, you who is the father of my little one?* she asked. The questions hung in the air before a cold breeze came by and lifted her words off of her thin shoulders and took them off into the distance.

Déédyázhí shivered from the cold morning breeze, then forced herself to turn away from the ceremonial scene with which the sheep and goats blessed her. She turned toward the direction of the shed.

She quietly hurried along to avoid being seen by a soldier. All of a sudden, she heard a sound that caused her to stop in her tracks. Somewhere in the distance she heard a child crying. Then she heard a woman speaking her language, the Naabeehó *Navajo* language. Déédyázhí turned toward the sound but could not see into the distance because of the fog that appeared and hovered near the ground. She looked back at the sheep corral and saw that the fog had also engulfed the ceremonial rise and fall of the siil *steam.*

Dééd Yázhí was desperate to know who the Naabeehó *Navajo* woman and child were and where they were from, but she reminded herself that she was not alone. She had a little one to think of, so she forced herself to walk away from the crying child and hurried back to the shed.

After relieving herself in the crude outhouse, Dééd Yázhí entered the shed and covered herself with the thin blankets the tall, gray-haired one gave her. She closed her eyes tightly so she could concentrate on the sound of the tall, gray-haired one's voice as well as the voices of her mother and her father. She remembered their voices very clearly. She buried her face in the thin blankets to bring back the voice of the tall, gray-haired man who gave her a little one to love and care for. The blankets gave her warmth.

Chapter Eleven

A Taste of Home

As the days grew into weeks, Dééd Yázhí began to lose favor with the older officers and never gained the respect of the new officers who had come to take charge of the fort. Time passed and the officers' treatment of her became harsh and less protective. She found her old fears of the soldiers visiting her mind daily. She remembered back to when she had been kidnapped and sold, she had no idea where she was or how far her home was, let alone where home was. She felt completely alone.

The young Naabeehó 'ashkii *Navajo boy* was kept busy with the sheep the soldiers had confiscated from the Naabeehó people, which were herded into the fort daily. In order to see Dééd Yázhí, the young boy had to sneak away at night. Their visits had to be short because the weather was becoming colder by the day.

Every evening, Dééd Yázhí made sure she cooked a slab of jerky on the grate over the open coals. She never failed to save a large piece of grilled jerky for the young boy. Over their little meals, they shared stories that reminded them of home. She told the young boy about her mother and her father and her siblings. She loved telling him about her family. It seemed every time she talked about her family, they visited her in her dreams. She wanted the little one growing inside her womb to know its grandparents and its uncles and its aunts.

The young Naabeehó 'ashkii *Navajo boy* did not have much to share. He could not tell Dééd Yázhí much about his family because he had been kidnapped when he was small and his mother had been killed by a soldier, leaving him with only the memory of her death. The tall, gray-haired one had cared for him since he was brought to the fort. Dééd Yázhí worried about the young boy. He did not remember what his clans were, so she gave him her clans.

"Tó 'Aheedlíinii nílįį dóó Ma'ii Deeshgiizhnii bá shínílchíín. Áádóó Táchii'nii 'éí danicheii dóó Tó Dích'íi'nii dine'é 'éí daninálí. 'Éí binahjį' shitsilí nílįį dóó shí 'éí nádí nishłį. Na'niłkaadii Ts'ósí yinílyée doo. 'Éí nízhi' doo," *You are of the Water Flows Together people and you are born for the Coyote Pass people. Your maternal grandparents are of the Red Running into the Water people and your paternal grandparents are of the Bitter Water people. In this way, you will be my younger brother and I will be your older sister. Your name will be Slender Sheep Herder. That will be your name,* Dééd Yázhí said as she giggled at the name she gave the young Naabeehó 'ashkii *Navajo boy.*

The young boy was eager to learn about Dééd Yázhí's family, and at times, he began to talk about each member of her family with a sense of familiarity. After each visit from the young boy, Dééd Yázhí was always left with the feeling her family had come to visit her. She continued to hope her father would come looking for her and find her, then take her home to the base of Dziłíjiin *Black Mesa*.

****

Dééd Yázhí was feeling even more confusion and fear. Using the young boy as an interpreter, she was horrified when an angry soldier told her she could no longer wear her rug dress at all when she left the shed. The angry soldier gave her two long shirts with long sleeves as well as two long skirts that came down to her ankles. He further told her to wear her bright-colored bonnet at all times. She was terrified to hear she could not wear her rug dress outside of the shed any longer. Her mind was being tortured by the thought that her father might not recognize her if he came looking for her.

She was left with the clothes and was ordered to wear them every time she left the shed to go to the outhouse or when she wanted to visit the sheep. She was also ordered to "earn her keep." Putting his red, distorted face directly in her face, the red-haired soldier told her the soldiers would not be able to protect her if she wore her "her savage-looking dress." The young Naabeehó 'ashkii *Navajo boy* did his best to interpret for the soldier with his very limited understanding of English. What the young boy did not risk telling Dééd Yázhí was she would be killed by the soldiers if she was seen wearing her rug dress because they had declared war on the Naabeehó people, her people.

In their discussions, Dééd Yázhí and the young boy suspected that the soldiers did not want the Naabeehó people to see a Naabeehó woman freely walking around at the fort. They pondered the idea that the soldiers were very afraid

Naabeehó warriors would try to raid the fort to take back the daughter of a prominent Naabeehó leader if the warriors knew she was being held there.

In order to survive, Dééd Yázhí complied with the orders of the red-haired soldier. She knew first-hand what the evil soldiers were capable of. On the next day, a soldier came to escort her to the laundry house. Embarrassed, humiliated, and feeling extremely underdressed, Dééd Yázhí exited the shed. She put her head down and just simply put one foot in front of the other and followed the soldier. She wanted to place an extra covering over her abdomen because she did not want her little one to see her wearing the enemy's clothes. She closed her eyes when she saw the faces of her mother and her father in her mind. What would they think of me? she thought painfully as she wondered what her younger sister was wearing right now. She wondered if her father's strong, brave warriors had found her sister.

As she walked, she noticed the sheep corral which was within viewing distance. She was too embarrassed to look toward the corral because she knew the sheep would not recognize her in the enemy's clothing. She knew they would be judging her, accusing her of becoming one of the enemy. She felt so ashamed, which led her to feel a deep, deep sense of sadness and humiliation.

When she felt her abdomen, it felt as if her little one had no protection in the thin shirt and thin skirt. Her rug dress was thick and it provided plenty of protection, but the enemy's clothes provided very little protection. When she walked past a few soldiers, she felt they could see through the thin, flimsy clothes she was wearing. She believed she was betrayed by the wind in that the wind was laughing at her by demonstrating how thin her clothes were when it kept picking up the hem of her skirt and causing it to flounce up and down, exposing her brown legs and her ugly black boots.

Dééd Yázhí listened to her footsteps. They were loud. Her footsteps told the story that it was a clumsy person who was walking in the ugly black boots. She noticed she was walking with her knees slightly bent so no one could see her wearing the ugly black boots. She felt her face flush when she thought of the moccasins her maternal grandfather made for her. When she walked in her moccasins, her moccasins never made a noise to alert the enemy where she was walking, but the ugly, black boots announced to her enemy that she was near. Dééd Yázhí did not feel safe in the clothes she was wearing.

Instead of being left alone in the shed like she was used to, Dééd Yázhí was told through gestures, motions, and shoves to wash the bedding of the officers. Washing bedding was a lengthy and cumbersome process. The chore was made even more difficult by the clothes she was forced to wear, but she was glad to get out of the shed so she could look for the tall, gray-haired one and catch a glimpse of the sheep. When she was escorted to the laundry house, she listened for the voice of the tall, gray-haired one and the bleating of her lamb. It also gave her a chance to look into the hills for the possibility of seeing her father and her younger brothers who had come to look for her. The hard work she was assigned helped her forget she wore the clothes of the enemy, but she worried about her father not being able to recognize her because she looked like the enemy.

Dééd Yázhí began her workday washing for the officers or the soldiers. Each week, she was to begin her week by entering the smaller buildings on the northern side of the fort. Each building was square and identical in size, each containing two rooms and a kitchen. These buildings were reserved for the officers, and it was in one of the buildings in this row of smaller houses the tall, gray-haired one had once lived.

It is good most of the men in the blue clothes have left so I do not have so many blankets to wash, but did the tall, gray-haired one have to leave and be gone so long? Dééd Yázhí thought to herself. Whenever she entered the building the tall, gray-haired one lived in, she breathed in the scent that brought him close to her. He did not smell like this until he came to see me in the evenings, she thought and it was during the last evenings he was at the fort that they had their most intimate moments. Each time she entered this particular building, Dééd Yázhí rubbed her abdomen to wake up her child so the little one could get to know what was left of his or her father.

"Kóne'é nizhé'é kééhat'ịị́ nít'ę́ę́', shiyázhí," *It was in here that your father lived, my little one,* she would say as she gently massaged her abdomen through her thin clothes. Dééd Yázhí knew her little one sensed the reverence of the space, because she would feel an increase in her little one's movements. In answer to her little one's responses, she would breathe in deep, deep enough for the scent to reach her little one.

One day as she wandered around in the officers' quarters, she wondered in what area of the building her tall, gray-haired one slept. As she wandered around in the building, the eastern side seemed to come alive with his memory more than any other space. Dééd Yázhí, once again rubbed her abdomen and vowed to raise her child with the memory of his father.

My baby will get to know his father through me, she silently vowed one day as she faced the eastern wall. The memory of the gray-haired one's touch on her skin, his sensual voice, and the sound of his breathing seemed to become more intense. She felt embarrassed as she looked around her to see if anyone was near, because she felt the excitement of the tall, gray-haired one's strong body next to hers. For a minute, her mind stopped reminiscing when it stumbled on the thought that she had to protect the tall, gray-haired one with her own body.

Shaking her head, to rid it of its recent thought, Dééd Yázhí's mind drifted to the sensuous feel of his strange hairy chest against her smooth breasts. Her memory brought back the wet kisses he would leave on her body to be cooled by his breath. She could still see his eyes with their strange color of turquoise with their long gray lashes and short bushy eyebrows above them. A sense of embarrassment floated through her mind when she reminded herself of the time she first saw the tall, gray-haired one's eyes up close. She smiled out of embarrassment to think that she once equated his eyes with that of a horned toad's eyes.

Speaking quietly to her little one, she said,

"Ts'ídá t'ahdoo bíla' ashdla'ii ła' bináá' ákót'éego yiistséeh da nít'ę́ę́, t'áá hazhó'ó na'ashǫ'iiłbáhí dich'ízhígíí t'éiyá bináá' ákónoolningo néistsééh nít'ę́ę́. Nináá' shį́į hait'éego naashch'ą̨' doo, shiyázhí. Shí shináá'ígíí nináa'go 'éí nihidine'é doo yee naa daadloh da doo. 'Éí bich'į' shíni' íí'áh. Naa hą́ą́h

186

hwiinidzingo 'át'é, shiyázhí. *I had never seen a five-fingered one (human being) with eyes of that color before, it was only in the eyes of a horned toad that I had seen eyes of that color. I wonder what color your eyes will be, my little one. If your eyes are the same color as mine, our people will not make fun of you. That is what I worry about. You are thought of as being very fragile, my little one.*

After expressing her concern to her little one about the color of the tall, gray-haired one's eyes, Dééd Yázhí felt a sense of relief. She had finally voiced her concern to someone, even if the "someone" was her own unborn child. A sense of heaviness left her shoulders. She was immediately grateful to her child for being kind to her in that way. Her little one was already helping.

One morning, as Dééd Yázhí was cleaning the space where she felt the presence of the tall, gray-haired one, she heard herself breathe,

"Doolá dó' naadzólníi da, she'awéé' bizhé'é nílįįnii." *How handsome you are, you who are the father of my baby.* As soon as her whispered words drifted toward the walls, it seemed as if the air carried her words on a gentle breath, which came from behind and landed on her right shoulder. She whirled around in fright, and to her relief, found the room empty. It must have been the tall, gray-haired one, she thought as she quickly gathered the bundle of bedding that was left at the door and ran from the building.

Has he been killed? Was I in the home of someone who is no longer living? she questioned her thoughts as she shuddered. This was the first time she allowed herself to think that thought. Tears collected in her eyes. She vowed she would not allow her tears to escape until she was alone in the shed.

187

Dééd Yázhí found washing bedding and uniforms for the officers was an easier chore because there were only a few officers. She would gather all the bundles from the officer's quarters and take them to the laundry building. The laundry was a building with one large room, which contained several aluminum tubs, large slabs of cake soap, and several washboards. It was in this building all of the bedding and clothes of the officers were washed and pressed. Along one wall, was where the uniforms of the soldiers were stored. Shirts were placed on one side and pants on the other. A few hats lay on a small table. Once a week the soldiers were instructed to leave their uniforms for the Indian wife who washed clothes. A long clothesline was awkwardly attached to the building.

Washing for the soldiers was a cumbersome process because there were more of them. First, there were the barracks from which she had to collect bundles. Each bundle contained thin woolen blankets, muslin sheets, a rough towel, and a yellowed washcloth. A smaller bundle contained the clothes the soldiers had worn. Dééd Yázhí winced each time she picked up bundles that were associated with the enemy of her people.

The soldiers' dirty blankets and dirty clothes were first placed in tubs containing boiling water on the stove. Dééd Yázhí's job was to get the water hot enough to begin boiling the blankets and clothes. Once the items boiled a short while as they were stirred with a long stick, the items were taken out and allowed to cool on a long table. Once cooled, the blankets and clothes were wrung out, washed in the tubs in the next room, rinsed, and hung out on the metal clotheslines that stretched between two buildings.

There were several barracks, some on the west side and a couple on the east side of the fort. Separating the two sets of barracks was the parade ground where Dééd Yázhí remembered first hearing the tall, gray-haired one yelling at the soldiers in his loud, angry-sounding voice.

A building, with one large room, the same size as the barracks, was attached to the back of the barracks by a breezeway. The large room housed a place for cooking and a place for the soldiers to eat. Many long tables and long benches took up the entire space. There was also a storage room for dry goods and food.

Dééd Yázhí washed all the bedding and uniforms for the officers on one day and for the next three days she boiled and washed the bedding and uniforms of the soldiers. The final day of the week was dedicated to the pressing of the uniforms the officers wore. After she became used to what was expected of her, the work did not seem difficult; it was just tedious.

Dééd Yázhí welcomed the hard work. Her mind flew back to her mother's words, bringing them back with clarity to remind her that a Naabeehó woman is supposed to work hard during her pregnancy so that the delivery of the baby would be easy.

"Jooltsą́ą́go doo t'óó hayaa ni'diniihgo jizdáa da. 'Ákóho'dil'į́į́go t'óó bízhníldį́į́h. Aadóó wónáasii' awéé' t'óó hade'át'į́į́h. T'óó jizdáago 'éí 'awéé' hódiigháahgo doo chohoo'į́į́góó neezgai łeh áádóó ch'ééh ajiłchíí łeh. Yéego bił nijilnishgo 'ál'į̱," *When you are pregnant, you should not allow others to cater to you as you just sit around. If you are treated like that, you become used to it. Pretty soon the baby gets too big. If you just sit around and you go into labor, you will have*

189

a lot of pain and you will have a hard time delivering the baby. One is supposed to work hard during her pregnancy, is what Dééd Yázhí used to hear her mother tell the Naabeehó *Navajo* women who were pregnant for the first time. With her mother's words resonating in her ear, Dééd Yázhí was glad she had the chance to work hard.

Even though these men treat me like an enemy, they are making it easier for me to have my baby when it is time for me to deliver my little one, she thought to herself many times as her belly grew larger by the week.

On one of the cold days of the fall season when Dééd Yázhí was hanging up towels, she ran out of space on the clothesline to hang the towels. She was eager to finish her work because it was getting colder and her thin clothes were wet and not keeping her warm. She looked toward the fence nearby and wondered if she could hang the towels on the fence.

As she walked toward the fence, something caught her eye. Dééd Yázhí caught her breath. Just beyond the fence, on the sloping hill, she saw pinon trees laden with ripened pine cones. Many of the cones had burst open and had dropped their nuts on the ground around the trees. Hungry for the taste of the pinon nuts, she walked along the fence looking for an exit that led out of the fort. She noticed a guard watching over the opening in the fence. As she walked further up the hill, she noticed more sloping hills that contained many more pinon trees, all laden with bursting pine cones.

Wet and cold, she pointed to the trees then pointed to the gate. The guard recognized her and led her to the opening and said in a gruff voice,

"Don't try anything. I will be watching you!"

Dééd Yázhí walked to the first tree and inspected its cones then knelt down and began picking the nuts that had been scattered on the ground by the wind. As she picked up the pinon nuts, her maternal grandmother's pinon-picking song came back to her mind, and she automatically began singing the song. It was the song her grandmother sang when they went to pick pinons in the late fall. At first Dééd Yázhí did not recognize her own voice. She stopped singing and looked around her cautiously, surprised to find the voice belonged to her. She had not heard the song for over a year and yet, the words were coming to her mind rather easily.

When both of her hands were full of pinon nuts, Dééd Yázhí stuffed the nuts into the sides of the ugly black boots she was wearing and quickly picked more pinon nuts. She did not realize she had company until someone kicked her, knocking her off balance. Afraid to look up, she saw a soldier's ugly, black boot. Fear gripped her heart. She grabbed a few of the pinon nuts she had scattered on the ground when she lost her balance, then threw them into her mouth. She heard the soldier laughing. Frantically, Dééd Yázhí took a chance and grabbed more pinon nuts in her hands and began running toward the security of the fence. Her long, wet, flimsy skirt and her ugly, black boots would not allow her to run very fast toward the gate.

Once inside the gate, she looked back to see two soldiers shouting loudly to the young soldier who kicked her. The soldier with the mean boot thought she was a member of the group of Navajos who belonged to the notorious Navajo leader,

Manuelito. The young soldier was surprised to hear the woman he kicked was the wife of the officer who left to fight in the Civil War.

Having difficulty catching her breath, Dééd Yázhí entered the safety of the shed. She placed the pinon nuts on a piece of cloth, then spit the pinon nuts out of her mouth, adding them to the pile on the cloth then emptied out the nuts she had stuffed in her ugly, black boots and marveled at the pile of pinon nuts on the cloth. She smiled to herself, rubbed and held her abdomen tightly, then dug a hole in the soft sand and hid the precious bundle in the sand.

Her smile faded when she heard the shuffling of feet at the door of the shed. A young soldier stood at the door waiting to escort her to back the laundry house. Reluctantly, she followed to finish washing the bedding and uniforms.

The following evenings, Dééd Yázhí returned to her shed with a renewed interest. The song she sang to herself when she was picking pinons tugged on a melody she used to hear her mother sing when she was a child. During her busy day, she took several glances toward the western hill where the trees were laden with pinon nuts. She welcomed the cold fall winds because they freed the nuts from the cones when they shook the trees. With every glance, she imagined pinon nuts scattered on the ground at the base of the trees.

Every day for the next few weeks Dééd Yázhí passed the same guard, picked several handfuls of pinon nuts and stuffed them into her ugly, black boots, then returned to the shed. The pinons were kind to her. They were placing precious memories back into her mind. She would pat the mound of pinon nuts gently and thank them for bringing her Naabeehó family back to her. She desperately missed her mother and her father, but the pinon nuts took some of the pain away and replaced the pain with sweet memories.

Dééd Yázhí thought of picking pinon nuts as a child. She remembered her maternal grandmother's words of wisdom regarding the picking of pinons.

"Naakai dóó 'Anaałání dóó t'áá 'ániidgo Bił da'ahijigáanii bik'ijį' nidajibaahgo neeshch'íí' t'éí bikiin nidajibaah nít'ę́ę́', áádóó 'ałchíní dóó sáanii danilínígíí níléí dził tádaat'ahgóó nidazhnichéé nít'ę́ę́' háálá 'áadi neeshch'íí' t'óó'ahayóí hólǫ́ǫgo biniinaa 'áajį', dził bit'áahjį', anídazhnichééh nít'ę́ę́'. *At the time when the Navajos were fighting against the Mexicans and the enemy Indians and more recently with the (white soldiers), the Navajos' only means of subsistence were the pinon nuts, and the women and children would run into the folds of the mountains in search of safety. As they hid in the mountains, they knew there were plenty of pinon nuts there they could subsist upon.*

"Áko nidi neeshch'íí' náhádláahgi na'nitin t'áá béstł'ǫ́ǫgo 'át'é. T'áá hazhó'ó ła' nááhaijį' hodadínóołnah bíighahgo t'éí nínádajiidlahgo bee haz'ą́. 'Aak'eedgo neeshch'íí' náhádláah níléí t'óó 'índa hwee nídaadzasjį' t'áá 'ádíjį' nináda'jiidlahgo bee haz'ą́. Neeshch'íí' hats'ą́ą́' bik'i yidzasgo 'éí t'áá 'ádíjį' neeshch'íí' nídajiiláhígíí ni' kódajiił'įįh. Yidzasdóó 'éí neeshch'íí' ni'góó nidadeeztą́ądígíí naaldlooshii danitsaazígíí dóó naadlooshii 'ádaałts'íísígíí daabá, 'éí bee baa hojoozba'íígíí 'áté. Neeshch'íí' tsin t'ah t'áá daabą́ąhígíí 'éí doo hádajit'įį da, doo tsin nídazhniłhałgo neeshch'íí'ígíí nínádazhniłdah da, háálá bįįh éí bidee' yee tsin nídeinigohgo neeshch'íí' nínádeiniłdahgo yaa nidahodikai łeh. Nááná tsin neeshch'íí' t'ah t'áá daabą́ąhígíí doo dajigháad da 'ałdó', háálá shash neeshch'íí' yaa nidahodikaigo tsin deigháad łeh. Díí na'nitinígíí bééhániihgo 'éí t'áá 'aak'eed ná'ádleehígíí bik'eh neeshch'íí' bee nihaa dahojooba' dooleeł. *But the picking of the pinon nuts has teachings tied to it. One can only pick enough pinon nuts to last one year. It is in the fall season the people pick pinon nuts and they can only pick pinon nuts until the first snow fall. It is only up until the time that the pinon nuts are snowed upon that the people are allowed to pick the pinon nuts. Once it snows then the activity is to be set aside. The pinon nuts that remain on the ground after the first snow are to be left for the large animals and the small animals, left for their consumption. A person is not supposed to hit a pinon tree with a stick. To do so is to mimic the deer, which use their antlers to hit the tree and knock off the pinon nuts. To shake the tree is also forbidden because the bears are the ones who shake the tree to shake off the pinon nuts so they can eat the nuts. If a person remembers to observe these teachings, then the Navajos will continue to be blessed with an abundance of pinon nuts every fall season.*

Dééd Yázhí's maternal grandmother reminded her grandchildren the Naabeehó people revered the deer and the bear, and so the people could not imitate their actions.

It was like therapy for Dééd Yázhí to go out and pick the pinon nuts off of the ground, because it helped her remember the words of her elders, specifically her mother, her grandmothers, and her aunts. Further, the area near the pinon trees became a treasured spot because it shielded her from the officers and soldiers who barked orders she could

194

hardly understand. More importantly, it was under trees like these the tall, gray-haired one kissed her for the first time.

Dééd Yázhí found herself coming to the same spot at least every day. She felt closer to her family and her Naabeehó people. She also felt closer to the tall, gray-haired one whose child she had growing inside her. She felt sad that with each passing day, the sound of his voice was fading.

Chapter Twelve
A Visitor in the Cold

Dééd Yázhí woke up one morning to find the sounds of the fort muffled. She imagined herself at home with her mother's soft rug blanket wrapped around her. Soon, the comfort of her thoughts left her and she remembered she was alone. She looked through the cracks in the walls of the shed and noticed everything was white. It was a strange day. If it snowed, it should be cold, she thought, but it was not cold. She remembered the pinon trees laden with ripened nuts. Now, it was too late to pick any more pinon nuts, she thought. The land she walked upon in her ugly, black boots had experienced its first snowfall of the season. Through the night, the snow had quietly and gently greeted the earth.

She was sad. She became afraid because pinon picking was bringing back to her memory the songs of her mother and her maternal grandmother. She was also saddened because the pinon trees were bringing back the memory of the first time the tall, gray-haired one stuck his hungry tongue into her mouth after his tongue gently parted her lips.

"Bidaa' yilzhóólí ne'," *His lips were so soft,* she softly breathed.

A few days after the first snowfall, Dééd Yázhí heard a commotion in the direction of the parade grounds. Soldiers were yelling and laughing. She scooted to the crack in the wall and saw some young men. She looked again, and saw they appeared to be Naabeehó! Her heart began to beat loudly and faster. She squinted to see through the crack in the wall and focused on the young men.

"Naabeehó danilį̇́!" *They are Navajo!* she said slowly. Her heart began to beat even faster.

"T'áá'aaníí Naabeehó danilį̇́," *They truly are Navajo,* she whispered sadly. She knew they were Naabeehó by the way the young men wore their hair and by the weapons the soldiers confiscated and carried. In observing closer, she saw the young men were near her age. She winced when she saw the young Naabeehó men had large bruises and deep-looking cuts on their arms and legs.

Barely able to see the outline of the logs that made the walls of the sheep corral, Dééd Yázhí saw a long procession of people walking. They were coming closer! Followed by many soldiers, there were many children, women, and elders. The children were hanging on to their mother's rug dresses and the women were hanging on to their elders. The elders were bent over and walked with great difficulty.

"Yáadi shą'?" *What in the world?* Dééd Yázhí said in unbelief.

As the people were forced to walk into the parade grounds, Dééd Yázhí could see that the children were crying as they clung on to their mothers' rug dresses or their mother's blankets.

Dééd Yázhí gasped. There were many women in the procession who had no blankets! Immediately, her mind thought of how the nights were going to be much colder now because of the snow. She saw that many of the children themselves were scantily dressed, but it was the men who caught her attention. They were stripped of their clothes! Their clothes were used to tie their hands behind their backs and to tie their ankles together.

It was the sight of how the elders were being treated which made Dééd Yázhí catch her breath. They were being rushed, pushed, shoved, and because of the treatment, many tripped along. Never had she seen elders being treated this way, and it was hard for her to watch. Although it was not clear because of the distance, Dééd Yázhí desperately searched from one face to another, wondering if any of these people were her relatives. To her relief and great dismay, she did not see the faces of any person in her family. The hole in the wall was too small and the people were too far to clearly recognize anyone.

Tears rolled down her face. She thought of her mother, her father, her maternal grandmother and her grandfather. She thought of her brothers who were trained to be brave and strong. She knew for certain her brothers would put up a strong fight if anyone tried to hurt their mother, their father, or their maternal grandparents.

Dééd Yázhí was oblivious to the pool of tears that had collected on the floor in front of her. She felt so incredibly helpless. She hugged her little one as if to protect it even more from any harm. She closed her eyes very tight to try to get the image of her people out of her mind, but the sight before her had already been burned into her mind. All she could do was cry. She could not be consoled. This was the first time in months she had seen another Naabeehó beside the young Naabeehó 'ashkii *Navajo boy.* In vain, she chided herself to keep herself from crying in order to keep the promise she made to not cry until she saw her father again. She forced herself to look through the crack in the wall again. She wished the sun would stay up high in the sky instead of following its worn path toward the western horizon.

In the bright sunlight of the next day, Dééd Yázhí noticed the mean soldiers were organizing the Naabeehó people into groups. The officers, who had replaced the tall, gray- haired one, did not talk much. Instead they yelled, grunted, gestured, and poked at the people with the ends of their rifles.

With the arrival of the Navajo captives, Dééd Yázhí's activities were limited. She was relieved. She was too embarrassed to look at her people because of the clothes she was forced to wear. Her clothes and her bonnet hid the fact that she was Naabeehó. On the days she was forced to work in the laundry, she would collapse on the thin blankets at the end of the day, hoping her people did not notice her in the clothes of the enemy.

Dééd Yázhí was being watched more closely and not allowed to walk to the sheep corral since it was near the captives. The Naabeehó captives were confined to a space that was at quite a distance from the shed. A guard was always near her when she left her shed for work.

Why am I not allowed to speak to these people? Maybe they know my relatives, she wondered as her mind stumbled over the questions she would ask the people. There were so many questions to ask.

When the soldiers were not busy supervising the Navajo captives, they were ordered to stand in straight, long lines and were told to shoot their rifles at various targets. When they missed their targets, they were yelled at and told to stay in the line longer for more practice. Dééd Yázhí assumed this was a way of intimidating her people, a way of showing them the strength of the soldiers.

The Naabeehó *Navajo* captives remained as quiet as possible. In the quiet of the night, Dééd Yázhí could hear the adults telling their children not to cry, laugh, or talk. More soldiers were arriving at the fort, riding in on horseback, and the five long barracks were beginning to fill. After a few days of training at the fort, the soldiers would leave and come back with more Naabeehó families. There seemed to be no order in the way the Naabeehó *Navajo* people appeared. Dééd Yázhí cried when she saw that some of her people had arrived without clothes, moccasins or blankets. Some people had articles of clothing to shield them from the harsh cold while others in the same group would have none. Her people sat huddled around fires, many sharing the same rug blanket.

More soldiers arrived from the east with their leader, a short man with curly hair. He was not impressive looking, but he had the attention of the soldiers. He spoke a few Navajo words, more than the white soldiers who had been stationed at the fort for some time. Whenever the short, curly haired one came back to the fort, more Navajo people were herded into the fort as if they were sheep.

The weather was getting colder. Dééd Yázhí looked around her. She had a fireplace and thin blankets to keep her warm. When she studied the faces of her people who camped west of the sheep corral, she could barely see their expressions. She saw hatred in the eyes of her people. They had hatred for the short man with curly hair.

"Adilohii" *Rope Thrower*" or "Bi'éé' Łichíi'ii" *the One with Red Clothing* was what they called the man named Kit Carson.

When the fort became crowded with Naabeehó captives, Dééd Yázhí searched their faces for familiarity. Her people did not appear healthy. Most of the captives were women, children, and elderly people. Dééd Yázhí's eyes filled with tears and her heart began to ache when she thought of her mother in that condition. With her tears blinding her eyes, she desperately searched the wave of faces that moved about. She moved to different areas of the shed to look through different cracks, and when she did, she saw even more Naabeehó people.

Whoever forced these Naabeehó *Navajo* people, my people, to walk here must be related to the men who brought me here, because these Naabeehó people look like they have been tortured, just as I was ..., she thought as she remembered the day when she was first brought to the fort.

Dééd Yázhí wondered how her people could keep warm as the days grew even colder. She thought of all the blankets she washed in the laundry. If I had known, I would have taken blankets the mean white men do not need, she thought to herself. She could hear children crying at night. It was sad to hear them saying they were hungry and cold.

As she listened to the innocent voices, she rubbed her abdomen, where her own little one grew. Will he ever be crying like that? she worried as the rate of her heartbeat increased even more. Will I be able to give him what he needs? she thought. She touched her breasts, which now seemed heavier with the realization that they would have to keep a little one alive.

The questions that relentlessly surfaced in her thoughts were, Why are my people being kept here? What have they done? Were they captured just as my younger sister and I were captured and then sold to these mean soldiers? she wondered as questions interrrupted her confused thoughts. She remembered what the young Naabeehó 'ashkii told her about Naabeehó warriors who were accused of raiding and stealing, but what were the women and children and elders accused of? When the nights grew even colder, the cries of the children became louder. Listening to the pained cries of the children made her want to bolt out of the shed and run to the laundry, to where she knew she could find many warm blankets. Dééd Yázhí fought a sense of desperation that was building in her mind.

She shook her head and closed her eyes real tight. As she did so, her father's instructions began to march through her mind, distracting her from the pained sounds of children and women and elders suffering. Dééd Yázhí remembered how her father taught her and her siblings to predict the weather quite accurately by looking at the position and the appearance of the moon. He taught them to especially watch the position the new moon appeared in. She regretted not noticing the latest new moon. She thought of the many nights when she could not see how the moon appeared because she was locked in the shed, which had prevented her from predicting the weather.

Dééd Yázhí was so desperate. She wanted the moon to tell her all about the immediate weather conditions because of the predicament her people were in. She was determined to help because when she needed help, the tall, gray-haired one came to her aid. Just like the tall, gray-haired one, she could not listen and watch any longer without finding a way to help her people. She also knew her father would go through hardship just to help his people. She was his daughter and she would risk her life for her people. She knew what she would do. She was motivated by the cries of the children and the elders.

Dééd Yázhí believed seven dah yiitą *new moons* had appeared in the night sky since she had seen the tall, gray-haired one. Her abdomen had grown quite large now. Besides, she thought, he left when the miniature leaves were just peeking out. The beginning of that month is referred to as T'ą́ą́chil *little leaves (April)*. Now it had to be the beginning of the new year, Ghąąjį' *the summit, (October)*, because the pinon nuts have ripened and the first snow has fallen, she reasoned.

Deed Yázhí smiled when she remembered the first snow of the fall season had appeared. The first frost or the first snowfall is the sign the Creator gives to the Naabeehó *Navajo* people to tell them the time has come to begin telling the little ones Winter Stories.

With her eyes shut, and her mind focused upon her father and her maternal grandfather, Dééd Yázhí could hear them telling Winter Stories. They would begin by saying,

"Shooh, áłchíní, kwe'é dinohbįįh. Haigo baa dahane'ígíí ła' bee nihił hashne' ..." *Little children, give me your attention, sit down right here. Let me tell you a Winter Story ...*

Silent hot tears made their way down Dééd Yázhí's face.

"Shizhé'é dóó shimá dóó shité'ázíní bił nída'ahiideestsééł," *I will see my father and my mother and my extended family again,* she whispered. Rubbing her abdomen, she continued,

"Nicheii dóó nimá sání k'é nididoonįįł, shiyázhí. Nité'ázíní 'ałdó' k'é danididoonįįł, shiyázhí." *Your maternal grandfather and your maternal grandmother will greet you, my little one. Your extended family members will also greet you as their relative, my little one.* Dééd Yázhí hugged her abdomen when she felt her little one move inside her.

"'Ayóó 'áníínísh'ní, shiyázhí," *I love you, my little one,* she whispered. She felt her little one move even closer to her heart as if her little one was telling her it loved her too. Her little one gave her the stamina to bear the sounds of her people suffering from the cold and hunger.

****

The closeness of the sound of a child crying woke Dééd Yázhí, interrupting her dreams of home. She sat up when she heard the sound of fear in the child's cry. Through the crack in the wall, she saw a little Naabeehó *Navajo* girl who had wandered away from the others. The little girl was crying so pitifully. Placing her mouth near the crack in the wall, Dééd Yázhí called to the little girl.

"Hágo. T'áadoo nichaaí. Ních'aad, hágo. T'áadoo náníldzidí," *Come here. Don't cry. Don't cry, come here. Don't be afraid,* she pleaded. When she first spoke, the little girl stopped crying, looked around, and began whimpering. Dééd Yázhí called to the little girl again, saying,

"Shd." *(A term to get a person's attention).* When the little girl turned around to face the shed, Dééd Yázhí quickly said,

"Kojí." *Over here.* Instead of following the sound of Dééd Yázhí's voice, the little girl turned toward the sheep corral and disappeared into the dark night. Dééd Yázhí desperately wanted to help the little girl. She decided to give one of her thin blankets to the little girl. Later that night, Dééd Yázhí got the attention of the guard, letting him know she needed to relieve herself before she settled down for the night. She took her thin blanket with her and walked from the shed to the crude outhouse. On her way back she dropped the blanket just outside the door of the shed and walked in. The guard quickly placed the lock on her door and left. Becoming more bold about wanting to help the little girl, Dééd Yázhí called to anyone who could hear her later that night.

Before long, the little girl began to cry. A little boy heard Dééd Yázhí. After hearing her Navajo words, he came near the shed and said,

"Ha'át'íí lá?" *What is it?* Dééd Yázhí closed her eyes to increase her sense of hearing the sound of another person speaking Navajo. It was music to her ears. She shook her head to bring her mind back to the present. She knew the little boy was taking a chance in coming near the shed.

"At'éé yázhí hanáchahígíí bimá shą' háadi naaghá?" *Where is the mother of the little girl who is crying?* she asked the little boy.

"Hóla." *I don't know,* was the boy's answer as he turned to leave. Dééd Yázhí was desperate as she begged the little boy to come back.

"At'éé yázhí bimá shá hágo bidiní, t'áá shǫǫdí." *Tell the little girl's mother to come here for me, please.* Without another word, the little boy was gone.

A while later, Dééd Yázhí heard someone scratching on the wall of the shed. She listened intently to decipher the side and place she heard the scratching sound coming from. Cautiously she moved to a crack in the wall near the place where she heard the scratching sound. Whispering, she said,

"Ha'át'íí lá? *What is it?*

From the faint light of the midnight moon, she saw the faint outline of a woman sitting on the cold ground near the shed with the little boy next to her. Dééd Yázhí asked the woman,

"Da' niísh at'éé yázhí hanáchahígíí bimá nílį̃? Deesk'aaz nidi kǫǫ́ tádígháah łeh, yichago." *Are you the mother of the little girl who cries? Even though it is cold, she walks around here crying.*

The woman responded by saying,

"Ei 'at'éé yázhí bimá dóó bizhé'é dóó yił háájéé' Bi'éé' łichíi'ii dabíígháą́. Éí biniinaa t'óó yichago tádígháah łeh. Bik'éí daats'í ła' ch'ééh hainitáago, hajooba' íinízingo, t'óó yichago tádígháah łeh. T'áadoo baa 'áhóolyą́ą́łígóó biniinaa t'óó baa 'áháshyą́. T'óó shił baa hojoobá'ígo biniinaa. Shí dó' t'áá bígi 'át'éego shą̨ąh áhásdįįd." *That little girl's mother and father and her siblings were all killed by the one with the red shirt (Kit Carson). That is why she walks around crying. Wanting sympathy, she walks around crying, probably looking for her relatives. There was no one to take care of her, so I am taking care of her because I felt sorry for her. Just like her, I have also lost relatives.*

206

Through tears and anguish, the woman further told Dééd
Yázhí,

"Hastiin iiná bił ásh'ínée nihe'anaa'í, bináá' nááná łahgo
'ádaat'éhígíí, yik'iji' nidoobah yiniiyé 'ííyáhę̄ę t'áadoo nihaa
nádzáa da. 'Áádóó sha'áłchíní 'éí doo béédahoozin da. 'Ashkii
yázhíígíí 'éí bimá doo bééhoozin da 'áádóó bizhé'é seesyį́í dóó
yił háájéé' danoochéełgo 'ałtso doo béédahoozin da. 'Áko
'ashkii yázhí 'éí yisnááh ábi'diilyaa dóó t'áá sáhí ch'éétłizh. T'áá
sáhí naagháago dóó t'áadoo baa 'áhoolyą́ąłígóó biniinaa t'óó
'ádíistsood. K'ad éí t'óó 'ałk'ídahwiilta'. T'áá shí sha'áłchíní nilį́
nahalingo baa 'áháshyą́." *The man I made my life with left to
go fight against the enemy with different colored eyes, and he
never came back. And I do not know where my children went;
they disappeared. The little boy ended up alone when his mother
disappeared and his father was killed, and no one knows what
happened to his siblings when they were running away from
the enemy. He was alone with no one to take care of him, so I
just held him close (took him in). Now we just watch over one
another. I am caring for the children as if they were my own.*

Dééd Yázhí could barely comprehend what she was hearing.
Tears rolled freely down her face. She felt incredible sorrow for
the three people as well as for herself. She remembered her thin
blanket. She told the woman,

"Ch'é'atiingi beeldléí 'áłt'ą́ą'íígíí ła' ni'góó siłtsooz.
Nídidííłtsosii' bee nídanohjah doo. T'áá shǫǫ da bee t'áá deesdoi
doo." *At the entrance (of the shed), there is a thin blanket on
the ground. Get it, you can all use it when you sleep. It may
keep you warm.*

"Éí łą́ą. T'áá shǫǫ shį́į́ bee deesdoi doo. Doolá dó' nihaa jiisíníba' da. Díí yee' doochohoo'į́į́góó hak'az bik'ee ti'dahwii'nííh. Nizhónígo shį́į́ nihik'ésti'go bee nídaniijah doo. T'áá 'awołíbee baa 'ahééh danidzin." *That's what was needed. You have certainly blessed us. We are severely suffering from the cold. It will nicely cover us when we lie down to sleep. We are extremely thankful for it.*

For the next few nights, the little boy, the woman, and the little girl who cried were Dééd Yázhí's nocturnal visitors. The woman was from the Łeejin Haagééd *Coalmine* area and the little boy was from Jeeh Deez'á *Low Mountain* area, and the little girl's family lived in the Tó 'Ałch'į́dí *Dilcon* area. Five days before, they had been forced to walk to the fort by the short man with curly hair whose name the Naabeehó people spit out when they spoke it, Bi'éé' Łichíi'ii *Kit Carson.*

Dééd Yázhí told the woman she had been captured by some mean men, then sold to the men here. She took a huge leap of faith in asking the woman to bring the children to visit her and keep her company. She promised the woman she would do what she could to get the woman and children what they needed for themselves by saying,

"T'áá bíneesh'ánígi t'aadoo le'é nihá hásht'į́į dooleeł." *I will do whatever I can to get you what you need,* she told the woman. The woman happily agreed to accept what was given her and the children.

The woman stopped smiling and her face took on a sad tone. With great sadness in her voice, she told Dééd Yázhí,

"Shité'áziní ła' yisnááh ádabi'diilyaaígíí Naasht'ézhí bikéyahgóó 'adeineeshcháá' ..." *My relatives who were taken captive were chased into Zuni country...*

208

Dééd Yázhí interrupted her by asking,

"Háíshą' nidahoniłchéego? Da' nihí nihidine'é yisnááh ádabi'diilyaa? Yisnááh ádabi'diilyaaígíí shą' háadi kéédahat'įį nít'ę́ę́'?" *Who are the ones who are chasing them? Is it our people who have been taken captive? Where did the people who have been taken captive live?* Dééd Yázhí asked as the questions tumbled out of her mouth. This was the first time she had heard her people were being sent southward instead of being brought to this fort. Her mind flew to her family, her mother and her father. She prayed to the Creator asking that her family remain safe in the folds of Dziłíjiin *Black Mesa.*

The young woman scratched her head and said,

"Ła' Kin yis'áanii bikéyah dóó shádi'áahjigo kéédahat'įį nít'ę́'ę́ę̨,'éí yisnááh ádabi'diilyaa, jiní." *It is said, some were ones who lived south of Hopi country who are the ones who were captured.*

Dééd Yázhí breathed a sigh of relief as the woman continued,

"Nááná ła' éí níléí Dinébito'dóó nihidiné'é ła' dah deidíníiyood, jiní." *And then some of our people who lived in the Dinebito area were the ones who were chased out of that area, it is said.*

Dééd Yázhí's ears began ringing and her heart stopped at the mention of the last location. Her family lived just a half day's ride from where the woman said the people were taken as captives.

"Háíshą' nihidine'é 'áádóó yisnááh ádayiilaa?" *Who took our people from that area captive?* she asked loudly.

"Hastiin Bi'éé' Łichíi'ii deiłnínígíí. T'áá 'óolyéego nihidine'é doo yaa jooba' da. Ch'ikéí da yił nidahadeełgo t'óó'ahayói 'ákót'éego 'atídayiilaa. Nihidine'é t'óo'ahayói tídadidzaa." *The one they call Red Shirt (Kit Carson). He has no sympathy for our people. He even caught many of our young girls, then raped them and tortured them. Many of our people were badly mistreated.*

Dééd Yázhí gasped. From her own experience, she knew what the young women were going through. She wondered where her younger sister was and if she was being cared for. She desperately wanted to know if her mother and her younger sister were safe.

The young woman told Dééd Yázhí the Naabeehó *Navajo* people held at the fort were not permitted to mingle. They were required to stay in the groups they had been assigned to, and because of the requirement, the woman could not look for her relatives.

Dééd Yázhí finally had the courage to ask. She asked the woman if she had heard of her father, and the young woman reported she had not heard of him.

"'Ei shįį níléí Naabeehó dine'é náás daazlį́'ígíí ła' nizhé'é yéédahósin. Bínidabidídéeshkił." *It could possibly be that some of the older people may know him. I will ask them,* the woman said.

The woman visited regularly with Dééd Yázhí long into the night as long as the light of the moon was hidden by clouds. She shared stories while Dééd Yázhí shared food with the woman and the two children by placing the food outside the shed in the late evening.

One night the woman came to the shed. She reported they had been told they were being sent to another fort, far away from their homes because the Naabeehó *Navajo* had been kidnapping, raiding, and murdering white people, Mexicans, and several Pueblo Indians.

The young woman said the Naabeehó *Navajo* interpreter told the people about an 'ałgha'deest'ą́ *an agreement* (a previous treaty), but many of the Naabeehó people held at the fort had not heard of the agreement. The soldiers further told the Navajo people the treaty had been broken over and over by the Navajo people. The woman reported the Naabeehó people wondered what was being referred to, and they were confused about the reason they were being held captive at the fort at gunpoint.

"Dabikéyah yę́ęgóó dóó dabighanígóó t'éí nídabí'ni'. Náasjigo 'éí dooda. T'ahdoo yéego diłk'áásdą́ą' danihighan nihits'ą́ą' táádeishchxǫ' yę́ę hasht'éédadiilnííł daaní, níléí diné. T'áá nihí nihikéyahdi t'éiyá hazhó'ó hasht'e' ninádiikah, daaní. Nihidine'é ch'ééh dadeeskai dóó daadlóóh dóó dichin dabi'niighą́ą' dóó yéé' yik'ee ti'dahoonííh," *The people just want to go back to their own land and to their own homes. They do not want to go forward. They said they want to repair their homes, which were destroyed by the soldiers, before the weather gets too cold. They said it is only on their own lands that they will be able to rebuild their lives. Our people are tired and cold and hungry and they are suffering from fear,* the woman reported with sadness.

Dééd Yázhí listened and grieved with the woman. She further explained how the enemy soldiers told them through interpreters that they will be taken to a place which has plenty of water, a lot of free land, and a place where a lot of plants grow. There was excitement in the woman's voice when she explained it was supposed to be warm there. She added, they were told they could grow their own food there and have plenty to eat. The people who have gone on before, to the place near the Pueblo Indians, are waiting for us to catch up to them, and then we will be taken to this place where we may rest once again.

"Shí 'éí 'ákǫ́ǫ́ shíni'. Ei shį́į́ sha'átchíní 'áadi 'atah naazdá. Sha'átchíní bił nída'ahiideestséełįį' t'éí shíni'. Sha'átchíní hadínéeshtaałgóó t'éí shíni'," *I want to go there. It could be that my children are there among them. I just want to see my children again. I just want to go where I can look for my children,* the woman said.

This was the first time Dééd Yázhí had seen the woman show a sign of weakness. The woman was crying silently. She looked up into the sky and noticed the winds had moved the clouds and the moon was beginning to shine brightly. Dééd Yázhí watched as the bright moonlight made a small rainbow in the large tear that clung to the woman's chin before it fell onto her dark blue rug dress.

Dééd Yázhí heard the little girl stir in the woman's arms and begin to whimper. To comfort the little girl and not wanting the little girl to start crying, the woman untied her rug dress at her left shoulder and lifted a flat breast toward the little girl's mouth.

"Shibe' ásdįįd, doo hazhó'ó 'ashą́ą́ da léi'." *I have no breast milk because I have not been eating much.*

212

Dééd Yázhí saw the woman wince with pain as the little girl began making loud sucking noises as she took in the woman's depleted nipple. Dééd Yázhí reached up and felt her own rounded breasts that had become larger because of her pregnancy. She massaged her protruding abdomen to caress her little one. She had to concentrate to listen to what the woman was saying. She was tired and wanted to go to sleep, and hoped her dream would tell her that her father and her mother were safe at home at the base of Dził íjiin Black Mesa. She also thought about her tall, gray-haired one.

"T'ah nidii daats'í shénálniih éí doodai' daats'í nááná ła' asdzání háadi shį́į́ yił ałhééhooszįįdgo yik'é na'níláá dóó baa náhoołtį?" *Does he still remember me or was he given to another woman he had become acquainted with and wanted and paid for?"* These questions kept her awake long after the woman and the children had left.

At full daylight and when she was allowed to leave the shed to relieve herself, Dééd Yázhí left a bundle for the woman and the children to pick up. Inside the bundle was another thin blanket, some bread, and a few pieces of jerky.

"Díí bił daalkan dooleeł," *They will like these,* she said with a sad smile. Dééd Yázhí's smile grew when she remembered the way the young woman loudly smacked her lips when she ate the food she shared with them.

The next day Dééd Yázhí heard a lot of commotion coming from the sheep corral. She heard soldiers yelling. Horses were neighing. Children were crying. She scrambled out of her thin blankets and looked through the nearest hole in the wall. It was just after sunrise. To see the horizon, Dééd Yázhí moved to another spot to look through another hole in the wall to see exactly where the sun was. The sun was still hugging the eastern horizon, but it was up in the sky far enough to cast light on the ground and on the activities near the sheep corral.

Dééd Yázhí noticed a procession of Naabeehó *Navajo* people was forming rather quickly. There were many orders being shouted at the people before the procession left. The procession began with a group of soldiers on horseback, next a group of Naabeehó people, next wagons, another group of Naabeehó people, wagons, and another group of Naabeehó people, followed by many soldiers on horseback. The entire procession was surrounded by soldiers, placed at intervals, as the group began moving toward the eastern direction. The shouts of the soldiers echoed throughout the beautiful valley. Dééd Yázhí looked out at the landscape before her and could not reconcile the angry shouts of the soldiers with the beautiful valley before her. She shook her head in sadness.

When Dééd Yázhí watched the last of her Naabeehó people leave, she felt a strong despairing sense of loneliness fall upon her. The silence was too much for her to bear. She closed her eyes so she could hear her language being spoken again in her thoughts. The sounds of her Naabeehó people brought the sounds of her mother's home back to her mind. Now, she was even more lonesome than she was before her people were forced to walk to the fort.

When the cold night air closed in on the fort, Dééd Yázhí waited for the woman and the two children to come and visit her. No one came to visit. She remembered she looked to see if the bundle was gone when she went to the outhouse earlier in the evening. The bundle was not there.

The fort was very quiet. Dééd Yázhí cried then fell into a deep sense of loneliness. Instead of loathing the sense of loneliness, she greeted it by saying,

"Yá'át'ééh, ch'énáh. Háádéé'shą' yínááł? Níhosésa' nít'ę́ę́' lá." *Greetings, loneliness. Where are you coming from? I missed you.*

She resented the fact that she gained friends who would then leave and she would not know where they had gone to. The first to leave was the tall, gray-haired one, then the Naabeehó 'ashkii *Navajo boy* as well as her little lamb, then the thin woman and the little girl and the little boy.

Dééd Yázhí was sleeping lightly when she heard a sound late that night. Someone was scratching at the outside wall of the shed. She sat up to answer the sound, glad that her loneliness was going to be chased away. She heard the scratching again.

"Ha'át'íí lá?" *What is it?* she asked in a loud whisper. From the sound of his whispered voice, she recognized him. It was the little boy who brought her the woman and the little girl.

"Sínídáásh?" *Are you home?* he whispered.

"Aoo', ha'át'íí lá?" *Yes, what is it?* Dééd Yázhí repeated.

"T'óó yee' ásht'į. Dichin nisin," *I am here for no reason. I am hungry,* the little boy forced himself to say. Dééd Yázhí pushed a couple of pieces of jerky through the hole in the wall. She felt the boy snatch them and in a second he was gone.

She did not have the chance to ask the little boy why he was still at the fort when all the other Naabeehó people had left. Although the little boy did not stay to chat, Dééd Yázhí was so happy she had someone with whom to visit.

She was glad the little boy was brave enough to stay while his only relatives, the thin woman and the little girl, had left.

Dééd Yázhí slept while it snowed silently in the darkness.

Chapter Thirteen
A Visitor

It was many days before Dééd Yázhí heard from the little
boy. It was on a very cold dark night when the little boy showed
up again. When she heard his familiar scratch at the wall, she
smiled to herself. She missed her little friend. Before she gave
the little boy any food, she asked him why he was still at the fort
and not with the thin woman and the little girl.

"T'óó yee' ninaagóó naasháa dooleeł biniiyé. Nizhí
shimáhígíí bizhí nahalingo diits'a'. Nizhí t'óó shił nizhóníyee'.
Shich'į' yáníłti'go, t'óó shimá shich'į' yáłti' nániisdzįįh. Éí
biniinaa t'áá kǫ́ǫ́ sistee'." *I just wanted to be around you that
is the reason. Your voice sounds like my mother's voice. I like
your voice. When you talk to me, I think it is my mother who is
speaking to me. That is why I am determined to stay here.*

The little boy's explanation touched Dééd Yázhí's heart.
She felt an even stronger sense of responsibility for him. She
vowed to do all she could to help her little friend. She wanted
to give the little boy a blanket, but the lock on the door did not

217

permit that. She told him to look behind the shed for a blanket the next day. After swallowing a piece of jerky, the little boy happily agreed and was off again.

The little boy came to visit every night to give Dééd Yázhí news of more Naabeehó people who had been forced to walk to the fort. She, in turn, asked him to look for her family members. She told him their names and rewarded him with food every time he came late at night with any piece of information. She was thankful for his company.

****

Late one night, Dééd Yázhí heard someone scratching at the wall. It sounded like two men were quietly arguing and she became afraid. She listened quietly not responding until she heard Navajo voices. It was the little boy. It sounded as if he was trying to hang onto someone with a man's voice. She crawled to the larger hole and asked what they were doing.

The little boy told her he was hungry. Dééd Yázhí worried she would not be able to feed him and the person he brought with him. The little boy continued quietly,

"Dichin nisin. T'ahdoo 'asháágóó díkwíí jį shįį 'azlįį'. *I am hungry. It has been several days since I last ate.*

"Na', díí t'éí shich'iiyą'. Díí dohsįįł. Yiskáągo 'índa shaa nááʼíkaah." *Here, this is the only food I have. The two of you can eat this. I will not be getting food until tomorrow.*

With some difficulty, Dééd Yázhí pushed the two slices of cooked meat through the small hole. The little boy pulled the pieces of meat out of the hole, and she heard him offering some of the meat to the person he was with. While still smacking his lips, the little boy casually told her,

218

"Díí hastiin shikéé' níyáhígíí Dziłíjiindę́ę́' naaghá." *This man who followed me is from Black Mesa.*

At the name of her home area, Dééd Yázhí's heart stopped and she held her breath. Peering through the hole in the wall to see the face of the young man, she hoarsely asked,

"Háíshą' bighandóó naniná?" *Whose home are you from?*

The young man offered no information. After a long moment of silence had passed, the young man told her he was the son of Hashké Yił Naabaah *the One Who Goes to War Scolding.* Dééd Yázhí gasped and a sob escaped her lips.

"Háí bighandóó diní?" *From whose home did you say?* she asked loudly, then in a hoarse whisper she asked the question again.

"Háí bighandóó?" *From whose home?*

Dééd Yázhí could not breathe as she waited for the young man's answer. Once again, the answer was the same,

"Shizhé'é Hashké Yił Naabaah wolyé. Dziłíjiindi kéédahwiit'į́į́ nít'ę́ę́'." *My father's name is the One Who Goes to War Scolding. We used to live in the Black Mesa area.*

Dééd Yázhí was afraid to breathe. She covered her face with her hands to hush a gasp that began at the back of her throat and felt as if it would choke her. She leaned forward until she felt her forehead rest on the floor of the shed. Slowly and clearly she said,

"Shí dó' Hashké Yił Naabaah shizhé'é," *Me too, my father is the One Who Goes to War Scolding.*

At her response, she heard the young man gasp then she heard a loud scuffling sound. With tears streaming down her face, she waited for the young man's response. She waited but no sound could be heard. Confused, she asked the little boy,

"Dinééh bich'į' yáshti'ę́ę shą'?" *Where is the young man I was speaking to?*

The little boy said,

"T'óó náhidiitah dóó háajigo shį́į́ dah yiitxe'. Hadínéeshtaał, ya'?" *He just jumped up and ran off somewhere. I will look for him, alright?* Without waiting for Dééd Yázhí's answer, the little boy could be heard leaving the side of the shed.

Dééd Yázhí tried recreating in her mind what just happened. She wondered, Da' t'áásh aaníí shitsilí be'iinéé' diséts'ą́ą́'? *Did I really hear the sound of my younger brother's voice?* She became extremely sad. Her heart filled with fear. Questions began to torture her as they marched through her mind. Shizhé'é dóó shimá daats'í bi'diiltsoodgo 'atah yisnááh ábi'diilyaa? Shité'áziní danilínígíí da shą' hái 'ałdó' yisnááh ádabi'diilyaa? Da' t'áásh aaníí shitsilí shich'į' haadzíí' dóó bich'į' haasdzíí'. Haa lá hóót'įįd? *Were my father and my mother captured and made captives along with the others? What other members of my extended family were captured? Did my younger brother really speak to me and did I speak to my younger brother? What happened?*

Desperate for some information, she held her heart because it was hurting. Her tears would not stop flowing. She was so afraid her mother had been captured as well and was being mistreated by the angry white men.

She could not hold her head up anymore. She allowed her body to roll to one side and allowed herself to remain in that position for the rest of the night. Sometime during the night, she woke up to find her body shaking. She realized her body was shaking from the cold. Covering herself with the thin blankets did not warm her. Sleep finally crept up on her.

In the morning, the warmth from a small patch of a sunray warmed her face. She could not wait until nightfall, the time when the little boy knew it was safe for him to visit her without anyone noticing him. She waited all night for the little boy and her younger brother to come back, but they never did. She was afraid they had been caught sneaking away from the Naabeehó prisoners. Dééd Yázhí desperately wanted to see her brother again.

Suffering from embarrassment because of her attire, Dééd Yázhí dragged herself through the day as she worked and completed her daily chores. She was not allowed to get close enough to the Naabeehó *Navajo* prisoners to see if she could catch a glimpse of her family members. From afar, she searched the faces of the saddened Naabeehó people looking for her younger brother, but she was not sure if he really was her brother.

Is it possible the little boy wanted to cheer me up so he told the young man to say he was from Black Mesa and claimed to be the son of Hashké Yił Naabaah? she asked herself.

After all, I told the little boy the names of my father and my mother, she reasoned in her thoughts.

Nearly two weeks later, when her little one dropped lower into her abdomen and upper pelvic area, the little boy and the young man came back to visit Dééd Yázhí. It was late at night when she heard the familiar scratching on the wall of the shed. Scared but excited, she answered,

"Ha'át'íí lá?" *What is it?*

"Nihí 'íit'į," *It's the two of us*, the little boy answered.

Dééd Yázhí held her breath. Not wanting to scare the young man away, she asked,

"Deesk'aazísh? Ooyą́ą́'ísh? Háájísh oo'áázh? T'óó doo nihéé hoozin da." *Is it cold? Did you eat? Where did you go? You just disappeared.*

She could not stand it any longer. Without waiting for an answer, she asked the young man what his mother's name is. She held her breath and held her abdomen with both hands while she waited for his answer. The young man reverently said,

"Shimá 'éí Nínáániibaa' wolyé," *My mother's name is Nínáániibaa' (Woman Warrior Who Went to War and Came Back Again).*

Dééd Yázhí became sick to her stomach. Kneeling on the floor of the shed, she steadied herself by holding onto the chair the tall, gray-haired used to sit on. Afraid her knees would give way under her as she knelt, Dééd Yázhí felt around her, searching for her thin blankets onto which she could collapse if she needed to. While silent, sad, lonesome tears made their way down her face, she sat heavily down on the floor and scooted toward the wall so she could sit with her back to the wall for support. She was oblivious of the constant flow of tears that were making patterns on her face.

After a long silence, the young man asked her,

"Háish ánít'į?" *Who are you?*

Dééd Yázhí sat up straight. To her surprise, she realized she had never asked the young man for his name. She could not answer the young man who could be her younger brother.

Instead she began sobbing. She kept choking on the sobs and could not answer. Finally she voiced her name, saying,

"Shí 'At'ééd Yázhí Naazbaa' dashijiní." *They call me Little Girl Who Went To War and Came Home.* She could not believe she was speaking her name. This was the first time since she had been kidnapped that someone had spoken her name. She felt her identity had been stripped of her and her name was to be voiced only to another Naabeehó person. She began to cry bitter tears. She covered her mouth to keep from alerting anyone at the fort that she had visitors.

Without warning, she heard herself naming her family members. She had no control over her tongue and her mouth. The names and words just kept spilling out as she said,

"Shí dó' shimá Nínáánibaa' wolyé. Shitsilí 'aláájí' naagháhígíí Nahat'á Yinaabaah wolyéé dóó shideezhí 'éí 'Asdzání Yázhí Naazbaa' wolyéé dóó shitsilí 'akéédéé' naagháhígíí 'éí Tł'ée'go Naabaah wolyé." *Me too, my mother's name is Nínáánibaa'. The oldest of my younger brother's name is the One Who Goes to War Around Plans, and my younger sister's name is Little Young Woman Warrior Who Came Home and my youngest brother is called the One Who Goes to War at Night.*

Dééd Yázhí heard the young man begin to cry then she heard a loud thud and felt him fall against the wall that separated them. After many tears had found their way to the ground, the young man whispered his name amid sobs. Dééd Yázhí heard him say,

"Nahat'á Yinaabaah yinishyé." *My name is the One Who Goes to War Around Plans.* He was her younger brother! Dééd Yázhí and her brother cried quietly and uncontrollably until the soft pale moon was no longer shining. They continued to visit and cry until the eastern sky shoved the night sky up to show a thin sliver of a faint white light above the horizon.

All of a sudden, Dééd Yázhí realized she needed to ask about her younger sister. The questions tumbled out of her mouth without giving her younger brother the chance to answer each question as they came falling off her tongue.

"Nihideezhí shą'? Bénáhoosdzinísh? Hooghandiísh nádzá? Yá'át'éehgoósh nihaa nádzá?" *What about our younger sister? Was she found? Did she come home? Was she alright when she came home?*

Although she could only see the faint outline of her brother, Dééd Yázhí sensed a heaviness that came over her him. He took a deep breath, hesitated, then sadly said,

"Nihideezhí t'áadoo bénáhoosdzin da. Sháhaniih kwe'é bí 'ałdó' bi'dótą' lá ni. Hádą́ą́' shą' nihideezhí t'áá yiniłtsą́ą́ nít'ę́ę́?" *Our younger sister was never found. I thought she was being held here with you. When was the last time you saw our younger sister?* her brother asked in a pained voice.

There was a long silence that followed the information Dééd Yázhí had been given regarding her younger sister. Only the sound of a little breeze doing its best to shake the earth awake could be heard. Her younger brother interrupted the sound of the breeze when he told her he and his younger brother had stayed home to care for their mother who became very sick after her daughters were kidnapped.

"Nihizhé'é dóó binaabaahii ya'ólíhígíí díkwíidi shį́į́ ch'ééh ni dóó nihideezhí nihíkánidanitáago haa'íshį́į́ doo nínikai da. Nihizhé'é t'óó bąąh nináháka'go hooghandi nináhádááh nít'ę́ę́'.

'Áádóó nihimá ni dóó nihideezhí yisnááh ánihi'diilyaaígíí yik'ee kadeeyá. T'áadoo yá'át'ééh nídoodleełįį' anáhálzhishgo nízaad nihoolzhiizh. Nihimá t'óó nihaa náchahgo nahashzhiizh. Wónáasii' doo nidi 'anízin da silįį' nít'ę́ę́'. T'óó yéigo nihits'ą́ą́' bííts'iiní. T'óó baa hojoobá'ígo baa tsídadeekééz. Shí dóó nihitsilí t'áá hooghangi ninánihi'di'niłgo nahashzhiizh, nihimá bikí'hółta' nihi'di'níigo. Nihizhé'é 'éí bí dóó binaabaahii ya'ólíhígíí yił tánídadibahgóó hadanihinitáago nízaadgóó nahashzhiizh."

"Shí dóó nihitsilí doo ts'íí 'át'éégóó nihíhosiilza'. Doo chohoo'įįgóó bik'ee ti'hwiisii'nii'. Ts'ídá t'áá'ániit'é tídadiidzaa."

Our father and his most trusted warriors searched to far places for you and our younger sister on many occasions. Our father would just come home so disappointed.

Our mother became very sick when you and our younger sister were kidnapped. For a long time, it seemed as if she would never get better. Our mother would just cry over the two of you. Pretty soon, she came to the place where she did not want to eat. She became very thin. We all felt so sorry for her. For quite a while, our younger brother and I were left at home to care for our mother to make sure she was cheered up. Our father and his trusted warriors never stopped searching for the both of you whenever they went into warfare.

My younger brother and I missed you in an extreme way. We really suffered because of it. All of us were hurt by it.

Dééd Yázhí heard what she had been wanting to hear for a long time. She learned her father searched for her and her younger sister for a long time, and not only him but his most trusted warriors looked for them as well. She learned her mother had yearned for her daughters' presence and she further learned her mother had become helpless because she missed her daughters.

Dééd Yázhí felt a heavy burden had just been lifted off of her shoulders. She sat up straighter. She lifted her head and looked up. She straightened her back and felt the weight of her unborn baby shift. Her father and her mother and her younger brothers missed her and her younger sister.

Cool tears of relief began to completely wash away tears that once burned with questions that asked if her mother and her father and her brothers missed her and her younger sister. Dééd Yázhí knew in her heart her father would not give up looking for her and her sister, but for the past several months she had to fight the questions that torturously marched through her mind every night about whether her father and her brothers were looking for her, because they had not come to the fort to look for her.

The sun had pushed the night sky back to further expose a thick faint line of a pure white light when Dééd Yázhí and her younger brother decided it was not safe to continue their reunion. Her brother lifted the little boy who had fallen asleep on his lap and held him in his arms as he stretched his legs before he stood up.

Dééd Yázhí remembered the food she had saved for the little boy and her brother. In a quick motion, she shoved the food through the hole in the wall and told her brother to be careful, saying,

"Nihe'anaa'í t'áá baa 'áhólyą, shitsilí. Doo ts'ííd ádaat'ée da. 'Ayóo danihijoołá." *Be careful of our enemy, my younger brother. They are terrible. They hate us.*

Dééd Yázhí giggled when she saw that the hole in the wall had expanded over time. With her last words of advice, her brother shoved the food in his mouth and saved some for the little boy before he ran toward the far fence to return to the place where many Naabeehó *Navajo* people were being held.

Dééd Yázhí lay down on her thin blankets and allowed her mind to bring back the words of her younger brother. He told her he was captured by Nóoda'í *Utes* at the base of the Kin yis'áanii *Hopi* mesa. She remembered he told her the Nóoda'í, who spoke Navajo, told him he was going to be held to be used as bait to capture his father and his warriors.

Dééd Yázhí jumped when she remembered her brother told her the Nóoda'í *Utes* knew of the capture of his sisters and that they were also being held as bait for the capture of their father and his warriors. She began to cry when she remembered her brother telling her the Ute scout told him one of his sisters had been sold to the Mexicans and the other sister was probably dead. He was further told,

"Ni dóó nizhé'é dóó nizhé'é binaabaahii danilínígíí naaltsoos bee 'ałghada'sidoot'ánée doo bida'oł'įįgóó biniinaa k'ad nááná ła' kéyahdi 'ąąhéeshjéé' danohłįgo 'ánihi'di'doolnííł. Éí biniinaa yisnááh ádaniilyaa. Nizhé'é 'ayóo béého'dílzin. T'áá'íídą́ą́' nizhé'é ba'áłchíní naakigo bąąh yist'įįd, nilahkéí bąąh yist'įįd, áko k'ad shį́į́ 'éí t'aadoo da nidi, níkánootáał dooleeł. Éí 'éí baa 'ákodaniidzin háálá nilahkéí ch'ééh yíkáhaineeztą́ą́'. Nizhé'é níká nootáałgo dóó nik'íníyáago bí dó' bi'di'dooltsoł áádóó bí dóó binaabaahii 'ałdó' yisnááh ádadiilnííł." *You and your father and his warriors have not kept the promises you made in the treaty and for that reason, you are being taken to another place to become a prisoner. That is the reason you have been captured. Your father is well-known. Your father already lost two children. He lost your two sisters, and now he will for sure come looking for you. We know, because he searched for your sisters in vain. When your father comes searching for you, he will walk into our trap then we can capture him and we can capture his warriors as well.*

Dééd Yázhí shuddered. She knew firsthand what the Nóoda'í 'anaa'í *enemy Utes* were capable of. Once her younger brother had been informed of the plans of the Nóoda'í, he was tied up, rolled up in a blanket and thrown over a horse.

Her brother told her although their mother had barely survived her daughters' disappearance, she regained her strength and adopted four orphaned children they found hiding in the crevice of a large rock formation while returning home from a leadership gathering.

When Dééd Yázhí remembered the last bit of information, she sat up straight while her thin blankets strained against her to keep her in her make shift bed. Her ears were ringing. She became sad because her mother had taken in other children and the children were given the love she and her younger sister had been craving for. She did not know whether to cry out of anger from having been deprived of her mother's love, or cry because she was glad her mother was able to love other children. Dééd Yázhí's emotions came and went in waves of anger, feeling deprived, and then feeling glad. She shook her head to release the thoughts, which caused her to become sad, and tried desperately to think about how the adopted children helped her mother heal.

Dééd Yázhí felt her little one move in her abdomen. She hugged her abdomen and said,

"Ayóó'áníínísh'ní, shiyázhí." *I love you, my little one.* Once again, she repeated, "Ayóó'áníínísh'ní, shiyázhí." This time, she remembered the way her mother's voice sounded whenever she heard her say,

"Ayóó'áníínísh'ní, shiyázhí." Dééd Yázhí began to cry. Her shoulders shook with sobs, bringing her mother's love for her back to her.

The next night, her younger brother and the little boy came to visit her when the bright moonlight was hidden behind thick clouds. Through tears, she told her younger brother of their capture and recounted each event as if they had occurred the day before.

In telling her story, Dééd Yázhí realized the hatred she had felt for the events had been ever so slightly replaced by the love shown her by the tall gray-haired one. With great difficulty, she told her younger brother she was carrying the child of the enemy. She told him she did not want it known that she was carrying a baby for the enemy because her Naabeehó *Navajo* people would grossly mistreat her child. She also knew the soldiers would also mistreat her little one.

Dééd Yázhí took more blankets from the laundry room and took some food to give to the younger brother she still had not fully seen but with whom she had lengthy nightly conversations. It is good that I am big and pregnant because my stomach hides the blankets and food I am taking from the soldiers, she thought as she gently tied the supplies to her waist, then covered her belly with the flouncy blouse and skirt.

With the last visit from her younger brother, Dééd Yázhí became very sad. He announced he was going to steal away to return to find their mother and their father to let them know she was safe. She wanted to go along but she knew it was impossible for her to even entertain the thought of escaping from the fort.

Not knowing the night when her younger brother stole out of the fort, Dééd Yázhí knew in her heart he was on his way home. She asked the Creator to protect her younger brother. She also thanked the Creator for the knowledge that her mother, her father and her youngest brother were safe.

Visits with her brother made her miss her family even more. Thinking about her family made the days and the nights unbearable. As soon as the sun came up, the faces of her family members vividly marched through her mind. Now that she was carrying a little one, the nights were even more painful to bear. Before her brother's visit, she had not heard anyone telling her they loved her or that they missed her.

It was when the fort was quiet and the moon shone through the holes in the wall of the shed that Dééd Yázhí missed the tall, gray-haired one. Even though she did not understand the words he spoke when he looked deeply into her eyes or when he gently touched the parts of her body that were covered by her rug dress, she knew he was telling her he loved her the way a good man loves a woman. The soft moans of love he voiced in the dark when their bodies moved as one rang in her ears in the darkness. She never wanted to forget the tall, gray-haired one's moans when he demanded more of her body as he held her down when her body rode his. Many nights, she wondered how many Naabeehó women covered their man's body with their own when love was being made.

Dééd Yázhí felt an extreme sense of loneliness. She missed the tall, gray-haired one even though he used to make her protect him with her body when their love was being made. She felt a sense of embarrassment come over her. She wondered if she was the only Naabeehó woman who had protected a man's body when she was the most vulnerable to her enemies.

Did the tall, gray-haired one really love me? Was I only there to satisfy him and protect him when love was made? Wasn't he the one who protected me when the mean white men raped me over and over again? He spared me, she reasoned once again. With accusatory thoughts marching through her mind, she felt abandoned once again.

Dééd Yázhí cried herself to sleep every night. Her eyes were swollen from the tears she cried throughout the night. She missed her mother. She missed her favorite parent, her father. She missed younger brothers. She missed her younger sister. She missed her family.

She missed the tall, gray-haired one even though he abandoned her and their child.

Chapter Fourteen
A Relative to Stay at Last

Since her younger brother left, Dééd Yázhí fell into deep sadness and loneliness. The knowledge that the soldiers were searching for her father caused her to lose the last few nights of sleep. The thought that her father had searched for her and her younger sister coupled with the thought that their mother and her brothers missed them so much brought her a sense of great relief.

The visits of the little boy brought her happiness. He visited with her and told her stories about her Naabeehó *Navajo* people who were being held as prisoners near the sheep corral. She needed her rest but her mind would not let her rest. The cold and long nights of winter magnified her anguish.

On a cold windy night, Dééd Yázhí slept rather soundly, mainly out of exhaustion. In her dream, she dreamed about riding a wild horse that would buck when it rounded a bend in the path she wanted the horse to follow. She had no reins to hold on to as she bounced from one side of the horse to the other! Men who belonged to the 'anaa'í *enemy* of the Naabeehó *Navajo* people were chasing her. They were making eerie sounds which rose and fell with the hills she was riding amongst.

Her dream would fade away and her mind would find peace, then all of a sudden the same dream would begin again. With each recurring dream, she found herself riding a different horse, one that was wilder than the one she had been riding.

"Ha'át'íísh biniiyé t'áá sáhí díí łį́į́' yishǫǫhgo baa naashá? Shizhé'é shą'?" *Why am I the only one to be taming these horses? Where is my father?* she asked, as the horse bucked wildly once again. Along with each kick of the horse, the pains in her pelvic region became stronger. She held onto the mane of the horse so as not to fall off.

"Shizhé'é! Shizhé'é!" *My father! My father!* she hoarsely called out, being careful not to alert the 'anaa'í of her whereabouts.

Just before she was about to get on another wild horse to escape from the 'anaa'í *enemy* who was chasing her in her dream, a strong wind hit the shed with such force it woke her out of her disturbing dream. It was early in the morning.

Dééd Yázhí breathed a sigh of relief.

"Dííjį doo naashnish da," *I do not work today,* she breathed.

Settling back onto her thin blankets, she felt deep pressure building in her pelvic area. She could not believe her baby had moved into her birth canal and her muscles were in the process of moving her pelvic bones apart to allow her little one to be born. She was aware of this process because she helped her mother during the season when the sheep and goats were having their lambs and their kid goats. She could not believe it was happening to her. She shut her eyes tight and asked rhetorically in disbelief,

"She'awéé' shídiiyáá dó'ísh łé!" *I wonder if I am experiencing labor pains?*

She felt helpless. She had witnessed the birthing process where a Naabeehó woman held onto a sash belt that was suspended from the ceiling. The woman was suspended in a semi-squatting position, allowing gravity to aid in the birthing process.

Dééd Yázhí studied the thin ceiling beams in the shed. The beams were too close to the ceiling to loop a sash belt around it. To make matters worse, the one sturdy beam she wanted to loop her sash belt around was too high for her to reach.

In unbelief and fear, she wondered, why didn't I find a beam from which I could hang my sash belt earlier in my pregnancy? She silently chided herself. Carefully, she climbed up on the table in an attempt to loop her sash belt around the one beam. She stretched as far as she could, barely reaching the top of the sturdy beam with one hand and with the other hand, she hugged the bottom of her extended belly to provide support for her little one.

"Nááná shą'," *I have to try again,* she said, straining, hoping her words would stretch her arm farther toward the top of the beam. On the second try, she felt her skin tear and she doubled over in pain. Her sash belt fell down around her. Helpless and desperate, she looked down to find herself standing in a pool of water streaked with blood.

"Shisis łichí'í doo bąąh dah sétį́ígóó shą' hait'éego shił náhoniigahgo bínísdzil dooleeł?" *Without being able to hang onto my sash belt, how am I going to have the strength to withstand the labor pains?* Dééd Yázhí whispered hoarsely, as she looked helplessly at the limp sash belt that lay immersed in blood and water near her feet. She had no control over the clear fluid that ran out from between her legs as she heavily and clumsily sat down on the table.

She closed her eyes tightly as she tried to gain control of the frantic thoughts which mercilessly shouted as they marched through her mind. She concentrated on her mother's face to bring her mother's teachings back to the forefront of her mind. Next, she began to concentrate on her maternal grandmother's face to bring to mind their conversations surrounding childbirth.

Haash jiit'įįh? *What does one do?* Her mind shrieked! She felt helpless! She picked up her soiled red sash belt her mother had lovingly woven for her and draped it over the back of the chair. She remembered she and her younger sister had been invited to watch their cousin have her twin babies, but they were reluctant to witness something so scary so they declined, and decided to play with their lambs instead.

Looking toward the rays the sun cast through the holes on the eastern side of the shed, Dééd Yázhí felt a sense of relief flow over her. No one comes to bring me food and wood until close to noon, she thought to calm herself. She was relieved. She did not want a man to see her in this state. She helplessly glanced at her bed as tears of fear began to surface to make large pools under her eyes.

She comforted herself with the thought, if only I was not pregnant, I could just be lying in my slightly warm bed. At that thought, her little one reminded her that he or she was getting ready to meet her. A dull labor pain started at the small of her back and intensified as it moved toward her pelvic area. She hugged her abdomen and begged her little one, saying,

"T'áá hazhó'ígo! 'Ayá! Shiyázhí, ayá!" *Slowly! Ow! My little one, ow!* She moaned in pain as she hugged her slightly smaller abdomen. Her little one heard her and the pain began to subside.

Just when her labor pain subsided, a strong gust of wind hit the shed and shook it, making the door rattle. Dééd Yázhí noticed the wind began to howl more fiercely and she could feel the cold air seeping in through the holes in the walls, through which she pushed food to give to her visitors.

Climbing off of the table before another labor pain attacked her, she wrapped herself in a thin blanket and slowly lowered herself down onto the floor to wait. An intensely strong labor pain settled in her lower back and moved slowly toward her pelvic area again. She closed her eyes and felt faint. Suddenly, she heard her mother's voice.

"Awéé' hódiigháahgo bił nijilnishgo 'ál'į. 'Azhą shį́į́ hoł náhoniigah nidi, t'óó bił ájít'ée łeh." *When one goes into labor, one should work with the pain. Even though the pains are intense, one should just bear it.* Dééd Yázhí looked around. No one was with her.

Disappointed, she slowly got up and took off her soiled rug dress then wrapped herself in the clean thin blanket the tall, gray-haired one gave her before he abandoned her. To distract

236

herself from her labor pains, she started washing her rug dress that had become drenched when she sat down on the table that was covered with water and blood.

The water in her washbowl was frozen, but the coals in the tiny stove were still warm, so she rekindled the fire and watched the ice thaw as her labor pains became progressively intense. Her hands shook from the pain as she wet a rag and cleaned her soiled rug dress. She turned the dress inside out and wiped it off. More water ran down her legs, cooling her body. She was shivering from the cold and the pain.

From the sunlight that filtered in from the smoke hole in the roof, Dééd Yázhí figured it was midmorning. Water mixed with blood was still running down her legs at intervals. When she began to warm up more water to wash her body, she experienced excruciating pain. It felt like someone had tied her red sash belt around her stomach and had pulled it tight and was making it even tighter. Soon her breath was being squeezed out of her. The room began to turn. She moved toward her thin blankets on the floor, felt around and wadded up some material and slowly sat down on it. She felt intense pressure in her lower back and pelvic area.

Quickly she jerked her legs apart and laid back to wad up the material some more. Her breath was being squeezed out of her again. *Who is tying me up? They need to know I cannot breathe!* she thought as she looked around confused. Her breath was being pushed out of her lungs, into her abdomen and down into her pelvic area.

"Tó 'ádejidlį́į́h, áko tsį́į́łgo 'ajiłchííh." *One drinks water until they can drink no more and in that way one delivers her*

237

baby sooner, she heard her maternal grandmother say. Dééd Yázhí sat up and started to get up to get a cup of water when she felt the sash belt being tied around her chest and abdomen again. This time, the person who tied the sash belt around her was using a wider sash belt forcing the air out of her lungs faster. The pressure stayed in her pelvic area and would not leave. She could not take in more air into her lungs. Soon with more blood and water running out, the pressure was released and she could breathe again.

Dééd Yázhí was becoming afraid of the ones who were tying her up with her sash belt. She started drinking water out of the jug very fast when someone tied her up again. It was too tight!

"Yéego shini' yistxih, shá bidiní. K'adí! K'adí!" *Tell them it is too tight. That's enough! That's enough!* she barely whispered. When she could not hold her breath any longer, the sash belt was released again and she could breathe.

"T'óó bił ánít'é, shiyázhí," *Just bear the pain, my little one,* she heard her father tearfully say. This was one of the few times she heard her father's voice so clearly, and she began to cry. It was her mother and her father who were tying the sash belt around her. She was feeling betrayed by them. Once again, they were tying the belt around her, and this time her mother said,

"T'áadoo t'óó díních'aaí. Bił anildzííł. Yéego! Yéego! Kooshídéé' yee'..." *Close your mouth, don't keep it open. Push. Hard! Hard! It is so close!*

She heard her mother say.

" K'ad háánílyjjh," *Now rest.*

Dééd Yázhí laid back, trying to catch her breath. Without warning, she heard her father say,

238

"Nááná shą́. T'ááłáhídi nááná. Bił ha'íínílní, shiyázhí." *Once again. One more time. Just bear with it, my little one.* She felt her lungs being crushed once again by the sash belt her father had tied around her chest. Next her abdomen was being crushed, then her pelvic region, and after a lengthy struggle to breathe, the pressure was released, but she could not get enough air into her lungs!

Why isn't my father releasing the belt? Dééd Yázhí thought frantically. She tried reaching out for her father but she did not have the strength. She could not speak. Neither could she breathe. Her father tied the belt too tight. She felt her body was being crushed again when she heard her mother and her father crying. In the midst of her mother and her father's cries, she heard a faint, weak wail.

The belt was loosened. Dééd Yázhí could breathe again. Once again, she heard the faint, weak wail. Slowly and weakly, she sat up to find her little one laying on its side. It was being kept warm by her legs. She looked at her little one. Her little one looked helpless and it was trembling. Quickly, she picked up her newborn infant and raised her head to look into her father and her mother's faces, but she and her little one were alone. Tucking her little one and the afterbirth into her thin blanket, she searched the small room for her mother and her father.

Dééd Yázhí and her baby were alone. There was no sound other than the howling of the wind. She began to cry bittersweet tears. Her mother and her father were here with her. They helped deliver her little one.

"Shimá dóó shizhé'é doo kǫ́ǫ́góó shą, haa yisdzaa nít'ę́ę́?" *What would I have done if my mother and my father were not here?* she asked as she hugged and held her little one close. Once her newborn baby was warm again, she lifted the blanket to look at her little one.

Dééd Yázhí was amazed her little one brought her father and her mother's words close to her ears once again. She clearly remembered the words of her father. Every year, during her birth month, her father told her the words he spoke to her when she was born. With tears in his eyes, she would hear him say,

"Ni'dizhchíneedą́ą́' kónidíiniid ne', shiyázhí. Háshinee', shiyázhí. Ma'ii Deeshgiizhnii dine'é bá shínílchíín. K'ad dóó kodóó shiyázhí nílį̗ dooleeł dóó k'ad dóó kodóó shiyázhí nidishníí dooleeł. Tó 'Aheedlíinii dine'é 'éí nílį̗... *When you were born, I said this to you, my little one. Dear one, my little one, you are born for the Coyote Pass people. Now and from now on, you will be my little one, and I will call you my little one. You are of the Water Flows Together people ...*

Dééd Yázhí lifted the blanket off of her little one's face to greet her little one in the same way her father greeted her. She knew her mother greeted her when she was born because her father told her what her mother said to her. Dééd Yázhí cleared her throat. With tears streaming down her face, she looked into the swollen eyes of her little one and softly said,

"Háshinee', shiyázhí. Tó 'Aheedlíinii dine'é nílį̗..." *Dear one, my little one. You are of the Water Flows Together People...* Dééd Yázhí winced when she said,

"Nihe'anaa'í ła' bá shínílchíín. Azhą́ shį́į̃ nizhé'é nihe'anaa'í nílį̗ nidi, nizhé'é 'ayóó jooba'go 'át'é. Ma'ii Deeshgiizhnii dine'é 'éí danicheii nááná nihe'anaa'i 'éí daninálí. K'ad dóó kodóó shiyázhí nílį̗ dooleeł áádóó k'ad dóó kodóó she'awéé', shiyázhí nidishníí dooleeł." *You are born for one of our*

240

people's enemies. Although your father is one of our enemies, your father is a very kind man. The Coyote Pass people are your maternal grandfathers. One of our enemies are your paternal grandfathers. Now and from now on, you will be my little one, and I will call you my baby, my little one.

Her little one listened to her voice as she spoke and seemed to understand what she said. Her little one closed its eyes and lay still and contented in her arms.

Remembering how they tied the umbilical cord and cut the afterbirth off when a little lamb was born, Dééd Yázhí tied her newborn's umbilical cord quickly just like they did for the little lambs, then cut the cord to release the afterbirth and buried it nearby to be taken out later. Her little one slightly moved, and she felt a slight warmth in her breasts that began at her shoulders and moved down and concentrated in her nipples.

She quickly offered a soft breast to her little one. At the feel of softness gently nudging its lips, her newborn's lips parted and took in her darkened extended nipple. As her little one slowly sucked on her nipple, she felt slight contractions in her abdomen and felt more liquid run out between her legs. She did not move. She did not want to disturb her baby with dark hair and light skin.

Dééd Yázhí held her baby close until the morning to keep him warm. The faint light of dawn stopped the wind and hid the usual noises around the outside of the shed. She leaned backward slightly to look out through a hole in the wall and found the ground was covered entirely by snow. She thought of her brother and the young boy. She worried about them but was glad she had taken the blankets for them.

She heard footsteps approaching the shed. The guard came to unlock her door. He said something in English when she did not come out, then waited at the door. When she did not come out of the shed, the guard looked in the door and motioned for her to come out.

"No," she quietly said and turned back to her little one. The soldier peered in, turned, and quickly left.

Dééd Yázhí was staring at her son feeding at her breast when she heard noises at the door. The soldier had not only brought food and wood for her, he had also returned with one of the officers.

"Damn it! She was one of our best workers! Have you taken a glance at the baby? Is it Folton's baby? I wonder. You can never tell with these savages! Well, let her rest. We'll get Folton's other savage to take over her work. Go get that Navajo boy who takes care of the sheep. Maybe she can tell him how to take over her work. This baby could not have been born at a worst time. But if the child is Folton's, we will have to be careful. We have our orders!" the officer shouted.

Three cold nights passed before her younger brother visited again. Surprised he was still at the fort, Dééd Yázhí wondered if he had been caught trying to escape to return home to let their mother and their father know she was alive and being held at the fort, the place the Naabeehó people called Tséhootsoh. Her brother explained,

"Ch'ééh aadéé' shíni' nít'ę́ę' nidi nihe'anaa'í ts'ídá t'áá 'awołíbee nihaayadahooliihgo biniinaa t'áadoo 'áádę́ę' naa náaniit'áazh da. Nihimá dóó nihizhé'é bich'į' yóó 'adínéesht'įįł dishnínée t'áadoo bi'iishłaa da háálá nihí dinééh dóó hastóí daniidlíníígíí t'áá kóníghánídéé' nihe'anaa'í nihik'idadéez'íį'go biniinaa t'áadoo yóó 'aneesht'íį' da. Nihe'anaa'í, bitsį' daalgaiígíí díkwííshį́į́ t'áá'áłahíjį' nihik'i dadéez'íį'go 'ádayósin, áko doo haada jónééh áhoot'éégóó nihił hoo'a'. Ayóo dahashké daazłį́į' ałdó'. T'áadoo hooyání dóó t'áadoo hasinígi be'aldǫǫh hach'į' yił hadaadił. T'óó náhádzidgo nihił hoo'a'. *I have been wanting to come back to come see you, but our enemy do not trust us at all and so that is the reason we did not come back to see you. I did not escape as I said I would to return to our mother and our father because our enemy has been watching us very closely. Several of our enemies with white skin have been watching us at all times, so it came to the place where I could not do anything. They have also become very mean. Without warning and without notice, they bring out their guns, ready to shoot us. It has come to a time that is very scary.*

"Nihidine'é shį́į́ haa dahoolaago 'aadéé' ła' ałyóídę́ę́', nihikéyahdę́ę́' nihidine'é yah adeiniyoodgo yaa nínáádiikai. Ha'át'íishį́į́ 'óolyé naaltsoos bee 'ałgha'diit'aah, éí doo bida'oł'į́įgóó biniinaa kódanihi'dil'į́ danihiłníigo yinahjį' nihidine'é ti'dayiyoołníih dóó ti'danihiyoołníih. Nihizhé'é 'éí naaltsoos bee 'ałgha'diit'aah éí t'áá ła' yiyiiłtsą́ągo yee nihił nahasne'. Íídą́ą́' éiyá nihinaat'áanii nihe'anaa'í ła' yił ałghada'deest'áa ne'. Éí 'éí bee nihił hane'go bénáshniih. Díí nihe'anaa'í bitsį' daalgaaígíí shį́į́ hádą́ą́' bił ałghadazhdeest'ą́ągo 'ádaaní. 'Éí daats'í Naat'áanii Sání dabijinínée yił ałghada'deest'áneedą́ą' bikéédóó nihiNaat'áanii Sání yił da'deesdǫǫh ha'nínée 'ááh deiłní, 'áko jó nihí da bee'ałghada'sidoot'ánée doo bida'oł'į da danihijiníigo nihik'ídahoji'ááh. T'áá hó bee 'ałghadazhdeest'ánée t'áadoo nidi hoł yíłį̇įdgóó nihinaat'áanii 'ayóó 'át'éé nít'ę́'ę̨ę nihits'ą́ą́' dajiishxį. 'Éí haniii doo béédajilniih da." *It is uncertain what our*

243

people did to them. They have begun the practice of forcing our people who come from different areas of our land to come here. Our people were chased out of their home areas to this place. We are being told we are not abiding by something called a paper holding an agreement, and that is why we are being treated like this, and they are torturing our people and torturing us. Our father has seen a paper of agreement, and he told us about it. It was at a time when our leaders made an agreement with one of our enemies. I remember being told about that. Our enemy with white skin are talking about an uncertain time when our leaders made an agreement which was made on paper with them; that is what they are referring to. Maybe that was the agreement they made with the Old Leader (Narbona) where, after the agreement was made with him, they shot him, and they blame us for not abiding by the agreement. It was them who did not have any respect for their own agreement so they killed our great leader. Don't they remember that?

"Doo chohoo'įįgóó nihee nídiiłk'aazígíí biniinaa 'ałdó' t'áadoo nihimá dóó nihizhé'é bighangóó yóó 'aneesht'įį' da. 'Ashkii yázhí bich'į' shíni' íí'áago biniinaa t'áadoo bits'ą́ą́' dah diiyáa da. Yéego nihíká 'eelwod. T'óó shił baa hojoobá'íyee'."
I did not run away from here to return to our mother and our father's home because it became extremely cold. I was worried about the little boy and that is another reason I did not leave. He really helped us. I have so much sympathy for him.

After a long silence, Dééd Yázhí announced,

"She'awéé' hazlį́į́'. Díkwíí yiskánídą́ą́' awéé' shídiiyáago she'awéé' shéłchį. Nihimá dóó nihizhé'é kwe'é shaa ní'áazhii' shíká 'ahi'noolcháá'. Shiyáázh hazlį́į́'. Nida' hazlį́į́'." *I have a baby.*

244

A few days ago, I went into labor and I had my baby. Our mother and our father came here and helped me deliver my baby. I have a son. You have a nephew.

Confused, her brother twirled around to face the wall of the shed and clumsily asked, "Da' ne'awéé' hazlį́į́'? Naabaahii ła' nihee nááhásdlį́į́'." *You had a baby? We have another warrior.*

Dééd Yázhí smiled at her younger brother's declaration. There was a comfortable silence that existed on both sides of the wall of the shed.

The sound of her baby whimpering brought her brother's attention back to the newborn infant. He asked,

"Niyáázh, shida' yázhíísh yízhí bá 'íinilaa?" *Did you give your son, my little nephew, a name?*

Because of all of the excitement, Dééd Yázhí had not named her son yet. She blurted out,

"Níyol Yił Naabaah wolyéé doo háálá t'óó bi'dizhchínéedą́ą́' doo chohoo'į́į́góó chííl bił deeyol. *His name will be the One Who Makes War with the Wind because he was born when the wind was blowing real hard as it snowed.*

Her younger brother liked the name of the infant because his name contained portions of her brothers' and her father's names. She gave her younger brother some of her food that was left over and told him she was tired. Her brother thanked her for bringing his mother and father's family another warrior. Then he stood up to go back to his camp to try to sleep in the extreme cold.

"Díí nídeezidígíí bii' kót'éego nihee nídíłk'asígíí shį́į́ biniinaa nihidine'é Yas Niłt'ees yee dayíízhi'. Ayóo dó' beełt'é." *Within this month it gets very cold like this. That is probably the reason they named this month Crusted Snow (January). It is appropriate since the cold wind creates a crust on the surface of the snow,* she whispered as she listened to the sound of her brother walking carefully on the frozen, crusted snow as he walked away from the shed.

Dééd Yázhí lay quietly concentrating on her mother and the words of wisdom she had spoken when she was teaching young mothers. The silence began to come alive with her mother's words as they drifted around in the room, then settled in her ears.

"Awéé' bits'éé' ni'diikǫsgo t'áá haa'ígi da hooghan binaagóó, dibé bighan bitsį́į́góó da, 'éí doodai' táchééh bíighahgi da łeeh jitį́į́h. Hwe'awéé yázhí bá 'ákó'jiił'įįhgo ch'ikę́ę́h tsíłkę́ę́h yileehgo hooghan doo yits'ąą nízaadgóó dah nídiidááh da. T'áá hooghan binaagóó na'anishígíí binaanish áyiił'įįh." *When the little piece of umbilical cord that was attached to your newborn baby falls off, you need to bury it near the hooghan or near the main post of the sheep corral or near the sweat hogan. When you do this for your newborn baby, he or she will not wander very far away from home when they become a young woman or a young man. She or he will do the work that needs to be done around the home.*

"Dibé bighan bitsį́į́góó hayázhí bits'éé' łeeh jitį́į́hgo 'éí hwe'awéé' at'ééd yázhí nilį́įgo 'éí ch'ikę́ę́h yileehgo dibé dóó tł'ízí bił na'anishgi binaanish áyiił'įįh. Doo nízaadgóó bilį́į' yits'ą́ą́' dah nídiidááh da doo. 'Áádóó hayázhí 'ashkii nilį́įgo tsíłkéí yileehgo 'éí béégashii dóó łį́į' bił na'anishgi binaanish áyiił'įįh. Bilį́į' doo nízaadgóó yits'ąą dah nídídááh da doo." *When you bury the little piece of your little one's umbilical cord near the sheep*

corral, when your little one is a girl, then when she becomes
a young woman she will make caring for the sheep and goats
her livelihood. She will not wander very far from her sheep and
goats. And if your little one is a boy, when he becomes a young
man he will make raising cows and horses his livelihood. He will
not wander very far from his livestock of cows and horses.

"Nááná hayázhí bits'éé' ni'diikǫsgo táchééh bitsį́igi łeeh jitį́įhgo 'éí ch'ikę́ę̨hjį' dóó ts'íłkę́ę̨hjį' aniséehgo bina'nitin łą́ą̨go hólǫ́ǫ dooleeł. Nihidine'é neinitingo bits'ą́ą̨dóó nihi'í'ool'įįł dóó nihe'oodlą' niłdzil dooleeł." *When you bury your little one's little piece of umbilical cord near the sweat hogan, the little one will have many teachings to share when he or she becomes a young woman or a young man. As they teach their people, our people will have a strong cultural and spiritual foundation.*

"Ne'awéé' hazlį́į́'go, 'íishją́ą́ bá 'ákó'jiił'įįh." *When you have a little one, make sure you do that for your child,* Dééd Yázhí had heard her mother say many times.

"Shiyázhí bits'éé' ni'diikę́ę̨zgo t'áá naashtin dooleeł. Shá 'ashja'iilaígi t'áá hooghangi, Dziłíjiin bitsį́igi shiyázhí bits'éé' bá łeeh deeshtį́įł. Shimá dóó shizhé'é shíká'ahi'dí'nóołchééł. Íishją́ą́shį́į́ dibé bighan bitsį́igi daats'í shiyázhí bits'éé' łeeh dootį́įł didooniił. Táchééh bitsį́igi daats'í łeeh dootį́įł didooniił. Táchééh bitsį́igi bá łeeh yítą́ą̨gogo 'éí shiyázhí bicheii nahalingo łą́ą̨go bina'nitin hólǫ́ǫ dooleeł." *When my little one's little piece of umbilical cord falls off, I will keep it. The first chance I get, I will bury my little one's piece of umbilical cord for him at home on Black Mesa. My mother and my father will help me. We will see if they want to bury my little one's piece of umbilical cord near the sheep corral. Maybe, they will say, bury it at the base of the* sweat hogan. *If it is buried near the sweat hogan, then my little one will be just like his maternal grandfather and have many things to teach.*

"Shimá dóó shizhé'é bizaad k'ehgo shiyázhí bá 'í'doolnííł. Díí 'éí bee nihoní'ą́ą dooleeł." *It will be according to the words of my mother and my father that we will do this for my little one. This is a promise I have made.*

"Azhą́ shį́į́ shiyázhí nihe'anaa'í bitsį' daalgaiígíí yáshchíin nidi, shiyázhí Naabeehó nilį. T'áá'íídą́ą́' Diné k'ehjígo k'é bidííniid. Bizhé'é 'éí t'áadoo k'é bidíiniid da, t'óó bik'iníícháą́'." *Although my little one is born for our enemy with white skin, my little one is a Navajo. I already greeted him through his clans in Navajo. His father did not greet him, he just abandoned him.*

****

When her little one's umbilical cord fell off, Dééd Yázhí carefully wrapped it up and tucked it away because she did not want to bury it anywhere near the fort, a place that represented so much hatred for her and her people. It was a place that represented so much hurt. She did not want her son to take on the attributes or characteristics of the enemy.

Dééd Yázhí promised to raise her child at the base of Dziłíjiin *Black Mesa.* That was where she decided to bury the little piece of his umbilical cord. It was her desire to watch her grandchildren play and live there too. Deep in her heart, she knew she would return to her home in Black Mesa.

Chapter Fifteen
The People Are Moving

Dééd Yázhí received an unexpected visitor. Standing at the door was the young Naabeehó 'ashkii *Navajo boy* who took care of the sheep at the military sheep corral. Since the new soldiers moved the corral to the far side of the fort toward the southern direction, she had not seen the young boy in a long time. She missed him. Besides the tall, gray-haired one, he was the first one to treat her as a friend when everyone else wanted her dead. He was also at her wedding so he was a part of the family.

Dééd Yázhí invited the young Naabeehó 'ashkii into the shed by demanding,

"Shitsilí, tsį́į́łgo 'aadę́ę́' yah anilyeed!" *My younger brother, hurry and come on in!* Before they spoke another word to one another, she held up her little one for the young boy to see.

"Yáa! Shádí, ne'awéé'ísh hazlį́į́'?" *Wow! My older sister, did you have a baby?* was all the young boy could say as he stared first at Dééd Yázhí, then at her little one, and back at her.

"Aoo', shiyázhí hazlį́į́'," *Yes, I had a little one,* she answered with a smile.

Out of excitement, the young boy asked a question that was against Navajo cultural protocol. He asked,

"Da' hastiin nineez dóó bitsii' łibáhéęísh ne'awéé' bizhé'é?" *Is the tall, gray-haired man your baby's father?* As soon as the words were out of his mouth, the young boy covered his mouth with his hand as if to stop the words from floating throughout the room. With an embarrassed look, he added,

"Ne'awéé' éí hastiin t'óó bíyó yinoolnin." *Your baby kind of looks like that man.*

Ignoring the young boy's embarrassment, Dééd Yázhí answered,

"Aoo', azhą́ shį́ nihe'anaa'í nilį́ nít'ę́ę' nidi 'éí she'awéé' bizhé'é nilį́." *Yes, although he was our enemy, he is the father of my baby.* Her reply was in a voice that seemed to apologize for the fact that she had borne a baby for the enemy.

"'Éí hastiin háájí shį́ 'ííyá," *It is uncertain where that man went,* she continued with a faraway look in her eyes.

"T'ah nít'ę́ę' t'óó doo bééhoozin da," *He just went missing,* she said.

"Ne'awéé' nizhóníyee'. Ashkiiísh? At'éédísh?" *Your baby is beautiful. Is it a boy? Is it a girl?* the young boy asked shyly as he held his breath while he gazed at the little one. The baby was indeed a beautiful child.

"Shiyáázh bee shaa hojoozba'," *I have been blessed with my son,* Dééd Yázhí said as she looked into the eyes of her child with reverence. Without looking up, she thought, the tall gray-haired one would have been proud of his son. Her thought remained silent as she smiled at her beautiful infant son.

Drawing her eyes away from her child, she focused upon the young boy facing her and spoke in an accusatory voice.

"Háájísh ííníyá?" *Where did you go?* she demanded. "Díí bizhé'é nahalingo, ni dó' t'óó doo nééhoozin da. Níhósáahgo díkwíí shį́į́ yiská." *Just like this one's father, you disappeared. I missed you for several days.* The young boy interrupted her by blurting out the reason for his visit, saying,

"T'aadoo lé'é biniiyé naa níyáá nít'ę́ę́'." *I came to see you for a reason.*

Dééd Yázhí demanded an answer from the young boy when she repeated,

"Háájíísh ííníyá, nidishní? T'óó níhosésa'. T'áadoo shaa néínídzáa da. Níhósáahgo díkwíí shį́į́ yiská. Nich'į' shíni' íí'áá nít'ę́ę́'. Háájíísh ííníyá?" *I said, where did you go? I missed you. You never came back to see me. I missed you for several days. I was worried about you. Where did you go?* her voice demanded.

Without addressing her questions, he turned and ran out the door yelling,

"Áłtsé ...," *Wait ...*

His words trailed after him, then he disappeared around the corner. Dééd Yázhí heard the sounds of a person exerting strength. It was the young boy who was pushing a rather fat sheep through the door, and with great effort he pushed the sheep into the shed.

"Díí nidibé yázhí yę́ę 'át'é!" *This is what used to be your little lamb!* he said excitedly. The fat sheep did not seem to remember Dééd Yázhí, but it stood patiently near her as she petted it. She sat down on the floor near the sheep and leaned toward it. There were times when she wondered if her lamb had been killed for meat or for its thick pelt. She buried her face in its thick wool and wept.

251

The scent of the wool brought to her mind vivid memories of her father, her mother, her family and the tall, gray-haired one. The sheep seemed to remember her and allowed her to fully lean on it as it stood patiently and firmly, supporting her weight as sad tears shook her body. The tall, gray-haired one was the one who gave her the sheep when it was a little lamb. She noticed it seemed as if her little one and her lamb knew she needed them. Her baby remained quiet and the sheep stood still and waited for her to regain her strength.

Memories began to flow. The sheep pulled her memory back to the time when she was little and when she used to sit on the clean dirt floor of the hooghan *hogan* near her mother as she wove on her loom. She thought of how she loved playing with the many colored balls of yarn made of wool her mother kept for the designs she wove into her beautiful rugs.

Dééd Yázhí looked at her hands, now calloused and cracked. Tears dropped on her hands in an attempt to heal her cracked hands. She remembered her little hands were fat and very clumsy, so her mother encouraged her to organize the balls of yarn in the basket that sat near her mother's loom. She loved watching the balls of yarn roll across the hooghan *hogan* floor as she played with the balls of yarn instead of organizing them. She also remembered how she giggled when she watched her father chase the round balls of yarn. She loved to hear her mother lovingly scold her father for getting the balls of yarn dirty, which would only encourage her father's silly antics, making her laugh until her whole body would shake up and down from her laughter as she sat on the floor.

Looking at her tears forming little puddles in her palms, Dééd Yázhí's thoughts brought her mother close as she remembered back to the time when her mother taught her how to card wool. She loved the soft wool that lay around her in little tufts and mounds that covered the floor near her mother's loom. She could not count the number of times she had watched her mother card wool. Her mother used the short bristles of a plant to make a specially made bé'ázhóó' *brush* to align the soft wool fibers in preparation for spinning. As her little hands did their best to card the wool, she was taught to sing a song for carding wool.

"Niyiin hólǫ́ǫgo dóó bee ni'dí'a'go doo ch'ééh nídídáah da dooleeł, shiyázhí," *Have a song to sing and you will not get tired when you sing your song, my little one,* is what Dééd Yázhí heard her mother tell her many times in one day. Dééd Yázhí began to hum the song as more tears poured into the palms of her hands.

She remembered how the lanolin on the wool fibers made the bé'ázhóó' *brush* become sticky and heavy while the dirt on the wool made the bé'ázhóó' turn a dark color. She loved to wash the bé'azhóó' *brush* with yucca soap because she loved the smell of the yucca plant. Dééd Yázhí and her father would stand outside swinging the bé'ázhóó' lightly in the crisp air to dry the bé'ázhóó'. During these times, her father made up little silly songs about what they were doing and her father's funny songs made her chores more enjoyable.

The cooing of her little one brought Dééd Yázhí back to the present. She shook her head and smiled at the young boy who patiently waited for her. Once her tears stopped flowing, she told him about her duties at the laundry during the day.

"Ákǫ́ǫ́ 'ałnááshi'dil'aahgo ch'ééh hánidésh'įį' łeh. Ei shį́į́
nihe'anaa'í haada daniilaago biniinaa doo neesh'įį da nisin
nít'ę́ę́. Éí doodai' da nihidine'é nááná łahgóó 'adeiniłkaadgo
daats'í ni 'ałdó' akéé' dah danídíníiłcháą' nisingo t'óó naa shíni'
nít'ę́ę́." *When I was sent there, I tried looking for you. I thought
I had not seen you because our enemy had done something to
you. Or, I even thought they had sent you along with our people
when they forced them to leave for another place. I was so
worried about you.*

The young boy told Dééd Yázhí he lost favor with the new
soldiers and was not allowed to leave the corral except at night
to sleep.

"Dibé bighan yídashiistł'ǫh. T'áá 'ákwe'é dibé baa
'áháshyą́ą́go 'ádashiilaa. Shí dó' ch'ééh aadę́ę́' nich'į' shíni'go
díkwíí jį shį́į́ 'azlį́į́'. T'óó 'áádę́ę́' nídísht'įįhgo 'aná'át'ááh nít'ę́ę́.'"
*They tied me to the sheep corral. They left me there to care for
the sheep. I also wanted to come and see you for several days. I
would just glance this way every day until the sun went down.*

Dééd Yázhí wiped away a tear. She looked at the boy and
thought, I love him as a younger brother. Without speaking, she
just stared at the young boy.

"Ha'át'íí lá?" *What is it?* he asked when he noticed her
staring at him.

Not wanting anyone to know, it was with great trepidation
that she told the young boy about her younger brother who was
being held prisoner along with the many Naabeehó people.

"Shitsilíké naaki. Shitsilí 'aláąjį' naagháhígíí koji' yah
abi'doodlóóz. Kwe'é 'atah ąąhéeshjéé' nilį́. Tł'ée'go kwe'é nihaa
nádáahgo nihésdáah łeh nít'ę́ę́, níléí haiłkáahjį' anáhálzhishgo

254

'índa níléígóó 'anáhályeed nít'ę́ę́'. Doodjłígíí ha'oh ninádaniłnah, jiní. Łah da naashnishdę́ę́' ch'iiyáán bá ch'éénísh'į́įh nít'ę́ę́'. Tł'óó'dóó nihésdáago ná'ádį́įh łeh ne'. Naabeehó 'ashkii t'ah ashkii yázhí nilį́įgo shitsilí yił ałhééhooszįįd dóó 'áádę́ę́' shitsilí yił shaa ní'áázh." *I have two younger brothers. My brother, who is the older of the two, was brought here. He came here as a prisoner of war. At night, he would come here and sit near us until it was nearly morning, which is when he used to run back. The food that was given to them would run out before he could get any, he said. Sometimes, I stole food for him from my work. He would sit outside and eat while he visited with us. There was a little boy who came to know my younger brother, and he is the one who brought my brother to me.*

The young Naabeehó 'ashkii listened carefully and asked a few questions. As he prepared to leave after their short visit, he promised Dééd Yázhí he would return and visit her more often. He pushed the fat sheep out the door, then left, placed the lock on her door before he stepped off the porch.

The sun had moved farther toward the western sky when Dééd Yázhí heard someone knocking at her door. With fear rising in her heart, she quietly said,

"Ha'át'íí lá?" *What is it?*

"Ch'iiyáán yee' ła' naa níką́," *I brought you some food,* the muffled voice said.

Dééd Yázhí heard footsteps leaving her porch. She thought, doesn't the person know there is a lock on the outside of my door? She wrapped her baby tightly and covered him just in case the person wanted to kidnap her little one. Some time passed. Sounds could be heard outside her shed. With her heart beating loudly, she heard loud footsteps coming back again. Someone with heavy feet was knocking at her door again. Her fast beating heart kept time with the knocking sound at the door.

She stared at the door and held her breath. She heard the lock being slid out of its place. The door slowly opened. It was someone who was wearing a big thick coat with a hat on his head to hide his face. She hid her baby with her body. The person brought her more food. With the door closed and the person inside the shed, Dééd Yázhí fearfully asked,

"Háísh ánít'į́?" *Who are you?*

"Shí 'ásht'į, shádí. Sháą́' naa nídeeshdááł nidíiniid ne'?" *It is me, my older sister. Remember I told you I would come back?* It was the voice of the young Naabeehó 'ashkii *Navajo boy.*

"Ha'át'ííshą' biniiyé 'akót'éego hadínít'é? T'óó yee néésísdzíid," *Why are you dressed like that? I was scared of you,* Dééd Yázhí scolded.

The boy responded, saying,

"Díí yee' nitsilí ch'iiyáán ła' bá né'į́', éí biniinaa kót'éego hadiisdzaa. Nihe'anaa'í t'ah t'óó'ahayói kǫ́ǫ́ nidaakai. 'Ei shį́į́ ch'iiyáán nish'į̨hgo dashiidoołtséél nisingo biniiyé kót'éego hadiisdzaa. Nihe'anaa'í yá da'oo'ínígíí Bitsį' Yishtłizhii danilį́. ' Éí kót'éego háádadiit'įįh. Éí 'oo'íinii ła' bi'éé' bits'ą́ą' né'į́'. Díí 'éé' nitsilí baa díinił áko díí yee hadít'éego nihe'anaa'í yits'ą́ą' yóó 'adínóot'į́ł nisingo biniinaa né'į́'."

I stole some food for your younger brother that is why I dressed up like this. There are many of our enemies who are still walking around here. I thought they might see me stealing food, so that is why I dressed up this way. Our enemy uses

256

Indian scouts. The scouts dress like this. I stole one of the scouts' clothing. I thought you could give these clothes to your younger brother so he could wear these clothes and run away from our enemy. That is also the reason I stole the clothes.

Dééd Yázhí reached out to the young boy and drew him into her arms. She closed her eyes tightly and said softly,

"Shizhé'é binaabaahii sínílį́į́'. Binaabaahii sínílį́'ígíí 'ayóo bił nílį̇ doo. *You have become one of my father's warriors. He would be so honored that you have become his warrior.*

Dééd Yázhí was touched by the young boy's bravery. She knew he risked his life for her younger brother. She was amazed at how thoughtful he was. He asked if he could stay a while, to which she heartily agreed.

"Háshinee', shitsilí," *Dear one, my younger brother,* was all Dééd Yázhí could say.

The young boy broke the silence by asking if he could hold her little one.

"'Áłtsé, ni'góó nídaah, ákohgo 'índa nílák'e deeshtééł." *Sit down on the floor first. Then I will place him in your hands.* The young boy giggled, as he held out his hands.

"Ha'át'íí shą'?" *What is it?* she asked.

"'Awéé chí'í ts'ídá t'ahdoo ła' nídiishteeh da nít'éé'. T'áá hazhó'ó dibé yázhí dóó tł'ízí yázhí naashjaahgo t'éí bínéshdin." *I have never picked up a newborn baby. I am only used to carrying little lambs and little kid goats.*

Dééd Yázhí giggled then wrapped her baby securely and placed her little one gently in the young boy's lap for him to hold.

257

"Hait'éego shą' awéé chí'í dah joołtéeł łeh?" *How do you hold a newborn baby?* he asked. Dééd Yázhí watched as the young boy locked eyes with her little one who had just awakened. Her little one settled easily into the arms of the young Naabeehó 'ashkii.

"Shí dibé yázhí t'éí naashtée łeh, tł'ízí yázhí dó'…" *I only carry little lambs, little goats also…* he said as his voice trailed off. Dééd Yázhí's eyes began to tear up. The young boy was only the second person whose face her baby had looked into.

"T'áásh ákót'éego dah yishtééł?" *Am I holding him right?* the young boy whispered.

"Aoo', jó doo yichah da." *Yes, well, he is not crying,* Dééd Yázhí said to reassure the young boy who was mesmerized by her little one. She found herself missing her younger siblings. She wanted so much to be sharing this time with them, but for now, she was content to watch her little one looking into the eyes of the brave young boy.

With tears in his eyes, the young boy told her he had to leave before the soldiers noticed he was not among the sheepherders.

"Ahéhee' nihaíníyá. Nihik'ihółta'go hodiina'. Ná 'ashja'iilaago nihaa náádíídááł." *Thank you for coming to see us. You cheered us up. As soon as you get a chance, come and see us again.* In that instant, Dééd Yázhí decided to adopt the young Naabeehó 'ashkii as her own son. To confirm her wishes, she said,

"Nitsilí shá dah yíłtéeł doo." *You can hold your younger brother again.*

"Da' shitsilí yázhí nilį́?" *Is he my younger brother?* the young boy shouted with excitement.

258

"Aoo', nitsilí hazlį́į́. Éí bee shiyáázh sínílį́į́." *Yes, you now have a younger brother. In that way, you have become my son.* Without warning, the young boy flung his arms around her neck and held her tight as his body shook with silent sobs. In between sobs, he cried,

"Shimá! Shimá! Shimá! Shimá!" *My mother! My mother! My mother! My mother!*

Dééd Yázhí held the young boy close to her as he cried. She found tears running down her face as well. Her own newborn son had given her another relative, the young boy.

He turned back to the baby and said,

"Hágoónee', shitsilí yázhí. Yiską́ągo naa náádeeshdą́ą́ł. Hágoónee', shimá," *Goodbye, my little brother. I will come back to see you tomorrow. Goodbye, my mother.*

"Aoo', yiską́ągo shį́į́ nída'ahiidiiltsééł." *Yes, we will probably see each other tomorrow.*

****

That night, Dééd Yázhí's younger brother came to visit. She had been patiently waiting for him. She told her brother she would place a bundle for him and identified the place near the shed. After naming the contents of the bundle, her younger brother said,

"Áłchíní nidi naabaahii daazlį́į́. Háshinee'go dó' ájít'į́. Shida' shá 'ahéhee' bididíiniił. K'ad éí nihimá bighangóó shá 'ashja'iilaa." *Even children have become warriors. Dear one. Thank my nephew for me. Now I have the chance to go to our mother's home.*

Dééd Yázhí smiled. Her younger brother immediately claimed the young Naabeehó 'ashkii as his nephew. His words warmed her heart.

259

Her younger brother told her the Naabeehó people who were forced to walk to the fort were to be taken to a place far from the fort, and that they would be walking there. They were told they would have to travel fifteen miles a day regardless of the surrounding conditions. Because he did not want to think about it, he finally told Dééd Yázhí he had a young wife and he did not know where her parents were, but he left his new wife behind to care for their maternal grandmother. He did not know where their mother and father were, nor did he have a chance to say goodbye to his new wife. He hoped she was with their mother and father, but he was worried about her. She was the oldest sibling of the orphans their parents had adopted. He said he had tried so hard to fight his growing affection for her but had lost completely. She had won.

This man, Bi'éé' łichíi'ii *Kit Carson,* (her younger brother spat when he spoke the name of the notorious enemy of the Naabeehó people) has no heart, her younger brother told her. He claimed he was very worried for his wife's safety. The woman he loved is beautiful. Kit Carson and his men look for beautiful women to mutilate. He told Dééd Yázhí he did not want to go with his Naabeehó people without knowing whether his wife and the rest of his family members were all right.

Dééd Yázhí encouraged her brother not to run away, but the news of his older sister and her baby, and the desire to see his parents, and his longing to see Tsék'iz Naazbaa', the woman of his dreams, caused him to call upon his bravery and begin plans to sneak off into the mountains to return home to look for his family. Dééd Yázhí and her younger brother encouraged one another through tears. Her brother was very afraid for her little one. He was afraid because he believed soldiers would mistreat him or take him away from his sister or worse yet, their Naabeehó people would mistreat and hate her little one because he was born for the enemy who was causing them so much hardship now.

Dééd Yázhí did not expect to see her brother again. He is so brave, she thought as she watched him leave to return to the rest of the captives.

****

The morning was filled with officers shouting orders at their soldiers who, in turn, shouted at the Naabeehó people. Before noon, the procession was near ready to leave. Dééd Yázhí felt a deep loneliness that made her heart hurt. She picked up her little one and placed him over her heart and lay motionless. She looked out through the hole in the wall, she saw a group of Naabeehó people being shoved, pushed, and hit. Even the tall, brave, proud men were being shoved about by the mean soldiers as they were placed at the front of the procession of Naabeehó prisoners.

A group of Naabeehó were sent off down the dusty road that led eastward. Next came a set of wagons filled with supplies, barrels filled with water, food, bags of flour, tools, and ammunition, followed by another group of her Naabeehó people. Several wagons separated the next group of Naabeehó prisoners. The entire procession was surrounded by soldiers, who placed themselves at intervals as the sad confused group slowly moved down the road that led them toward the eastern direction.

Once her Naabeehó people left, the silence was even more pronounced and left Dééd Yázhí very lonely. Life was cruel to her once again. Once again, she was losing someone. Her brother was taken out of her life. Would she see him again? she wondered. She vowed not to allow herself to get close to anyone, other than her family, if more Naabeehó *Navajo* people were forced to come here. It was too painful. She had to survive the disappointments in her life for her little one's sake. He was her life now. He was a testimony of her love for the tall, gray-haired one.

The new set of officers who took over command of the fort did not recognize Dééd Yázhí's status as an officer's wife. They had their orders. The Navajos were bad people and needed to be removed from the area to Fort Sumner. They took their orders literally. Just like the other Naabeehó prisoners, Dééd Yázhí was fed only once a day. She could see the gradual decline in the quality of food she was being sent. She was grateful but guilty that she was allowed to stay in the shed while her people were suffering on the outside and she could do little to help. Where was her tall, gray-haired one? she wondered.

The coldest part of the winter was near the end of the winter season. Very few Naabeehó people *Navajos* had been forced to walk to the fort and Dééd Yázhí wondered why. She assumed the young Naabeehó 'ashkii *Navajo boy* was not allowed to give her food or help her anymore. She was grateful for her work at the laundry house. It made the sun float across the sky faster. She carried her little one in a sling under her arm when she did not have a large load of laundry. She was careful where she carried her little one, she did not want him to come in contact with the filthy laundry.

Feeling sorry for her people, Dééd Yázhí took various items of clean clothing from the laundry room in hopes she would find a Naabeehó person to give the clothes to. She could not imagine the full impact of the cold outside. Although it was very cold in the little shed, she stayed warm as long as she felt her little one's warm body against her. As long as their hearts beat together, she knew they would survive the cold, the hunger, and the nastiness of the new soldiers.

Dééd Yázhí had not heard the first thunder ushering in the spring season but she knew they had entered the season when the little leaves on the trees were beginning to show signs of new life. The new spring season had arrived and the month was T'ą́ą́chil *April*.

One day when Dééd Yázhí was wearily entering the shed, she saw a piece of material stuck in the crack of the southern wall. She cautiously opened it and found in it four large sticks of jerky and a smaller piece of moldy bread. She had not had mutton in a long time. She devoured the first piece while she allowed her little one to suck on another piece of jerky. After having devoured the first piece, she looked around in a confused fashion and began to wonder who brought the jerky to her. It must have been the young Naabeehó 'ashkii *Navajo boy*, she decided, then warmed up water to drink so she would be able to produce milk for her little one.

More Naabeehó were being forced to walk to the fort by the soldiers who were on horseback. These Naabeehó *Navajo* people looked wild, older, very hungry, colder, and more desperate than the groups she had seen come and go. The new soldiers seemed to be in a hurry to chase the Naabeehó people on to the next place.

The little gifts of jerky appeared once again in the cracks of the shed. One day while walking to the laundry, Dééd Yázhí saw the young Naabeehó 'ashkii carrying a large load of laundry. She walked with him. Without acknowledging one another, she asked the young boy if he was the one who left her the jerky and pieces of bread. The young boy was puzzled and did not claim to be the bearer of the gifts of food. The little pieces of jerky continued to arrive every so often. The jerky always seemed to arrive when Dééd Yázhí was most tired, most hungry, and most lonely; but the question that nagged at her tired mind was "who was bringing the jerky and bread?"

The weather had become warmer. The long, cold winter had passed and the new buds on the trees began to push out their contents by unfolding the tender leaves they had painstakingly cared for. The tender leaves began to reach maturity when another large group of Naabeehó people were forced to walk to the fort, then forced to walk down the road toward the eastern direction.

When the green color in the tender leaves became more pronounced, Dééd Yázhí noticed even more soldiers were arriving, but she did not recognize any of the faces. The new soldiers had no sympathy for her nor did she have status with them. All hope began to vanish as the soldiers' treatment of her was becoming one of disdain. She only wanted to protect her little one. She promised her little one she would not let anyone harm him.

The new soldiers' activities were becoming increasingly oppressive as they ordered a new group of Naabeehó people through the day's activities. One warm day, as preparations were being made to leave the fort, a soldier pushed the door open when Dééd Yázhí and her little one were resting on the floor after a long day of work at the laundry. Her eyes flew toward the bundle of clothing and blankets she had taken for her Naabeehó people. She became afraid that the soldier had seen her take the clothing and blankets.

The soldier recklessly packed a few of her belongings, along with the items she took from the laundry and threw the bulging bag out the door then he turned and grabbed her around the waist and shoved her toward the door and on out onto the porch of the shed.

"'Áłtsé, she'awéé' bi'éé' t'ah ákóne' sinil. Éí nídiishníłł," *Wait, my baby's clothes are still in there. Let me get those,* she pleaded. She slipped out of the soldier's grip, ran back into the shed and had only enough time to grab a few of the things the tall gray-haired one gave her. She also grabbed her little one's sling, stuffed their thin blankets into a thicker blanket, rolled it up and stepped outside. She quickly placed her little one in the sling. He lay tucked away, hanging under her arm, just above her hip in the cloth sling she made from fabric her tall, gray-haired one had given to her as a gift so long ago

Would the person who brought me and my little one pieces of jerky know we do not live here anymore? she wondered. Would my tall, gray-haired one come to look for us here? What if my younger brother came back, how would he know where to find me? Does the Naabeehó 'ashkii know I am also being forced out of here? she silently asked.

Dééd Yázhí felt a deep pain when she thought of her father. She asked herself, will my father try to come here looking for me? If he does, how will he know I am not here any more? Will my father ever see my little one, his grandson? she thought as the questions marched single file through her mind.

Stopping to cover herself and her little one with the thin blanket the tall, gray-haired man gave her, Dééd Yázhí stuffed all her belongings into a light blanket, then tied the ends tightly together and heaved all of her possessions over her shoulders, and began walking in the direction in which the soldier pointed his gun.

****

Dééd Yázhí could not believe she was pushed in the direction of where her Naabeehó people were gathered. She was so excited! Finally, after so long, she was able to fully look into the eyes of her people. She was shocked as she looked from one face to another. The wrinkles on the faces of the Naabeehó elders made deep ruts in the smoothness of their beautiful, light brown skin. She saw new scars that were healing. The younger Naabeehó people took on the posture that was only allotted to the elders. They were stooped. They were not stooped because they carried a heavy load on their backs; instead, their load was the memories they carried, memories of the young and old being tortured into submission only to become prisoners of the strange enemy with white skin. Just from looking at the posture of her people, she could see the deep scars that wrapped themselves around the heart of each one of her people. She saw the hungry and terrified look in the eyes of her people.

Dééd Yázhí searched the faces of her people intensely. She searched for any signs of recognition. She looked for her mother and her father and her brothers and her younger sister. Relief and sadness poured over her heart when she did not see her mother, her father, or her siblings. Tears began to pool in her eyes, not wanting to spill over to expose her relief and extreme sadness. She looked up into the sky in hopes that her tears would run back into the sockets that held her eyes in place, causing her nose to run. When she sniffled, several Naabeehó women looked at her.

She wanted to stomp her feet. Instead, she took several determined steps as she thought, it is dangerous for me to show any emotion or to call any attention to myself. I cannot risk the life of my little one who was born for one of the enemy with white skin whose plan it was to kill my people. She wanted to wipe the memory of the tall, gray-haired one from her mind. As she stepped determinedly, she woke her little one from his peaceful slumber, and he squirmed and began to whimper. Quickly and with great care so as not to shift the heavy load on her back, Dééd Yázhí reached inside her rug dress and lifted one breast and pushed it through the hole in the shoulder of her rug dress. She then lifted her little one and felt him nudge against her breast as he searched for her erect nipple. Feeling her little one's moist lips surrounding her nipple, she once again took several determined steps to remind herself not to be careless and attract attention to her and her little one.

Dééd Yázhí realized that keeping her little one hidden from view was more difficult than she imagined. She knew the white enemy's treatment of her Naabeehó people had put hatred for the enemy in her people's heart. For her people to see that her little one was born for their anaa'í enemy, she knew her people would have hatred for her little one as well. She knew the enemy with white skin would also have disdain for her little one because he was Naabeehó and born for one of their men.

She looked for the young boy who took care of the sheep at the fort, the one who brought her pieces of jerky. Hearing gunshots, she raised her head to look farther ahead to look into the faces of the mean soldiers, then lifted the thin piece of material that held her little one close to her. He was sleeping now. His long eyelashes resting on his cheeks reassured her he was unaware of the danger he was in.

Dééd Yázhí had many questions but the only representation of certainty that she could claim was right in her arms. She pulled her little one close to her body and said ever so softly,

"Shiyázhí, Naabeehó nílį. Nihe'anaa'í 'atxídanihił'ínígíí bá shínílchíín, áko nidi nizhé'é 'éí 'ayóo shaa jooba' nít'ę́ę́'. Ni dó', nizhé'é nahalingo nidine'é baa jiiníba' dooleeł. Háshinee', shiyázhí." *My little one, you are Navajo. You are born for our enemy who are torturing us, but your father was very kind to me. You will also be kind to your people in the same way your father was kind. Dear one, my little one.*

What would these people think if they heard me? she gasped. She held her little one close to ensure his comfort and safety.

With conflicted thoughts, Dééd Yázhí proudly joined her people on their walk toward the east. Little did the procession of prisoners know they would be haunted daily by the questions of the children wanting to know the answers to questions such as:

"Háágóóshą' yiikah?" *Where are we going?*

"Hahgoshą' áadi niikááh?" *When will we get there?*

"Ha'át'íísh biniinaa t'áá 'áníiltsoh deekaiígóó yiikah?" *Why are we all going at the same time to the place where we are going?*

"Ha'át'íísh dabi'niidą́ą́'?" *What are we going to eat?*

"Nihilį́į́' shą'?" *Where are our horses?*

"Nihidibé shą'?" *Where are our sheep?*

"Ha'át'íishą' biniinaa nihicheii dóó nihizhé'é 'atíbi'dil'į́?" *Why are our maternal grandfathers and our fathers being treated so badly?*

"Ha'át'íishą' biniinaa yiikah?" *Why are we going?*

"Ha'át'íishą' biniinaa doo łį́į́' nihił deiyíjeeh da?" *Why are we not riding horses?*

The soldiers riding on horses set the pace for the people, pushing for fifteen miles per day. The ground was dusty from the groups of wagons, horses, and people that were traveling up ahead, forcing Dééd Yázhí to walk toward the outside of the procession. She was glad for the excuse of walking away from the others, telling those around her,

"Łeezh bił dah oojołígíí bik'ee ch'ééh disdziih. T'óó háádiskosgo 'ánáshiil'įįh." *The dust in the air makes it hard for me to breathe. It just makes me cough.* With those words, she moved to the outside of the procession.

Dééd Yázhí loved being on the outside of the procession. She never had the opportunity to see such a great expanse of land in such a long time. She was in awe of the myriad colors splashed across the landscape before her. The clouds kept her busy as she watched for shapes to appear that reminded her of her world when she was a child.

At the end of the first day of walking eastward, many older Naabeehó were complaining of their feet hurting. Others complained of hunger, while still others spoke of fatigue from having been forced to run out of the mountains and then being forced once again to walk. Dééd Yázhí felt sorry for her people. She felt guilty that she had a spring in her step. She did not feel the weakness her fellow prisoners felt because she was so excited to be outside of the shed while watching the sun make steady steps across the vast blue sky toward the west. Thinking of food brought thoughts of the young Naabeehó 'ashkii who took care of the sheep.

Dééd Yázhí was thankful her work schedule at the fort was strenuous because she was able to keep up with the pace set by the soldiers. She was also thankful for her tattered rug dress. It was testimony of her status as a prisoner of war. She was further thankful for her moccasins, which were still in good condition. She was glad for the warm wraps the tall, gray-haired one had given her. Inwardly, she smiled to herself knowing that she was kept warm with the memory of the tall, gray-haired one. The thickness of the blankets were very burdensome, but she knew they would come in handy when she and her little one slept on the hard ground.

The Naabeehó people were told to make camp in a valley bordered by tall mesas on the south and north sides. The soldiers gave only the Naabeehó men a medium-sized pouch, which contained flour that had lumps in it. Dééd Yázhí was overlooked because she was not represented by a man. Instead, she took out her own personal pouch in which she carried several pieces of jerky given to her by the mysterious person, another pouch of pinon nuts, and a little container of water, the container that was a gift from the tall, gray-haired one. She was grateful to the Creator that she had the mind to keep these items bundled in one place.

As the soldiers ordered the Naabeehó people to settle in for the night out in the open valley, Dééd Yázhí could hear the lonely cries of the coyotes. Looking out over her people, she was reminded of home and the fall season when her family went out in groups to gather pinon nuts and juniper berries in preparation for the long winter. She remembered how she could see several small fires lit, which were kept burning throughout the night to let the night creatures know the Naabeehó people were in the vicinity.

This time, it was the soldiers who kept their fires going around the perimeter of the Naabeehó people's camps. Occasionally, Dééd Yázhí could hear a soldier walking through the camps of the people. Naabeehó mothers were asked by the elder men to keep their children quiet, so as not to attract the attention of the soldiers.

One old Naabeehó man said,

"Nihe'anaa'í doo 'ádahalyą́ą da. T'áadoo hooyání t'áá'áníiltso nidanihidooltsił. Áłchíní baa hą́ą́h danohsin. T'áadoo daachaaí. Hazhóó'ígo bich'į' yádaołti'. Ch'iiyáán ádin nidi ch'il daadánígíí nihinaagóó dahóló. 'Éí ch'il daadánígíí bá hádaoht'į." *Our enemies are not wise. They are capable of killing us all (without warning). Be mindful of the safety of the children. Don't let them cry. Talk to them in a nice way. Although there is no food, there are plenty of edible plants around us. Obtain those plants for them.*

Dééd Yázhí closed her eyes as she listened to the old
Naabeehó man speaking. She could see her father's face and
hear him speaking the same words of kindness to his people.
Her father loved children. She knew her father's heart would
be filled with love for her little one. Her mother, if she were
here, would help her take care of her little one by hiding him
from their Naabeehó people. Tears made their way down Dééd
Yázhí's face. Trying to shake the thoughts of her people being
mistreated by the mean soldiers, she shook her head.

The elder Naabeehó women told the girls and young
women to make their hair dirty by mixing fine dirt and mutton
tallow together and rubbing it in their hair and on their faces,
arms, and legs. The elders reminded the girls and young women
that it would be up to the young women and girls to keep the
number of their people strong. As Dééd Yázhí listened to the
older women talking, she thought, sheep take care of us in
many different ways. Their tallow is protecting us now from our
vicious enemy. They give us a soft pelt to sleep on. Sheep feed
us with their nutritious meat. They clothe us with their soft,
warm wool. Dééd Yázhí thought of her fat lamb and felt an even
deeper appreciation for her lamb and the sheep at her mother's
home.

"Háshinee', shidibé. Háadi da shạ' naaghá. Naabeehó 'ashkii
daats'í shá yik'idéez'įį́'. Ashkii daats'í 'atah bi'di'noolchééł? *My
dear sheep. I wonder where it is? Maybe it is watching over the
Navajo boy for me. Is the young boy also being forced to walk
among the people?* she silently wondered.

The soft voice of a sad, worried older leader interrupted
Dééd Yázhí's reminiscing when he said,

"Nihidine'é t'óó'ahayói doo béédahoozin da. Yéigo danihich'eekę' baa 'ádahołyą. T'áadoo t'áá sáhí bíni' naazdáhí. T'áadoo t'áá sáhí ni'ohgóó 'anídaakahí. 'Amá danohłínígíí, danihich'eekę' t'áá bikéé' nidaohkai. Danihich'eekę' danilínígíí binahjį' Naabeehó dine'é náásgóó dahólǫǫ dooleeł." *Many of our people have disappeared. Take good care of our young women. Do not leave them alone. Do not allow them to go alone to relieve themselves. Those of you who are mothers, follow your daughters closely. It is because of the young girls and women that our Navajo people will continue to exist.*

Dééd Yázhí loved hearing the cadence of her spoken language as it painfully slipped off of the Naabeehó leader's tongue. For many months, Naabeehó words were only in the form of her thoughts and whispers. She wanted him to continue speaking. She could not get enough of the beautiful sound. Dééd Yázhí found herself dizzy as she heard the sound of her language floating softly in the air. She wanted to hear her language being spoken in the morning and at noon and in the evening. She especially wanted to hear her language being spoken at night.

Looking at the distant mountains that were covered by the last purple and orange rays of the setting sun, Dééd Yázhí reached up and felt her hair. It was also stiff with mutton tallow and dust and it smelled bad. She jumped at the question that her mind stumbled upon when it asked whether her tall, gray-haired one would recognize her in this state. Thinking back to the time when she first met him, she knew he would recognize her, because at that time, he had rescued her from the dirty, mean white men. She was dirty and yet he saw her under all the dirt that covered her and he showed her kindness.

He will know me! she thought as she nodded in determination to answer her own question. Dééd Yázhí watched in sadness as the soldiers poked, hit, ridiculed, and shouted angry words at her Naabeehó people. She did not see her tall, gray-haired one in any of the mean men. She also searched the faces of her people, looking for the face of her brother and the Naabeehó 'ashkii as well as the little boy. She remembered what her brother looked like when they were still at home, but when he came to visit her at the fort, she had only seen him in the moonlight. She kept her mind alert so she would not miss the face of any one of her relatives or the two boys she had adopted.

Although darkness brought uncertainty, worries, and fear, Dééd Yázhí kept her distance from the rest of her people. She still had a few pieces of jerky left. She and her little one subsisted on what she had rationed out to herself. She was comforted by the night sky that arrayed itself before her. She could not keep her eyes off of the beautiful stars that winked playfully at her and the beautiful moon that held her secrets in its deepest shadows. Dééd Yázhí felt safer knowing that her family was seeing the same stars she was watching as the constellations moved in unison across the late night sky. She did not fall asleep until the last constellation had disappeared behind the high rising rock formations that surrounded her and her people.

Early the next morning, Dééd Yázhí and her Naabeehó people heard several gun shots. The soldiers were on their horses and were riding through the Naabeehó camps, firing their guns into the air. The people who were familiar with the sounds quickly moved and began gathering their few belongings. Naabeehó elders and children could be seen huddled in little groups, crying. The sound of the guns being shot into the air put fear into their hearts. It was at the sound of the gunshots that they had seen their relatives fall in their tracks only to die a painful death later. To the Naabeehó people, the gunshots meant loneliness, depression, and death.

The Naabeehó people fell obediently into place. The procession became longer and longer. Soon, the procession took on the form it had when the people were first forced out of Fort Canby.

Dééd Yázhí kept watching the soldiers intently, wondering if one of them could be her tall, gray-haired one. How was he supposed to know she had been forced out of the shed and was being forced to walk toward the east along with her people? Even her younger brother was unaware of her absence from the fort. She wondered who would tell her younger brother she had been chased out of the shed and forced to walk along with her people. Dééd Yázhí began to wonder if her tall, gray-haired one had made her well just so she could endure this journey. Was this his way of getting back at me? she thought. She felt betrayed by the tall, gray-haired one.

What will I tell my son when he begins to ask questions about his father? What am I supposed to tell the other Naabeehó when they find out about the color of my child's skin and his hair? None of the soldiers walked with a limp the way my tall, gray-haired one did. The last thought comforted her. As she studied the faces and forms of the soldiers, they all looked alike, but they lacked the kind expression of her tall, gray-haired one.

Dééd Yázhí placed herself at the end of the procession and near the outside once again. The sun was warm and the wide dirt road they walked upon was dusty and rocky. Looking eastward, she could see several hills and mesas that offered themselves as allies of the enemy in that the landscape provided a natural barrier on the north and on the south, forcing the Naabeehó people to walk through a wide dusty valley.

Several warriors reported they had been this way when they followed the Naakai men who took their women and daughters to be sold at the Indian slave markets. Through the beautiful valley the people walked. Dééd Yázhí lost count of the number of days they had walked.

The Naabeehó men reported the mountain that rose in the distance before them was named Tsoodził *Mount Taylor,* their sacred mountain of the south. Dééd Yázhí recognized the name of the mountain as the one that established the southern boundary of the land the Naabeehó people claimed as their own. She had heard her father speak of the great mountain called Tsoodził *Mount Taylor.*

To prepare his people, the leader of the Naabeehó people was telling them to be respectful of their mountain of the south. He told the women to keep their babies from crying as they walked along the base of their mountain. He also told the men and the women not to scold their children as they walked past their mountain of the south.

"Bíni'dii nihada'áłchíní nihidził, Tsoodził, k'é dabiłní. Nihidził bíighahgóó nihidi'noolkałgo, t'áadoo nihada'áłchíní bich'adahoshookéhí. Bíni'dii nihada'áłchíní bidził k'é deiłní 'ałdó'. Nihídó' nihidził k'é dabidohní. Nizhónígo nihaa 'áhályą́ą dooleeł.

Ayóo jooba'ii 'óolyé, Tsoodził. Doo nihaidiyoonah da. T'áá kwe'é
nihiba' hólǫ́ǫ dooleeł. Nihidi'noolkałgóó nihaa 'áhályą́ą dooleeł.
Binahjį' nihikéyah biih nídiikah."

*Allow your children to be greeted as a relative by our
mountain. As we are forced to walk past our mountain, don't
scold your children. Allow your children to also greet their
mountain. You also, greet your mountain. It will take good
care of us. The mountain that is called Mount Taylor is a kind
mountain. It will not forget us. It will remain here for us.
Wherever it is we are being forced to walk to, it will take care of
us. By means of it we will come back into our own lands.*

Dééd Yázhí's shoulders ached from the large pack she
carried on her back, but hearing words that were very similar to
the ones that would have been spoken by her father gave her
much comfort. Although the pack she carried was heavy, she
sensed herself standing more erect and proud.

She watched the birds flying overhead and listened to their
wings pressing against the wind, then declared to herself that
it was a beautiful sound. She watched in wonderment as she
lowered her eyes to watch little bugs and rodents scuttle away
from the long procession of Naabeehó people. These were new
sights and sounds she had not heard or seen in a long time. She
lifted her head and silently thanked the Creator for her freedom.

Near noon, Dééd Yázhí heard a loud commotion. All the
Naabeehó people were stretching their necks to see what or
who was causing the commotion. All she could hear was the
angry voices of the soldiers barking orders at someone up
ahead. She was relieved when the procession of people, horses,
and wagons stopped. Painfully, she lowered her heavy pack and
gently set it on the ground then silently waited.

The procession of sad Naabeehó people, angry soldiers on horses, and horse-drawn wagons began to slowly move again. Dééd Yázhí picked up her heavy pack and followed along, swinging it onto her back as she began walking, still maintaining her distance from her Naabeehó people.

The soldiers cracked their whips to get the attention of the Naabeehó people, but the sound of their whips was ignored. Dééd Yázhí jumped when she heard loud gunshots, waking her little one. Quickly, she gently began to rock her body hoping her little one would not start crying. With fear in her heart, she looked ahead to see soldiers shooting their guns in the air. Looking up to see whom the soldiers were shooting at, she saw only the clear blue sky.

As the group of Naabeehó people began to slowly move forward, she looked upon several children and elders lying on the ground, suffering from a severe attack of diarrhea. In desperation, the sick children held out their hands to the people passing by. Mothers whose babies were sick on the side of the road wanted to stay and comfort their little ones, but the soldiers whipped them, kicked them, and fired shots in the air. The women were torn from their children and were forced to walk away from their suffering children. Dééd Yázhí could hear the mournful cries of the mothers of the sick children and the painful cries of the children who still sat on the side of the dusty road. Through Indian scouts, the soldiers told the women the sick elders would care for the children and the babies. As the people marched on, they could hear the cries of the little ones and the elders begging them to come back and not to leave them. Two soldiers were ordered to go back to "take care of the sick savages."

The two soldiers rode back to the roadside where the sick elders and children had been left. Then as the people rounded a slight bend in the road, Dééd Yázhí heard several gun shots. Some loud screams were heard. More gunshots. Then complete silence.

A young mother walking just ahead of Dééd Yázhí whirled around, nearly knocking Dééd Yázhí off her feet. With a wild look in her eyes, the young mother ran back to the children, babies, and elders left behind. A soldier tried jerking her back, but instead, tore her loosely fitting buckskin top and lost his grip on her arm. She ran, screaming,

"Shiyázhí! Shiyázhí! Shiyázhí!" *My little one! My little one! My little one!* When the young mother reached the bend in the road, a soldier lifted his rifle and shot her in the back. The young woman continued running, then staggered, fell down, and still dragged herself behind the bend in the road. The sounds of the desperate mother dragging herself back to her baby was the last sound Dééd Yázhí heard before the soldier fired at the young mother once again. Horrified, the women gasped. Children began to cry.

Dééd Yázhí thought, we were just told by the Naabeehó leader not to scold the children or make the children cry, and now all the women and the children are crying. She looked eastward toward their mountain with a helpless look on her face as hot tears made their way down her face.

She looked around her. The women lowered their heads and sobbed. Babies and children began to cry even louder. The men cried in their hearts because they had been rendered helpless. They were born to be the protectors of their women and their children and yet they had been stripped of their inheritance.

279

Someone was heard to hoarsely whisper,

"Háíshą' ádaat'į?" *Who are these people?* The rhetorical question was carried off to the distant hills and onward toward the great Mount Taylor by a slight breeze that also brought chills to the Naabeehó people.

After this incident, the Naabeehó people were forced to walk faster. It was as if the soldiers were angry with the people for loving the children and elders who had been left behind, and for having felt remorse for the ones who had been killed by the soldiers. After walking long hours under the hot late afternoon sun, the people were ordered to stop to camp for the night.

Lumpy yellow flour and foul-smelling bacon and containers of water were given to the Naabeehó men who returned shamefully to their camps with the meager supplies. The women mixed the water and the flour together and cooked the hard mixture over live coals then cooked the bacon by placing the slices of bacon on the end of sticks. Dééd Yázhí noticed the fat from the bacon caused the evening fire to burn blue. She looked at the fire as she thought, what is this food our enemies are trying to feed us? This food makes the fire jump and become a strange blue color! After our people eat the enemy's food, they become sick, she thought with horror in her eyes. Just at that moment, a Naabeehó woman walked through the camps whispering hoarsely,

"Díí ch'iiyáán nihitaa daas'nii'ígíí yáadishį́į́ 'át'é. 'Ei nihe'anaa'í bich'iiyą', t'áadoo daohsání. 'Ei shį́į́ nihité'áziní dayííyą́ą'go yits'ą́ą́dóó bitsą́ dahodíinii'. Yíiyá! Yíiyá! Hatíhíláane'ęę'. Nihí dó' ei ch'iiyáán bits'ą́ą́dóó danihitsą́ dahodidoołch'ih. T'áadoo daohsání!" *This food that has been*

given to us is disgusting. Do not eat the food the enemy gave
us. That is probably what gave our relatives stomach pains after
they ate it. Scary warning! Scary warning! It is unthinkable. You
will get stomach pains as well from eating the food. Don't eat it!
Still, the Naabeehó people who were weakened from the long
walk of the day and extreme hunger ate the food.

Dééd Yázhí moved away from her people. She reached into
her little pouch and brought forth two pieces of jerky, ten pinon
nuts, several juniper berries, and two pieces of dried yucca fruit.
With her mouth dry from the earlier experience, she chewed
and chewed her food hoping the chewing would bring forth
moisture from her saliva to wash down her food. Her little one
needed nourishment.

Two more days of walking was wearing on Dééd Yázhí's
resolve. Her people who once walked faster were beginning
to slow down. The Naabeehó men told the Indian scouts to
tell the soldiers they had to walk more slowly because of the
elders, but the soldiers did not seem concerned as they pushed
the people forward and quickly. At the end of the second day,
the Naabeehó people were asked to settle down for the night
in a wide, green valley. Food was once again rationed to the
Naabeehó prisoners, but as before, Dééd Yázhí was overlooked
by the soldiers because she was not represented by a man.
She did not mourn the fact that she did not receive the deadly
rations and she vowed never to eat the food of the enemy again.

She became worried because she was eating the last of the
jerky that had been brought mysteriously to the shed at Fort
Canby. After eating the jerky and drinking the last of her water,

she settled down for the night, comforted by the number of pinon nuts and juniper berries she had in her pouch. As she lay looking up at the stars, she told herself,

"Dichin wolyéi baa 'ákonisin háálá dichin bii' tádííyá. Bii' tádííyáa nidi t'áadoo shik'eh deesdlį́į' da. K'ad nidi doo shik'eh didoodleeł da. *I am well aware of hunger. I have walked through hunger. Although I walked through hunger, it did not overtake me. Even now, it will not overpower me.* Although she vowed, her mind was apprehensive. She had her little one to care for. She kept thinking about food and made herself believe she was full and satisfied.

The stars set out their patterns in the sky lulling Dééd Yázhí to sleep. She dreamed of having meal after meal of delicious ribs of lamb. How many sheep did my mother butcher? she wondered in her dream as she filled herself with the delicious, fat slices of blue corn bread. Streams of fat flowed from her wrists down to her elbows from the fat pieces of meat she held in her hands. The water she drank tasted like the water her father obtained from the spring that spouted clear, sweet water.

"Na', shiyázhí," *Here, my little one*, she heard herself say as she held out a fat piece of meat attached to a lamb rib.

Chapter Sixteen
Let Me Carry Your Heavy Pack

Dééd Yázhí was jerked awake when she felt a strong hand, the hand of a man which was placed over her mouth. Not wanting to wake her little one, she struggled silently with the strong person who was holding her down with his other hand.

Because of the struggle, her precious little one rolled out of his little wrap and rolled onto the hard ground. He began to cry loudly. Quietly, the person holding her down told her to pick up her little one.

"Niyáázh nídiiłteeh." *Pick up your son.* Her mind obeyed by guiding her hands. She wanted to scream. She expected to be tortured by one of the soldiers, but not at the hand of one of her own people! her mind screamed silently.

"T'áadoo 'íits'a'í nániteeh." *Lie back down without a sound.* She turned toward the sound of the voice that was telling her to lie back down and be quiet. Although shaking violently, she remembered her little one and turned toward him and offered him her breast to quiet him. Her little one struggled against her shaking hand. Dééd Yázhí could not get control of herself.

Her fear was getting the best of her. When she felt her little one slip her nipple into his mouth, she felt a slight sense of comfort begin to release her fear.

When the quietness of the night returned, the man asked her,

"Da' niísh At'ééd Yázhí Naazbaa' yinílyé? *Are you the one who is called Little Girl Warrior Who Came Home?*

She weakly answered in a shaking voice,

"Aoo'. Háísh ánít'į̱?" *Yes. Who are you?* With her answer, the man released his harsh hold on her.

Putting his mouth against her ear, the man told her,

"T'áá kwe'é sínídá." *Remain sitting right here.* As fear and questions flew through her mind, Dééd Yázhí remained motionless and quiet. Tears of fear ran in a steady stream down her face and dripped onto the face of her little one.

In the pale moonlight, Dééd Yázhí saw a dark figure gliding toward her. It was a man. Her breath quickened out of fear as her thoughts raced through her mind. Are the soldiers going to kill me because of the tall, gray-haired one? Are they here to take my baby? Will I end up like the young woman who desperately tried crawling back to her baby, only to end up dead a few feet away from her little one? she thought in desperation.

She was breathing so hard and so fast she was afraid she was going to faint when she heard someone whisper her name. She turned toward the voice. It was the voice of a man who held out his hand toward her, but she rolled away from his hand. The dark shadow said,

"Shádí, shí 'ásht'į̱, nitsilí, Nahat'á Yinaabaah." *My older sister, it is me, your younger brother, One Who goes to*

284

War Around Plans. Dééd Yázhí was afraid to trust the man's voice. She had not seen her brother in many, many days. She asked herself, *how could he know where I am?*

She sat up and waited in anguished silence. She felt hot tears rolling down her dusty face. In the worst way, she desperately wanted this person to be her younger brother. The young man at her side whispered the names of the people in her family.

"Nihizhé'é Hashké Yił Naabaah wolyé. Nihimá 'éí Nínááníbaa' wolyé. Nihideezhí Dzání Yázhí Naazbaa' wolyéé dóó nihitsilí 'éí Tł'ée'go Naabaah wolyé." *Our father's name is One Who Goes to War Scolding. Our mother's name is named Woman Warrior Who Came Back Again. Our younger sister is named Little Young Woman Warrior Who Came Back and our youngest brother is named One Who Goes to War at Night.* Dééd Yázhí heard a gasp escape her lips. Sobs came to the surface which she could not muffle. The voice continued to reassure her it was her brother and he meant her no harm. Her younger brother said,

"Shįįgo 'éí Dziłíjiin bighą́ą́'di kéédahwiit'į́į́ dóó haigo'éí Dziłíjiin bitsį́įdi kéédahwiit'į́į łeh." *We live on the summit of Black Mesa in the winter and in the summer we live at the base of Black Mesa.* He continued,

"Nihe'anaa'í bitsį' daalgaiígíí bił haz'ánígi tł'éego naa néiit'ash nít'ę́ę́', shí dóó 'ashkii yázhí léi'. Niyázhí, shida', éí Níyol Yił Naabaah wolyé." *The little boy and I visited you at the place of our enemy with white skin. Your son, my nephew, is called the One Who Fights with the Wind.*

Slowly, Dééd Yázhí's breathing began to slow down.

"Shitsilí, háshinee' dó' ánít'į. K'asídą́ą́' yee' yéé' bik'ee

shijéí niiltłah. Doochohoo'įįgóó náhádzid. T'áá sáhí, shí dóó
shiyázhí, 'ałk'íhwiilta'go 'atah nihidi'noolkał. Dichin biih niidee'
t'áá 'óolyéego. Da' niísh ałk'íniilgizh shá 'ánéinil'įįhgo shá
nínádíł'įįh nít'ę́ę́'. T'áá 'éí t'éí nihich'iiyą'go 'atah nihidi'noolkał.
Shiyééł ayóo nidaaz nidi t'áátáhígi 'át'éego 'akéé' yishjił.
Nihe'anaa'í doo bíla'ashdla'ii danilį da. Yáadishį́į' ádaat'é." *My
younger brother, dear one. My heart nearly stopped as a result
of fear. It is extremely terrifying here. We are alone, me and my
little one, we have been keeping each other company as we are
being forced to walk along with the others. We have truly fallen
into hunger. Was it you who made the mutton jerky and hid it
for me to find? That is all we have been eating as we are being
forced to walk along with the others. Even though my pack
holding our belongings is heavy, I keep carrying it as we follow.
Our enemies are not of the five fingered ones (the human race).
They are something awful.*

Dééd Yázhí cried silently out of relief. She focused upon
the pieces of jerky that were left for her when she whispered
excitedly,

"Da' éí ni 'ánít'į? Da' ni nihaná'íłtso' nít'ę́ę́'?" *That was you?
It was you who fed us?* She felt so much love wash over her and
her little one. It was her younger brother who left her the pieces
of jerky and the yucca fruit. She reached out into the dark and
hugged her younger brother.

"Háshinee', shitsilí. Nida' yázhí 'ayóó'ííní'níí lá. 'Ahéhee',
niniiłt'aa nihikáa'jį' hazlį́į'," *Dear one, my younger brother. You
truly love your nephew. Thank you, it is because of you that we
have survived extreme hardship,* she said referring to the pieces
of jerky that mysteriously appeared in the cracks of the shed at
Fort Canby.

Her younger brother whispered into her ear,

"Aoo', éí shí nihaná'ástso' nít'ę́ę́'. Ákwe'é nánísdzáá nít'ę́ę́' doo naagháhí da. T'óó hook'ee haz'ą́ą́go bik'íníyá. Ha'a'aahjigo Naabeehó dine'é dah náádeidíníiyood ha'níigo 'aadę́ę́' nihikéé' eeshkahgo kodi 'índa nihik'íníyá." *Yes, that was me who used to leave you the food. I went back there and there was no one there. I just found the place empty with no one living there. I was told they had chased more Navajo people this way, so I began tracking you and I found you here.*

Possibly because she was so hungry, all Dééd Yázhí could think about was how excited she was to know it was her brother who had taken care of her and her little one after he left the fort. He was the one who gave them jerky and other food to nourish her and her little one. Her heart was afraid to feel a sense of relief.

Her younger brother told her of how he returned home to see their mother, their father, and his young beautiful wife. The visit was short, he told her, because their mother and their father sent him back to the fort to take care of her and her infant son.

Dééd Yázhí leaned against her younger brother at the news of the safety of her mother and her father as she asked,

"Nihimá dóó nihizhé'éésh bitah yá'áhoot'ééh? Nihitsilí shą'? Nihideezhí shą'?" *Are our mother and our father well? What about our younger brother? What about our younger sister?* she felt pain when she asked about her younger sister.

"Nihimá dóó nihizhé'é bitah yá'áhoot'ééh. Áko nidi, nihimá 'éí yisnááh ánihi'diilyaaígíí t'ah nidii t'áá yéego yik'ee ti'hoonííh. Nihideezhí 'éí t'áadoo bénáhoosdzin da. Nihitsilí 'éí bitah yá'áhoot'ééh. Nihimá yaa' áhályą́ą́ dóó yik'ihałta'." *Our mother and our father are well. Our mother is still suffering greatly from the two of you having been kidnapped. Our younger sister was never found. Our younger brother is well and he is taking care of our mother and keeping her company.*

"Asdzání 'iiná bił áníł'inígíí shą'?" *What about the young woman you make your life with?* Dééd Yázhí asked timidly. She had never known either of her brothers as a married man, and so to ask of the well-being of his wife brought a nervous giggle to her lips.

"'Asdzání 'iiná bił ásh'inígíí 'éí bitah yá'áhoot'ééh dóó nihimá yik'ihałta'go hooghandi yił siké. 'Ayóo nihimá yaa jooba'." *The young woman I make my life with is doing well. She is keeping our mother company at home. She is very kind to our mother.*

"Jó nizhónígi 'át'éé lá," *She is a good person,* Dééd Yázhí quietly answered.

Her younger brother continued telling her of his time away from her and her son. Instead of re-entering the fort, he lived in the hills above the fort and hunted to accumulate skins and to make jerky. He did not want to venture into the fort except when there was no light from the moon and when it was safe. It was upon the return from their last hunting trip that he and his friends found her and her little one gone and the shed vacated. He told her of how much he worried about her and her little one's safety because the shed appeared as if a struggle had taken place.

Her brother told her he kidnapped the little boy when he found him sleeping near the sheep corral. With his latest bit of news, Dééd Yázhí cried again. From the fort, her younger brother and his friends followed the tracks left by the procession of Naabeehó people and followed at a distance, traveling mostly at night.

He further reported that his father had promised their mother they would gather his people together and travel to the fort to find their oldest daughter. Her brother explained that at the time of his leaving their home in Black Mesa, their mother and their father and the young woman of his dreams and her adopted siblings were going to move the rest of the family higher into the mountains of Black Mesa to be safe a while longer while more rugs were being woven for clothing and blankets and while more jerky was being prepared. The family did not want to consume any sheep or goats because their father wanted to save the herd for his family and his people to eat while they were traveling to the fort. The young warriors were told to hunt animals for their meat and fur for warmth.

Dééd Yázhí could hear her father's voice as he demanded more of his warriors. She remembered what he would say,

"Ádínáasjį' doo 'ééhózin da. Nihist'e' t'áá nihídaastł'óǫgo t'éí dah didiikah. *Our future is uncertain. We will not leave until we have enough food to take with us.*

Dééd Yázhí started to cry. She had not felt the protective hand of her father for so long. The memories of her father's strength flooded her mind with so much love for him and her mother and her sister as well. At these memories, her mind seemed to collapse. She heavily leaned against her younger brother and fell into a bothersome sleep forgetting her hunger and her thirst.

As the faint white light of dawn in the eastern sky cast a glow on the eastern horizon, Dééd Yázhí stirred, not wanting to wake from her sleep. In her sleep, she dreamed her younger brother had come to visit her. When her mind became more alert, she kept her eyes shut to remember their conversation. Tears flowed as she remembered her mother and her father and her younger brothers and her younger sister. *If I could just have someone take care of me just for one day, I know it would bring back more memories of my family,* she thought as she kept her eyes shut tight.

She opened her eyes and looked toward the faint light in the eastern sky and spoke prayers of gratitude to the Creator. She thanked the Creator for bringing each member of her family closer to her in her dreams. She thanked the Creator that her younger brother had visited her in her dream. She thanked the Creator that she was stronger now and could continue to walk and protect her little one. She also thanked the Creator that the heavy burden she carried would be much lighter after having rested well for one night. Her last thoughts in her prayers were of her younger sister.

Slowly she voiced her daily morning prayer, saying,

"T'áásho̜odí, shiTaa', shizhé'é shá baa 'áhólyą́ą dooleeł. Shimá 'ałdó' shá baa 'áhólyą́ą dooleeł. Shilahkéí shá baa 'áhólyą́ą dooleeł. Áádóó shideezhí 'ałdó' shá baa 'áhólyą́ą dooleeł..."
Please, my Spiritual Father, take care of my father. Take care of my mother also. Take care of my brothers. Take care of my younger sister also...

Her prayer was interrupted when her little one began to stir. With his sleepy movements, Dééd Yázhí became mindful of her surroundings.

If only I could have protected my younger sister, maybe she would be here and we would be making the journey together, she thought as she held her little one so close he began to squirm and whimper. I have to remain alert, she thought as her eyes flew open. I have no more food! I have no more water!

Reaching for her little container of water, which held the last of her water supply, her hand bumped against something. Looking down, she found a bundle of long, soft pieces of jerky and another bundle of ripe juniper berries. Bundled together were freshly picked plants holding little bright red flowers that held sweet liquid in the base of the flower. She pulled off the petals of the flowers one by one and sipped on the delicate drops of liquid. Near her son was another bundle of jerky.

"Da' t'ah nidiiish neiiseeł?" *Am I still dreaming?* she whispered as she cautiously looked around her.

Her hopes of survival were interrupted with the sound of several of her Naabeehó people wailing. Soldiers were barking orders. Once again, the men were told to line up for their supply of rations. Dééd Yázhí saw the faded figures of men with stooped shoulders walking toward the wagons laden with the food supplies. Several women and children continued to cry. Once again, the fear that was her daily companion came back to visit her. She watched as her little one bravely fed at her breast.

How long can I keep him safe? she asked herself. Tears of fear filled her eyes as she watched the long line of men waiting to receive their rations. So far, the soldiers were satisfied in asking the men how many women and children they were with.

When will they become more curious and begin to count the people individually? she silently wondered. Tears of fear filled her eyes and spilled over onto her nursing son.

291

Dééd Yázhí watched as a young man walked toward her as she was bundling up her thin blankets and new supply of food. She shook out of fear.

Ch'iiyą́ą́n kǫ́ǫ́ sinilígíí daats'í yiyiiłtsą́ą́go 'aadéę́' nídiilwod? Nihich'iiyą' nihighaidoo'nił daats'í yiniiyé 'aadéé' yigááł? *Maybe he saw the food that was sitting here and so that is why he is coming this way? Maybe he is going to try to take our food from us?* she wondered as she watched the young man walking straight up to her. He approached her and said,

"Na', kǫ́ǫ́ tó sik'azígíí ła' díídlį́į́ł." *Here, drink some cool water.*

Dééd Yázhí looked at the young man, looked at the container of water, then reluctantly looked away. She grabbed the container and gulped the water down then dipped her hand into the water and sprinkled it on her face. She was going to place drops of water on her little one's lips, but she remembered her people who were getting sick!

"'Ei shį́į́ díí tóhígíí yits'ą́ą́dóó shidine'é kanidaakai," *It could be this water that is making my people sick!* she whispered to herself, regretting that she drank the water. She whispered to herself,

"Díí yee' doo shą́ą́htéeh da. Díí tóhígíí yishdlą́ą́' nidi doo haada shidoolííł da, 'áko nidi shiyázhí 'éí t'áá yéego baa hastxi'. *I am healthy. Even if I drank this water, it will not do anything to me. But, my little one is not to be exposed to this water.*

She quickly gave the container of water back to the young man who then tucked it into his pouch. Becoming bolder, knowing she may have placed her health in jeopardy, she asked,

"Háísh ánít'į?" *Who are you?*

The young man bravely answered,

"Nizhé'é binaabaahii nishłį́į́ nít'ę́ę́'. Bá naashnish nít'ę́ę́' ałdó'. Bá na'nishkaadgo naaki nááhai. Nizhé'é ba'ałk'ee sédáago néyą. Nizhé'é bilį́į́' ałdó' bá baa 'áháshyą́ą́ nít'ę́ę́'. Nizhé'é na'abaah bits'ą́ą́dóó baa 'ákoniizį́į́' dóó bíhooł'ą́ą́' áádóó nizhé'é binaabaahii nishłį́įgo díkwííshį́į́ náhááh k'ad. Nilah 'aadę́ę́' ashíłł'a', nihaa 'áháshyą́ą́ dooleeł biniiyé. Nizhónígo nabidi'neeztą́ą́'. T'áá'ałtsogóó 'ayóo bił bééhózin. Shí 'éí t'ah íhoosh'aahígíí biniinaa 'áádę́ę́' ashi'dool'a'. Shádí dóó shida' nihá baa 'áhólyą́ą́ dooleeł shidíiniid nitsilí."

I was one of your father's warriors. I used to work for him as well. I herded sheep for him for several years. I grew up staying at your father's place. I also used to take care of your father's horses. I became aware of warfare and became a warrior under your father's teaching. I have been your father's warrior for several years now. Your brother sent me here to take care of you both. He has been trained very well. He is very knowledgeable about things. Me, I am still learning, that is why I am the one who was sent here. Take care of my older sister and my nephew for us, is what your younger brother told me.

Dééd Yázhí looked toward the eastern sky and whispered a prayer of gratitude to the Creator. She looked back at the stranger with tears of relief and gratefulness in her eyes. She decided the young man's eyes expressed kindness. The skin on his face was as smooth as her child's face. His eyelashes held tiny pieces of dust particles as he looked at her without blinking his eyes. His hair was pulled back and held in a loosely tied tsiiyééł *hair bun*. His eyes held her attention. She looked deeply into them, then quickly looked away and saw him do the same.

Their attention turned to the barking of orders from the soldiers and to the frantic cries of women and children. A woman was heard to hoarsely cry out,

"Dooda! T'ááshǫǫdí, dooda!" *No! Please, no!*

More commotion was heard, then more pleading from several Naabeehó people. The people gasped when they heard several gunshots. Dééd Yázhí saw many soldiers riding on their horses in a wild manner, whipping at the people's legs and yelling at them. The Naabeehó people who stood near her quickly picked up their few bundles, then slung them over their shoulders and stood ready to begin their walk once again. Dééd Yázhí turned to grab her heavy pack but found it missing. The young man stood waiting for her with the large pack on his strong, wide back. Her pack was pulling on his buckskin shirt. Dééd Yázhí felt guilty. Sensing her guilt, the young Naabeehó man said,

"Díí biniiyé shi'deel'a'. Shiláąjį' yínááł, t'ahdoo nihich'į' hodiwoshdą́ą́'." *This is the reason I was sent. Walk ahead of me before we get yelled at.* The kindness of the young man brought memories of her father that flooded into her mind, making her extremely homesick.

Her thoughts of her father were interrupted, when she heard the commotion again and saw that the soldiers had roped two people and were dragging them away from the procession of Naabeehó people. The people being dragged by the rope were an elderly couple. They were doubled over in pain as they clung onto the rope while being dragged. Dééd Yázhí became sick to her stomach when she saw her Naabeehó people trying to help pick up the elderly couple, but when they did, they were whipped by the soldiers with long horsewhips. The soldiers fired warning gunshots into the air, warning the rest of the Naabeehó people to stay away from the poor, sick elders.

As the Indian scouts were shouting confusing orders, Dééd Yázhí watched as the old man who had been dragged reached over and tried to pick up the old woman, who was possibly his wife. Seeing the act of compassion, a mean soldier pulled the couple to the side of the road and down a steep embankment. The old man slipped out of the rope. Seeing the woman being dragged away, he fell to his knees and cried hoarsely. Dééd Yázhí could see from his clothes that he too, like the people who were killed before, was suffering from an extreme attack of diarrhea. The soldiers whipped and barked at the Naabeehó people if they slowed down or made any attempts to help the wounded ones.

Dééd Yázhí felt hot tears fill her eyes as she heard a little girl screaming,

"Shimá sání! Shimá sání! Shimá sání!" *My maternal grandmother! My maternal grandmother! My maternal grandmother!*

Dééd Yázhí and the Naabeehó women gasped. How could her tall, gray-haired one be a part of this group who tortures her people? she wondered in pain as she felt dislike build up even more within her. She chose to walk at the end of the procession and because of her place in the procession, she could hear the helpless cries of the elderly people as they were left behind. The sick elders were left to die on the side of the dusty road.

Dééd Yázhí looked past the procession of Naabeehó people ahead of her and saw a stout, sturdy mountain. She heard her people whispering about this mountain being their mountain of the south. She also heard the men telling their sons their mountain of the south was the mountain which represented the turquoise of the midday sky.

She closed her eyes for a second and envisioned the beautiful turquoise stones that made up her father's necklace and his turquoise earrings. They were what this mountain represented. Her emotions sent her on a wild ride for the rest of the day as she saw their mountain coming closer while the big bright yellow sun rode its path through the sky toward the west.

She was in awe of the mountain and yet she was confused, angry, and disappointed. She remembered her father telling them their mountain of the south represented childhood in the cycle of life. She questioned, how could this mountain that represented childhood, within the cycle of life, disregard the suffering of the Naabeehó children as they watched their grandmothers and grandfathers being left in the dust to die a slow death? How could this mountain watch as the children were suffering from the soldiers' harsh treatment? How could this mountain not care that the children were starving and dying from thirst and fatigue? As she questioned the mountain of the south, she gave her mountain a pouty look with each question that marched through her mind.

She was mesmerized by the majestic appearance of their mountain. With every footstep, she brought her mountain closer to her.

"Doolá dó' ayóó 'ánoolnin da." *It is breathtakingly beautiful,"* she said as her voice brought thoughts that returned to their velvet softness once again.

"Eidí ga'," *I know,* was all the young Naabeehó man said.

This mountain does give me a sense of calm in the midst of all this confusion and meanness, Dééd Yázhí thought as she watched the mountain come closer and closer with each weary step.

She glanced back at the young man following her. Although the young man was carrying her cumbersome pack, she still felt a heavy burden on her shoulders. She knew for miles that the farther she walked toward the eastern direction, the farther she was walking away from her father and her mother and her youngest brothers and especially her younger sister, as well as the memories of the tall, gray-haired one. The little warm bundle she kept hidden under the light blanket she wrapped around her and her little one comforted her.

I should not have to hide him, she thought. He should be raised Naabeehó. He should be raised by his elders. Dééd Yázhí stopped, spun around on the soft heel of her moccasin and stopped to face the young Naabeehó man.

"Shizhé'éésh ił ahojooba' yínanineeztą́ą́'?" *Did my father teach you kindness?* she demanded to know.

"Aoo', ha'át'íí lá?" *Yes, what is it?* the young man answered as he looked past her to see if the soldiers noticed they had stopped walking while the Naabeehó people had continued walking.

"Shiyázhí ił ahojooba' yíhwiidooł'ááł, nisin," *I want my little one to learn kindness,* she claimed.

"Ne'awéé' bicheii yits'ą́ą́dóó 'íhwiidooł'áałgo 'át'é. Nizhé'é t'ah nihił hóló̜. Nizhé'é t'ah nidii níkanitáago 'át'é. Nideezhí 'ałdó t'ah yíkantáago 'át'é. T'áadoo nihaa yooznah da. Nizhé'é bił ná'ahiiniltsǫǫgo bicheii yázhí neidínóotįįł. T'áadoo nizhé'é bigáál dah nídiit'i' nahalingo yáníłti'í," *Your baby will learn from his maternal grandfather. Your father is still with us. Your father is still looking for you. He is still looking for your younger sister. He never forgot you both. When you see your father again, he will teach his grandson. Don't speak as if your father is no longer living,* the young man said with gentleness in his voice.

The young man leaned closer to her and said in a near whisper,

"Azhą shį́į́ ne'awéé' nihe'anaa'í ła' yáshchíin nidi, niyázhí Naabeehó nilį́. Tó 'Aheedlíinii nilį́." *Although your little one is born for one of our enemies, he is a Navajo. He belongs to the Water Flows Together People.*

Dééd Yázhí raised her eyes to meet the kind eyes of the young man. She was surprised the young Naabeehó man knew her clans. Her younger brothers and her father must have spoken of their clans often. Her heart was filling with joy.

A man knows who I am! her mind screeched. She wanted to tell her little one, but she kept the content of her heart hidden away. The gentle voice of the young Naabeehó man soothed her heart as he continued by saying,

"Niyázhí nihe'anaa'í 'éí dabinálí nidi Ma'ii Deeshgiizhnii dine'é 'éí dabicheii. 'Éí béénílniih. T'ahdoo nihe'anaa'í danihiiłtsééhdą́ą́' yówohjį' nááś yínááł. Nihe'anaa'í 'ayóo bádahachį'." *Although your little one is born for our enemy, his maternal grandfathers are of the Coyote Pass People. Remember that. Before our enemies see us, go on and walk forward. Our enemies are very angry.*

298

Dééd Yázhí's mind was reassured with the words of encouragement from the young man. As her heart settled down, she turned around and proudly followed the procession of her people.

When the sun began its slow descent toward the western horizon after casting a faint peach glow over the Naabeehó people, Indian scouts who served as interpreters announced they had come to a narrow crossing where the dusty road they traveled intersected with a wide shallow river. The soldiers were heard barking orders, wanting the people to stop walking so the soldiers could replenish their supply of water from the clear shallow river. The soldiers tried in vain to get the attention of their prisoners as they yelled angry shouts and repetitive gunshots. The people ignored the orders of the soldiers and rushed toward the shallow bank of the river as they carried any container they could use to collect water. For a short time, the tired, hungry, worried Naabeehó people forgot they were prisoners and collectively drank the cool water, then laughed and played in the shallow water under the watchful eye of their majestic mountain of the south.

Shifting the weight of her little one, Dééd Yázhí knelt down near the river's edge and reached into the water and watched as the water made a miniature waterfall as it ran over her hands.

"Yá'át'ééh, shik'éí. Tó 'Aheedlíinii nishłį." *Greetings, my relatives. I am of the Water Flows Together People.* In answer, the water tickled the palms of her worn hands, hands that were tired from carrying a heavy burden on her back for miles before the burden was lifted by the young man. The heavy burden of being a Naabeehó prisoner was lightened by the cool water.

With the young man's help, Dééd Yázhí sat down on the shallow bank of the river and slipped off her soft worn moccasins, then slowly lowered her feet into the water. Once again, she greeted the water by saying,

"Yá'át'ééh, shik'éí. Tó 'Aheedlíinii nishłį." *Greetings, my relatives. I am of the Water Flows Together People.*

When all the large barrels were filled with the river water, the soldiers fired several shots into the air to get the attention of their Naabeehó prisoners. Hearing the gunshots, the people became disheartened as they took their places behind the wagons and the soldiers.

Feeling her feet refreshed, Dééd Yázhí did not want to follow in the steps of her fellow prisoners. The road was damp from the water dripping out of the barrels. As she walked in the wet sand, she felt the water continuing to greet her as she followed the damp path before her that led to the wagon crossing.

In crossing the shallow river, the soldiers tied ropes between thick poles that were planted in the sandy river. With the ropes as a safeguard against the current and the quick sand, the Naabeehó people slowly crossed the river and continued on their sandy journey.

The soldiers ordered the people to stop for the night when the sun cast darkened orange rays on Mount Taylor. When Dééd Yázhí and the young man opened the pack in which their food supplies were kept she noticed a large bug crawling on the outside of a bag that someone's lumpy flour was kept in. Dééd Yázhí watched an elder man squeeze the life out of the bug. Inspecting the flour, he found large lumps in the yellowed flour. He picked out a lump and picked at the hardened flour. What he

300

found made Dééd Yázhí sick. The hardened lump was a bug just as fat and as long as the one he crushed in his hand.

Was this what her people ate that made them sick? her mind screamed. She told the Naabeehó people camped near them about their discovery. The people looked back at her with no sense of concern in their faces. She thought their look was a strange reaction to their discovery. The people sarcastically replied,

"Dichin yee' danihi'niighą́ą́'. Ha'át'íísh dó' dadiidį́į́ł? T'áá yee' ei t'éiyá bikiin nihi'di'noolkał." *We are dying of hunger! What else could we eat? That is all that we have to live on as we are being forced to walk.*

The women described the way they picked out the bugs and mixed the bacon grease with the flour, explaining how the flour gets hard if it is not eaten right away. They explained that trying to prepare the yellowed flour in the similar ways they prepared their beautiful ground corn was not an easy task. The women said the flour had no taste to it and became sticky like mud when mixed with water. Each Naabeehó woman knew their ground corn maintained a coarse consistency that remained pliable during preparation, but disdained the yellowed flour that turned into hard balls which were difficult to work into bread. The people who ate the flour either became constipated or had diarrhea. The children and the elderly Naabeehó people suffered the most from the pains of either illness. Mothers helplessly watched as their elders and their children suffered.

Dééd Yázhí heard the men beg to be allowed to leave the group to go look for herbs or to look for other sources of food.

"This land is foreign to you Navajo people. Because of that, it will only cause you men to take more time in searching for the medicinal plants and food sources," one soldier scolded. In sadness and in silence, the Naabeehó people resigned to their suffering.

Déédí Yázhí was aware the Naabeehó men could not look into their children's eyes because the children saw their father as their source of food, but the men were forbidden to hunt. Using slingshots, rocks, and sticks, the men did their best to catch prairie dogs, rabbits, and large rats when the animals ventured close enough to the people.

The young Naabeehó man waited until the attention of the people around him and Déédí Yázhí was directed elsewhere before he dug a shallow hole in the ground and buried the flour and all its bugs. Déédí Yázhí felt guilty for burying the flour, but she was not taking any chances in getting sick or making her little one sick. Without a second look, the young man covered the shallow grave with little twigs and walked away from it.

Déédí Yázhí appreciated the actions of the young Naabeehó man. She chided herself for joining him as he buried the flour, in doing so they were attracting attention to themselves. Their actions made her little one vulnerable to her people. She was fully aware of the hatred her people had for the soldiers. She drew her light blanket close around her and rejoined the young man.

The soldiers ordered the people not to move around in their camps but to settle down for the night. When their sacred mountain disappeared into the blackness of the night, several Naabeehó men stole away to gather herbs.

At full daylight, a rare occurrence took place. The men and the women and the children were counted. Usually, it was only the men who were counted. Once all the people were counted, the soldiers shouted orders and the Naabeehó people were ordered to continue eastward.

The people were told through Indian scouts they would be stopping at a small settlement that evening to rest. The soldiers warned the men and boys against stealing away, bothering the residents of the area, or raiding the fields of the people who occupied the valley. To keep the Naabeehó people under control, the men and boys were ordered to spend the night in a make-shift corral. The women were told not to build fires to keep them warm. The people were further told they would not receive their ration of food until they had completely passed the small settlement the next day.

A blanket of sadness was thrown over the entire procession by the words of the soldiers and the Indian scouts. Children searched the faces of their mothers to catch a glimpse of bravery, but the women stared back with unanswered question. No one slept that night.

Chapter Seventeen
Pueblo and Lava Country Lead to the Big River

The Naabeehó were not prepared for the scenery which came into view when they walked around the bend. Indian scouts told the Naabeehó people not to attempt to steal away to raid the surrounding villages because the Pueblo Indian people who lived in the area were treasures of the deities.

Dééd Yázhí was glad to concentrate on the landscape before her instead of the sharp lava rocks that pierced her feet through the soft moccasins her maternal grandfather made for her. She carefully picked the places where she stepped to preserve her beautiful moccasins.

When the little square Pueblo houses came into view, Dééd Yázhí forgot the sharp lava rock formations that made walking so difficult. The source of her pain changed. Looking at the scene before her, she felt an overwhelming sense of homesickness when she saw the Pueblo homes huddled against the rolling hills and lazy sloping sides of the low mesas. Her sense of homesickness was elevated when she saw lazy streams of smoke exiting the slightly slanting rooftops. Juniper trees did their best to stand tall as they dotted the rocky landscape, bringing to mind the scent of cedar.

Her mind flew back to the Kin yis'áanii dine'é *Hopi people* who also lived in square houses made of hewn sandstone built on top of mesas that rose from the landscape, which could be found a day's horse ride to the south of her beautiful Black Mesa. As tears made their way down her smooth, dirt-covered face, Dééd Yázhí closed her eyes. She could hear her father bartering with an older Kin yis'áanii hastiin *Hopi man* as they discussed a trade over hot bread that was baked inside a little outside oven on top of a high Hopi mesa.

Her memories brought her father's image close to her mind. She saw the load of firewood piled high on the travois her father brought to the Kin yis'áanii Mesa for trading. She could smell the sweet scent of the wood that had been cut from a dried juniper tree. She sniffed the air around her to solidify the scent of the freshly cut juniper wood. The scent was faint in her mind but strong enough to hold her lovely memory.

With her eyes still closed, Dééd Yázhí saw the beautiful stack of pale blue Kin yis'áanii piki bread that sat on the rough table at which her father and his Kin yis'áanii *Hopi* neighbor sat. In her mind, the older Kiis'áanii man was placing more things on the table for trade when he saw the many rabbits her father hunted, skinned and brought for bartering. She saw the bag of parched corn being plopped on the table. Her memory of the scent of parched corn heightened her sense of smell as her mouth began to water.

Dééd Yázhí licked her lips and when she did so, her salty tears made their way into her mouth to replace the memory of the taste of parched corn.

The sound of the young Naabeehó man asking,

"Ha'át'íí lá?" *What is it?* brought Dééd Yázhí out of her beautiful, memory.

"Shizhé'é yee' t'áadoo hooyání bénááshnii'," *All of a sudden, I remembered my father,* she replied softly as tears made their way down her face, carrying the dirt that lay in their path in miniature rivulets down her face.

She kept the memory of her father to herself to keep it safe in her mind so she could visit it later that evening when her people settled down for the night. Dééd Yázhí allowed her eyes to visit each little Pueblo house that hugged the hills and breathed a whisper of gratitude to each home for bringing the memory of her father close.

Tears continued to cleanse her face as her eyes visited each home. She knew a family sat inside each square home made of hewn rocks. She yearned to be a part of a family again and desperately wanted to sit and leisurely eat a meal and listen to stories of the various happenings during the day. She wanted to hear women scolding their husbands or their children as the sound of the women's voices echoed through the square house.

She envied the Pueblo people for living so close to her mountain of the south. She looked toward the mountain, which was now directly north of them. It was even more breathtakingly beautiful in the early evening sun.

Lost in the thoughts of her family, Dééd Yázhí noticed the young Naabeehó man was sitting on the ground and was leaning against her large heavy pack. He tenderly looked back at her and said,

"Nitsilí bił ná'ahiiniltsą́ągo bee háádíídááł. Nitsilí dó' nił ná'ahiiltsą́ągo yits'ą́ą́dóó bitah yá'ánááhoot'éeh dooleeł. Ayóo nidziilgo 'áté. Níni' ałdó' ayóo bidziil. Nízhánee', nizhé'é dóó nimá nizhónígo niyaa hooł'a'. Doo 'íits'a'ígóó t'óó nidine'é bikéé' yínááł. Díí shį́į hait'éego t'áá sáhí yíyééł nít'ę́ę́'. T'áá shí nidi shił nidaaz. Yówéé 'át'éego nidziil lá, t'óó nisin, níighahgi yisháałgo. Niyéél nidaaz nít'ę́ę' nidi ne'awéé' t'áá néshjee'go yíłtééł. Asdzání yá'át'éehii nílį́." *When you see your younger brother again, you will feel better. When your younger brother sees you, he will also feel better. You are very strong. Your mind is also very strong. You are fortunate that your father and your mother have raised you well. Without a sound, you just walk after your people. It is uncertain how you were able to carry this pack all by yourself. It is even heavy to me. I just think you are really strong as I walk beside you. Although your pack was heavy, you still kept your baby right next to you. You are a young woman who is good.*

Dééd Yázhí heard the words of the young Naabeehó man and his words made her feel stronger, but she was also surprised by the amount of information he told her. She decided he told her those things because he felt sorry for her, or more likely, because he saw her as an older sister. With slight embarrassment, she quietly answered,

"Doo saad honishłǫ́ǫ́góó t'óó 'nihidine'é bikéé' eeshjił nít'ę́ę'. Ei shį́į hait'éego da saad honishłǫ́ǫgo nihidine'é ła' shidiizts'ą́ą'go dóó shíká 'eelwodgogo, she'awéé' yidoołtséél nisingo biniinaa, t'áadoo 'íits'a'í t'óó 'akéé' eeshjił nít'ę́ę'.'"

307

I did not complain as I followed our people, carrying my pack
on my back. I was afraid that if I complained, one of our people
would have heard me, and if that person helped me, I was
afraid they might see my little one, so I just carried my pack and
followed in silence.

Dééd Yázhí did not realize the young Naabeehó man truly
admired her strength. She looked up at him and smiled at him.
He in turn, offered his tender smile she loved seeing. He tickled
her heart. She sadly realized the tall, gray-haired one's smile
did not tickle her heart the way the young Naabeehó man's
smile did. Slowly and thoughtfully, she rhetorically said quietly
whispered to herself,

"Dooda. She'awéé' bizhé'é nihe'anaa'í nilį́į́ nít'éę́'. Doo nidi
bił ahidiists'a' da nít'éę́'. Díí dinééh éí bił ahidiists'a'. Díí dinééh
shijéí nidaazgo yaa 'ákónániidzįįh. Shijéí bił hózhǫǫ́go 'ánáyiil'įįh.
Bizaad yee shaa jooba'. Shich'į' yáłti'go chánah nishłį́įgo
'ánáshiidlaa. Doo shik'éí nilį́į́ da nidi, shiyéél shá yooyééł."

No. My baby's father was our enemy. I did not understand
his language. I understand the language of this young man.
This young man notices when my heart is heavy. He makes my
heart happy. He is kind to me by means of his words. He has
rejuvenated me through his words. He is not related to me and
yet, he carries my pack for me.

Dééd Yázhí noticed the young Naabeehó man was looking
at her when she glanced at him. He was sitting on the ground
resting against her large pack. She wrinkled her nose at him.
The young man wrinkled his face as he looked back at her and
they both laughed at one another. Dééd Yázhí wanted to laugh
again. She wanted her little one to hear her laughter. She felt a
lightness since the young Naabeehó man came to help her.

When the golden light of the sun was enveloped by the western horizon, the soldiers rode their horses in circles, surrounding the people, and forcing the people to move in closer to one another. Once the Naabeehó people settled closer to one another than they had on previous nights, the soldiers dismounted their horses after which an Indian scout led the horses away while the soldiers unrolled their bedding on the hard, lava-crusted ground.

The orders the soldiers shouted were crisp and impatient as they made further preparations to camp. The people were told that if they tried to escape, they would be shot without a warning. Mothers could be heard as they scolded their sons in subdued tones, telling them to behave because their families could not bear any more pain from the loss of another loved one.

Dééd Yázhí unfolded her bedding and sat down on the ground. Small, black, round, sharp rocks were strewn across the floor of the wide valley. Placing her moccasins under her head to serve as a pillow, she heard the young Naabeehó man moving about. She looked over and in the dim light she saw him rubbing his back against the sharp, black rocks that served as his bed. She heard him say,

"Doolá dó' bik'e' ahwiihgo tsé hadaaz'áhígíí shíígháán deighaz da. 'Aaah. Ayóo! Tsé hadaaz'áhígíí shik'i nida'iizǫ́ǫz. K'ad éí t'áá shǫǫh shi'éé' biníkáních'ih doo. K'ad éí ghaazh dooleeł." *Doesn't that feel good as the rocks that stick out scratch my back. Aaah. Ouch! One of the sharp rocks cut a hole in my clothes. Now, at least the breeze will come through the holes. Now, it is sleepy time.*

Dééd Yázhí smiled at the young man's expression, "K'ad éí ghaazh dooleeł," which is an expression a parent speaks as an endearment. She slept in spite of the sharp black rocks that became a mattress for the many Naabeehó families who lay in the shallow crevices of the red earth to avoid sleeping on the rocks.

The Naabeehó people and the soldiers got little rest that night. Even the air was carried about in a restless manner by the faint breezes that appeared from nowhere. Everyone released a sigh of relief when dawn was announced by the faint, white light of the sun. Wanting to get the Naabeehó people out of the valley in a hurry, the soldiers commanded their orders. The people were not allowed to make preparations for a meal after the long, tense night.

"This valley belongs to the Pueblo people! There will be no wandering away from the campsite! There will be no stealing from the peaceful Pueblo people. Anyone one found wandering will be shot!" the people were told by the soldiers. Wanting to put fear into the hearts of the Naabeehó people, the Indian scouts added additional information in their translation than what was expressed by the soldiers because they disliked the Naabeehó people.

The long procession of soldiers on horses, Naabeehó people, and horse-drawn wagons was being rushed along the wide dirt road by unfeeling soldiers. Toward noon Dééd Yázhí heard a commotion up ahead. With a heavy heart, she expected someone to be sick or to have been killed by the heartless soldiers. The young Naabeehó man put his burden down and ran ahead to see what caused the commotion. Soldiers could be heard yelling at some people as they poked the people recklessly with their rifles, urging them to move forward.

After a long span of time, the young man rejoined Dééd Yázhí and told her of the predicament the Naabeehó people found themselves in. The lava beds the procession had approached were associated with tragic incidences in ancient Naabeehó history. The people were unwilling to tread over the lava beds, and yet the dusty road they traveled wound in and around the lava beds, making the people fearful. How could they make the soldiers understand that traveling over the lava beds was taboo and that there would be retaliation for disturbing the place? The children, having become extremely curious, were insistent in asking questions about the apprehension of their elders. The elders impatiently told the children the retelling of the tragic story was limited to the winter season. Elders pacified the youngsters' curiosity by promising to tell them a condensed version of the story once they had passed the dreaded lava beds.

The soldiers forced the people to follow the dusty trail that led eastward. Three men were killed because they refused to follow the first set of wagons that went through. In fear, the people cautiously stepped onto the large solitary lava field. Great anxiety taxed the strength of the Naabeehó people.

By the time Dééd Yázhí, the young Naabeehó man, and the few people straggling behind made their way through the sharp flesh-piercing lava beds in distress, the sun's weary light cast deep purple shadows from the western horizon. Dééd Yázhí wished the people ahead would move faster to put more space between her and the petrified valley. When she looked down at the path before her, she saw blood collecting in pools in the crevices on the ground. The blood was from the many Naabeehó people whose flesh on the bottom of their feet had been cut and torn by the sharp lava path.

She shivered out of fear and anxiety. She longed for the bravery of her father and her younger brothers. Her father would know what to say to put her fears to rest. Looking toward the mountain, she felt the strength of the Naabeehó stories her father told her when she was younger.

The soldiers ordered the Naabeehó people to make camp for the night. As Dééd Yázhí had feared, they had not put enough space between themselves and the drama of the lava beds. She anticipated she would not be getting any rest for her tired body.

While she settled down to her nightly dinner of jerky and water, Dééd Yázhí found her tired, distressed mind making the blood in her head pulsate loudly, causing her to imagine the pounding came from the ground. When darkness covered the ground, she was jerked awake just as she was falling asleep to hear and feel the tragic details of the ancient story.

Without considering the safety of her child, Dééd Yázhí wished she was in the midst of the crowd of Naabeehó people ahead. When she could finally separate imagination from reality, she found their surroundings to be quiet and very peaceful. Parents must have told their children bits and pieces of the ancient story because there was the absence of the sound of children crying, whining, or complaining. No one was making a sound. Dééd Yázhí found the quiet that surrounded her eerie but peaceful.

The young Naabeehó man announced he was going to relieve himself. In his absence, Dééd Yázhí was about to scream from the heavy deafening silence she became acutely aware of. Soon, she found herself desperately in need of relieving herself as well. She waited. She tried to distract herself from her body's persistence by naming the constellations that appeared above but once she named them all, her swollen bladder forced her to get up. She tied her little one in the sling and rushed away from her slumbering people. She stumbled past a soldier who held out his rifle, warning her not to go much farther. Glad that she did not have to be alone in the dark, she swung her little one onto her back and quickly squatted as her body shook from chills that attacked her body. Quickly she stood up, lowered her biil éé' *rug dress*, kicked dirt onto her still-warm urine, then turned around and raced past the soldier with her little one bouncing at her side. As fast as she could, she slid under her thin blanket and placed her little one beside her. To comfort herself, she offered her little one her breast. Her heart beat less wildly when she fed her little one.

"Háádę́ę́'sh náádááł? Kodi nánísdzáá nít'ę́ę́' doo kǫǫ 'oołhosh da. Nihich'ị' shíni' íí'áá nít'ę́ę́'," *Where are you coming back from? When I came back, the two of you were not sleeping here. I was worried about you,* Dééd Yázhí heard someone say in a hoarse whisper.

"Jįįdą́ą́' tó 'ádeiyishdlą́ą́' lá," *I drank too much water earlier today,* she whispered in embarrassment.

"Nihe'anaa'í kǫǫ nidaakai. T'áadoo t'áá sáhí níléígóó nídídáhí," *Our enemies are around here. Don't go out there by yourself,* the young Naabeehó man said quietly.

"Hágoshį́į," *O.K.,* was all Dééd Yázhí could say. She smiled to herself. She loved having someone care about her safety. She thought of their little humorous exchange of wrinkling their nose and face at one another and smiled. Her heart felt warm.

Staring into the black, starry sky, Dééd Yázhí asked the young Naabeehó man if he was still awake. Quietly, he turned toward her voice, asking her,

"Ha'át'íí lá?" *What is it?*

Without responding, she moved closer to him just so she could feel the warmth of another person other than her child. The young man sensed her need for comfort and stretched out his arm and placed it under her soft tsiiyééł *hair bun*, and with his other hand, he covered her with an additional thin rug blanket.

Dééd Yázhí had been without the comfort of another person for so long. She could not move, she lay there and allowed an occasional tear to run from her eyes and fall into her hair. She tried in vain to memorize the closeness of the young man. Frustration filled her mind. Her imagination was working overtime. She could not erase the sound of heavy footsteps pulsating in her head!

Wait … she thought. She was afraid to, but she forced herself to listen to the pounding sound again. She felt relief. The pounding sound she heard was the sound of the young Naabeehó man's heartbeat as his pulse pounded in her ears. She had forgotten the sound of another person being so close, close enough to hear the steady beat of their heart. Dééd Yázhí moved closer to him to feel his warmth and to hear his heartbeat. She fell asleep with a faint smile on her face.

Dééd Yázhí was so relieved to see a faint white light in the eastern sky. She finally relaxed her body and allowed sleep to visit her without interruption. The gentle nudging of the young man awakened her to a full sunrise. He had set out jerky and water for them to eat and had beaten some juniper berries into a plum-colored soft mush. Grateful for the attention he gave her, she ate in silence and thanked him for helping her through the night.

****

Three more days the Naabeehó people were forced onward toward the east, walking nearly eleven miles a day. The soldiers wanted the people to walk fifteen miles a day, but the elders, the sick ones, and the few sheep and goats the people were herding slowed the long procession. On the third day, after having left the lava beds, the soldiers told the Naabeehó people they were once again in the territory of another group of Pueblo people.

Once again, the Naabeehó people were warned not to leave the camp. Seeing the large cultivated fields of corn and melons reminded the people what they had been forced to give up. The sad look in the eyes of the Naabeehó men told many stories of their own great fields of corn, which they were privileged to have planted near their homes in Dinétah *Navajoland.* Seeing the vast cultivated fields reminded the Naabeehó people of their plight in the absence of corn, melons, squash, and beans.

The feeling of remorse and desperation was being compounded with every step as the people walked from the edges of one cornfield to another. In haste, the soldiers herded the people onward, fearful of losing control of the

Navajo people. The hungry people filled their empty stomachs with their saliva that collected in their mouths as they passed one cornfield after another.

On the late evening of the third day, the soldiers who were not assigned to guarding the Navajo people stood in a huddle and laughed about how fast they made the people walk.

"We know we got fifteen miles out of these savages," jeered one soldier as the other soldiers congratulated one another for only losing three people.

"We lost one pregnant woman who was bleeding, I think because she miscarried," one soldier stated as he laughed.

"Well, hell, we couldn't slow down for her, so Slim here shot her," another soldier announced proudly.

"That's two savages we don't have to worry about!" the soldier announced.

"What about that disgusting old man you shot. He was dying anyway because he had an attack of diarrhea. We could not have him slowing us down. We are behind in our schedule in getting these savages to Fort Sumner," another soldier said as he caressed his rifle.

"We averted a war with the Pueblo band of Indians by firing on the man who was trying to steal some melons, don't you think?" a young soldier asked.

"How many more filthy Navajos are we going to have to shoot if we have to run them this fast again?" one young soldier asked, smiling, as he squatted on the ground drinking water. The other young soldiers laughed at his comment and prepared to settle the people down for the night.

"Remember, you are young recruits! Just because you signed up to fight in the Civil War does not mean you have to shoot these Navajo Indians. This is a real delicate task we are attending to. We are supposed to get these marauding Navajo Indians to Fort Sumner, even if it means we have to put our hate for them aside. Do you understand?" an officer demanded.

"Yes. Yes, sir" was the unanimous reply from the soldiers.

"Then disperse! Take your places as we lead them onward!" was the last command.

The next day, the soldiers set a slower pace for the people and left the wide, dusty road for a narrower road that turned slightly southward. The weather became warm, making the Naabeehó people more fatigued, hungry, and thirsty. The shallow, wide river they crossed several days ago was still their constant companion as it meandered near the dusty road, then wandered away from it again, only to run alongside it again.

If the people had to leave the shallow, wide river in this heat, the soldiers were sure they would have lost many of their prisoners, but when their prisoners saw the river meander southward in the same direction as the new road, the Naabeehó people were easily turned southward. Without warning, the people realized the little river they were following had intersected with another river.

The soldiers had slowed down and wanted the people to settle into groups. Once again, the people had to cross a river. This time, the river ran deeper, wider, and more swiftly. The anxiety of the people began to run very high. The people looked back at the little river they had followed for miles. They were content to walk beside the little river and drink from its bounties. The Indian scouts announced the people would have to cross the swiftly running river. Watching the swift current flow past made the Naabeehó people dizzy.

Before she even reached the river, Dééd Yázhí could hear cries of,

"Yíiyá! Yíiyá! Yíiyá!" *Scary! Scary! Scary!*" as the words echoed toward the back of the long procession.

"We will begin crossing the river tomorrow," the people were told. As the people prepared to camp for the night, they were further told to stay close to one another because they had entered dangerous territory. Indian scouts told the people they had entered the territory where the Mexican slave traders ran loose.

The Naabeehó men who had participated in retaliation raids in search of their captured Naabeehó children and wives were familiar with the slave traders. The Naabeehó men told of stories where they had tracked the Naakai *Mexican* slave traders as far as the great river. The tired Naabeehó people had heard their elders warning them of the great Rio Grande River, but the people never dreamed that the harmless little river they followed for several days led to the great river.

****

The Rio Grande River was the natural boundary over which Naabeehó people were never to cross. The great river was on the eastern side of the land the Diné 'Anaa'í *Enemy Navajos* occupied.

The older men who were once great warriors knew they were being chased to a bad place. They were aware of the danger that lay as close as the next hill. They knew of the danger

318

that lay just across the great river. The strong men trembled with fear. They knew they had been trained for warfare and hardship, but their women and their children were not prepared for the harshness of the lands the enemy occupied.

Out of habit, the men looked around to see if they had entered Diné 'Anaa'í territory, while the women and children looked into the hills to look for a prairie dog or a rabbit their fathers could kill for dinner. The children could taste the meat of the little animals as they tightly held their sunken abdomens.

The Diné 'Anaa'í *Enemy Navajos* were also Naabeehó people. They spoke the same language as the Naabeehó, but they lived very near to the great river. Looking for land in the east, they went as far as the great river but they never crossed it. In the beautiful hills just west of the great river was where the Diné 'Anaa'í made their home.

The Naabeehó men remembered stories that were told of how fiercely the naabaaahii *warriors* raided to get back their women and children who had been stolen by the slave raiders. As raids of retaliation by the Naabeehó naabaahii *Navajo warriors* became more violent, the Spaniards, the New Mexican troops, and the ranchers who wanted to punish Navajo raiders found the Diné 'Anaa'í *Enemy Navajo* settlement west of the Rio Grande easy prey for the Spaniards, troops, and ranchers who wanted revenge.

The Diné 'Anaa'í became the target for the many real enemies of the Naabeehó, causing even the Diné 'Anaa'í to turn against their Naabeehó people. Soon the Diné 'Anaa'í began to lead the troops and ranchers west into Tséyi' *Canyon de Chelly,* an area considered by the soldiers to be a stronghold of the southwest and in the midst of Naabeehó territory. Without the help of the Diné 'Anaa'í the New Mexican ranchers would not have been able to point out the troublesome Naabeehó raiders who lived in Dinétah *Navajoland*. There were times when the Diné 'Anaa'í, themselves, raided the Naabeehó people because they were so angry with them for causing the New Mexican troops and ranchers to come after them instead. Their only fault was that they lived in a vulnerable area. They suffered because they lived not far from the main dusty road that led into Naabeehó country.

The children heard the men quietly discussing the Diné 'Anaa'í. Without fear, the children had many questions to ask. This new knowledge of another group of Navajos took their minds off of their hunger and fatigue for several hours as they waited for the loud bark of the soldiers.

****

The little river the procession had followed for many days was the Rio San Jose, which joined the Rio Puerco quite a distance to the north. The Naabeehó people had bravely crossed both rivers. The crossing of the two rivers took two whole days. The people were faced with the crossing of another river, a big wide river.

Naabeehó leaders could not keep the information to themselves. They told their people they had been warned many times during the Leadership meetings never to cross the big river because that was where their protection from their four sacred mountains ended. The Naabeehó people tried begging the soldiers not to force them to cross the river, but the soldiers were deaf to their pleas.

The wagons carrying food and water and ammunition were loaded onto short rafts which were floated across the big wide river with very little difficulty. Witnessing this, the people settled down a bit. Once all the wagons were on the other side, the soldiers pushed the Naabeehó people, who had been ordered to gather in groups, onto the rafts.

No one group wanted to be the first to cross the river on a raft. One brave young woman, one who had been raped by two soldiers and one Indian scout in the lava beds, was so overcome with grief from the violent incident that she saw the river as the answer to her dilemma. Since leaving the lava beds, the young woman found it difficult to live with the humility.

While sitting on a make-shift travois on the bank of the river, the brave young woman told the women she could not force from her mind the memories of how the evil white men and the evil Indian scout had cut her biil éé' *rug dress* off of her body with such force her dress burned her skin as it was ripped away. Forced to walk a ways away from her fellow prisoners, the woman reported she was left naked. Crying, the woman told how she sat down on the ground as a means to conceal her lower body but the soldiers whipped her and forced her to run behind a small hill. There, they ripped into her body, tore at her hair, bit her tender skin, and grunted loudly in her ear. The rocks under her back, her buttocks, and the back of her neck cut into her skin as the determined soldiers pushed down heavily on her. Each scream she attempted to make was met with a handful of sand and rocks, the woman said as tears ran down and mixed with the dirt on her face to make patterns on the woman's cheeks. The woman told of how the two soldiers left her in a helpless state, as she defenselessly felt the Indian scout repeat the beastly act upon her. When the Indian scout stood up, he kicked sand in her face, angry that she did not put up a fight.

Crying, the heartbroken woman told about her mother and sisters who rushed behind the hill to her side when they saw the men return. They covered her with a coarse blanket and helped her get up. Not wanting the soldiers to kill the woman they raped, her family prepared a travois to transport her.

Having relived the memory again, the young heartbroken woman looked deep into the swirling water below the sandy bank and without a word pushed herself out of the make-shift bed her mother and sisters had prepared for her. Several women and children screamed as they watched the crying woman disappear under the raft that rested near the river bank.

The Naabeehó women and children helplessly looked downstream in disbelief. The women screamed when the woman's head surfaced, bobbed up and down with the current. They continued to watch with tears flowing down their faces as the woman disappeared.

The warning, "Naabeehó are not to cross this river," echoed in the Naabeehó people's ears. This is why they said that. It was because of death, Dééd Yázhí thought as pains of sorrow gripped her heart.

How many more people have to die before the soldiers decide we have been punished enough? she thought as she heard echoes from the Naabeehó people who were asking the same question. Little did she know that their suffering had just escalated.

The rafts carrying children safely glided across the swift-running river and were unloaded, then sent back to the opposite shore to transport more Naabeehó people across. Dééd Yázhí stood frozen in her tracks on the sandy bank, unwilling to budge because she had not been given the opportunity to greet the flowing water. She stepped closer to the river bank and softly said,

"Yá'át'ééh. Shí Tó 'Aheedlíinii dine'é nishłį́. Shiyázhí shéstł'ónígíí 'ałdó' Tó 'Aheedlíinii dine'é nilį́. Nihaa 'áhólyą́ą doo." *Greetings. I am of the Water Flows Together People. My little one who is tied to me is also of the Water Flows Together People. Take care of us.*

With those few words, Dééd Yázhí felt safe enough to cross the river. She hesitated, looking behind her to look for the young Naabeehó man, but she did not see him. Instead, she felt his breath on her hair. Straightening her back, she looked for a safe place to step down. Not wanting to attract attention to herself and her little one, she tightened her grip on her little one in her blanket and quietly jumped onto the unsteady raft. The young Naabeehó man took a big step onto the raft. The weight from his body and the large pack he carried caused the raft to sway, making it become unsteady. Women screamed as the raft swayed. More people were being herded onto the raft. Dééd Yázhí was glad she and the young man were already on the raft where they claimed their spot. Others had to precariously cling to the raft as they settled into place.

The more the Naabeehó people pleaded with the soldiers to leave them there on the western bank of the river, the more impatient the soldiers became. With the ends of their rifles, the soldiers shoved the Naabeehó people onto the rafts, hollered at the dirty white men maneuvering the rafts, then shoved the rafts off with long poles.

Dééd Yázhí looked around her, then down at the water and immediately became dizzy. She reminded herself that she had greeted the flowing water and noticed the beating of her heart had slowed a little. She wobbled, and steadied herself against the large pack the young Naabeehó man carried. Her little one squirmed in her tight hold and started to squeal. Loosening her grip on him, she leaned more of her weight on the large pack.

"Áłtsé," *Wait,* the young Naabeehó man whispered into her hair as he steadied her. He set the large pack down on the raft, then grabbed her shoulders and said,

"Shinahjį' nitah hółdzil," *Lean against me to strengthen yourself,* he whispered. Dééd Yázhí leaned against the young Naabeehó man's words more than on the man. Leaning against his words and his strong body, she felt stronger. She became aware of his close presence. She felt his breath on her hair, which brought an emotion Dééd Yázhí had not felt since she and her little one had left Fort Canby, and more specifically, since the tall, gray-haired one still came to visit her. She closed her eyes tight at the thought that she wished she had washed her hair with yucca soap so the young man could breathe in the sweet scent of yucca soap instead of the smelly mutton tallow and dirt she applied to her hair and skin daily.

Embarrassed that she smelled like mutton tallow, Dééd Yázhí slowly turned and buried her face in the young Naabeehó man's chest. Many emotions began marching through her mind. There was the tall, gray-haired one who did not know he had a son.

There was the feel of having the tall, gray-haired one breathing on her hair when he lovingly held her in his arms. There was the longing look he gave her the last night they had spent together. Feeling guilty for thinking those thoughts, Dééd Yázhí shook her head violently.

Her mind raced back to their present predicament. Watching the young woman throw herself into the swirling current brought back to her mind clear memories of her younger sister.

Was my younger sister raped the way the young woman was raped? Did my younger sister cross this river too? Is she in the north, in Ute country? Overcome with grief, Dééd Yázhí leaned heavily against the young Naabeehó man as her body shook with sobs. The young man held her and her little one tight in his right arm as he kept his balance with his left arm.

Chapter Eighteen
A Stolen Baby!

The young man helped Dééd Yázhí turn around and told her to sit down on their large pack, which she did with such heaviness that the raft shook and caused the women to scream. Once they crossed to the other side, the soldiers grabbed the Naabeehó people by their hair, their arms, or their clothes to pull them onto the shallow bank.

Wanting to avoid the soldiers' forcefulness, Dééd Yázhí clumsily pushed herself off of the raft and stepped on a wide flat rock. Not wanting to lose her grip on her little one, she held tightly onto the sling where her little one lay quietly. Naabeehó women scrambled up the side of the shallow bank. A wild Naabeehó woman grabbed the back of the sling Dééd Yázhí had wrapped around her shoulders and waist and pulled herself up the side of the bank. Dééd Yázhí could not believe she was being pulled back into the water by the weight of the wild Naabeehó woman.

She leaned forward with all her strength. Her little one was being crushed by the woman's weight and Dééd Yázhí leaning forward. Her baby squirmed and squealed loudly. Feeling herself being pulled off of the rock on which she was precariously balancing one foot, Dééd Yázhí shifted her weight, throwing her hands up to keep her balance. To her horror, the sling holding her little one tore and snapped under the weight of the wild woman. In slow motion, her little one rolled out and landed on her foot, teetering before her. Dééd Yázhí struggled hard to keep her balance. She realized that if she moved her foot, her little one would roll into the water. The wild woman released her hold on the sling and fell back into the fast running water.

Dééd Yázhí heard her people gasp when they saw her little one. The Naabeehó women just stood in one place staring down at her little one. With no one holding her back, Dééd Yázhí regained her balance, reached down, picked up her little one and hugged him close as her body convulsed with quiet sobs. Tears of love and fright slid down her face and settled on her little one's soft skin. Quickly, she stuffed her little one into her loose rug dress and stepped onto dry ground. Her voice shaking and her entire body shaking, she whispered,

"Nikáa'jį' hazlį́į́', shiyázhí." *You have been spared, my little one.*

Her little one, not used to the rough feel of her woolen rug dress cried and squirmed but Dééd Yázhí held him tight as she quietly said,

"Ních'aad, shiyázhí, ních'aad. Doo lá dó' doo dahígi 'áhóót'įįd da! *Don't cry, my little one, don't cry. What a terrible thing to have happened!*

In the confusion, a little boy pushed against Dééd Yázhí and said,

"Na'," *Here*, as he held up her little one's sling, now dirty from the river bank.

Compared to her people, the color of her son's skin was pale and he had light brown hair. What Dééd Yázhí had painstakingly concealed from her Naabeehó people for so long, they now saw in broad daylight.

Dééd Yázhí looked for the young Naabeehó man, but he was hidden from her view by all the women who were yelling at her and spitting on her. Older Naabeehó women yelled at her, telling her she was a traitor. An older woman spat at her little one bundled in her arms, calling him names. Other women told Dééd Yázhí she should have not cared for one of the enemy's children, questioning her loyalty to her people.

"Ha'át'ííshą' biniinaa nihe'anaa'í be'awéé' ła' dah nííł'įįł?" *Why are you hiding one of our enemy's babies?* a Naabeehó woman demanded.

"Háadishą' dah nííł'įįł nít'ę́ę́'?" *Where did you hide him?* another asked.

"Háísh be'awéé' bił na'íłjooł?" *Whose baby are you hiding?* a young woman questioned.

"Háíshą' ei 'awéé' bee níní'įį'?" *From whom did you steal that baby?* an older woman demanded to know.

Dééd Yázhí trembled as her mind began to comprehend the reaction of her people, but she was not prepared for the reaction of the mean soldiers. Two young soldiers told their superior that a white settler's baby may have been kidnapped by a Navajo woman. Pushing aside the Naabeehó women, several soldiers surrounded Dééd Yázhí and her little one then called for the Indian scout to interpret their message.

328

"Ask her to produce the baby," the officer ordered.

The Indian scout ordered,

"Awéé'. Awéé'," *The baby, the baby.*

"Dooda!" Dééd Yázhí said with bravery as she tightly hugged her little one.

"Awéé'. Awéé'," the scout yelled once again.

Dééd Yázhí put her head down as if she were protecting her little one with her head and refused to answer.

"Where's that sheep-herding boy who can interpret? Maybe he can get some information for us. We don't want to get these savages riled up. Maybe this is the kid some savage was reported to have had for Lt. Folton," the officer carelessly yelled out.

"Who is Folton?" a young soldier asked.

"He is a decorated officer who was reassigned to join the Union soldiers in the South. He is the reason we can't overlook this child, even though the child looks more like the savage than Folton. That child could be Folton's. We have our orders!" the officer reported.

"Did anyone see the child?" a soldier asked.

"Where is that little savage boy? We need him before these people really get riled up and start getting themselves killed. We reported their numbers before we left Fort Canby so we can't lose too many, even though we don't care who survives. Get that little sheep-herding boy, now!" demanded the officer, at which the soldiers scattered to search for the young boy.

"They are already riled up from crossing the river, sir," a young sympathetic soldier added.

"I can't wait until we get *all* these savages across the Rio Grande so we can turn back to Fort Canby," the officer huffed.

The officer angrily pushed Dééd Yázhí to a clearing, away from the Naabeehó people and the soldiers. While soldiers were busy transporting more Navajos across the river, Dééd Yázhí sat under a grove of cottonwood trees. She was so upset with herself. Tears danced in her eyes, threatening to fall out of their little pockets in her eyes. In trying to hide her little one she only attracted attention to him, and now his little life was in danger. Tears for her little one found their way down her dirt-and-water-stained face.

Dééd Yázhí became worried when she noticed the sun had slipped downward to get closer to its resting place on the western horizon. She wondered what they were going to do with her. In the distance, she saw the young Naabeehó man standing on the outskirts of the maddened crowd of women. The group was closely watched by soldiers so the young man could not leave the group to join Dééd Yázhí and her little one. Dééd Yázhí noticed the young man was guarding the large pack he carried for her.

Dééd Yázhí felt a gentle tug at her skin. She looked down and watched her little one nursing at her breast. The sight before her brought her comfort but her comfort was short-lived when she remembered she had not eaten for the entire day. She was glad her little one had not started eating food yet. She never trusted the soldiers' food. Dééd Yázhí made a promise to herself, to keep feeding her little one so he would not become sick like so many of her Naabeehó people.

Her admiration for her son was interrupted when she heard a young voice she had not heard in a long time. She jerked her head up when she heard a young voice say,

"Shimá." *My mother.*

A gentle smile of recognition began at the corners of her lips and slowly spread across her face. She wanted to yank the young Naabeehó 'ashkii *Navajo boy* into her arms and hold him close, but she was afraid the soldiers would take him away from her. She gently touched the young boy's arm and felt strength surge into her fingers, then flow into her arm and extend slowly throughout her body. She knew her little one also felt the strength that surged through her body. Dééd Yázhí hugged her little one and in doing so, she was hugging the young Naabeehó 'ashkii *Navajo boy* as well. Tears quickly made their way down her face as if they were looking for a place to hide from the soldiers.

"Da' niísh ałdó' akéé' yínááł?" *Are you also being forced to follow the others by walking?* the young boy asked, looking at her with tears in his eyes. Dééd Yázhí closed her eyes to memorize the voice of the young boy she had been looking for and missing and worried about.

"Háádę́ę́'shą' yínááł?" *Where are you coming from?* Dééd Yázhí asked him without answering. Fighting her desperate desire to jump up and hug the young boy, she reminded herself she had to be careful not to show any sign of love and closeness as she watched a soldier approach them.

The officer gripped the young boy by the shoulders and stared into his face. Shaking the boy by the shoulders, he demanded,

"Ask this woman where she got the baby she is holding."

"Her baby," the young boy answered bravely.

"Ask her who the father of the baby is. Ask now. Do you understand me?" the officer yelled.

Without hesitation, the young boy answered the officer by saying,

"Folton."

"Who is this savage? Who is she married to, do you know?" the officer demanded. Once again came the answer,

"Folton. Folton woman," the young Naabeehó ashkii *Navajo boy* answered bravely.

Hearing the answer, the officer rubbed his face with his hand, then stepped backward a couple of steps. Turning around, the soldier kicked a pile of sand into the air causing it to spray onto two soldiers' boots. Quickly, the officer announced,

"We have a problem. The young boy identified the Navajo savage as Folton's spouse! She was to remain at Fort Canby. The officers had their orders to protect the decorated officer's wife. She was never supposed to be sent along with the rest of the Navajo people. By whose orders was she ordered to vacate her quarters?"

"I do not know, sir. We joined this group of Navajos near Fort Fauntleroy."

"Well, soldiers, we have to escort her back to Fort Canby. That baby she was accused of stealing is Folton's baby. Folton is a decorated soldier with the Union Army," the officer said in a determined tone.

"Let's sleep on it. Who is going back to Fort Fauntleroy? Maybe the ones going back can escort her as far as Fort Fauntleroy and from there get another escort to take her back to Fort Canby."

"What a mess!" a young soldier was heard to say.

"Isn't that the truth! I am glad it wasn't any of my men who forced her out of the fort. This baby complicates the situation. Not only do we have to offer her protection, we have to keep the baby from starving."

The officer started laughing when he said,

"Aren't you all glad you didn't try anything on her? The Army was supposed to house and protect her."

The question was met with silence. No one answered. The young soldiers who stood in the circle became afraid. With that loud announcement, other soldiers standing nearby turned in unison and looked in Dééd Yázhí's direction.

"Let's get back to the task of getting all the prisoners across the river and then we will decide what to do with Folton's savage," the officer ordered.

Overjoyed to see a familiar face and one she could trust, Dééd Yázhí told the young Naabeehó 'ashkii *Navajo boy* about her and her little, letting the young boy know what happened to them since she last saw him. Looking to see where the soldiers were, she talked fast, saying.

"Ch'ééh níká désh'íí' nít'éé'. Naah shíni'go hooghan bii' kééhwiit'ínée yii'dóó hadanihineeshcháá'. T'áadoo 'áhánéhígóó t'óó 'aadę́ę́' akéé' dah a'diiłjid. T'óó 'áłtsé dah nihi'dí'níilkaad yéędą́ą́' éí t'áá sáhí nitsilí yázhí dóó shiyéél yishjił nít'éé'. Doo chohoo'íígóó shá nidaazgo bąąh nináshdááh nít'éé', azhą́ 'ákót'ee nidi nitsilí dah neesh'íįł nít'éé'. Nihidine'é nitsilí yázhí dayiiłtsą́ągogo shits'ą́ą́' haada deidoolíił nisingo biniinaa dah neesh'íįłgo bił asdisgo yishtééł nít'éé'. T'ah nít'éé' dinééh léi' nihíiyáá dóó shiyéél shá dah yidiiłjid. Shitsilí 'éí 'ei dinééh baa hashne'ígíí nihainíł'a' lá. Nihik'i déez'íį' dooleeł biniiyé nihainíł'a' lá. 'Éí dinééh shitsilíké dóó shizhé'é yił tánídadibah nít'ę́ę́' lá. 'Ayóo shíká'análwo'. Bee t'áá yédígo shik'i hooldoh.

I tried looking for you. I was worried about you when they chased us out of the home we lived in. I had no choice, I just started following them (the people) as I carried your baby brother. When we were first being chased along, I carried your baby brother and my pack all by myself. I would get very tired because the burden was very heavy for me. Even though it was like that, I still hid your baby brother. I was afraid if our people saw him, they would in some way hurt him so that is why I hid him by wrapping him up. I carried him that way. Without notice, a young man joined us and he started carrying my heavy pack for me. My younger brother sent the young man to us. He sent him so he could watch over us. He was a warrior with my younger brothers and my father. He really helps me. Because of him, I felt a great deal of relief.

Dééd Yázhí shook her head once she realized she was talking too much. Thinking of the young boy, she demanded,

"Háadi'shą' nanináá nít'ę́ę́? Níhósááh nít'ę́ę́'. Nich'į' shíni'íí'áá nít'ę́ę́'. Ashkii léi', t'ah áłts'íísí léi' ałdó' shaa nálwo'go shił nahalne'go 'ałk'íhwiilta' nít'ę́ę́'. Éí 'ashkii shitsilí yił shaa ní'áázh. K'ad éí 'ashkii yázhí bich'į' shíni'íí'á. Yéigo bich'į' shíni'íí'á. Háadi da shą' atah bi'di'noolkał nisingo t'óó baa nitséskees łeh. T'óó shił baa hojoobá'íyee'.

Where were you? I missed you. I was very worried about you. There was a little boy who also used to come to visit me and we comforted one another. He is the one who brought my younger brother to me. Now I worry about him too. I am really worried about him. I just wonder where he is being chased to. I have so much sympathy for him.

Dééd Yázhí worried about whether she should have told the young boy about the young Naabeehó man. She remembered the young boy was used as an interpreter. She was afraid the soldiers would try to force the information out of the young boy, after all, she had been talking to him for a length of time.

Dééd Yázhí watched in fear as soldiers returned to them. One soldier took the young boy by the shoulders and pointed toward a group of Naabeehó people and ordered him to get back to the people he was traveling with. Dééd Yázhí watched the young boy slowly walk away to join a group of Naabeehó people. Soldiers pushed the Naabeehó people toward the eastern direction, forcing them to walk in the light of dusk.

Dééd Yázhí's heart filled with hope when she saw the young Naabeehó 'ashkii running toward her carrying her large pack. He dropped the pack on the ground next to her then turned and ran back to join the people who were walking away from her. She watched the young boy put his head down and fall into place, putting one foot in front of the other as he walked with his people.

She lost sight of the young Naabeehó man. Soon, she could not see the sad image of the young Naabeehó 'ashkii. She felt vulnerable, scared, alone, and worried. She worried about her little one. She worried about being separated from the young Naabeehó man. She worried about the young boy who just left her, and she worried about the little boy.

Dééd Yázhí looked into the sky and noticed the clouds had changed from a pale white to a peach-colored glow. Helplessly, she looked into the clouds to find the face of her mother and her father and that of her younger sister and her younger brothers. She missed her family in the worst way. She shook her head, and turned her thoughts to the boys and the man in her immediate life. She hugged her little one and comforted herself with the thought that she was glad to see the young Naabeehó 'ashkii again. Thinking of all the people in her life, she softly whispered,

"Háshinee'." *Dear ones.*

Still thinking of the young Naabeehó 'ashkii, she looked at the water flowing by. In sadness, Dééd Yázhí knew she was one river farther away from her mother and her father and her siblings and her land.

By nightfall, all the Naabeehó people, the soldiers, most of the horses, sheep, goats, and cattle had been transported across the river to land on the eastern bank. Sounds of the Naabeehó people being chased away from the river into the warm desert were all that could be heard. Lights from crude kerosene lamps were drifting farther away from Dééd Yázhí and her little one. She felt around her. The sand was still warm from the sun. The family who lost the young woman by drowning wanted to remain there for four days to grieve the young woman's death, but they were forced at gunpoint to move on. Dééd Yázhí could hear cries of unbelief and mourning.

Dééd Yázhí listened as her people were chased eastward. In her mind, she could see the young Naabeehó man and the young Naabeehó 'ashkii.

Soldiers told her through an Indian scout she could not leave. She had many questions to ask but they remained unvoiced. She was afraid to ask questions. Different scenarios rushed through her mind. What were the soldiers going to do with her? What were the soldiers going to do with her little one? Would she be raped? Would she be killed? She shuddered at the scenario of each question that tortured her mind as they marched through one by one.

Dééd Yázhí kept an eye on the moon rising in the east. Her fear grew as the shape of the moon was completely exposed above the eastern horizon. Darkness set in. Afraid, Dééd Yázhí sat still. She covered herself with her rug blankets the young Naabeehó 'ashkii placed near her.

A short, young soldier gave her two blankets. She decided to sleep on the soldiers' blankets while she used one rug blanket to keep herself and her little one warm. With the additional rug blanket, she comforted herself. She found a place where the sand was still warm from the sun and covered herself and her little one.

Afraid to allow herself to fall asleep, Dééd Yázhí held her little one and sang a little song to her child. It was the song her father used to sing to her and her younger sister when they were little, one they continued to hear their father sing as they grew older. The song comforted her and gave her strength. Looking up at the stars, she breathed,

"Ahéhee', shizhé'é. Ha'ííníshníigo 'ánáshiinidlaa. Niyiin she'awéé' bich'į' bee ni'dish'a'go bee shidziilgo 'áshiinilaa."
Thank you, my father. You have comforted me once again. Singing your song to my little one has made me strong.

****

Dééd Yázhí was held hostage overnight near the river's edge. The soft early morning dew settling on her face woke her from her nap. The sun announced its appearance in a soft white light that hugged the eastern horizon. When she turned to lie on her side, she felt for her little one. He was not hugging her the way he had when she drifted off into her nap. Panicking, she gasped and sat up, desperately feeling around her for the presence of her little one. The blankets the soldiers gave her were the same color as the ground, making it difficult for her to see in the faint light. Dééd Yázhí withdrew her hand in fright when she felt a hard bundle beside her feet.

"Shiyázhí! Shiyázhí! Shiyázhí!" *My little one! My little one! My little one!* she hoarsely whispered as she frantically felt for the soft body of her little one. Pulling on the blanket that lay crumpled next to her shoulder, she heard her little one whimper. Out of relief, tears made their way down her face as she picked up her little one. Quickly, she reached into her loose rug dress and offered her little one her breast that was the fullest.

Hearing her little one's soft sucking noises, she looked up to notice the stars had retracted into the early dawn. Looking into the sky, she breathed a silent prayer, thanking the Creator for the safety of her little one. She could feel her own body beginning to warm up as she held her little one close and chided herself for falling asleep.

Bothered by the hard bundle she felt when she was feeling around searching for her little one, she looked in the direction of the hard bundle. She shuddered when she remembered she had thought the package was that of her little one's dead body. She decided to wait until the light from the eastern direction had brightened the ground around her to inspect the package. In the meantime, she threw a blanket on top of the it, afraid it may be a dead animal with which the soldiers were torturing her.

In the full light of the sunrise, Dééd Yázhí looked around. She saw mounds lying on the ground between her and the river's edge. Sleeping soldiers created the mounds.

Cautiously uncovering the hard package she felt earlier, she noticed the hard bundle was wrapped in a thin piece of woven material. Puzzled, she partially uncovered the bundle and saw it was tightly laced with a rope made of braided yucca leaves. Immediately, she recognized the braiding. It was the signature braid of her father and his warriors.

"Yáa, shitsilí t'ah nidii nihaa 'áhályą́ą́ dóó nihik'idéez'į́į́. Háshinee' dó' ájít'į," *My younger brother is still taking care of us and he is still watching over us. What a dear one,* she softly whispered in gratitude.

The kindness of her younger brother made her cry. The loneliness she felt for her mother and her father and her younger sister and her younger brothers increased. Unwrapping the bundle, she could not see the contents of the package through her tears. Wiping away her tears, she found boiled meat, tanned rabbit furs, thin strips of jerky, and pieces of yucca root wrapped in its leaves.

She lifted the yucca root to her nose and felt her nostrils flare from the scent of the yucca root. Softly, she whispered,

"Shimá. Shideezhí. Háshinee'." *My mother. My younger sister. Dear ones.*

The scent of the yucca root immediately brought scents and sights of home. Dééd Yázhí closed her eyes and allowed her mind to feast upon the memory of the safety of her mother and her father's presence and the safety of her mother's home. She wondered where her younger brother was. In vain, she searched the distant horizons looking for his image, yet she felt the comfort of his presence. She did not feel alone anymore. She felt safer and stronger.

Déédd Yázhí was reminded of her little one when he pulled on her tender nipple with his lips as he urged her milk glands to release more milk. She reached under her blanket to lift her little one so he could nurse from her other breast, in doing so, she realized he was wrapped in a soft blanket made of rabbit fur.

"Éí ga' biniinaa shiyázhí doo shíighahgi siłįį da nít'ęę' lá, *That was why my little one was not lying beside me,* she said in a grateful whisper. A light smile drifted across her lips. Pulling her blanket close around her and her little one to hide the contents of the package, she found a container of water near the rug blanket she used to comfort herself. Picking up the container, she drank the sweet-tasting water to keep her milk from becoming depleted.

"Doo t'áá sáhí kǫǫ́ siikée da, shiyázhí. Shitsilí, nidá'í, nihik'i déez'įįgo 'át'é. Háshinee' dó' ají'į." *We are not alone here, my little one. My younger brother, your maternal uncle is watching over us. What a dear one,* she voiced.

"Ahéhee', shá bididíiniił. Nihá baa 'áhólyáą dooleeł," *Thank him for me. Keep him safe for us,* she breathed in a quiet prayer to the Creator as she glanced toward the eastern sunrise.

She took out the wrapped yucca roots and lifted them to her nostrils once again. As before, her nostrils flared from the beautiful scent of the yucca roots. Déédd Yázhí looked longingly toward the flowing river water. She promised herself she would wash her hair as soon as she could.

"ShiTaa', ayóó 'át'éego nich'į' ahééh nisin. She'awéé' t'áadoo shighadeistįį da. T'ah kǫ́ǫ́ shił hólǫ́, *I thank you greatly, my Spiritual Father. They did not take my baby away from me. He is still here with me,* Dééd Yázhí prayed as she hugged her little one and thanked the Creator for not allowing the soldiers or the angry Naabeehó women to take her little one away from her.

****

Dééd Yázhí sat on the sloping river bank just above the water level and watched the swiftly flowing water. She was hoping the water would flow clearer and no longer carry debris. In the worst way, she wanted to wash her long flowing black hair.

Noticing the water had cleared of debris, she selected two rocks, one wide and flat and the other fat and round. With the fat round rock, Dééd Yázhí pounded on the plump yucca roots her younger brother left for her. As she pounded on the roots, the sights and sounds of her mother's home permeated her mind, stirring and saturating her memories.

Dééd Yázhí closed her eyes. She could hear the sheep and goats greeting the day with their loud bleating. She could hear her father singing his songs as he gathered wood for the early morning fire. She could see her mother grinding blue corn in preparation for a breakfast of blue corn crepes wrapped around tender pieces of roasted lamb or goat meat. She could hear her father bellowing from the doorway,

"Dighádóhjeeh, shiyázhí dóó she'awéé' danohłínígíí." *Run toward the east, those of you who are my little ones and those of you who are my babies.*

Dééd Yázhí knew while they were running toward the east, their mother was at home washing her body with a soft woven cloth. She also knew her mother took the sheepskins her children slept on the night before and spread the sheepskins on the ground to be flooded by the light of the sun which cleansed the sheepskins of anything which would cause a body harm. Later, her mother shook the sheepskins to fluff them, then rolled them up and stacked them against the wall. Before Dééd Yázhí and her siblings arrived at home their mother would have also swept the hooghan *hogan* floor after she sprinkled droplets of water all around on the soft earthen floor.

Her nostrils flared at the memory of the sweet dizzying scent of the dampened earth that made the floor of her mother's hooghan *hogan*. Her mind was brought back to the present when she felt tears running down her face then being cooled by the breeze that softly blew by. Dééd Yázhí did not wipe her tears away. She was afraid that by wiping her tears she would wipe away the beautiful memories of being safe at her mother's home.

More tears ran down her face and joined the waters of the fast flowing river. Dééd Yázhí noticed the presence of a soldier as she nestled her little one and their precious bundle between some rocks for safety. She could not wait any longer. She loosened her hair out of its tsiiyééł *Navajo hair bun* and gathered her hair in her hands, and then slowly lowered the ends of her hair into the water.

She heard the soldier murmur,

"Mmmmmm," when he saw her long black hair.

Dééd Yázhí snickered at the soldier, thinking of the awful smell of the dried mutton tallow mixed with dirt that clung to her long hair. Ignoring the soldier who stood watch over her,

342

she moistened her hair with the fresh water then lathered her hair with a few pieces of pounded yucca roots. She could feel the roots of her hair come to life as it was being nurtured by the yucca root it had been yearning for. She could feel her worried thoughts being washed away along with the dirt that had clung to her hair for so many days. She wanted to hum the song her mother used to sing when her mother washed their hair in the warm mornings, but the presence of the soldier kept the song from exiting her lips.

With her hair washed and rinsed of the many coats of mutton tallow and rinsed of all the dirt that had collected in her hair, Dééd Yázhí felt youthful, free, and new. She wanted to wash her body but pushed her thoughts of a clean body into the back of her mind. She took the long thin strip of fabric she used as a sling to carry her little one and dipped it into the water then rubbed pieces of yucca root into the soft fabric and washed it. She was surprised at the new vibrant bright color of the soft fabric, which brought a giggle to her lips as she thought of her little one being wrapped in such dirty fabric.

To complete the cleansing process, Dééd Yázhí reverently washed the tsiitł'óół *the long hair tie made of spun strands of white wool* that held her hair in a tight hair bun. The cleansing of the tsiitł'óół required reverence because the hair tie held her thoughts, self-control, and her people's language in place as it was wrapped around her hair. Her hair covered her head, the part of her body that housed her thoughts, self-control, language, and the teaching of her Naabeehó elders. As she held up her hair tie for the breeze to dry, she thanked her hair tie for helping her maintain good thoughts, self-control, and her

Naabeehó language that provided her with strength. She then thanked her mother for lovingly creating her beautiful hair tie. Dééd Yázhí was amazed at how white her hair tie was when it was washed. She wiped her baby's little round face with her hair tie then held the hair tie close to her heart, as she softly said,

"Shiyázhí, nimá sání ninii' yideelnii'. Háshinee' dó' ájít'į."
My little one, your maternal grandmother has just touched your face. She is a dear one for doing that. At her words, her little one took in a deep breath to fill his lungs with the gentle, faint presence of his maternal grandmother.

Feeling cleansed, Dééd Yázhí carried her little one along with their precious bundle back to their camping area. Under the warmth of the sun, she rubbed her little one's body with the moist, soft fabric to bathe her son. Out of the safety of his tight wraps, her little one wailed and flailed his arms and legs until he was back in his warm comforting wrap.

Feeling a lightness about her, she took out some pieces of jerky and berries and softly hummed a song to her little one as she ate her meager lunch. The song was another song one her father used to sing to her. A soldier brought her some food, and stood watching her for a minute then left to rejoin the soldiers. As usual, Dééd Yázhí secretly dug a hole in the ground and dumped the soldiers' food into the hole and covered it up. She was safe eating her own food.

After eating, she felt stronger. Her head felt lighter. Her mind flew back to her mother's home. She thought of the way their goats would act after they had been sheared in the late spring season. She giggled remembering the way the goats romped, bumped into one another, and shook their heads and their bodies when they noticed they felt lighter after being sheared. Without hesitation, Dééd Yázhí shook her head and shook her body to mimic the newly sheared goats. She giggled again.

"Háshinee', anánídloh," *Dear one, you are laughing,* she told herself as she extended her arms to wrap them around herself and hugged herself.

Dééd Yázhí lifted her face to the bright sun to heal her soul as she used her fingers to comb her hair to align the strands before she placed them in her tsiitł'óół, which provided her with good thoughts, self-control, her language and the strength she would need for the following days.

Chapter Nineteen
A Family At Last!

Being forced to camp alone near the bank of the river
for several days, Dééd Yázhí was surprised to wake up to the
sounds of whistles being blown and guns being fired. In fear,
she wrapped her little one tightly and covered herself and held
her little one close. The sun had risen and the warmth from the
early morning sunrays made her aware of how much the dew
covering the ground had cooled the earth as well as the place
where she and her little one slept. Shivering, she listened for the
sounds she heard earlier. Silence.

Dééd Yázhí made sure the soldiers who were watching over
her were busy with their breakfast activities before she opened
the little package her brother left for her during the night. She
took a piece of nutritious jerky and ate it slowly along with the
roots and berries, which were enclosed in the package. The
berries provided her with precious liquids with which to produce
breast milk for her little one. My brother knows what I need, she
thought.

"Háshinee'," *Dear one,* she softly breathed with a smile.

She wrapped her package tightly, then wrapped her little one and stuffed their precious package inside her little one's wrap. Afterward, she got up to walk to the low bushes to relieve herself.

I am glad I have water and juice to drink so my little one can be fed, she thought as she squatted behind the bushes. Her little one lay near her on the ground. She could hear he was waking up. Before he fully woke up, Dééd Yázhí scooped him up and placed him in his sling to return him to the cozy spot next to her. She made sure she felt two bumps next to her, one being her little one and the other their package containing their precious jerky and berries.

Just when she returned to her camping spot, she heard the whistles again along with the neighing of horses. Next, she heard the cries of people, she heard sounds of her people. Dééd Yázhí missed hearing the Naabeehó language being spoken. Being alone with the soldiers forced her mind to place her back in the shed once again where there was the absence of the sound of Naabeehó being spoken.

"Diné k'ehjí doo yáshti'góó dóó shizaad doo diist'a'góó ch'énáh shéé'niilyééh." *When I do not speak Navajo and when I do not hear the Navajo language being spoken, loneliness begins to kill me,* she blurted out.

She shook her head to clear her thoughts, and reminded herself of the fact that although she had been suffering right along with her people as they were being chased eastward, she was glad to be out in the open where she could see the stars and watch the moon march across the night sky. When I was living in the little shed, I did not see the stars or the moon for many months. My songs come to me a lot easier when I can see the moon and stars, she thought.

That evening when she could not sleep, she sang the little songs her father used to sing to her. Once her ears heard the words and music of the song, Dééd Yázhí felt relatively safe and comforted.

The sounds from the river interrupted her thoughts. She was shocked to see many Naabeehó children and toddlers being transported across the river on rafts. The same traumatic scenes she had witnessed when her people were forcefully transported across the river were unfolding before her eyes as she looked from one horrified face to the other.

She felt the need to be near the young Naabeehó man and the young boy she had not seen in several days. She felt the weakness in her knees become more pronounced as she watched the children desperately hang on to the shaky raft. She caught her breath when she saw that many of the children were naked and very thin.

Instinctively, she felt for the little package her younger brother left her. She did not have enough food to feed all the children, but she wanted to. She warned herself that if she gave the children some of her jerky and berries, the soldiers would find out someone was bringing her food and the soldiers would not allow her to be alone at all. Dééd Yázhí had to remind herself that the survival of her little one was of utmost importance.

She gripped at her heart every time she saw the children scream when the raft shook from the debris that floated in the path of the raft. She could see how thin the children were as their chests heaved up and down with each scream.

Children who could barely take care of themselves were holding on to little toddlers whose mouths were open wide with terror. The little toddlers clung to the arms of the little boys who were hanging on to them. Dééd Yázhí clutched her abdomen. She felt sick with terror as she watched the raft sway abruptly just before it reached the eastern bank of the river. She gasped, and felt sickened as she watched two little boys tumble over the side of the raft only to be dragged alongside the raft by the debris that pushed the raft downstream.

When the raft reached the bank of the river, the soldiers waiting on the bank threw a rope to lasso the two little toddlers out of the debris. The soldiers quickly pulled the two little ones out of the debris and carried them to where Dééd Yázhí stood and plopped them down on the ground at her feet.

A red-faced soldier bent over to look her right in the eye and yelled words she could not understand. She figured the soldier was talking to her when he yelled,

"You better hope they die! It would be better if they die! There'll be food for you if they die and two fewer savages for us to look after! If they live, they are your responsibility! Hear me?"

The soldier spun around and ran back to the riverbank to drag more children off of the swaying raft. Dééd Yázhí could not move her body. She looked at the two little children lying in a heap at her feet. If she had not watched the scene unfold, she would not have known the little heap was two toddlers. Their bodies were covered in debris. Their long hair which was tangled around their faces held the debris close to their faces.

Dééd Yázhí was frozen in place. Her mind was not functioning. Watching the little ones tumble over the side of the raft had paralyzed her. All she could do was hold her little one closer to her body.

Her little one pushed against her as he lay crushed inside her thin rug blanket. It was as if her little one was prompting her to help the two toddlers. She looked at the little heap at her feet. Her mind was confused and her thoughts were trudging through her mind at a slow pace.

Her first terrifying thoughts were, what if these little children are dead? I cannot have any contact with a dead person's body! I have a little one to care for, his life is of utmost importance to me. I cannot jeopardize his little life for these two little ones I do not even know. My little one is in a struggle for his life too.

Another thought that began to inch through her mind was based upon her father's teaching:

"Háida 'ayóó'ábi'dó'níigo doo bee nijinée da dóó nááná ła' da doo bich'į' nahojiyiiłnáa da, háálá bimá 'ayóó'ábó'ní." *You are not to make a person cry and you should not cause hardship for another person because he or she is loved by its mother.* I know they have mothers who love them just as much as I love my little one, she thought. I should try to help them because their mothers love them. The final thought that pushed her into action was, What if these two little ones are related to me by clan? If they are related to me, I can't just stand here and watch them struggle for their lives? Her jumbled thoughts kept her from concentrating. She felt so helpless. She looked up. The two soldiers were no longer standing nearby. They were at the water's edge forcing all the terrorized children off of the raft.

Dééd Yázhí heard herself whisper in desperation, "Shimá, shíká 'anilyeed." *My mother, help me.* Just that little plea brought memories of her mother saving the lives of newborn lambs and kid goats born in the cold nights of the spring season. Dééd Yázhí remembered watching her mother removing the membrane off of the newborn animals' snouts, then breathing gently into the nostrils of the little lambs and kid goats. After breathing life into the newborns, her mother massaged the newborn lambs and kid goats then covered them with a rug blanket and carried them inside her home to keep them warm.

Dééd Yázhí placed her little one on the ground near her and covered him with her thin blanket, then turned to tend to the two toddlers near her. She prayed, asking the Creator to spare the lives of the two little children because she did not want to be touching dead bodies for the sake of her own little one.

Carefully, she removed the debris from the faces of the little toddlers and used a thin short stick to carefully clear their nostrils and their mouths of debris and course sand. Their little bodies were so very thin. Tears surfaced in her eyes as sobs shook her body when she lifted one toddler. Reluctantly, she tore a narrow strip off of the sling she carried her little one in and placed the narrow strip gently over the nose and mouth of the first little toddler and breathed gently into the toddler's nose and mouth. Three more breaths were gently blown into the toddler's nose and mouth. She then turned to the second toddler and gently breathed into his nostrils and mouth through the narrow strip of material. She turned back to the first toddler and breathed again.

Dééd Yázhí remembered the times when her mother worked to revive the newborn lambs and kid goats. Her mother never gave up. Every newborn was precious to her. Dééd Yázhí vowed to be strong like her mother and help these little ones if they were still alive.

Not intending to, her hand pressed against the first toddler's stomach which was very hard. She instinctively pushed down on the toddler's stomach and chest area. Out came a fountain of debris. Quickly pushing the toddler on its side she watched as the toddler continued to vomit the contents of its little body. The toddler began shaking. Dééd Yázhí massaged the toddler's little body with one hand and with the other hand, she placed the thin material over the second toddler's mouth and nostrils and gently breathed into the little one's nostrils and mouth. She pushed on the second toddler's stomach and chest area and out spouted debris and sand. With the two toddlers on their sides, she massaged their little bodies. The two little toddlers were shaking. Dééd Yázhí covered them with her worn rug blanket and continued to massage their little bodies to warm them up and to bring life back into their cold bodies.

With tears running down her face, she whispered,

"Ahéhee', shimá, shíká 'íínílwod. Áłchíní yázhí 'iiná biih nááłyá." *Thank you, my mother. You helped me. Life has been placed back into the little ones.*

The survival of the two toddlers released pent up thoughts of her mother and her father, thoughts that were testimony of her mother and father's unconditional love for her.

Dééd Yázhí hugged herself with thoughts of her mother and her father as she continued to massage the two little toddlers.

She comforted herself in knowing her mother and father loved her and her younger sister. She knew her father loved them not only because they were his children but also because they were their mother's daughters. Dééd Yázhí knew her father had been looking for them. She remembered the many times he went looking for his warriors who had not come home. She had witnessed the many times he went searching for his horses when they were not in the corral. She knew her father had never stopped looking for her and her younger sister. She vowed to care for her little one in the same way her mother and her father cared for and loved her and her siblings.

Looking toward the clouds in the sky, she quietly said,

"Ahéhee, shiTaa'. Shimá dóó shizhé'é 'ayóó'ashó'ní. Shideezhí shá baa 'áhólyą." *Thank you, my Spiritual Father. My mother and my father love me very much. Take care of my younger sister.* Turning to the little ones, she added,

"Ahéhee', shiTaa'. Áłchíní yázhí bikáa'jį' hazlį́į'." *Thank you, my Spiritual Father. The little children have been spared.*

She turned back to the little toddlers. Their skin was still clammy, but they were breathing. She picked up the remnant of the thin fabric she used when she breathed into their mouths. She felt sad that the fabric was all that she had to use. Her tall, gray-haired one gave her the long thin fabric when he still lived at the fort. She treasured the fabric and never wanted to place a tear in the fabric he had given her.

She was surprised. She had not thought of the tall, gray-haired one in many days. She felt a sense of guilt wash over her. She looked back at her little one who was sleeping soundly, nestled in his covers. She stopped her thoughts by telling herself,

353

"T'áá hó nihits'ą́ą́' dah jidiiyá. Shí t'áadoo nówohjį' hodíiniid da. *It was he who walked away from us. I never told him to leave.*

Embarrassed, her thoughts turned toward the young Naabeehó man who carried her large pack without complaining. He did not even know her, yet he took care of her and her little one. She felt a great sense of warmth. Even away from her mother's home, she was surrounded by the ones who loved and cared for her and her little one.

Dééd Yázhí felt guilty because many of the thoughts close to her were thoughts of the young Naabeehó man. He was kind to me. He was kind to my little one. He protected us. He was our warrior. The soldiers forced him to walk away from us, she reasoned. She knew he was thinking of them and was worried about them.

Her thoughts became sad when she thought of the tall, gray-haired one abandoning her. I shared the most intimate moments with my enemy, then he walked away, she thought in confusion.

The sound of children crying brought Dééd Yázhí back to her immediate plight, that of the two little toddlers and their survival. She could hear soldiers yelling commands the Naabeehó children did not understand. She watched more children stumbling off of the raft and onto the riverbank. Several toddlers were nearly trampled by older children who were so eager to step onto solid ground. Many children, sick from the swaying motion of the raft, were bent over on the bank heaving, trying to vomit out food they had never eaten.

She stood up to see what the commotion was about after she heard the sounds of high screams coming from the river.

354

A second raft came into view transporting crying and screaming women. She looked back at her little one to make sure he was covered then turned her attention to the screaming women. The women reached out to their children who were on the bank. The children, nearly tumbling back into the river, reached out to their mothers. Without much trouble, the women were forced off of the raft and forced onto the eastern bank of the river. Once safely on the solid bank of the river, the figures of women and children crashed into one another and merged with one another. The cries of the Naabeehó women and children were loud. Their eerie cries were carried down the river by the brisk breeze.

Dééd Yázhí searched the faces of the women as they rushed off the raft, looking for the face of her mother and possibly the face of her younger sister, if she had been found. She felt a deep sadness along with a sense of relief knowing her mother was not among the women transported across the river. It was her deepest hope that her mother was still in the safety of Dził́íjiin *Black Mesa.* Dééd Yázhí lifted her face to the sky and asked the Creator to preserve the safety of her family and her Naabeehó people.

With the all the Naabeehó people safely across the river, which had taken the entire day, the number of soldiers increased. Dééd Yázhí felt her level of anxiety rise to a new level as more soldiers were transported across the river. Each soldier looked just like the last and they were dressed alike, worse yet, each soldier was just as mean as the last. Dééd Yázhí's heart became very fearful and desolate.

Dééd Yázhí anxiously waited for a mother, a father, or a grandparent to come and claim the two little toddlers who were lying near her on her dampened blankets. She noticed the sun was disappearing behind the ridge that rose into the western sky across the river.

She heard the Indian scout who served as the interpreter tell the Naabeehó people to stay in one place to be counted. She searched the faces of her people, waiting for one of them to claim the two toddlers. No one came to ask about or claim them. No one appeared to be looking for a child. Dééd Yázhí looked down at her own little one who was peacefully sleeping and felt a deep sadness for the two little toddlers who remained unclaimed.

The soldiers hitched the horses to the wagons and asked the Indian scout to let the Naabeehó people know they had to start walking again. The Indian scout hollered at the people in his own language, which was foreign to the Naabeehó people. The soldiers were satisfied their message had been conveyed to the Navajo people.

Dééd Yázhí waited patiently with the children. The thin women, men, and children quietly settled on the ground waiting for the next command from the soldiers. She wondered how far these people had been forced to walk. Listening to their sparse conversations, she kept hearing place names near their great mountain of the west. She guessed the people were from as far away as Dziłabéí *Gray Mountain* near the great Dook'o'oosłííd *San Francisco Peaks*.

When the Naabeehó people did not begin walking toward the eastern direction the way the soldiers asked, the soldiers lifted their rifles and fired a few shots into the air. They shouted at the Naabeehó people telling them to follow the wagons. Yelling at the Indian scout, an officer said,

"Tell these people we have to get as far as we can. We will follow the wagon trail. The horses will be our guides so the people *have* to keep up with the horses, or be left behind in the dark. We can't protect them when they fall behind. Tell them that. Once we stop, we will give them some food. Tell them that. That should make them walk faster."

Believing the Navajo people understood the message of the Indian scout, the soldiers riding horses shouted at the people, telling them to begin their walk once again. The people responded by organizing themselves into a long procession of families.

The soldiers did not direct their attention toward Dééd Yázhí. She wondered if she was to join the families as they began their walk eastward. She stopped a young man and asked him to carry the two toddlers. Picking them up, the man disappeared into the crowd of Naabeehó people. With her little one in his sling, Dééd Yázhí quickly gathered her still-damp rug blankets, but found they were much heavier than she imagined. She rolled them up but the blankets were cumbersome, she knew she would have trouble carrying them. She unrolled them, then wrapped the blankets around her as she awkwardly joined the Naabeehó people who fell in line at the end of the procession. Happy to hear the Naabeehó language again, she felt safe, but she remained mindful of her little one and his safety. She worried about the two toddlers.

Dééd Yázhí had great difficulty walking because of the damp rug blankets she wrapped around herself. Every time she took a step, the thick rug blankets rubbed against the back of her legs. With a smile breaking over her face, she thought, even my rug blankets are wanting me to walk faster, they keep hitting the back of my legs telling me to take faster steps. She wished the young Naabeehó man was with her to keep her company and carry her blankets. She was glad her little one was back in his sling so she did not have to worry about carrying him in her arms.

The people walked quickly in the dark, putting one foot in front of the other. To remain on the path they were to follow, the people listened for sounds to lead them as they walked the in the dark. The Naabeehó people at the front of the procession listened for the sound of the horses' hooves pounding on the worn path while the group behind them listened to the sound of worn moccasins or bare feet softly caressing the ground as the people ahead of them walked the worn path. The people at the end of the procession, including Dééd Yázhí, listened for the sound of the people in front of them taking deep breaths as they walked. Each group carefully listened to the sounds of the people ahead of them so they would not fall behind or get lost. They also listened for the sound of the people walking ahead so as not to trample on the children or the old people who walked slow. At the end of the procession were soldiers, Indian scouts, and livestock.

Dééd Yázhí recognized the voices of several soldiers who rode their horses behind her. They knew she was the wife of an officer. They were also the ones who knew she hid a baby in her arms, a baby who looked more white than Navajo.

Periodically, Dééd Yázhí looked up into the dark sky to check the position of the major constellations as she walked along in the dark. The constellations gave her a sense of the direction in which they were being forced to walk. The placement of the constellations also let her know how far into the night they had walked.

At intervals during the night, Dééd Yázhí heard herself say, "Hiłiijį́į́'." *Dusk has arrived.*

Chahóółhéél." *Darkness has set in.*

Tł'éé' hazlį́į́'. *It has become nighttime.*

It was the time of tł'éé' hazlį́į́', *it has become nighttime,* when the soldiers told the people they could rest but no fires could be built to prepare what little food the Naabeehó people were given. Dééd Yázhí was exhausted. Her hands hurt from gripping the rug blankets and her arms were shaking from holding up the heavy rug blankets to keep them wrapped around her. The backs of her legs were chafed from the rug blankets rubbing against her calf. Her shoulders ached from the weight of her little one as he hung in the sling she wrapped around her neck and shoulders. Her scalp was hurting because she had tied her tsiiyééł *Navajo hair bun* so tight. Her nipple hurt from her little one sucking on the same breast because she had no way of repositioning him so he could nurse at her other breast. Her feet hurt from walking on the pebbles hidden on the path. Listening for signs of life, she fearfully made her way away from her people.

Naabeehó men could be heard clearing the areas where they and their families would camp for the night. Cries of children who were hungry could be heard. Women were heard comforting their children. Elders could be heard humming the tune of a familiar song. Soon, the moonless valley was covered with a pitch black blanket of darkness. The Naabeehó people were quiet.

Although fearful of what was hiding in the dark, Dééd Yázhí settled some distance away from her people to protect her little one. She felt an uneasy sense of safety knowing the soldiers who were camped nearest to her were the ones who knew she was an officer's wife.

Dééd Yázhí released her rug blanket and felt it to fall to the ground. She followed by falling on top of her blankets as she held her little one securely. After resting for a little, she unrolled the blankets. She was so disappointed to find her rug blankets had not dried; they were still wet from being trampled by the Naabeehó people as her people jumped from the shallow water on to the riverbank. For warmth, Dééd Yázhí tucked her little one into her loose rug dress as she lay down on one side of the damp blanket. To allow her mind to rest, she loosened her tsiitł'óół *hair tie* so it was not so tight and felt immediate relief. She looked up into the sky and prayed to the Creator for a warm night.

For protection, she felt in the small package her younger brother left her when she was camped near the river. She found the slingshot her younger brother made for her hidden among the food. She felt around to gather small pebbles in case she would need to use her slingshot during the night. With the pebbles safely under her rug blanket, Dééd Yázhí took out one piece of jerky and a few sumac berries and some juniper berries. With these in her stomach, she closed her eyes to give her mind and body much needed rest.

Dééd Yázhí felt a sense of heaviness, waking her out of a sound sleep. A heavy person was lying on the rug blanket she used as an inside covering! Her first thought was for the safety of her little one. She felt for him, he was safely tucked inside her rug dress, sleeping.

Shaking, Dééd Yázhí held her breath to heighten her sense of hearing. No sound could be heard. Someone who is tall must be on my blanket, she thought, feeling the heavy person lying near her feet as well. Her ears were ringing, blocking out all sounds.

Dééd Yázhí looked up to see where the constellations were positioned in the sky. She figured it was the pronounced darkness that reigns just before the faint light of dawn overpowers it.

Once again, she felt the weight of a heavy person pulling on the rug blanket she used as an inside covering. Someone was inside her rug blanket! Dééd Yázhí was paralyzed by her thoughts. How can I fight off a strong soldier when my little one is tucked inside my rug dress? her mind frantically questioned.

Sitting up in the dark, her mind flew back to the time when she was sold to the soldiers at the fort. Her mind returned to the pain and humiliation she felt from being raped over and over again by one soldier after another. Fear was getting the best of her! Where is my younger brother? her mind screamed.

Grabbing the slingshot, she grabbed the pebbles she gathered earlier. Stuffing a pebble into the slingshot, she held the weapon tightly in her hands. She needed to lift her little one out of her rug dress and place him on the blanket near her but she did not dare let go of her slingshot while the heavy person was still in her coverings.

The stars had disappeared. Dééd Yázhí was beginning to feel disoriented. Where was the sun that was supposed to announce its arrival with a pale white light in the eastern direction? Not wanting to wake the person sleeping on her blanket, she sat completely still, desperately hoping her little one would not wake up. Her body was very tired. Her back hurt. Her shoulders and her arms hurt. Her legs hurt and her feet hurt. Most of all, her head hurt from the desperation she felt.

She sensed that the person sleeping on her blanket was having a restless sleep. He kept moving. Desperately she searched for the eastern white light of dawn. Finally, a faint light appeared. She peered at her bedding but could not make sense of the scene before her.

When her baby whimpered, she gently lifted her little one to offer him her rather flattened breast. Satisfied with the closeness of his mother, her little one fell asleep again. As the predawn light shed more light on her unwelcomed visitor, Dééd Yázhí kept an eye on the person sleeping on her bedding while she aimed her slingshot at the man's head.

When the sun fully exposed the scene before her, she yanked her rug blanket off of the person sleeping under it. To her complete surprise, there were four little thin undernourished children sleeping on her bedding. They were nestled head to foot along one side of her blanket. Two of the four little children were the toddlers she rescued the day before. They were still in a weakened state and could barely sit up. After questioning the two older children, she found they had been invited by and followed their younger siblings in joining the woman who saved their lives.

Déédd Yázhí learned the children became orphans when their mother and their father were killed by Indian scouts near the wide canyon west of Dinétah *Navajoland*. As she guessed, the Naabeehó people had been forced to walk from an area beyond Dziłabéí *Grey Mountain*. She had heard the people mention that area when they softly spoke to one another.

Suddenly, Déédd Yázhí felt a weight fall on her shoulders. How was she going to feed herself and four additional children? She wondered if her younger brother even knew she had moved farther eastward during the darkness of night. Would her brother be able to feed the four little children too? Where was the young Naabeehó man? Where was the young Naabeehó 'ashkii *Navajo boy*? Where was the little boy who brought her younger brother to her when she lived in the little shed at the fort? Her head hurt from thinking too much. She loosened her tsiitł'óół *hair tie* and rubbed her scalp. It eased her mind.

She felt so helpless and alone although she had five little children surrounding her. Four children sat facing her, waiting for her an invitation to join her. Déédd Yázhí straightened her back and reached into her precious package and broke the pieces of jerky into small pieces. She told the children,

"Díí 'atsį' ałk'íniilgizhígíí bíni'dii nihizéé' si'ą́ągo daohts'ǫǫs. Doo halniih da silį́į́'įį' índa hazhóó'ígo dadooh'aał. Hazhóó'ígo daots'ǫǫzgo dóó bikéédóó hazhóó'ígo dao'aalgo t'áá shǫǫ nihizhéé' bee nídadínóohchał. Tsxį́įłgo 'adasołna'go 'éí t'áadoo hodina'í dichin bik'ee ti'náádahooh'níih dooleeł. Díí 'atsį' nihitaa deeshnihígíí t'áá díí t'éí bikiin náás nihidi'noolkał dooleeł. 'Áłts'íísígo 'ałts'á dahaasts'i'go 'éí t'áá shǫǫ nihich'iiyą́go díkwíí jį́įįį' nihidínóołnahgo danihich'iiyą́' dooleeł. T'áadoo nihist'éí baa daholne'é. 'Ei hastóí danihijoołáhígíí nihist'e' nihighadeidoojih. *Suck on this piece of jerky as you keep it in your mouths. Once the taste has left the jerky then you can chew it very slowly. If you chew it slowly, you will eventually get full with your saliva. If you chew it fast, you will be suffering from hunger quickly. This jerky I am giving each one of you is all I have. You will have to survive on these little pieces of jerky as we are being forced to walk onward. If the jerky is broken into little pieces, we will at least have it for food for several days. Don't tell anyone about our food. The men who hate us will take the food away from us.*

Shik'eh dahonoł'įįgo t'éiyá shiniiłt'aa nídanihiilkáah dooleeł. Áádóó, shooh, t'áałá'í nootínígo da'íínółjiid dooleeł. Nihí nohneezígíí nihitsilíké wołjił dooleeł. K'asídą́ą́' shį́į́ tó bííghą́ą́'. Doo bitah hółdzil da. Yéego yá'át'ééh násdlį́į'go 'índa t'áá bí 'akéé' ahi'noolchéeł dooleeł." *Obey me. That is the only way you will be able to stay under my care. And, listen, each one of you will be carrying something. You who are taller will carry your younger brothers. They almost drowned. They are not strong. When they are much better, they will be able to walk on their own as they follow.*

The children looked at her with big tears in their eyes. Their eyes reflected the fear and hurt they had already experienced in their young lives. No one had given them hope before. They vowed to obey. Looking into the eyes of the four children, Dééd Yázhí told herself she would want someone to take her little one and claim him as their own child if he ever became an orphan.

Each boy was missing an article of clothing. One toddler had no shirt. One of the taller boys needed a pair of deerskin pants. One of the little toddlers had no moccasins and the tallest boy only wore strips of material that were wrapped around his buttocks and abdomen. Their hair had not been brushed and placed securely in a tsiiyééł *Navajo hair bun.* Looking at the boys, Dééd Yázhí thought, if I took their clothes off of them and put all the clothes on one boy, that boy would have a whole outfit to wear. Compassion overtook her heart. She vowed to become a parent to the young boys. To show their strength, the boys stood before her and stuck out their chests, determined to help their new mother.

To keep her vow, Dééd Yázhí began searching the nearby landscape for signs of roots and edible plants. She knew she and the little children would have to survive on their environment. She wondered if her younger brother knew she took in four children.

****

The Naabeehó prisoners slowly began to move around after the soldiers counted the men and distributed the rations to them. Dééd Yázhí ignored the counting and rationing activity, knowing she was not affected by either. As the Naabeehó men returned with their meager rations, Dééd Yázhí felt the package her little one carried under his wraps. It had become thinner because she fed the four boys as well as herself. She decided she would save the berries and roots for herself to ensure she had a continuous flow of breast milk for her little one. She looked up into the low sloping hills wondering if her younger brother was watching them. She hoped so.

When the Naabeehó people ahead of them quickly began to move forward, Dééd Yázhí's adopted children nearly tripped over an older man who had fallen because he could barely

365

keep up with the people. Although Dééd Yázhí was afraid of the soldiers who were following close behind her little family, she forced herself to stop and help the old man. She noticed the soldiers waited impatiently as one of them whipped at the weeds that lined the path.

She stopped the boys by saying,

"Áłtsé. Nihicheii bíká'oohjeeh. T'áadoo t'óó danółʼíní. Háida bichʼįʼ nahwii'náago doo t'óó jinéłʼįį da. T'áadoo kótʼé ha'níní bíká 'ajilwo'. *Wait. Help our maternal grandfather. Don't just look at him. When someone is having a difficult time, you are not to just look at the person. Without a word, you help him.*

The little boys could not do much because of what they carried. Still, at her word, they stopped and waited for the old man to be helped up by Dééd Yázhí.

"Shíla' yiiłtsóód, shicheii. Yiizįįhgoósh bíninil'ą́?" *Take my hand, my maternal grandfather. Can you stand?* she asked in a gentle voice.

The old man muttered,

"Aoo', shitsóí. T'áá ni t'éí jiiníba' lá. Nihidine'é t'óó shik'i naaskai," *Yes, my granddaughter. You are the only one who is kind. Our own people just walked over me,* the old man said as he steadied himself and brushed the dust off of his worn out deerskin pants and tattered deerskin shirt.

Dééd Yázhí replied,

"Nááś bi'di'noolkał, éí shį́į́ biniinaa. Doo 'éí t'áá 'ákódaniléehgo 'ádaat'įį da. Bí dó' baa dahojoobá'í. *Our people are being forced to walk on, that is probably why. They did not treat you that way on purpose. They need sympathy too.*

366

In her thoughts, Dééd Yázhí expressed how her Naabeehó people were beginning to take on the characteristics of the mean, uncaring soldiers. Without asking, the old man joined Dééd Yázhí and her children. He criticized the soldiers, saying,

"Ei nihe'anaa'í, t'ah chaama'ii danilínígíí, doo dajooba' da. T'ahdoo nihéédahoosįįhgóó nihich'į' nidahwiiłnáago yaa nídiikai. T'áadoo nidi nihich'į' ádéédahoolzįįd da. Haashį́į́ dahwiilyaago doo chohoo'į́įgóó nihik'eedadeeznih. Nihí 'éí t'áadoo haada yit'éego da 'atídahwiilyaa da. Hó 'éiyá 'áháchxį' hwii' daahéełgo nihik'ijį' nídazhdiibaa'. Hastói naabaahii danilínée yéédaaldzidgo danihitsíłkéí', t'ah na'abaah yídahooł'aah yę́ę, jó 'éí da yik'ijį' nídadiibaa'. Aadóó t'áá náá bíláahdi danihizáanii dóó nihada'áłchíní yik'ijį' nínáádadiibaa'. Yáadishį́į́ 'ádaat'éé lá. Doo naabaahii yá'át'éehgo baa nitsídahakeesígíí danilį̨į da. Háíshį́į́ nidabineeztą́ą́go 'ádaat'į́. Naabaahii nizhónígo dóó yá'át'éehgo nidabidi'neeztą́'ígíí 'éí doo sáanii dóó 'áłchíní yik'ijį' nídadidoobah da. Shí shitsóóké shits'ą́ą́' yisnááh ádayiilaa. 'Asdzą́ą́ bił iiná 'ash'ínée shits'ą́ą́' be'iina' bii' haalyá. 'Aadę́ę́' nihidi'noolkałgo shits'ą́ą́' kadeeyá. T'áá ch'ééh yishjiłgo shits'ą́ą́' ádin. Nihe'anaa'í doo dabiishxįį da."

Those who are our enemies (the soldiers), the ones who are still kids, they are not kind. Without getting to know us they began to make things difficult for us. They did not even greet us by telling us their clans. It is unclear what we have done to them to make them hate us so much. We did not do anything to them that would torture them. They were already full of hate when they began to make war with us. They were afraid of our warriors so they turned against the teenage boys who were just learning about warfare and they fought against them instead.

And even worse, they began to fight against our women and our children. It is unclear what they are. They are not thought of as warriors of good quality. It is uncertain who trained them. Warriors who have received quality training and have been trained well will not fight against women and children. They kidnapped my grandchildren, my daughter's children. My spouse, the one whom I made my life with, had her life taken out of her. She became sick as we were being chased this way. As I carried her on my back, she left me. She was not killed by our enemies.

Dééd Yázhí felt sorry for the old man. All she could manage to say was,

"Yáa, yáadilá 'óolyé, shicheii." *What a happening, my maternal grandfather.*

She looked at his feet. The old man was not wearing moccasins! His toes were exposed and bleeding. Dééd Yázhí noticed the man had what looked like a thick sole under his feet. It made the sound of a new pair of moccasins when a person walks in them on hard ground. The old man did not limp or wince whenever he took a step, he just tried to keep up with her and the four little children.

Dééd Yázhí wondered what the old man wore on the bottom of his feet. Finally, she asked,

"Shicheii, nikélchíísh bii' háínílwod? Díí tsé 'áwózí bik'i jidiiltałgo 'ayóo bik'e'ashch'íí'." *My maternal grandfather, did you wear out your moccasins? It really hurts when you step on one of these pebbles.*

The old man replied,

"Aoo', shitsóí. Haash dó' deeshníįł. Shikétł'ááh neezgai nidi 'atah yishtł'ééł." *Yes, my granddaughter. What else can I do? The bottom of my feet hurt but I am running along with the others.*

The old man shared the reason he joined the group of Naabeehó who were forced to walk from Dziłabéí *Grey Mountain.* He said,

"Nihitsóóké hadíníitaał niidzingo biniinyé 'akéé' dah diit'áázh, shí dóó 'asdzą́ą́ bił 'iiná ásh'ínée." *My wife and I began following the others because we were looking for our grandchildren, my daughter's children.* Dééd Yázhí listened to the old man's stories of his grandchildren but she could not help but hear the sound made by the soles of the man's feet as he walked along the dusty pebble-ridden path.

The whistles and snapping of whips interrupted her concentration on the old man's footsteps. One of the Indian scouts hollered at the Naabeehó people asking them to stop because the soldiers needed to rest their horses. Dééd Yázhí searched the face of the old man.

In frustration, he said,

"Yáadilá 'óolyéé dó'. Łį́į́' ch'ééh nídadikah ha'níigo biniiyé' nihiyéél ni' nidanohnííł nídanihidi'niih. Nihí naadiin tsosts'id yiskánídą́ą́' dah nihi'dí'níilkaad, níléí Dziłabéí bitsį́į́dóó. T'ááłáhígi 'át'éego nihidi'noolkał. Ch'ééh adidááh bik'ee ti'dahwii'níih nidi, 'áłtsé, háádaołyį́h, t'áadoo nihi'doo'niid da. Nihe'anaa'í t'áá hazhó'ó bilį́į́' t'éí bił danilį. Nihí 'éí doo nidi hoł da'niidlį da, ádin. T'óó t'áá hooshch'į' nihik'eedadeeznih. Haashį́į́ dahwiilyaa sha'shin, hóla. Da'ni'įįhii danohłį danihiłníigo, háí shį́į́ bee da'neet'į́į'go bee nihik'ídahoji'ááh. T'óó náás nihidi'noolkał. Háágóó shį́į́ nihi'di'noolkał sha'shin, hóla. Shikélchí nidi bii' haíyá díí."

What a happening. They tell us to put our burdens down because the horses are tired. Twenty-seven days ago, they began chasing us from the base of Grey Mountain. We have been chased without any rest. We have been suffering from exhaustion but they have never said, 'Rest yourselves first'. Our enemies respect only their horses. They have no respect for us, none. All of a sudden they just began to hate us. We do not know what we did to them, I don't know. They accused us of being thieves, we do not know who we stole from, but that is what they are blaming us for. We are just being forced to walk, it is uncertain where we are being forced to walk to, I don't know. I have walked out of my moccasins.

Curious, Dééd Yázhí asked,

"Ha'át'íísh nikétł'ááh sitą́? Ninádíl'isgo ha'át'ííshį́į nitł'izgo nikétł'ááh sitą́ yiits'a'." *What is underneath the sole of your feet? Whenever you take a step, it sounds like something hard is underneath the sole of your feet.*

"Yáadilá 'óolyé," *What a thing to say,* the old man answered as he sighed with a slight chuckle.

"Díí yee' tsé 'áwózí da'digishígíí bik'i nihidishtaałgo tsé 'áwózí shikétł'ááh ałtsoh nidayiishgizh. Shidił bee séí shikétł'ááh bínídiiłjahgo wónáasi' séí ditą́ągo shikétł'ááh niníką́ę́z. Áádóó azhį́į́h ła' shóiséłt'e'ii' shikétł'ááh bínáádiiłjéé'. K'ad éí hakélchí hóló̜ nahalingo 'akéé' yishwoł. Neezgai shį́į doo nít'ę́ę' nidi t'áá shǫǫh tsé 'áwózí da'digishígíí bik'éédadiishtał nidi doo baa 'áháshchįįh da," *When I stepped on the sharp pebbles, the pebbles cut up the skin on the soles of my feet. Sand that mixed with my blood stuck to the soles of my feet. Pretty soon it got so thick, it covered the soles of my feet. I also got ahold*

370

of some tree bark and made it stick to the bottom of my feet. It probably would hurt, but I don't feel it when I step on the sharp pebbles, the old man said with a smile that seemed to express "they tried to hurt me but I came back".

Dééd Yázhí asked,

"Nikélchí bik'ésti'ígíí yéęshą' hainilaa? *What did you do with the top covering of your moccasins?*

The old man responded,

"Ei 'áłchíní yázhí ła' bik élchí 'ádaadingo t'óó 'ałts'á héłgizh áádóó 'áłchíní yázhí dabikétł'ááh bá bídahéłtł'ǫh. T'óó shił baa dahojoobá'ígo biniinaa bá 'ákóshłaa. *There were some children who did not have moccasins, so I cut the piece apart for them and tied the pieces to the bottom of their feet. I felt sorry for them, that's why I did that.*

Dééd Yázhí looked at her newly adopted children's feet. They had no shoes.

"Shooh, shicheii, díí 'ashiiké 'ei nikétł'ááh béshjé'ígíí ła' bá 'ákódadíiliił, ya'? T'óó baa dahojoobá'ígo shikéé' deiyílyeed. Doo nidi saad dahał'įįgóó shikéé' deiyílyeed." *My maternal grandfather, make the covering that you made for your feet for these boys, alright? I feel so sorry for them as they run following me. They don't even complain as they run following me.*

The old man promised,

"Hágoshįį, shitsói. T'áadoo lé'é dijé'ígíí bik'íníyáago shįį ła' bá 'ádadeeshłiił." *Okay, my granddaughter. When I find something that's sticky, I will do that for them.*

****

The soldiers whistled at the Naabeehó people once again to force them to start walking again. The old man looked at his feet and smiled. He told Dééd Yázhí many of their people were wearing the same shoes made of dried mud. Waiting for the procession of Naabeehó people to begin moving again, Dééd Yázhí shut her eyes, and breathed a prayer of gratitude to the Creator, saying,

"ShiTaa', shicheii Dziłíjiindi kééhat'ínígíí shá baa 'áhólyą́. Shikélchí nizhónígo shá 'áyiilaago t'ah nidii bii' sé'eez." *My Spiritual Father. Take care of my maternal grandfather who lives at Black Mesa. He made my moccasins so well that I am still wearing them.*

Remembering her maternal grandfather caused her loneliness to surface and overflow in the tears that made a constant stream down her face. The old man reached up and gently touched her shoulder and whispered,

"Ha'íínílní, shitsóí. Niyázhí bá ha'íínílní." *Be strong, my granddaughter. Be strong for your little one.*

Dééd Yázhí was comforted by the old man's words and his presence. Slowing down her pace, she closed her eyes and imagined it was the voice of her own maternal grandfather who was speaking to her. She noticed her feet felt stronger and her back felt stronger when the procession began moving forward. Dééd Yázhí wondered what the old man would say if he knew her little one had light skin, skin that was similar to the enemy who was forcing them to walk toward the east.

The soldiers pushed the Naabeehó people at a faster pace after they stopped to rest the horses. Dééd Yázhí looked back at the soldiers, wondering why they pushed her people with urgency. She noticed the soldiers were glancing toward the northern direction with worried looks. She followed their gaze and looked to the north. Large dark clouds were looming in the northern sky. The clouds had been a part of the northern horizon for the past few days.

Dééd Yázhí remembered the shape of the new moon that had risen several nights before. The shape beautifully displayed a white silvery slice of the moon. The two pointed sides of the moon were high. She remembered saying,

"Dah yiitą́ą la'. Bidee' la' deez'á. Níłtsą́ yaa halne'. Nihee nináháłtįįh dooleeł lá. Háágóó da shą' nihidi'noolkał? K'adę́ę daats'í 'áadi niikááh? *There is a new moon. Its horns are pointed. It tells us about moisture. It shows we are going to have some rain. I wonder where we are being chased. I wonder if we are almost there?*

Looking down at her little one, she whispered,

"Nihidine'é 'ąąhéeshjéé' danilį́įgo dabi'dótą'ídi daats'í nizhé'é 'atah bóhólnííh. Áadi daats'í nizhé'é bił ałhééhodíilzįįł." *Maybe your father is an authority figure at the place where our people are being kept prisoners. Maybe you will get to know your father there.*

Her soft spoken voice was interrupted by the sharp snapping of the soldiers' whips. The soldiers' orders were for the people to walk faster. In listening to the old man's loud footsteps, she could tell he was walking faster. The Naabeehó people started to complain.

Dééd Yázhí noticed an old woman stumble and fall into the path of the Naabeehó people behind her. People stopped to help the old woman but two mean soldiers rode their horses to the place where the old woman lay on the sandy path. Others tried to help as well, but the soldiers whipped at anyone who attempted to help the old woman. An inconsolable crying little boy sat next to the old woman. His little fingers were locked around the fraying ends of the old woman's thick rug dress.

Looking back at the soldiers behind her, Dééd Yázhí noticed they were frantically looking toward the northern direction. Their frantic glances kept them impatient as they chased her people in a southeasterly direction.

Dééd Yázhí gasped when she saw a soldier ride his horse into the marching crowd of Naabeehó people and throw his lasso around the old woman who had pushed herself up to a sitting position. When the rope fell around her torso, the soldier dragged her toward the side of the well-worn path.

The little boy wrapped his arms around the blind woman's waist and screamed,

"Shimá sání! Shimá sání! Nił yish'ash. Ná 'eesh'į́į́go yee' akéé' yiit'ash. Háíshą' ná 'oo'į́į dooleeł? Áłtsé, shimá sání! Níká 'iishyeed! Shimá sání! Shimá sání!" *My maternal grandmother! My maternal grandmother! Let me walk with you. I am the one who helps you see as we follow along. Who will help you see? Wait, my maternal grandmother! Let me help you! My maternal grandmother! My maternal grandmother!*

With pain in her voice, the old woman said,

"Níláah nimá bikéé' yílwoł, shitsóí. Nimá bíká 'anánílwo'. Nimá bich'į' nídílyeed. Shí t'áá kwe'é 'áłtsé hanáshyį́į́h. Doo chohoo'į́į́góó ch'ééh déyá," *Go on, run after your mother, my grandson. Help your mother. Run back to your mother. Let me rest right here first. I am extremely tired,* the old woman said in a feeble effort to comfort her young grandson. The little boy's strong arms could not be peeled from his maternal grandmother's frail body as soldiers pulled the old woman along with the rope as she half-walked and was half-dragged to the side of the road. The little boy was dragged along as well as he clung to his grandmother's thin waist.

Dééd Yázhí heard a crowd of old women telling the little boy to return to his mother. A red-faced soldier held his lasso in the air and twirled it above his head, making the air rush in circles above his head. The women screamed as the red-faced soldier roped the little boy and pulled him away from his grandmother.

The little boy stared after his maternal grandmother as she was dragged past the crowds of Naabeehó people. Helplessly held by the rope around him, the little boy held out his outstretched arms as if his grandmother would return. The little boy's loud cries for his grandmother brought tears to the eyes of the Naabeehó people who were a witness to the sad scene that unfolded before them.

The soldier dragged the old woman through the sand and past bushes that lined the worn path. The old woman's body was twisting as it was dragged farther away from the path. Without warning, a loud piercing gunshot rang out above the crowd of helpless Naabeehó people. A loud scream bounced off of the bushes that lined the path. The old woman gasped as she cried,

"Ayá! Ayá!" *Ouch! Ouch!* Silence followed. The little boy bolted forward and tumbled when the rope around his little body jerked him back. His little body shook with silent heavy sobs. Several soldiers pointed their guns at the men who stood ready to fight for their people. Warning shots were fired into the air. The snapping of many whips made the air above the Naabeehó people jump to attention.

The old man shouted,

"Ei 'ashkii yázhí shą' háí be'awéé'?" *Who does the little boy belong to?* Dééd Yázhí jumped at his loud demanding voice.

"Ei bimá tó nílínígíí yiih hítłizhgo tó biishxį," *His mother fell into the water and was killed by the water,* a scared young woman said. Without warning, the old man bravely left Dééd Yázhí's side and took several long steps toward the little boy who was still held by the rope. The little boy stared forward in shock.

"Hágo, shicheii yázhí," *Come here, my little grandson,* the old man said in a gentle voice. Without a thought for his own safety, the old man reached for the rope and pulled it up over the little boy and threw it toward the soldiers. He picked up the little boy and carried him back to where Dééd Yázhí stood waiting and watching. The people urged Dééd Yázhí to keep moving forward and not stand in one place.

"Ni dó' danidiyoołhééł," *They will kill you too,* her anxious people warned her as she stood directly in the path of the soldiers on horseback. She held her little one tight. She could not move her feet. In desperation, she wondered how her child's father could be a part of such hatred. She could hear her heart beat loudly. She thought of the tall, gray-haired one who spared her life when the mean enemies wanted to tear it out of her. He was kind to her when the others were so angry. He gave her a little warrior who would take care of her when he grew older. Her heart continued to beat the same message as it beat loudly in her ears.

The soldiers laughed when a young soldier joked.

"The old man still has some life in him,"

376

Within a couple of steps, the brave old man brought the inconsolable little boy to Dééd Yázhí's side and said to him,

"Shooh, shicheii yázhí, díí 'asdzání nimá nilį́į dooleeł. Naa 'áhályą́ą dooleeł. Ayóo jooba'. Ni dó' naa jooba' dooleeł. Shí 'éí nicheii nishłį́į dooleeł." *Look, my little grandson, this woman will be your mother. She will take care of you. She is very kind. She will be kind to you also. I will be your maternal grandfather.*

Dééd Yázhí turned around and looked into four sets of eyes belonging to the four boys she had adopted. How will I be able to care for five little boys and an old man as well as my little one and myself? she asked herself. All of a sudden she felt crushed. Her burden had become very heavy.

"Shimá shą' haidzaa doo ni'?" *What would my mother have done?* she asked herself as she placed a hand on the little boy's head.

"Shimá doo bił naaki nilį́į́góó díí 'ashkii yázhí t'áá bí be'awéé' nilį́ nahalingo yaa 'áhályą́ą doo ni'. Shizhé'é nidi 'ałdó' t'áá 'ákódzaa doo ni'. Shimá dóó shizhé'é 'ayóo 'áłchíní yaa jooba'," *Without question, my mother would have taken in this little boy and treated him as if he was her own and she would care for him. My father would do the same. My mother and my father are very kind to children,* she reminded herself, as she thought of what her younger brother told her when he visited her at the fort. He told her their mother and their father had taken in three little boys, an older sister, as well as a baby sister.

As if she needed to voice her thoughts to someone, she looked down to tell her little one,

"Shizhé'é, nicheii, naat'áanii nilį́, 'éí biniinaa bidine'é 'ayóo yaa jooba'. Áłchíní yázhí 'agháago yaa jooba'. Shimá dó'

377

t'áá'ákót'é. Shí dó' doo shił naaki nilį́į́góó díí 'ashkii yázhí t'áá shí she'awéé' nahalingo baa 'áháshyą́ą́ dooleeł." *My little one, your maternal grandfather is a leader; that is why he is very kind to his people. He is especially kind to children. My mother is also like that. Without question, I also will take in this little boy and care for him as if he were my own little one.*

Turning to look at the four little boys who came under her care, she promised herself,

Níléí 'ashiiké yázhí 'ałdó' baa 'áháshyą́ą́ dooleeł. K'é beego shik'éí danilį́. Baa dajiinishba' doo. *I will also care for the little boys. They are related to me by clan. I will be kind to them.*

Turning back to the little boy who lost his maternal grandmother, Dééd Yázhí said,

"Txį', t'óó naahojoobá'ígo nichah. Nik'éí 'ádin nahalingo nichah. Ních'aad, ních'aad. Hak'éí 'ádingo t'éiyá 'ei 'akót'éego jichah łeh." *Let's go. You are crying in such a pitiful way. You are crying as if you do not have any relatives. Don't cry, don't cry. A person cries like that only when they do not have any relatives.* Dééd Yázhí stopped in her tracks.

"Ha'át'íísh dishní! *What am I saying!* she said, chiding herself for being so unsympathetic. This little boy has lost his relative! she thought. In a soft tone, she said,

"Nihí nik'éí daniidlį. Ních'aad, nihíighahgi yínááł." *We are your relatives. Don't cry, walk beside us.* To acknowledge the little boy's pain, Dééd Yázhí audibly told herself in a rough manner,

"T'áá 'ákónéehee jichah. Nihe'anaa'í hamá sání hats'ą́ą́' dayiishxį̈. " *He has every right to cry. Our enemy killed his maternal grandmother.*

Although worn out from the fast pace he kept up, the old man picked up the little boy, held him in his arms and started walking. Dééd Yázhí could hear the clip clop sound of the old man's shoes as he walked.

The impatient soldiers yelled at the people. Dééd Yázhí heard and felt the leather whips snapping loudly above her head. She was aware the soldiers were riding their horses a few feet behind her and her little expanding family. She was deeply saddened by the thought that the soldiers were angry with her Naabeehó people before they even met them.

The soldiers continued to whip at the feet of the Naabeehó people to make them walk faster. With each crack of the whip, the sad crowd of people took a few quick steps then slowed their steps down. Dééd Yázhí looked into the faces of her people. They looked back at her with sunken eyes. Their smiles had disappeared many days ago.

Dééd Yázhí watched her new family scurry along. The two older boys carried their weak younger brothers who nearly drowned. The two little boys who were carried tightly held her neatly rolled up rug blankets. She knew the rug blankets were heavy and cumbersome. She was quick to admit the young boys bought her and her little one comfort. Now, there is another little boy who will bring me comfort as well, she thought. Once again, she looked into the eyes of the brave little boys walking beside her.

The little boys looked back at her and smiled dusty, tired smiles. She smiled back, but in her heart, her smile was sad. She missed the young Naabeehó man. She missed the young Naabeehó 'ashkii. She missed the little boy.

Chapter Twenty
Keeping Little Ones Alive

Dééd Yázhí remembered her mother as an elegant woman, one who walked with pride. Even if the forced walk was difficult, she knew her mother would carry herself with respect. A straight back. Head up. Her arms carrying a child who could not walk. Her words comforting and motivating others around her

Thinking of her mother's straight posture forced Dééd Yázhí to straighten her back. She lifted her chin to tilt her head up. She took proud steps. Through her actions and her words she wanted her children to be proud of being Naabeehó.

****

The sun was setting, the shadows of the people walking eastward were becoming longer and longer. Dééd Yázhí made a game out of seeing whose shadow could become the longest by stretching her body every time she took a step. Her adopted children laughed as she walked in a hilarious manner. She cried when she heard her children laugh.

Long after the sun had set and a heavy covering of dusk had set in, the soldiers ordered the Naabeehó people to stop and make camp. They told the people there was no need to hunt because they had meat in the wagon. The men were told to stand in a line near the wagon that held the food. Dééd Yázhí heard the people say the wagon smelled bad. She heard the old man loudly say,

"Tł'ízí chǫǫh bitł'aajį' hanii t'éí dajíyeeh. Ayóo dó' niłchxongo bich'į' nisiidzį." *They must be hauling the hind end of billy goats. It really stinks as we are all standing around it.* Some Naabeehó men laughed. The women sat patiently on the ground. Dééd Yázhí watched the old man receive a little piece of meat and some onions. When he brought the meat and onions back to Dééd Yázhí and the little boys, she told him to throw the meat away.

"Nichxǫ', t'áadoo daołchiní. We'! Wée'! Wééee'!" *Don't, don't smell it. Yuck! Yuuck! Yuuuck!* She became nauseated from the smell. She heard a whizzing sound above her head, and then heard a soft thud in the distance. The old man announced,

"Tł'ízí chxǫǫh bitł'aajį t'óó níléijigo bee 'adzíiłne'. Háni'dii ma'ii yaa nahodikai." *I threw the billy goat's hind end that way. Let the coyotes eat it.*

Dééd Yázhí gathered her children around her. She tore off a piece of jerky and placed it in her little one's mouth. She smiled when she heard sucking noises coming from her little one. She took out another piece of jerky and tore it into small pieces and asked each little boy to place the piece of jerky in his mouth and suck on the meat until it fell apart. Each little boy did as they were told except for the little boy who lost his grandmother. Dééd Yázhí touched his shoulder and said,

381

"Diich'ééh." *Open your mouth.*

The little boy started to cry because he swallowed the little piece of jerky. Dééd Yázhí gave him another small piece of jerky and told him,

"Díí t'áá nizéé' si'ą́ą doo. 'Awółneeh lágo. T'áá díí t'éí nihist'e'. Nizhéé' bee náninchaadgo 'índa 'adííłnah áádóó tó 'ałch'į́į́dígo nihitaa deesił. Éí bikiin da'iidoołhosh. Díí niha'níłtsoodígíí t'áadoo baa dahołne'í. Ts'ídá dooda! Nihe'anaa'í nihighadeidoo'nił." *Keep this in your mouth. Don't swallow it. This is all we have for food. When you get full from your saliva then you can swallow the meat and then I will give you a little water to drink. You can go to sleep on that. Don't tell anyone about what I gave you to eat. Absolutely not! Our enemy will take it away from us.*

After each boy was given a little piece of jerky, the older man graciously accepted a little piece of jerky and placed it in his mouth, saying,

"Díí lą́ą, shitsóí. 'Ayóo nihaa jiiníba'." *This is what I want, my granddaughter. You are very kind to us.* To get the attention of the little boys, the old man said,

"Shooh. Kojí, shooh," *Look. Over here, look.*

When five pairs of eyes were focused upon him, the old man licked the palm of his hands and said,

"Nihí dó' ákódaohnééh." *You, also do the same.*

The little boys licked the palms of their hands in unison, then waited for the old man to speak again. The old man rubbed his knees and his legs, saying,

"Kódadohní. Díí sha'ííníłtsoodígíí bikiin ayóo dinishwo' dooleeł." *Say this. With what you shared with me, I will run real fast.*

Déed Yázhí felt her heart melt as she watched the little boys follow the old man's actions and words. The old man licked his fingers and rubbed his calves and his ankles and his feet and said,

"Kónáádadoh'ní. Díí bikiin ayóo dinishjááda dooleeł." *Now say this also. With this, I will be able to run far.*

The little boys spoke the words with one voice. Tears threatened to surface in Déed Yázhí's eyes. The last time she had heard a man express the words was when she was still living in her mother's home. It was the way her father showed appreciation for the meal he ate. She was grateful for the darkness. Hot tears ran down her face.

In the dark, she organized sleeping arrangements for the little boys. She was glad the soldiers had given her some woolen blankets, which she shared with her sons and the old man while she and her little one slept on the thick rug blanket and covered themselves with her warm rug blanket.

In silence, she searched the sky for constellations and the bright moon but none could be found. A slight breeze came by to bid her good night, and then lifted the loose strands of her hair causing them to tickle her face. Déed Yázhí chuckled.

The old man sat straight up in his makeshift bed and said, teasingly,

"Awéé' ch'ídeeldlo'! Bá ni'doo'nih. Aadi, ch'iiyáán hádaohkai. T'áadoo le'é nidoo'nihígíí hádaohkai," *The baby laughed its first laugh! Let's give out gifts for her first laugh. Go, all of you, go find some food. Go look for things the baby can give out as gifts.*

The old man laughed and said to her,

"Shitsóí, 'anánídlohgo t'ahdoo diists'įįh da nít'éé'. Ániid anánídlohgo sidéts'áá'. Ts'ídá shił nizhónígo sidéts'áá'. Ahéhee'. Anánídlohgo bee nihik'i jiisíníba'. Háshinee', shitsóí." *My grandchild, I had not heard you laugh before. I heard you laugh a little while ago. It was a beautiful sound when I heard it. Thank you. You have blessed us with your laughter, my dear one, my grandchild.*

Dééd Yázhí was so touched by what the old man expressed. She reached into her little package and brought out another stick of jerky and tore it into pieces then gave the old man a couple of pieces and gave the little boys a piece, telling them to suck on the piece of jerky until there was no more flavor in the meat, after which they could chew on the meat. The old man held the piece of jerky up to his mouth and kissed it. In the dim light, the little boys placed their little piece of jerky against their lips and kissed the little piece of jerky they held in their little hands.

Dééd Yázhí felt her sense of responsibility rise to a higher level. She appreciated each child near her and she appreciated the old man. They had become a little family. She hugged her little one who contentedly sat on her lap. My son now has siblings and playmates, my son also has a great-grandfather, she thought.

In the dark, she could hear the little boys rubbing their legs and their feet as they whispered in unison,

"Díí sha'ííníttsoodígíí bikiin ayóo dinishwo' dooleeł. Díí bikiin ayóo dinishjáád dooleeł." *With what you shared with me, I will run fast. With this, I will be able to run far.*

Dééd Yázhí sent silent kisses to each little boy on the breeze that played with the loose strands of her hair as she softly said,

"Háshinee' dó' ádajiní. Shit'áahjį' adahizhneezhcháá'. Baa 'áháshyáą dooleełígíí bee nístsogo 'áshidííłíł, shiTaa'." *Dear ones, as they say that. They have come to me for safety and survival. My Spiritual Father, make me capable of caring for each one of them.*

She hugged her little one. She was touched by her new sons' bravery. Love flowed from her to her adopted sons and to her adopted grandfather.

"Shiyáázh nizhónígo nabídínóotįįłígíí nihíiyá." *A person who will teach my son well has joined us,* Dééd Yázhí whispered before she drifted off to sleep.

****

The Naabeehó men were kept separate from the women and children. They were being counted. Through the interpreter, a gruff soldier told the people they had to wait for food and water.

"How are we gonna control these savages without food and water?" a young concerned soldier asked.

"We just have to make an example of the one who gets out of hand, soldier," his officer replied.

"I don't like mistreating old people and … ," the young soldier began to say.

"What? Are you getting soft on these people you called savages, soldier?" the officer replied laughing.

"No sir, I just miss my family, that's all. I miss my mother …" the young soldier said sadly.

"Now, just don't go adopting one of the old women like Folton. They are unclean!" the officer warned.

"No, I won't, sir. I'm not that lonely. But we have done pretty good with these people, haven't we, sir? We have not treated them the way that Indian fighter Kit Carson treats his prisoners. Oh, I have been wanting to ask: What have the children done to us to deserve this? I don't like fighting children. I did not sign up for the Army to do that. I don't want to tell my family that I fought old women and children. I wanted to fight alongside my cousins in the Civil War. Not here!" the young soldier lamented.

"Well, soldier, General Carleton's orders are that we are to subdue all the Navajo Indians. We need to let the old ones die off. They are the ones who rob, raid, steal, and kill the prospectors, settlers and miners moving west. They are in the way of progress. Pretty soon, this whole area will be covered with wagon trains moving west. We need to keep our own race safe as they move west. You don't want these savages robbing the wagon trains or killing the women and the children, do you?" the officer asked.

"Excuse me, sir, but I have not seen any of them kill a woman or a child. Instead, they take care of one another. I don't see these people the way they are described," the young soldier bravely responded.

"Your job is not to think or reason or feel sorry for these savages, soldier. Your job is to get them to Fort Sumner. Do your job, soldier. Now don't go questioning our superior officers. General Carleton is considered an authority on Indian Wars. We don't question him. We just follow his orders. Now, let's get these savages to settle down before they get out of hand. There are stray savages still terrorizing the countryside. We have to stop them and send them on their way to Fort Sumner," the officer ordered.

"Yes, sir," answered the young soldier.

The soldiers turned their attention to counting the Naabeehó men. Usually the soldiers counted the men and then handed out food rations, but the men returned to their families empty-handed. Dééd Yázhí was glad she never became dependent upon the food the soldiers provided. She promised herself she never would.

It has been a while since our grandfather left our side to be counted, Dééd Yázhí thought as she worried about the old man. Relieved to see him returning, she noticed he was limping.

Dééd Yázhí had to admit her heart was fearful. She had two sticks of jerky left of the food her younger brother provided her several days before. She had eaten all the berries and the soft covering of all the juniper berries.

There was no water left in her water jug, the jug her mother made of thin pinon branches and pitch. She reached for the jug, lifted it and hugged it. The jug was her tangible link to her mother. Her younger brother was so thoughtful in bringing it to her when she lived in the little shed at the fort. In desperation she whispered,

"Shimá. Shizhé'é. Kodi, doo chohoo'įįgóó ti'dahwii'nííh. Dichin bik'ee ti'dahwii'nííh." *My mother. My father. We are really suffering here. Hunger is what we are suffering from.*

Dééd Yázhí felt her breasts. What was her baby going to feed on? Would her baby survive? Would her little sons survive? Would the old man whom she adopted as her maternal grandfather survive? Would she survive?

****

"Forward. March!" the short stocky officer announced in a loud, high-pitched voice.

"Náás dah dohkááh, jiní," the Indian scout hollered.

The Naabeehó people moved forward. Just like her people, Dééd Yázhí put one foot in front of the other and followed the procession. The people were guided in a northeastern direction. The landscape was sandy with slightly rising hills. Dééd Yázhí was glad for the sandy trail. The sand was soft on the old man's feet as well as the feet of her little adopted sons. As they walked far into the dark night, she wondered what kind of rodents and insects were watching them march by. She stepped on something soft and shuddered. She wondered what insect she had squashed with the soft sole of her moccasin.

The big, bright, round, yellow rising moon threatened to roll right over the procession. Dééd Yázhí missed the even sound of clip-clop, clip-clop when the old man walked on the narrow path. She heard people complaining up ahead, but her adopted children did not complain. The two older boys carried their blankets and rug blankets and the two young toddlers walked, even in their weakened state. The youngest of the boys, the one who had lost his maternal grandmother, held the old man's hand as they walked ahead of Dééd Yázhí and her sons.

The old man sang songs. Interrupting his singing, he said, "Hayiin hólǫ́ǫgo doo ch'ééh adidááh da. Joogáálgóó hayiin bee nizh'di'a'go 'ayóo hach'į' nahaldoh łeh. Nida'doh'a', shicheii yázhí danohłínígíí." *Wherever you are walking, you do not get tired when you sing a song. You can cover more ground when you sing a song. Sing, those of you who are my grandsons.*

Dééd Yázhí was greatly encouraged when she heard the words of the old man. She had heard the same words spoken by her father and her mother when they wanted to motivate their children. She felt as if her parents had come to visit her through the words of the old man. She thoughtfully said,

"Shizhé'é 'ayóo 'ákó nihijiníí łeh ne'. Nida'doh'a'. Nida'doh'a'go 'iłhóyéé' dóó ch'ééh adidááh dóó t'áadoo lé'é bik'e'íyée'ii nihá nahgóó kóyiił'įįh. Nida'niilkaadgo 'éí doodai' naadą́ą́' deiik'áago da nihimá nida'doh'a' nihiłníí łeh ne'. *I remember, our father used to tell us that. When you sing, it pushes away laziness and fatigue and the fear of unknown things. I remember whenever we herded sheep or when we ground corn, our mother told us to sing.*

Dééd Yázhí listened to the little boys singing the same song the old man had been singing. Her steps matched the gentle rise and fall of the melody her sons were singing. She felt lightness in her step and was not as tired. She smiled a weary, but confident smile. Looking up into the open black sky, she whispered,

"Ahéhee', shiTaa'." *Thank you, my Spiritual Father.*

Before long, the Naabeehó people were told to settle down for the night. The soldiers told the people they could not build a fire. The short, stocky officer told the interpreter,

"Tell them there have been reports of Mexicans in this area. The fires may attract them, so no fires!"

The Naabeehó people did not mind. They were so tired. The bright moon shed light on the landscape. It was flat. As far as the moon shed its light, it was flat. Dotted across the dimly lit landscape were little mounds that shimmered in the moonlight.

As if given a signal, the people dropped the bundles they carried and dropped themselves down on the flat ground. Dééd Yázhí and her family joined their people.

All of a sudden, the soldiers and the Naabeehó people jumped up from where they sat down. The soldiers were cursing loudly.

"Damn it!

"What is this?"

"Owwww!"

"Damn it! I got stuck by something!" The words echoed among the soldiers. The Naabeehó women were speaking loudly as different ones said,

"Yáadishą' bii' dineebin?" *What uncertain and disgusting thing did we sit in?*

"Yíiyá! Ha'át'íishįį shishshish!" *Yikes! Something stung me!*

"Náhidiitáád! Hosh bii' dineebin." *Jump up. We sat down in cactus.*

"Ayá!" *Ow!*

"Díí la' dooda! Ayóo!" *This is bad! Ow!*

"Doolá dó' doo da da!" *This is not good at all!*

Similar words and phrases were heard throughout the groups of Naabeehó people who were camped under the big bright moon. The soldiers did not know they had led the Naabeehó people into an area that was dotted with hundreds of different types of cactus plants.

"We will have to wait until morning to look at our map," the short, stocky officer said sheepishly. He did not want to admit he followed a trail that was not marked as having been well traveled on his crude map.

Morning arrived slowly. The children cried from the pain of the cactus needles. The sun exposed the skulls of horses and cows and possibly even people.

The soldiers studied the map. They were supposed to take the wagon road that ran south of the town of Albuquerque to keep distance between their Naabeehó prisoners and the small villages that hugged the town of Albuquerque, but the short, stocky officer was familiar with the less used, dangerous mountainous route, the route he forced "notorious Navajo marauders" to trudge through in order to punish them. Although the route was brutal and dangerous, the short, stocky soldier decided to take this group of Navajos through the mountainous route to save a few miles.

"We have veered off course. I am familiar with this route but not at night in the dark. We will have to backtrack and get back to the main route," the short, stocky soldier announced. The soldiers shook their heads. They could not look at the Navajo people. They were following orders--orders to punish old people, women, and children by forcing them to walk through the grueling route.

"Think of these people as our prisoners. Once you do that, it will make your job easier. We are behind schedule as it is. We will have to make them walk fifteen miles a day. Farther in the places where the path is less treacherous," the short officer yelled in his high-pitched voice.

Dééd Yázhí could not believe she and her little one had survived the past few weeks only to come to a place where the path had been baking in the sun. The eastern landscape before them was flat, very flat.

Even the bushes have been beaten down into the ground by the dry air, she thought as she looked around her. Walking near the edge of the path, she noticed the sides of the path were lined with many small cactus plants. Some plants were so small, she had to inspect the place where she stepped before she put her foot down to avoid stepping on a dangerous cactus plant. She pulled tiny cactus needles out of the skin of her little adopted sons every chance she could.

"Háadish ádeiit'į?" *Where are we?* she asked in disgust. She felt betrayed by the tall, gray-haired one. She did not want her little one to meet his father. She believed the tall, gray-haired one was just as mean and as hateful as the soldiers who were forcing them to walk through cactus fields as they walked farther toward the east in the dark.

Confused, she wondered why her own father repeatedly told his children to run toward the eastern direction to accept the bounties of the day offered by the Creator. Dééd Yázhí felt betrayed by the eastern direction. Morose thoughts began to get the best of her. No wonder our leaders told us never to cross the great river, she thought.

"Hatxíhíláa ne'ee'," *What sorrow,* was all she could say.

Refusing to allow her mind to think, Dééd Yázhí placed one foot in front of the other, ever mindful of the cactus plants that threatened her safety. She walked near the edge of the path and told her children and her grandfather to follow in her footsteps because she did not want them to step into the waste of her people. Many of her people were very sick from eating rotten meat.

She looked at her people around her. Many had no covering for their feet and no clothes with which to cover themselves. To make a desperate situation even more desperate, she realized a hole had appeared in the sole of each of her moccasins.

To avoid hurting her foot, Dééd Yázhí started walking on her tiptoe. Realizing she became tired rather easily, she decided to return to walking her normal walk, heel to toe, heel to toe, ever mindful of the hole in her moccasin.

Naabeehó men told their people to walk as if they were not tired. They warned the people they had to get past the place of the cactus before they could allow themselves to rest. Through the interpreter, the people were told,

"Shift your burdens you are carrying."

The people listened and bravely walked while the soldiers rode on their horses. When they finally left the area strewn with cactus plants, the air smelled different. The people sniffed the air. In the dim moonlight, Dééd Yázhí could see low clouds hugging the ground in the distance. Fat clouds sat on top of the low clouds. Dééd Yázhí agreed with what she heard several of her people saying

"Níłtsą́ la' halchin." *It smells like moisture is in the air.*

The people felt hopeful as they put one foot in front of the other. It had been several days since they left the dangerous river. Dééd Yázhí thought about the river. She wanted to go back to it. She felt safe there.

After walking far into the night, the people were told to make camp for the night. The winds began to blow. Each stiff breeze that blew by brought with it the strong scent of moisture. The winds became stronger, saturating the air with the scent of moisture.

Dééd Yázhí and the old man quickly cleared an area for her adopted children to sleep. Her children looked at her and asked,

"Ha'át'íísh dabi'niidą́ą́'? Ałk'íniilgizhísh ła' t'ah t'áá yidziih?" *What are we going to eat? Is there any jerky left?*

The old man told the young boys to eat memories of food.

"Ch'iiyáán nihimá nihá 'ánáyiil'įįh yéę baa nitsídaohkees. Éí ch'iiyánígíí béédaołniihgo nihizhéé' bee nídadínóohchał." *Think about the food your mother used to prepare for you. As you remember, you will fill yourselves with your saliva.*

Dééd Yázhí took one stick of jerky out of her depleted package and gave each boy a little piece.

"T'óó daohts'ǫǫsgo nihizhéé' bee nídadínóohchał." *Just suck on it and fill yourselves with your saliva.*

The old man began to tell a story. He started by saying,

"Ałk'idą́ą́', jiní ..." *A long time ago, it is said* ... Dééd Yázhí did not hear the rest of the story. She was preparing her empty water jug, cleaning it out so she could set it out to collect rain water. The smell of moisture was becoming stronger. The people felt their nostrils flare as they took deep breaths. Dééd Yázhí could hear children crying. Old people were moaning. Mothers were speaking to their children in muffled words. The wind tried to take the words of the mothers to scatter them across the plain, but the mothers kept their words close to their hearts.

Dééd Yázhí could feel her baby becoming weak. His cries were telling her he was becoming dehydrated. The water the soldiers poured out for the people, earlier in the day, was of a light red color. The water can was also red inside from rust. Dééd Yázhí wished she had her goats to provide milk for her little one. All she had to offer him was her tears. She reached out to make sure her water jug was sitting upright. Her baby was crying. She felt helpless.

Dééd Yázhí fell asleep from exhaustion and dehydration. Someone was nudging her in a careless manner. She did not want her baby to wake from his slumber. Frantically, she felt for the pebbles she asked her sons to collect for her slingshot. The wind tugged at the rug blanket covering her. The nudging continued. It was very dark. The stars were hidden behind the clouds. The dust that rose and spun in the air also hid the fragmented light of the moon Dééd Yázhí needed to be able to see.

She quickly reached out to scare the person nudging her, slapping her rug blanket in the place she felt nudged. In hitting her rug blanket, she realized her five sons were fighting to be the one closest to her.

"Nihíighah nohjeehínee'. Wóshdę́ę́'," *Sleep by us then. Come on,* she said hoarsely. She welcomed the warmth the little boys provided her and her little one.

Dééd Yázhí fell asleep again. She was abruptly woken out of her slumber, someone was covering her mouth to keep her from screaming! His hands were very strong and very big. She struggled to turn over so she could put all her strength behind her fists. She heard a man whisper in her ear,

"Ge'! Shí 'ásht'į! Ge'! 'Áhodiilzééh!" *Listen! It's me! Listen! Stop!*

Dééd Yázhí stopped struggling. Her mind was screaming for relief. She could not quite identify whom the voice belonged to.

"Nihí 'ádeiit'į. Nitsilí bił tádiikááh nít'ę́ę́'. Tó nílínígíí bibąąhgi niba' tádiikááh nít'ę́ę́'." *It is us. We were with your younger brother. We were waiting for you near the bank of the river.*

Dééd Yázhí's slender, hungry body convulsed with gasps of tears. Relief! Disbelief! Relief! Disbelief! The emotions washed over her, one after another. She allowed herself to be held by the strong arms of the young Naabeehó man who was forced to leave her near the bank of the big river many days back. Tears of relief flowed from her eyes and into her ears and settled into her hair. Neither one of them spoke.

The young Naabeehó man fought back tears. The woman he fell in love with had become very thin. He missed her. He scolded himself for not joining her much earlier but he could not because the soldiers who followed the procession of Naabeehó people rode their horses on the heels of Dééd Yázhí and the children she was surrounded by. He reminded himself that if he was caught by the soldiers as a deserter, he could not have been able to provide for her now when she needed it the most. He vowed not to leave her for such a length of time ever again.

When Dééd Yázhí's heartbeat slowed down, the young man reached into his bag and brought out a handful of sweet succulent berries. One by one, he placed berries in her mouth. The berries resisted her bite, then burst in her mouth, drenching her mouth with sweet juices that slithered down her throat. She could feel each individual berry making its way into her stomach. Her body was parched as she opened her mouth for another berry. Her emotions were just as parched as she pushed her body closer into the young man's body. Closer, she wanted to be closer to him. She turned her head so she could hear the young man breathing in her ear. Dééd Yázhí wanted more. More berries. More of the safety of the young man's body. More of the intensity of his breath on her hair. More of the sweet water he brought her in a pine jug. The young man whispered in her ear,

"K'adí. K'ad háánílyį́į́h. Shinahjį' ánít'éego háánílyį́į́h." *That's enough. Now rest. Lean on me and allow yourself to rest.*

Dééd Yázhí felt the young Naabeehó man raise his arm above her body and feel for her little one. In the dark, she knew he was gently squeezing berries into her little one's mouth by allowing the sweet juice of the berries to slowly drip into her little one's mouth. She could hear her little one hungrily swallow the nurturing juice of the berries.

The young man finally asked,

"Díísh háí 'ádaat'į? Shą́ą́' t'áá sáhí be'awéé' yooⱡjiⱡ ne' nisingo ch'ééh hánidésh'į́į', i'íí'ą́ą́dą́ą́'. *Who are these people? As I searched for you earlier this evening, I remembered you were alone, carrying your little one.*

Dééd Yázhí did not answer. She turned her head toward the young man again so she could feel his breath moving the loose strands of her hair. Even in her confused state, her mind told her she was experiencing a sensuous moment, and that the moment carried with it memories she would carry with her for the rest of her life. As she pressed her body against the young man's strong body, he responded by pressing himself against her. They were breathing the same air. Dééd Yázhí could feel her body coming back to life.

When she heard the cries of her little one, she was brought back to the present. Quickly, she moved away from the young Naabeehó man. Her body wanted to remain close to him, but her mind reminded her of her little one's father.

Reluctantly, the young man released her from his embrace after she quietly said,

"She'awéé' bizhé'é hólǫ́." *My baby has a father.*

"Aoo', shił bééhózin. Nihe'anaa'í nilį́." *Yes, I know. He is our enemy,* he whispered.

Although many new moons had come and gone and Dééd Yázhí had not seen her tall, gray-haired one, she still felt a deep sense of loyalty to him. She had been taught the value of loyalty, even if the loyalty was to be expended on an enemy who spared the life of a Naabeehó. The tall, gray-haired one was kind to her. He saved her life. He gave her a son, a son who has caused her to fight even more fiercely for life. She was grateful to the tall, gray-haired one. The young Naabeehó man interrupted her thoughts when he quietly said,

"T'óó yee' nihaa 'áháshyą́ t'éí biniiyé kwe'é nihínísá. Nihíniikai yee'. Ashiiké yázhí 'ałdó' bił naashkai. Níléíjí shiba' siké." *I caught up with you only because I wanted to take care of you. Actually, we caught up with you. I am here with the two boys. They are waiting for me over there.*

Dééd Yázhí forgot about the tall, gray-haired one and sat straight up and peered into the darkness as she said,

"Háadi? Háadishą' ashiiké yázhí siké? Yéego bíhósááh nít'ę́ę́'. Háshinee' dó' ájít'į́." *Where? Where are they sitting? I really missed them. Dear ones, the two of them.*

The young Naabeehó man cleared his throat twice and listened. Once again, he cleared his throat twice. Dééd Yázhí could hear the sound of two sets of feet moving closer to her. Anticipating that the two little boys would be so happy to see Dééd Yázhí, the young man picked up her little one and held him in his arms as he sat cross-legged on the ground near her.

398

As he had anticipated, the two little boys fell into her lap and hugged her. Dééd Yázhí hugged them back. She noticed her blouse was wet in spots. She thought her breast milk had seeped out. After checking, she realized it was the tears of the little boys that moistened her blouse. Tears of joy freely flowed as the three bodies hugged one another in the dark.

"Háshinee', háshinee', sha'áłchíní yázhí nohłį́įnii. 'Ayóo nihíhósááh nít'ę́ę́. Biniinaa shijéí neezgai nít'ę́ę́. Shaa nánoo'áázh. Shaa nánohkai. Nída'ahiiltsánígíí baa 'ahééh nisin. 'Ayóo nihich'į' shíni 'íí'áá nít'ę́ę́. Hágo, 'ádínáánihiistsóód." *Dear ones, dear ones, you who are my little children. I really missed you. Because of it my heart was hurting. Both of you have come back to me. All three of you have come back to me. I am thankful we have seen one another again. I was really worried about you. Come here, let me hold both of you again.*

The young Naabeehó man interrupted the happy reunion by asking,

"Shí shą'? Shíísh ałdó' shíhosínísa'? *What about me? Did you miss me too?*

Dééd Yázhí quietly giggled and said,

"Aoo', ni dó' níhosésa. Hágo, ni dó' ádíniistsóód." *Yes, I missed you too. Come here, let me hug you too.* Dééd Yázhí and the young man hugged one another crushing the little boys between their bodies, but the two boys did not move away.

The young man asked them,

"Nihiyist'e' shą'. *Where is our lunch?*

"Kwe'é, ná dah yishjił," *I am carrying it on my back for you,* the young Naabeehó 'ashkii *Navajo boy* said.

The young man reached in the bag and produced a thick piece of jerky and gave it to Dééd Yázhí and then handed her a fat round biscuit. Without questioning, Dééd Yázhí tore a piece off of her biscuit and began eating it. She closed her eyes and savored the taste and the sense of having a family around her. She could feel love emanating from the young Naabeehó man and the two little boys. The young man handed her a jug of water. Dééd Yázhí drank water for herself and her little one.

Turning toward the young man, she said,

"Ahéhee', sha'áłchíní shaa néíní'eezh." *Thank you for bringing my children back to me.*

She stopped eating her biscuit and asked, "Nihíshą'? T'óó 'ayóo t'óó nihidáahjį' ashą́." *What about you? I am eating in front of you.*

"Íiyą́. Nihí t'áá'íídą́ą́' da'iidą́ą́'. Nitsilí bił da'iidą́ą́'. Níléídę́ę́', háádę́ę́' shį́į́ nitsilí hanihisííd. Ashiiké, dinééh danilį́į́ léi', yił naakai. Nidaalzheeh áádóó 'atsį'ígíí 'ałk'íniilgizh yee 'ánídayiil'į̇ı̇h. Gah dóó bįįh bikágí 'ałdó' hadaalzheeh, nihidine'é kélchí bá 'ádadoolniił biniiyé." *Eat. We already ate. We ate with your younger brother. He is probably watching us from somewhere. He is with some young men. They hunt and make jerky out of the meat they acquire. They hunt rabbits and deer for their skins so they could make moccasins for our people.*

Tears of relief revisited Dééd Yázhí's eyes as she quietly said,

"Ałk'íniilgizh nihits'ą́ą́' ásdįįd nít'ę́ę́'. Ashiiké yázhí 'ałk'íniilgizhígíí 'áłts'íísígo bá 'ałts'á nídaasts'ihgo t'áá 'éí t'éí nídeiidį́į́h nít'ę́ę́'. Tó 'ałdó' nihits'ą́ą́' ásdįįd. She'awéé' she'abe' bits'ą́ą́' ásdįįd. She'awéé' yázhí ch'ééh bi'iisht'o', áko nidi tó nihits'ą́ą́' ásdįįdgo t'áadoo bee bohónéedzání da silį́į́'.

Shiyázhí yéego bich'į' nahwii'ná." *We do not have any more*
jerky. I have been pinching the meat apart into small pieces
and that is all I gave the little boys and that is all we ate. We
also do not have any water. My milk ran out for my baby. I tried
breastfeeding my little baby but without water it is impossible.
My little one is really suffering.

Hesitant to leave Dééd Yázhí and her little one, the young
Naabeehó man slept near the seven little boys who nearly
suffocated him with their little bodies. The old man also slept
near the little boys to keep them warm.

Dééd Yázhí listened to her little one and her young sons. She
knew she and her little ones were going to survive. She looked
up into the cloudy sky and quietly said,

"Ahéhee', shiTaa'. *Thank you, my Spiritual Father.*

The winds blew hard that night. Before the white light of
dawn nestled on the eastern horizon to announce the beginning
of a new day, the Naabeehó people were pelted with large,
heavy raindrops. Dééd Yázhí noticed that none of her people
moved. They lay face up toward the dark sky with their mouths
wide open. The scent of the wet sand pulled Dééd Yázhí toward
it. She wanted to lick the sand and eat sand in the worst way,
but she restrained herself. All around, her Naabeehó people
were sniffing the air and filling their lungs with the rain-laden
fragrant air.

Dééd Yázhí shielded her little one from the heavy raindrops
but caught precious rain drops in the palm of her hand and
let the water to drip into her baby's mouth. Her little one
resembled a newly hatched bird with his mouth wide open,
waiting for more water to drip in.

In the northern direction, streaks of lightning brightened the sky. Thunder followed each strike of lightning as it rolled and bellowed across the dark northern sky.

Through the Indian scout, the soldiers announced the Navajo people were to stay where they were. The soldiers pushed the wagons away from their camping area and coaxed their horses to lie down on the ground. The soldiers frantically looked in their wagons searching for dishes to set upright to catch water.

"No rations until the rain and thunder and lightning have passed," one soldier announced.

Dééd Yázhí was snuggled under her thick rug blanket with seven little bodies pressed against her. She was warm. Her little one lay near her with his mouth wide open waiting for more water to drip into his little mouth. When her little one fell asleep, she let her mind rest as well. She could hear her Naabeehó people praying, thanking the Creator for the much-needed rain. She smiled when she heard the old man say,

"K'ad lá shikee' náhásdlįį' ni," *Now I have shoes once again,* he said in reference to the mud that would cake on his feet to serve as his shoes.

Before the morning light became any brighter, Dééd Yázhí heard the young Naabeehó man wake the two boys he brought to her. They left to join other Naabeehó people. He told her they would walk ahead in the procession of Naabeehó people so as not to attract attention to her and her little ones. He told her he would carry her large pack.

Dééd Yázhí heard the soldiers walking around on the water-soaked ground. She told her little adopted children to sit still and not to be walking around.

"Nahałtingo hozhdísingo 'ál'į. Hazhó'ó t'ááłáhígi nahísóotą. Hodíínáá'ígo niha'deestsoł." *When it is raining, one is to remain respectful. Sit nicely in one place. I will feed you in a little while.* Her little children quickly turned toward her when they heard they would have something to eat. They swallowed her words to fill their bellies.

****

Dééd Yázhí's loyalty was in question again. Her thoughts were returning to the young Naabeehó man more often and less often to the tall, gray-haired one. The young Naabeehó man was providing for her and her little sons as well as her own little one. Her breasts were filling up again. She could hear her baby generously swallowing her milk when she fed him.

Where is my tall, gray-haired one? she wondered.

The rains stopped. The soldiers prepared the wagons for moving on. Instead of turning eastward, the soldiers directed the people to walk in a northeastern direction. Walking in the thick mud was difficult and slow. The wagon wheels moved slowly through the mud, which meant the people could walk at a slow pace. Although very weak, the Naabeehó men offered their strong bodies to push the wagons through the sticky mud. At the end of the day, the soldiers found a widened path and the people walked in a long procession surrounded by soldiers on horseback. The terrain had become rocky. The people without moccasins found it difficult to walk. Many wanted to drop the bundles they carried so as to lighten the load on their feet. Higher and higher into the hills they were forced to walk.

The old man stayed near Dééd Yázhí. He could no longer carry the little boy who had lost his grandmother because the slabs of mud he had placed on his feet were not sticking to his feet. Dééd Yázhí noticed he walked much slower. She was worried about him knowing the soldiers carelessly shot and killed the people who were holding up the procession.

When the soldiers asked the Naabeehó people to stop to rest, the young Naabeehó man visited with Dééd Yázhí and the old man. In disbelief, the young man asked her again,

"Díí 'áshiiké yázhí shą' háí 'ádaat'į́? Nihahastóí shą' háí 'át'į́? Háádéé'shą' naagháago bił wohnééł? Sháą́' t'áá sáhí ne'awéé' yíłjił ne'." *Who are these little boys? Who is the older man? Where is he from? I remembered you were alone, carrying your little one.*

Dééd Yázhí told him how the children and the old man came to be in her care. Late that evening when he came to visit her and the children again, she told him about the old man's feet. She also told him about the holes in her moccasins and told him the five young boys she had adopted did not have shoes either.

The young Naabeehó man inspected the old man's feet from afar. That night he left the two boys with her, telling her he was going to meet her younger brother. Dééd Yázhí became sad when he disappeared into the night. She could not sleep. She worried about her younger brother and the young Naabeehó man.

The early morning light brought signs of life. Her people were moving around. The soldiers were talking but still lying on the ground. Near her were five little pairs of muddy slabs of what looked like bark mixed with mud. Dééd Yázhí inspected the slabs. The slabs were lined with rabbit fur. Her moccasins were not under her head. She became anxious. A pair of muddy slabs of bark was near the old man's head. Near her feet were her moccasins. She quickly sat up, grabbed her moccasins and put them on. She found the insides of her moccasins were soft. She slipped off one side and looked inside the moccasin and found it was lined with soft, white baby rabbit fur.

"Bí 'át'į," *It is him who did it,* she breathed.

Later in the day, the young Naabeehó man came to visit. Dééd Yázhí watched as he cut a rabbit's skin with a sharp, flat piece of flint. He shaped the skin by wrapping it around her ankles and heels then tied it in place. Then he slipped it off her feet and placed it inside her moccasins.

"K'ad łą́ą́ nízaadgóó bee yínáał nidi bíighah," *Now you can walk a long distance in these,* he said with a wide proud grin. He told her he made moccasins for the little boys and the old man. He further explained he covered the rabbit skin with bark and mud to make them look like old pairs of moccasins. Dééd Yázhí was grateful. She knew her younger brother was also watching over her and her little one.

As they walked the difficult terrain, she looked at the other Naabeehó people's feet. She saw an elderly couple whose feet were raw from the walk. When they stopped to rest, the young man looked at the couple's feet. He got up then walked to the couple and began conversing with them. Dééd Yázhí watched as he created two crude pairs of moccasins from the leftover pieces of rabbit's fur.

Just before they lay their weary bodies down to rest on the rocky terrain for the night, Dééd Yázhí watched the elderly man take his crudely created moccasins and tuck them under his head as he lay down, then he reached for his wife's moccasins and gently tucked them under her head as a pillow. How many more of our people can we help with the few provisions we have? she wondered as she pulled her little one close.

The young Naabeehó man announced to Dééd Yázhí he was going to hunt rabbits to obtain meat and fur. He declared he needed to repair some of their people's moccasins and create new ones for the older Naabeehó people. In the darkness of night, the young man prepared to leave Dééd Yázhí and her family. Before he left, he said,

"Tsįįłgo nihaa nídeeshdááł." *I will come back to you all in a hurry.*

"Tsįįłgo naa nídeeshdááł," *I will come back to you in a hurry,* he whispered in Dééd Yázhí's ear before he brushed loose locks of her hair away from her face.

"Ádaa 'áhólyą́ą́ dóó niyázhí 'ałdó' baa 'áhólyą́." *Take care of yourself and take care of your little one also.* With those last words, he squeezed Dééd Yázhí's hand and moved into the silence of the darkness.

****

Early one cool morning while the Naabeehó people were resting on a narrow trail high in the mountain range, commotion was heard between some Naabeehó people and several soldiers. Soldiers who usually stayed on the outskirts of the long procession were walking among the people who were sitting on the ground resting in preparation for the day's strenuous walk.

"Ha'át'íí lá hadeinitá?" *What are they looking for?* was the question that echoed among the Naabeehó people.

"Asdzání danilínígíí hadeinitá. 'Asdzání be'awéé' dahólónígíí hadeinitá. Haashį́į́ deiléehgo yiniiyé hadeinitá. Hatíhíláa ne'ę́ę́. Danihich'eekę́ bąąh dah shoojéé'. Nihits'ą́ą́' atídayólééh lágo.

Sáanii 'ałdó' bik'i dasídóo'įį'." *They are looking for young women.*
They are looking for young women who have babies. It is
uncertain why they are looking for them. What a fearful thing.
Hang on tight to your older teenage girls. Don't let them hurt
them. Keep a watchful eye on the women. That was the message
that was passed from the front of the procession to the back
where Dééd Yázhí and her family sat resting.

Dééd Yázhí saw soldiers who were assigned to watch
over the people. Although it was very difficult due to the
mountainous terrain, the soldiers surrounded the people as they
stood in pairs. Four soldiers and the Indian scout walked among
the people to conduct the search.

The elderly couple spoke loudly and said they had heard the
enemy were looking for the young woman who had the baby
with "fair skin and light hair." As the four soldiers came closer,
Dééd Yázhí's heart began to beat faster. Should she run? Where
was the young Naabeehó man? Terrified, memories began
flipping through her mind. She thought of the time when she
lost her footing and nearly fell while she was climbing the bank
of the river and dropped her little one, exposing his lineage.

The Indian scout and four soldiers questioned some women.
Two women pointed in Dééd Yázhí's direction. The soldiers came
closer. They stopped when they saw a woman holding her little
one in a cradleboard. They pulled the thick covering off of the
cradleboard and stared at the baby then moved on.

A desperate old woman yelled at the soldiers to get their
attention and said,

"Shooh. Asdzání hadanohtáhígíí níléíjí sidá. 'Awéé' léi' dah
yoołtééł." *Look. The woman you are searching for is sitting*

407

over there. She is holding a baby. The old woman pointed her crooked finger in Dééd Yázhí's direction.

Hoping the soldiers would not see her and her little one, Dééd Yázhí ducked when the old woman pointed at her. Her ears were ringing. Her little adopted sons were crying as they held their little hands in front of their faces. In a panic, she searched for the young Naabeehó man. The soldiers saw her turning her head from side to side and thought she was going to run. One soldier took several long steps and grabbed her and held her down to keep her from getting up from her sitting position. The old man stood up to offer protection but two soldiers pushed him to the ground, knocking the wind out of him. Dééd Yázhí could not believe the scene that was unfolding in front of her eyes.

She was relieved her little one was quiet. She regretted not tucking him inside her rug dress for protection. Instead, he was covered by her thin blanket as he lay in her lap nursing and dozing off. A soldier grabbed at her light blanket to expose her little one. He yelled,

"White baby! White baby!"

Dééd Yázhí yanked her light blanket out of the soldier's grip and covered her son. The soldiers were staring at her little one. She shut her eyes tight to erase the image of the enemies' eyes focused on her little one. Quickly, she reminded herself that she had already looked into the eyes of the enemy when she lived at the fort. She forced her eyes open. Her little one needed her to protect him.

Slowly she uncovered the face of her son nursing at her breast. The Indian scout recklessly pushed her little one's forehead away from her breast, causing her little one to wail. The soldiers poked at the baby, stuck their dirty fingers into her baby's mouth and laughed as he wrinkled his face at the taste of their filthy fingers. Dééd Yázhí heard several of her people gasp when they saw her little one. Her little adopted sons clung to her and cried out of fear. They did not want their mother and their baby brother hurt by the mean soldiers.

One soldier gruffly pushed the other and said,

"How do we know she did not get raped by one of our own?" A soldier replied,

"If that happened, do you think she would have kept the rat? If she had been raped, she probably would have jumped into the river just like that one savage that we lost in the raging river. You know, the feisty one," the young soldier said as the other soldiers started laughing.

The soldiers discussed Dééd Yázhí's baby for a while, then hit the Indian scout on the back and told him to tell Dééd Yázhí they would be watching her closely. The Indian scout yelled at her in a language she did not understand, turned and ran through the crowd.

Dééd Yázhí fell back on her pack and held her little one close. Her own Naabeehó people began spitting at her feet, saying she would get them in trouble.

"Díí yee doodagóó nihił haz'á. Béé'díínítsih yee'!" *It is already bad for us. You have added to our troubles!* the mean old woman scolded, and continued her accusations by saying,

"Háádéé'shą' yínáałii 'ánít'ị̈? Doo nihí nihikéyahdéé' ánít'ịị da. 'Ei 'awéé' shą' háádéé' nídiniłtį? T'áásh ni ne'awéé'? T'áásh ni shíníłchį? Nihiniinaa nihe'anaa'í hózhǫ́ yéigo txi'danihiyoołníih

409

dooleeł. Ei 'awéé' daats'í háádę́ę́' shį́į́ bił nídinilwodgo yisnááh íinilaa! Ge' shooh, nééhodoozį́į́ł!" *Where are you from? You are not from our home area. Where did you get that baby? Is it your own baby? Did you give birth to it? Because of you, our enemies will make us to suffer even more. You have kidnapped that baby from someplace! Watch, you will be found out!*

Overcome with fear, Dééd Yázhí started to cry for her little one. The soldiers now know I have a light-colored child and now my people know I have an enemy's child, she thought as fear continued to build up within her.

The old man placed his hand on her shoulder and threw a pebble at the loud old woman to get her attention and told her,

"K'adí! T'áadoo saad honíłóní! 'Akódínínígíí biniinaa 'ei bił da'ahijigáanii 'atxínáádanihidoolííł. Áłchíní dóó sáanii doo nidi baa nitsíníkeesgóó 'áháchį' yanéinigééh. T'áadoo 'ádíní, k'adí! Díí 'awéé' yázhí shą' haa niilaago jiiníłá? Bí hanii bizaad k'ehgo ti'hoyínííh. Ayóó 'ánít'éé léi' niyéél ná deiyíníiljiid. K'ad shį́į́ 'éí t'áá ni, niyéél yíłjił dooleeł." *That's enough! Stop fussing with your words! Because of what you are saying, the ones we fight with (the soldiers) will torture us more. Without thinking of the children and the women, you just keep dumping your anger. Quit saying that, that's enough! What did this little baby do to you to make you hate him so much? It was not according to his wishes that you are suffering. You are so great, and yet, we are carrying your bedding. Now, you can carry your own bedding.*

To the rest of the Naabeehó people, he said,

"Haashílá bíká'ajijah. Bini'dii t'áá bí biyéél yoołjił. Awéé' yázhí dóó 'áłchíní yázhí doo yaa yizid da. Doo bił ahojooba' da, díí nihidine'é danilínígíí yi'di'doołnah!". *Don't help her. Let her carry her own bedding. She does not care about little babies and little children. She does not have sympathy for anyone, she will spread her hatred to the others.*

The woman sat down hard on her rolled bedding and looked from one face to another. The Naabeehó people did not show her any sympathy. Their elder had spoken.

The old man bellowed,

"T'áadoo 'íits'a'ígo hasht'e' áda'doołnééh dóó náás náánéiikah. Díí 'asdzání 'ayóo bił ahojooba'. Áshiiké yázhí bąąh ádahasdįįd yę́ę́ néidii'eezh dóó t'áá bí ba'áłchíní danilį́ nahalingo yaa 'áhályą́ągo 'ashiiké yázhí yisdáyíí'eezh. Shí dó' shąąh áhásdįįd. Shizáanii shits'ą́ą́' ádin silį́į', aadę́ę́' nihidi'noolkałgo. Doo chohoo'į́įgóó yínííł bik'ee ti'hooshnííh nít'ę́ę́'. Cháąh nídíshgohgo ch'ééh 'akéé' yishtł'ééł nít'ę́ę́'. Nihí 'éí nihe'anaa'í béédaołdzidgo biniinaa t'áadoo shíká'oojée' da. Cháąh dégo'go t'áadoo nídashidoodzįįz da." *Without any sound, get ready and let's begin walking again. This young woman is very kind. The lives of little boys who lost their relatives were spared when she took them in and began taking care of them as if they were her own. I, also lost someone when we were being forced to walk here, I lost my wife. I was really suffering from grief. I kept falling as I ran following the people. You were afraid of our enemy so you did not help me. When I fell, you did not help me up.*

Pointing to Dééd Yázhí, the old man continued,

"Díí 'asdzání cháąh dégo'go shíká'eelwod. Nídiidááh, shicheii, shinahjį' nitah hółdzil, shiłníigo náshidiidzį́įz. T'áadoo shíká 'eelwodgóó shįį 'éí nihe'anaa'í t'óó 'atiin bąąhjį', honi'ąąji' shida'asnii' doo ni'. T'óó shįį ma'iitsoh dashoolghal doo ni'. Kǫ́ǫ́ nidabikéé'. Díí 'asdzání t'áadoo dajiinohłáhí, be'awéé' yázhí 'ałdó' t'áadoo dajiinohłáhí. Baa hojoobá'íyee'. Bí dó' hojooba' íinízin. T'ááshǫǫdí, baa nídanihooshkąąh, shidine'é. Shá k'é dabidohní."

This young woman helped me get up when I fell. She said to me, "Get up, my maternal grandfather, depend upon me for strength," as she helped me up. If she had not helped me, our enemy would have pushed me to the side of the path or over the hill and left me there to fend for myself. The wolves would have devoured my body. Their tracks are all around here. Do not have hate for this young woman. Do not have hate for her little baby. They deserve your sympathy. They want your sympathy. I plead with you, my people. Greet them through kinship.

The Naabeehó people listened. They turned their backs on the old woman. The mean old Naabeehó woman turned back to her bedding and muttered as she wrapped her belongings in a large bundle and swung it onto her back. Dééd Yázhí felt sorry for her. She wondered what her father would have done in the same situation. She figured he would have reacted in the same way as the old man.

****

Dééd Yázhí looked around frantically. She was afraid. She had not seen the young Naabeehó man since the night before. Her large pack lay on the ground. She wondered if she could even carry the heavy pack on her back. She hoped he had not been caught by the soldiers. She tucked her little one snugly in her rug dress. Holding him tightly with one hand and with the help of her young sons, pulled the largest bundle up and swung it onto her back. Her little children all carried something. The old man followed the little boys to make sure they kept up with the procession.

Chapter Twenty-one

Allies of the Soldiers

When the Naabeehó people were herded toward the mountain range, Dééd Yázhí felt someone pull the heavy pack off her back. She spun around to find the young Naabeehó man at her side. A sigh of relief escaped her lips.

She asked him where he had been. He looked at her and opened the large bundle tied around his waist. Inside were large pieces of fresh jerky, juniper berries, medicinal herbs, and edible roots. He had been hiding in a ravine up ahead and joined the procession without being noticed.

"Nitsilí hágo shiłníigo biniinaa nihits'ą́ą́' dah diishwod. Da'iighaazhgo dah yiishtxe'. Níléí dah náhásk'id léi'gi bínishwod." *Your younger brother was calling me, and that is why I left you. I left the group when everyone fell asleep. I caught up with him on top of a hill.*

Dééd Yázhí silently cried. Her little one was in grave danger because of the enemy and because her own people saw her little one as an enemy. She told the young man about the event that took place earlier that day. The young man placed one arm

413

around her shoulders and comforted her. Her loyalty shifted again, she needed her tall, gray-haired one's help in protecting their little one.

Dééd Yázhí caught herself looking for the large water jug the young Naabeehó man filled whenever he found water. A look of sadness came over the young man's face when he noticed Dééd Yázhí was looking for the large water jug. It had become a practice for him to peel the worn moccasins off of her tired feet and wash her feet with the cool, clear water from the large jug. He also made it a practice to massage her feet.

Dééd Yázhí remembered back to the first time the young man washed and massaged her feet. She smiled when she remembered what he said to each one of her toes as he washed them.

"Díí tá'ádidoogis. Haa'íshą' díí dó' tá'ádidoogis. Díí dó' nááná. Díí shį́ 'ałdó'. Díí dó' ch'ééh adidááh yik'ee ti'honíhígíí, tá'ádidoogis." *This one will bathe. What about this one, it will bathe also. This one too. Probably this one too. This one is also suffering from fatigue, it will bathe too.*

She remembered giggling when he playfully spoke to her toes as he washed each one. He brought out the child in her by tickling her feet to rejuvenate them. Dééd Yázhí and the young man were aware of the women who cast disapproving glances their way. They knew the Naabeehó women did not approve of what they were doing. They heard an older woman say,

"Nízhdiilgą́ązhgo hanii 'ájít'į́, 'ał'ąą." *They must both be having a nightmare, the two of them.*

Another woman who was watching them boldly said,

"Doo 'áłchíní bináał ahízhdílchid da. Haa lá woht'į́?"

You are not to be touching one another in the presence of
children. What are you two doing?

Dééd Yázhí remembered basking in the young man's
attention. She told herself the women who were criticizing her
had not been kept as a prisoner before they were forced on
this long march. They did not have to go days at a time without
hearing their beautiful Naabeehó language being spoken the
way she was forced to when she lived in the little shed at the
fort, nor did they fall asleep without seeing the beautiful round
moon in the black sky of night.

Dééd Yázhí was aware love was building in her heart for the
young Naabeehó man but she consistently reminded herself
that her little one had a father. Although her little one's father
had abandoned them, he still gave her life and she was thankful
to him for that.

"Besides," she thought, "he spared my life too." She vowed
to remain loyal to the tall, gray-haired one, in spite of the fact
that he was the enemy who abandoned her and their little one.

The young Naabeehó man's low, kind voice interrupted her
thoughts when he whispered in her ear,

"Shá 'ashja'iilaago tó ła' ádeeshłííł. Nikee' ná táádeesgis."
When it is convenient for me, I will get some water. I will wash
your feet for you. Dééd Yázhí nodded at the beautiful thought.
He continued,

"Tóshjeeh nitsaaígíí t'áá kǫ́ǫ́ beesénahgo biniinaa t'áadoo
tó ła' nihá nánílo' da. Shá 'ashjanááhoodzaago shį́į́ 'índa tó nihá
shóideesht'eeł." *I forgot and left the large water jug here so I*
was not able to bring us more water. As soon as I get a chance,

I will obtain water for us. Hearing his caring words, Dééd Yázhí cast a glance in the direction of the bossy old woman. Earlier, she noticed the woman was rubbing her feet.

****

Another day of walking in a northeastern direction brought the procession to the outskirts of a small settlement that was nestled in the mountain range. Additional soldiers were waiting at the settlement. The soldiers reported they had been sent to look for Navajos who had escaped the long walk to Fort Sumner or ones who had escaped from Fort Sumner.

The people were ordered to make camp for the night. The soldiers kept watch over the Naabeehó people throughout the night. A new interpreter, who spoke more Navajo than the Indian scout, joined the procession. Messages were readily understood, which left the Naabeehó people a little less fearful. The former interpreter, the Indian scout, was sent to Santa Fe. The new interpreter told the Naabeehó people the additional soldiers were to accompany the procession through the mountain trails so the people had to behave and obey the commands of the soldiers. The people were ordered to walk single file as they marched past the small settlement. A few people came out to jeer at the Naabeehó people.

Leaving the settlement, the people were herded eastward toward a higher mountain range. Two days later they arrived at another small settlement in the high mountains. Through the interpreter, the people were warned not to leave the single-file procession, and if they did, they would be shot. The Naabeehó people walked without looking toward the little settlement. No one came out to jeer at them.

416

The soldiers were fearful of Mexican raiders who would steal a Navajo woman or child to sell to at the trade fair in Taos so they forced their exhausted prisoners to walk at a faster pace. Looking at the procession ahead of her, Dééd Yázhí could see steam rising into the air when the people breathed out. She acknowledged the steam in stating,

"Deesk'aaz hazlį́į́', áyaaní da shidine'é nídahididziihgo siil bee dah náá'oojoł łeh," *It has become cold. Every time my people breathe, a cloud of steam can be seen.*

She remembered back to the cold winter mornings when her father came back from his early morning run toward the eastern direction. He would chase Dééd Yázhí and her siblings outside and tell them to look toward the sheep and horse corrals.

"Nihilį́į́' nídahididziihgo siil bee dah oojoł łeh. Siiłígíí dah nídiildohgo tó nádleeh, binahjį' nihee nináháltį́į́h, binahjį' nihee nádzaz. Tł'óo'di nidaohsj', siil hadaohsííd. Áádóó dighádóhjeeh. Sodadołzin." *When our livestock breathe, there is a cloud of steam that can be seen. That cloud of steam becomes water, by means of it we have rain. By means of it we have snow. Stand around outside and be a witness to the steam. After that, run toward the eastern direction and pray.*

Dééd Yázhí was thankful she was a witness to the steam that collected above the heads of her people. She continued to watch the cloud of steam grow and disappear, over and over. She looked toward the sky and whispered,

"Ahéhee', shiTaa', shizhé'é bizhí diséts'ą́ą́'. *Thank you, my Spiritual Father, I heard the voice of my father.* Tears of love for her father ran down her cheeks. In her heart, she knew she would return to Dziłíjiin *Black Mesa* to raise her son. She wanted her father and her mother to look upon her son and bless him with their love. She was confident her mother and her father would fall in love with her son.

Seeing how rapidly the steam built up and dissipated above her people's heads, Dééd Yázhí knew her people were breathing hard because of the rough terrain they were forced to walk through. She was grateful she was used to the high elevation. As she put one foot in front of the other she pretended she was at home in the folds of Dziłíjiin *Black Mesa.* Tears of loneliness made a steady path down her face, washing away the delicate pattern left by the tears that were brought forth by the memory of her father's words. Dééd Yázhí told her little children about her mother and her father and told them about her home. She used the memories of her home as her pillow as she slept soundly that night.

Dééd Yázhí had so much appreciation for the young Naabeehó man. For two days, while on the mountain trail, the young man carried the bundles of the old couple. Dééd Yázhí told the young man she could not see his face because of the many packs and bundles he was carrying. While coming down off of the mountain, the young man carried the old man after the old man twisted his ankle on a rock that jutted out in the path they had been following.

While camped at the base of another mountain range, the interpreter told the Naabeehó people they were less likely to be raided by slave traders if they followed the mountain trails. While trudging on the narrow trail, the old couple whose moccasins the young Naabeehó man created from rabbit skins

418

were forced to the side of a high trail and left behind. They were dehydrated and sick and could not keep up with their people. Dééd Yázhí forced herself to walk away from them. She had to survive for the sake of her little one. The young man placed his arm around her shoulders and said,

"Ha'íínílní. Niyázhí bá ha'íínílní. Ashiiké yázhí bá ha'íínílní," *Be strong. Be strong for your little one. Be strong for the little boys.*

The Naabeehó people cried more often as they trudged through the mountains. They cried when the soldiers forced them to walk away from their loved ones who could no longer keep up with the fast pace of the procession. Being at the end of the procession, Dééd Yázhí was tortured by the images of her people falling over while reaching out to the ones leaving them behind. She could hear the weak voices of the ones left behind as they called out to their loved ones, yelling,

"Hada'íínółní, shité'ázíní, hada'íínółní!" *Be strong, my relatives, be strong!*

The Naabeehó people gasped as gunshots rang out and echoed many times as the cruel sound of the gunshots bounced off of the numerous folds of the long mountain range. The people were crying deep, heavy sobs. Dééd Yázhí's heart was hurting. She wondered how much more she could take. She hurt for her people.

Still mourning the loss of the old couple whose moccasins her young Naabeehó man made, Dééd Yázhí remembered how grateful the old ones were for their new moccasins. She tried to shake the extreme sadness she felt. She wanted to hear comforting words coming from her mother's mouth.

She knew she could walk many more days if she could just hear her father's kind words that he spoke to his children. She listened to her thoughts. Her memories were bringing the sounds of her mother and her father's voices closer to her ears. With each footstep she heard her people take, another word came back to her mind, another sentence representing her mother and her father came to mind.

Dééd Yázhí leaned toward the comfort of the young man. Once again, she felt betrayed by the tall, gray-haired one. Where was he? she wondered.

After seven days of walking on the treacherous narrow mountain trails, the procession of Naabeehó people followed a trail down into a valley and traveled along the base of a curved sloping hill. The people were so exhausted, they were trying not to run down the steep widening path. Dééd Yázhí could see her people half-walking and half-running down the trail. She was anxious to leave the dreaded mountain trail so she also half-ran down the mountain path toward the valley with its welcoming flat terrain.

Her moccasins were in dire need of being repaired again, only this time there was no rabbit skin with which to repair them. The young man pulled out a shrub, flattened it with his hands, and laced the thick layer of the shrub to the bottom of one of Dééd Yázhí's moccasins. He found another shrub which he flattened then laced it to the bottom of her other moccasin. Dééd Yázhí found it difficult to walk but she forced herself to. Her feet were swollen and blistered. She did not want to be left beside the trail to die. She had to live for her little ones.

Dééd Yázhí was discouraged. Their bundle of food was diminished. Marching through the mountain trails made it difficult for the young man to meet her younger brother. The young man did not want to risk getting caught crawling up the mountainside or falling down the mountainside in the black darkness of night. The numerous soldiers made it very difficult for him to steal off into the night.

Dééd Yázhí looked back at the mountain. Although she greeted the mountain before they entered its folds, it never greeted her or her Naabeehó people. Instead, the mountain had become an ally of the angry soldiers. The mean Naabeehó woman had also become an ally of the enemy.

Dééd Yázhí and her little adopted sons and the old man survived on the abundance of water which helped them to save their juniper berries. The many springs that ran off of the mountain kept their supply of water in adequate supply, although the young man only filled the smaller jug with water. To have filled both jugs would have added too much weight to the burden the young man carried.

When the people heard the orders of the soldiers to settle down and camp for the night, the people were grateful. Dééd Yázhí and her little family had just settled down when they heard the sound of coyotes howling in the distance. She smiled, that was her brother's cry to announce he had food for them. The young Naabeehó man disappeared from their side and followed the sound of the howling coyotes. Dééd Yázhí looked off into the stark darkness. The darkness brought a sense of peacefulness to her, allowing her to rest her mind and her body. Sleep covered her with its welcomed blanket.

The stirring of her little one woke her. Turning to her little one to feed him, she felt warmth. Breaths of air gently stirred her hair.

"Shí 'ásht'į́," *It's me,* she heard the young Naabeehó man say.

The young man was lying next to her. He touched her hand that was searching for him in the dark. He lifted her hand and placed it on his chest and reported her younger brother was safe. The young man had time to visit and obtain information during his secret meeting with her brother. Her brother had placed one day between themselves and the procession of Naabeehó people. In following them, her younger brother and his warriors found the old couple on the narrow path preparing for death. The old couple was given food and water and was safe with her brother and his warriors, the young man reported.

Dééd Yázhí's soft sobs interrupted his report. Her heart hurt from the memory of having to leave the old couple by the side of the mountainous path.

"Nizhónígo baa 'áháyą. Nitsilí naat'áanii biłílíinii nilį́." *They are being cared for very well. Your younger brother is a leader who is respectful.*

"Ni dó' ákónít'ée dooleeł," *You will be that way too,* Dééd Yázhí assured the young man.

"Háshinee' dó' ádíní," *What a dear thing to say,* the young man answered.

He placed a small, thick piece of jerky in her mouth and promised to wash her feet. Dééd Yázhí fought off sleep because she wanted to greet the new light of dawn so she could thank

422

the Creator for providing for them once again and for protecting her younger brother and the young man as well as the old couple.

Although she was experiencing such difficult times, Dééd Yázhí felt she had much to be thankful for. She fought sleep in the arms of the young man. She dozed off and woke to find her moccasins lined with soft rabbit fur. Putting them on, she felt she could glide across the valley.

After several long days of walking, the procession reached a small settlement. Their water supply was replenished and the Naabeehó people were allowed to rest. Discolored onions sustained the people. Fewer Naabeehó people were getting sick. The old man said,

"Tł'ohchin éí t'áá níléídę́ę́' deidą́. 'Ałk'idą́ą́, t'áá nihikéyah bikáa'gi, k'é bił da'ahidii'niid." *We have been eating onions for a long time. We greeted them a long time ago on our own land.*

****

The Naaabeehó people became agitated because they were told they would have to cross another river. This time it was the Pecos River. The children crossed the river first and the women followed. Many soldiers stood near the poles on the bank of the narrow river and counted the children and the women as they stepped off of the rickety raft and onto the slippery rocks that were embedded in the river bank.

Dééd Yázhí looked back to search for the young Naabeehó man and the old man. She could not see them. All she could see was large bundles sitting on the rafts with an occasional leg or foot or head sticking out from among the bundles. She wondered if the young man and her grandfather were among the bundles.

A large group of soldiers was waiting for the procession. Dééd Yázhí was filled with apprehension when she saw the soldiers who forced her people to walk through the mountains turn back toward the mountain path. She thought of her brother who was hiding in the mountains.

Without returning the children to their mothers or relatives, the women and children were herded eastward, away from the river as the men were forced onto the rafts. The men crossed before the rest of the soldiers and the wagons crossed. Many women expressed fear. They noticed the soldiers on this side of the narrow river were more hostile than the ones who had forced them to walk over the mountainous route. An old woman complained, saying,

"T'ahdoo nidi nihéédahojoosjjhgóó nihich'j' hádahaazhchjjd." *They are mad at us even before they have come to know us.* The women shivered out of fear.

Into the cool evening light they walked, following the soldiers and herded by soldiers who rode on horses. The soldiers wanted the women and children to hurry, but the sandy terrain was difficult to walk on.

The setting sun cast a pale peach glow on the Naabeehó people as they followed the darkened trail. After a long distance, the soldiers ordered the women and children to camp for the night. The women were fearful. They feared for the safety of their children, they were also fearful of the new soldiers and the night creatures. The women were also fearful of the new land. Dééd Yázhí noticed the moon cast a silvery glow on the soft sand and the women and the children. During the night, she comforted herself with the thought that the landscape was not very different from the one her family claimed for their summer home and where her father maintained his dá'ák'eh *cornfield.*

In her anxiety, Dééd Yázhí tried to greet the land. The land did not respond to her. Instead, the land angrily pushed its inhabitants toward the Naabeehó people. When the people placed their bedding down on the ground, annoyed insects crawled out of their homes and attempted to send the invaders on their way. Long, angry centipedes, three times as long as the ones that occupied Dinétah *Navajoland,* surfaced to reclaim their land. The centipedes let the people know they were not welcome. The people feeling the sting of the centipedes were chased out of their bedding and when they stepped into their moccasins, they found that angry centipedes had already inhabited their moccasins. Large spiders irritated by the commotion joined the centipedes in chasing the Naabeehó people out of their much-needed resting place. Fat red ants charged the people to demonstrate their aggravation at having their homes disturbed, forcing the people to stomp on the ground to shed the ants that had attached themselves to the people's clothes and bedding. The Naabeehó people had nowhere to turn. They built fires, hoping to keep the harmful insects away. The warm morning sun brought out the last stubborn reptiles of the season. The dangerous snakes surfaced hoping to find a rock upon which to curl up and warm their long slithering bodies. Dééd Yázhí could not believe the land the soldiers chased them to was so dangerous. She heard her people asking if they could leave the area and move to lands that were safer than the one they camped upon. Dééd Yázhí and her children were grateful she did not have their bedding.

They sat on a flat rock, afraid to move, in fear of what would come crawling out from under the rock. Dééd Yázhí missed her mother and her father. They would know what to say to her to make her feel safe. She also missed the young Naabeehó man.

Once again, Dééd Yázhí found herself questioning her loyalty toward the tall, gray-haired one. Where is he? Does he think about me? she wondered. Does he have another woman? A woman who speaks his language? she shook her head at the last two questions her mind was contemplating. To stop her mind from thinking, Dééd Yázhí shook her head. She did not feel the presence of another woman. Her tall, gray-haired one was still alone. She just did not know where he was. Even more worrisome to her was the thought that the tall, gray-haired one did not know where she was either.

Two days after the women and children crossed the narrow river, the men caught up with them. When Dééd Yázhí reunited with the young Naabeehó man and the old man, she quietly greeted them. She was content to hug them with her words. She was cautious not to demonstrate her love for the two men, afraid the soldiers would use their love for one another to further punish them. She worriedly told herself she could not survive the loss of another loved one.

Looking into her eyes, the young Naabeehó man saw a young, beautiful woman who had lived the life of an older woman who had survived much sorrow. In two days, she seemed to have aged even more, he thought. He was worried. He did his best to comfort her. In doing so, he saw big tears in her eyes that were ready to spill over. He wanted to reach out and touch her face and wipe away her tears. He knew she was lonely for her mother and her father. She was also lonely for her sister and her brothers. Sorrowfully, he also knew she was lonesome for a man who left her so long ago, forcing her to fend for herself. The young Naabeehó man vowed to love her and one day take her and her sons back to her home in the safety of Dziłíjiin *Black Mesa*.

Traveling over the mountainous terrains kept the Naabeehó people preoccupied with sheer survival but now they that they were in relatively safe terrain, the people thought about their status as prisoners of the soldiers. Dééd Yázhí's mind returned to the question of the reason she and her children were being forced to walk to this desolate place. When she first joined her Naabeehó people as they began their forced walk from the fort, she remembered how excited she was to be among her people and to hear the sounds of the Naabeehó language being spoken so easily. She loved hearing the words roll off the tongues of her people. When she heard the language spoken, all she had to do was close her eyes and picture her mother speaking or picture her father speaking.

Without thinking, she tearfully said,

"Diné bizaad shimá dóó shizhé'é nilį. Shidine'é Diné k'ehjí yádaałti'go shité'ázíní shaa ninádayii'éésh." *The Navajo language is my mother and my father. When my people speak Navajo, they bring my relatives back to me.*

Noticing the tears running down her face, the young Naabeehó man reached out to her to remind her of the reason she had to survive. He lifted the thin blanket away from her little one she held in her arms, and in doing so, his hand moved against her breast. Although her breast was hidden behind a thick rug dress, the young man felt the firmness of her breast without meaning to. Dééd Yázhí, herself, felt a shiver run along her spine when the young man's hand brushed against her. This was the first intimate contact they had had. She wondered if the young man felt the same shiver of emotions she felt. She avoided his eyes.

The young man hoped she would look into his eyes. He wanted to let her know he had loved her ever since he first saw her. The young couple's silent unmistakable passion was interrupted by the soldiers who were shouting loud orders.

****

Out of fatigue, the Naabeehó people willfully obeyed the orders of the soldiers and started walking again. To leave the area of angry insects and reptiles was their immediate desire. Walking farther eastward, the people saw different vegetation, plants they welcomed. Short yucca plants dotted the landscape before them. The men, while still walking, reached down and yanked on the base of yucca plants and offered the plant and root to their women. The women held the short roots up to their nostrils to breathe in the mind-cleansing scent of the yucca root, but the scent seemed to have been bleached out of the plant by the hot sun. When the people were allowed to rest, the men found flat rocks the women could use to pound the yucca plant's root to release the soap-lathering properties of the roots. The women wanted to wash their hair with the pounded roots. The men wanted to smell the sweet scent of yucca root when they came in close proximity with their women. The children wanted to run water on the roots, then rub their hands together to watch the lather grow right before their eyes.

The Naabeehó people saw another welcomed sight but one that also gave them fright at the same time. A narrow river loomed in the landscape up ahead. The people camped near the bank of the river. Anxious to wash her hair, Dééd Yázhí gave herself time to greet the river, after which she loosened her long hair from its tsiitł'óół *hair tie* and watched her hair unfold and fall into the water. The water gathered her long hair and pulled it downstream until her hair was fully extended and the water could no longer pull her hair along. She dipped her hands in the water, tore off small pieces of the pounded yucca root, and rubbed the small pieces between her hands, all the while taking in deep breaths that were saturated with the faint scent of yucca root. Immediately, she became homesick but she pushed the emotion aside and prepared to wash her hair. Once a thick lather was built up on her hands, Dééd Yázhí rubbed the thick, sweet-smelling foamy lather into her hair and rubbed until she heard the individual strands of hair begin to squeak. She rinsed her hair in the clear, shallow water that ran past. Looking up, she saw other Naabeehó women washing their hair in the same fashion she washed hers. The scent of yucca-root soap was so thick in the air it made her dizzy when she inhaled a full breath of air.

Dééd Yázhí washed each of her adopted sons' hair and rinsed their hair. She smiled a gentle smile as she watched each little boy leave the river bank shaking his head from side to side like a goat that was just shorn. The young Naabeehó man also released his long black hair from his tsiitł'óół *hair tie* and watched it rest on the current of the clear running water before it was enveloped by the water. He also lathered his hands and washed his hair. He loved the scent of the yucca root. He thought of the sensuous scent of yucca root Dééd Yázhí's hair would carry. He wanted to stand behind her so a slight breeze could carry the luscious scent to excite his senses.

Dééd Yázhí watched the young Naabeehó man stand up from his kneeling position after he washed his long black hair. The sight of his long black hair lying on his light brown skin caused her to catch her breath. She remembered the touch of the young man's hand as it softly brushed against her breast. She shook her body and stomped her feet to rid her mind of the memory. The young Naabeehó man saw her little dance and quietly laughed. He enjoyed caring for her.

The rest of the day was devoted to transporting the Naabeehó people across the narrow, deep river on short narrow rafts. Dééd Yázhí greeted the water before she sat down on the raft.

Within a few days the people were herded onto a low mesa that overlooked the Fort Sumner Navajo Indian Reservation. On the western side of the Pecos River the people were plagued by insects, snakes, and vicious birds. In spite of being faced with new dangers, the people drank the water that ran swift and was sweet to the taste. Dééd Yázhí was comforted daily by the water that swiftly ran past them as they faced nature's hardships. Many times a day she thanked the water for its abundance.

The soldiers who forced Dééd Yázhí and her Naabeehó people to walk many miles to Fort Sumner were ordered to return to Albuquerque to bring more prisoners. The soldiers left without a word or a glance over their shoulder. Dééd Yázhí was grateful to the soldiers for not taking her little one away from her.

Chapter Twenty-two

A Relative at Last!

The soldiers who met the Naabeehó people at Fort Sumner were angry. Before they met their new captives, they were angry. With their long whips, they whipped at the feet of the people who just arrived. Dééd Yázhí kept her head down and put one foot in front of the other. Holding her little one tighter than usual, she gathered her seven little boys around her to protect them. The young Naabeehó man carried their heavy pack on his back and with his free arm he helped the old man who had become extremely weak.

Dééd Yázhí looked up to find many Naabeehó people facing them. The first excited thought she voiced was,

"Áłahjį' Diné bizaad bee yá'áti'go diists'a' dooleeł." *I will hear the Navajo language being spoken all the time.* But when she looked directly into the faces of her people, she gasped. The excitement on her face dissipated. She saw thin women holding naked babies. Children hugged their mothers. Women, men, and elders stood staring at them through sunken eyes, looking tired and very hungry. All Dééd Yázhí could say was,

431

"T'óó la' haa dahojoobá'ígo 'ałk'idahanii'." *They are pitiful as they stand several persons deep.*

Dééd Yázhí felt an arm brush against her. She turned to look. It was the young Naabeehó man letting her know he was right beside her to support her and her little one. He said,

"Yáadishą'! Háajj'shą' nihe'anaa'í ch'ídanihizh'eezh? Haash dahwiilyaago? Ha'át'íísh biniinaa ts'ídá t'áá 'awołíbee nihik'ee dazhdeeznih? Díí yee' dooda! Nihidine'é t'óó baa dahojoobá'íyee'. T'óó la' baa jóchaígi 'áhoot'é. Ła' shį́į́ nihité'áziní danilį́. Hatíhíláa ne'ę́ę́'! Shí doo 'ádá 'ádíshnii da. Ni dóó niyázhí dóó díí 'ashiiké yázhí bá 'ádíshní. Nihicheii dó' baa nitséskeesgo 'ádíshní. Shí naabaahii nishłį́. Ti'hoo'nííh bínísdzil dooleeł biniiyé nashidi'neeztą́ą́'. Nihí 'éí t'áadoo bínanihidi'neeztą́ą́' da. Hatíhíláa ne'ę́ę́'!

What uncertainty! Where have our enemies led us? What have we done to them? Why do they have such hatred for us? This is horrific! Our people are in such pitiful condition. One could just cry over this. Some of them are possibly our relatives. What frightening conditions! I am not saying it for myself. I am saying this on your behalf and on the behalf of your little one and for these little boys. I am also thinking of our maternal grandfather as I say it. I am a warrior. I was trained to withstand suffering. You were not taught that. What frightening conditions!

The soldiers whipped at the Naabeehó people who stared at Dééd Yázhí and her group of people who had just arrived by force at Fort Sumner. There was no room for Dééd Yázhí and her group to move forward. With each crack of the whip, the crowd of thin, starving, naked people made room. Dééd Yázhí had never seen so many Naabeehó people at one time.

Women reached out, staring into the faces of the group that just arrived. They were possibly looking for loved ones. Dééd Yázhí tried looking back into their faces to see if she recognized anyone, but she could not imagine any member of her family being there and looking like them. She refused to allow herself to think her mother or her sister or her father or any other member of her family was among the prisoners.

As they were marched past the sea of faces, Dééd Yázhí felt extremely guilty that she had shoes, blankets, and a little food, and that her hair was freshly washed. Many of the people had no shoes or clothes. Some had clothes that resembled torn rags.

Without warning, a loud, piercing cry broke through the crowd, separating the people who were peering into the newcomers' faces.

"Háádę́ę́'shą' nihidi'noolkał?" *From what area have you been forced to walk here?*

Someone in Dééd Yázhí's long procession answered,

"Dook'o'oosłííd biyaadóó, Dziłabéí hoolyéédę́ę́' ádeiit'į. *We are from the base of the San Francisco Peaks, from a place called Gray Mountain.*

A brave man leaning on a long stick hoarsely said,

"Yáa, yáa, yáa, sha'áłchíní. Nízaadę́ę́' ádaoht'įį lá. Háshinee' dó' ádaoht'į. Haashįį dahwiilyaago kwe'é 'ąąhéeshjéé' ádanihiilaa. Doo sohodoobéézhgóó ti'danihiyoołnííh." *My children. You are from a long ways away. Dear ones. It is uncertain what we did to them but they have made us their prisoners here. They are making us suffer in an extreme way.*

An older near-naked woman reached out and touched the young Naabeehó man's shirt made of deer hide. After feeling the soft hide, she said,

"Danihízhánee'. Danihi'éé' dahólǫ́. Díí yee' k'é dóó nihizaad t'éí bee hadadíníit'é." *You are fortunate. You have clothes. We are clothed only with kinship and our language.*

A younger woman who wore only strips of what appeared to have been a rug dress yelled,

"Nihí 'éí dichin dóó ch'énáh t'éí bee hadadíníit'é." *We are clothed only with hunger and loneliness.*

A middle-aged woman poked her head out between several destitute people and said,

"T'áá nihígi 'át'éego nihí dó' danihi'éé' dahólǫ́ǫgo kojį' adanihidi'neeskaad, áko nidi danihi'éé' danihik'ééyol. Níyol nidi nihe'anaa'í yił k'é 'ahi'doo'niidgo nihik'ijį' nídiibaa'." *We had clothes on when we were forced to walk here, but our clothes were blown off of us. Even the wind declared a kinship with our enemy and has declared war against us.*

Dééd Yázhí felt as if she were gagging on the words of her people as she muttered,

"Háadishą' ádeiit'į?" *Where are we?* Her tongue felt like it was swollen as she desperately tried to mouth the words, "Shimá ... Shizhé'é ..." *My mother ... My father...,* but the words refused to come out of her mouth to mingle among the destitute people.

An old man scolded the new prisoners, saying,

"Doo hiniih ádahołyą́ą da. Doo haniih Dook'o'oosłííd, nihidził diyinii, bit'áahjį' adanohchéeh da." *You all must not be very smart. You should have run toward the protection of the San Francisco Peaks, our sacred mountain.*

Dééd Yázhí felt as if she were spinning from the many comments the people were shouting at them. She wanted to ask someone where they were from but she was overwhelmed at

434

the number of people who were standing in their way. Impatient soldiers whipped at the poor, naked people. The curious people quickly retreated behind the person standing near them as they rubbed the red lines the coarse whip left on their bodies.

Dééd Yázhí held her little one very close. She wished with all her might that her little one were still safe in her womb, not yet born. She shook her head as if to deny the sight before her. Angry questions began marching through her mind.

Shimá dóó shizhé'é da shą' háadi naa'aash?

Kojį' daats'í 'atah abi'di'noolcháá'?

Háíshą' ts'ídá t'áá'awołíbee danihijoołá?

Ha'át'ííshą' biniinaa doo chohoo'įįgóó Naabeehó dine'é ba'áłchíní deijoołá?

Haash dahoolaago?

She'awéé' shą' haadahoolaago kojį' adajizlóóz?

Shí nidi, haashą' yisdzaago kojį' adashizhneeshcháá'?

Da' t'áásh aaníí díí dazh'neez'įį'go biniinaa kojį' adahodi'neeskaad?

Where are my mother and my father?

Have they been chased here along with the others?

Who really hates us?

Why do they really hate the children of the Navajo people?

What did the children do to them?

What did my baby do to them for them to lead him here?

Even me, what did I do for them to chase me here?

Did all these people really steal, and that is why they were chased here?

Díí shidine'é doo 'a'ni'įįhii danilįį da. Yóówéé 'át'éego t'áá'ájít'é dazh'neez'įį' dooleeł. Háíshą' bijéí 'ádinígíí kónihił'į?

My people are not ones who steal. It is unbelievable that all of them would be ones who steal. Who is the one who does not have a heart who is doing this to us?

Dééd Yázhí became dizzy from fatigue, hunger, disappointment, and the harsh questions that tormented her mind. She felt weak. Just when she needed him the most, she felt the strong arms of the young Naabeehó man. She did not need to look up at him to see if it was him who was breathing on her hair. She could sense his strong presence. She leaned back into the body of the young man who leaned over to keep her from falling.

"Nihimá baa 'ádahołyą," *Take care of your mother,* she heard the young man tell her little sons. The little boys who stared at the naked people turned toward Dééd Yázhí and buried their faces in her tattered rug dress and began to cry. Their little bodies shook as they cried leaning against her. They needed to have their attention turned from the many naked, sick, and desperate people who stared back at them. Although the young Naabeehó man had his hands full from the large pack he carried, he lowered the pack and picked up the youngest boys and pulled the older ones close and comforted them. The little boys hid their faces in his chest. The old man momentarily regained his strength and took the two oldest boys' hands and started walking in the direction the soldiers told them to walk. Dééd Yázhí could hear the old man speaking comforting words to the boys as he walked bravely forward. She felt comforted in watching her sons walk bravely with the old man.

Soldiers surrounded Dééd Yázhí and her people and directed them toward a large stone building, away from all the destitute people. Dééd Yázhí could finally breathe. She took deep breaths, wishing she could breathe for her little one. She lifted her thin blanket to find his eyes wide open. As soon as their eyes met, her little one smiled a big smile at her. Tears collected in her eyes. She wanted her son to be brave just like the young Naabeehó man who clearly demonstrated to her that he had fallen in love with her. She stomped her feet to clear her head of any thoughts of love with the young Naabeehó man.

The men were escorted into the building while the women and children were left standing outside. The young man brought the little boys to Dééd Yázhí and helped the old man who slid down in slow motion to the ground. He told the little boys to take care of their mother's beedí *bedding and belongings.*

As he turned to leave, he left additional orders, saying,

"Nihimá bibeedí bá baa 'ádahołyą. Bikáá' dah nahísóotą. Baa 'ádahołyą," *Take care of your mother's bedding. Sit on top of them. Take care of them.* He left a smile for each little boy, then looked into Dééd Yázhí's eyes and let his eyes communicate how he felt about her. Reaching up, he rubbed her little one's head before he turned to join the men who had been ordered to enter the big, square house. Looking back, he said,

"Nihimá dóó nihitsilí yázhí baa 'ádahołyą. Nihicheii dó' baa 'ádahołyą. Nihí dó' áłhaa 'ádahołyą. Tsį́įłgo nihaa nídeeshdááł." *Take care of your mother and your baby brother. Take care of your maternal grandfather also. You too, take care of one another. I will come back to you in a hurry.*

Dééd Yázhí watched the brave, young Naabeehó man join the men who were walking into the square house. He walked proudly.

Watching the young man leave left Dééd Yázhí feeling cold. She was glad the sun was shining and was shedding warmth on her people without clothes. Thinking about the young Naabeehó man warmed her heart.

The old man interrupted her thoughts when he turned toward her and said,

"Dinééh yá'át'éehii nilį́. Díí 'áłchíní doo bí ba'áłchíní danilį́į da nidi t'áá bí ba'áłchíní, bá daazhchį́, nahalingo yaa 'áhályą́. Nízhánee', shitsóí, dinééh yá'át'éehii naa 'áhályą́. Bił ałhaa ni'dee'nil nahalingo naa 'áhályą́. Shí nidi 'ayóo shaa jooba'. Na'azheeh dóó na'nitin dóó 'ił ahojooba', díí t'áá'át'é bił bééhózin dóó yee 'aajooba'.

He is a young man who is good. Even though these children are not his, he still takes care of them as though they were born for him. You are fortunate, my granddaughter, a young man who is good is taking care of you. He takes care of you as if you were put together in marriage. Even toward me, he is very kind. He knows how to hunt and has teachings and kindness. All these things he knows, and he shows kindness by means of them.

Dééd Yázhí was comforted by the words of the old man. She was glad the old man survived the long walk. She had the young Naabeehó man to thank for his survival. She remembered how the young man distributed the contents of the large pack that he carried among her sons, for them to carry. Then he picked up the old man and carried him in his arms for a long distance as they trudged up the steepest sections of the mountain paths. She also reminded herself of the time he carried the old man on his back when the old man twisted his ankle and could not walk. Dééd Yázhí could feel her heart filling up with love for the young Naabeehó man.

Thinking of the many times the young man risked his life to obtain food and water for her and her children and the old man, warmed her heart to the point that it was ready to burst. While they were in the midst of the activities of walking toward the eastern direction those many days, Dééd Yázhí realized she never stopped to truly think of the many ways the young Naabeehó man had spared their lives. She stomped her feet again to shed her mind of the thoughts of love with the young man.

Her sons noticed her stomping her feet and wanted to know if she was OK.

"Aoo', wóláchíí' yee' shikélchí yíijée'go biniinaa nikídíshtał nít'ę́ę́'," *Yes, red ants were running onto my moccasins and that was why I was stomping my feet,* was her weak answer. Her sons began looking around themselves to make sure the red ants did not attack them. She smiled at their frenzied actions.

Dééd Yázhí breathed a sigh of relief when she saw Naabeehó men pouring out of the large building. The young Naabeehó man bravely walked up to her and said,

"Haa'ígi shį́į́ nihá nídahodii'ą́. 'Aadę́ę́' nihidi'noolkałgo tó nílínígíí bibąąhgi ch'íniikai yę́ęgi nihá nídahodii'ą́ą́ lá." *They have told us they have a place for us to settle upon. It is near the river we traveled along when we were being chased here.*

Dééd Yázhí asked,

"Shitsilí daats'í kojį' anihidi'noolkaadígíí bił bééhózin?" *I wonder if my younger brother knows we have been chased here.*

"Nihaa 'ákonízingo 'át'é. Bééhodoozįįł," *He is aware of it. We will see,* the young man replied as he reached up and wiped away a tear that refused to leave Dééd Yázhí's face.

"Ha'íínílní, shiyázhí," *Be strong, my little one,* the young man said as the words naturally and easily slid off of his tongue. Wanting the young man to say the words again, Dééd Yázhí asked,

"Ha'át'íí lá díníniid? T'áadoo nidiséts'áą' da. *What did you say? I did not hear you.*

"Ha'íínílní, nidishníi yee'," *I told you to be strong,* he answered thoughtfully.

Dééd Yázhí was saddened when he did not repeat the word that told her he was claiming her. She chided herself for not thinking of her little one's father. She wondered what she would have done or said had the young man repeated the word, "Shiyázhí," *my little one.* It was the same word her father used to address her mother.

Dééd Yázhí felt a sense of extreme loneliness overcome her. She wanted to cry but she was afraid that if she allowed herself to cry, she would never stop.

****

The soldiers spilled out of the large, square building. Dééd Yázhí was very worried. Were the soldiers going to separate them, sending her adopted children in a direction, different from where they were sending her and the young Naabeehó man? Her thoughts nearly got the best of her when to her relief, the interpreter told the group she and her family traveled with to follow them.

"Hágo, nihi'di'ní. Kéédahoht'íí dooleełgóó nihi'deesht'eezh. Tsįįłgo 'akéé' wohkah. T'áadoo 'akéé' ninádadinohdleehí, danihiłní." *They said, come here. They are going to take you*

to the place you will live. Hurry along as you follow. Don't
get behind, they said, the interpreter said in reference to the
soldiers' words.

A middle-aged Naabeehó man was given a stick with a
bright mustard-colored fabric tied to it. The man raised the stick
high up in the air.

"Ei tsin ha'át'íishįį yéego łitsogo béstł'ónígíí hádasídóo'įį'.
Hastiin ei tsin yootłígíí 'éí nihinaat'áanii nilį́ dooleeł. Tsį́įłgo
bikéé' wohkah. Kéédahoht'į́ dooleełígi t'áá nízaadi bił haz'ą́ągo
'át'é. Look for the stick with the deep yellow colored fabric tied
to it. The man who is carrying the stick is going to be your leader.
Hurry after him. The place where you will live is quite far.

Dééd Yázhí and her people followed the soldiers who rode
on their horses, who were then followed by a Naabeehó man
who carried the stick with the mustard-colored fabric attached
to it. Dééd Yázhí wondered why they were going back in the
direction they had come from. The sun disappeared behind the
western horizon and dusk silently crept over the people. They
were still walking when it became dark. The soldiers lit their
lanterns and kept moving in a northern direction. Dééd Yázhí
could hear water running. The sound of the water was loud as
it rushed over the boulders that stubbornly huddled against the
banks of the swift-running river.

Every so often she noticed they were led past little shacks
the soldiers called picket forts, which were square with funny-
looking roofs. When the soldiers passed each picket fort, they
greeted soldiers who sat looking out at the long procession
of Naabeehó people. The little shacks were lit from the inside

441

and the shacks looked small in the dark. The picket forts were placed along the forty square mile border of the Navajo Indian Reservation.

Through the interpreter, the Naabeehó people were told they should be thankful a man named President Abraham Lincoln was kind enough to establish this parcel of land he called "reserved lands" for your people. You will learn the art of peace on this reservation, they were told. In response, the Naabeehó leader whispered,

"Dził dadiyinii biníí'gi t'áá nihí nihikéyah dahólǫ́. Díí kéyah éí doo nihí nihá da." *We have our own land in the midst of the sacred mountains. This land is not for us.*

Although they could not see in the dark, Dééd Yázhí could feel they were walking up a slight incline that led to a slow rise in elevation. The soldiers stopped and used a dull hatchet to pound the end of a long pole into the ground. They checked to see if the pole was securely stuck in the ground then they tied a mustard-colored piece of fabric to the top of the pole.

Dééd Yázhí looked back in the direction they walked. She saw a straight row of picket forts dotting the landscape. She did not realize the picket forts were placed along the entire perimeter of the Fort Sumner Indian Reservation. From out of a couple picket forts, she heard soldiers laughing, arguing, and talking loudly. She wondered what they were talking, arguing, or laughing about.

She looked into the shallow valley and viewed hundreds of small fires sending little spurts of bright lights into the darkness. The small fires dimly lit up the entire valley before her. The small fires rose higher with the elevation of the landscape to show the

camping areas of her people creeping up the sides of the rising
hills. Dééd Yázhí was encouraged by the serene night scene
before her. She could not see the Naabeehó people who were
suffering.

Although she could not see them, Dééd Yázhí could hear her
people crying and talking. There was no sound of laughter that
was carried from her people to her ears. She viewed the scene
before her to mean she was no longer a prisoner held in the
little shed where she could not see her people. The many fires
meant she was not alone, her people were near. Her language
was near. Her clan relatives were near. She could hear the
Naabeehó language drifting up to her ears as she listened to a
woman scolding her little ones. Dééd Yázhí decided that from
where she stood, she would look down into the valley to search
for her mother and her father and her siblings.

The terror she witnessed earlier when she saw her destitute
people facing her was slowly vanishing from her mind. It was
pushed back further when the young Naabeehó man came close
and stood behind her. She could feel his warm breath on her
hair. She closed her eyes. She felt a beautiful man behind her.
She also felt her little one nuzzling against her breast. She put
her hands out beside her and felt her little sons move closer
to be enfolded in her arms. She heard the soft sound of the
Naabeehó language being spoken. She heard the water flowing
nearby, near enough for her to greet it on mornings when she
became lonely for her family. She smelled the pungent scent of
smoke rising from the fires her people were gathered around.

The young Naabeehó man was confused. He could not
believe the serenity of Dééd Yázhí's demeanor.

"Haash nít'é? Ha'át'íísh biniinaa doo nihidine'é nahalingo yíníł biih yíníłlizh da? *How are you? Why didn't you fall into emotional pain like our people?*

Dééd Yázhí spent the entire night telling the young man the rest of the story of her imprisonment at Fort Canby and how she was deprived of her Navajo language by not having anyone to speak to. She told of how alone she was the entire time because she was kept in a little shed. With the light of dawn illuminating the eastern sky, the young man understood how Dééd Yázhí remained so strong during their long walk. He was also able to understand her contentment in being close to her people. His respect and love for her grew.

Before the constellations disappeared by slipping behind the western horizon, Dééd Yázhí finally asked the young man the name his family gave him. He answered with shyness and laughed as he said,

"T'ah ánísts'íísígo shibízhí Kiizhóní yee shíizhi'." *When I was still little, my paternal aunt named me Pretty Boy.* Although Dééd Yázhí knew the answer, she interrupted him by asking,

"Ha'át'ííshą' biniiyé 'éí yee níizhi'?" *Why did she give you that name?*

"Hóla, t'óó daats'í bił nishzhónígo biniinaa. Shibízhí shíizhi'ígíí 'at'ééké t'éiyá ba'áłchíní nít'ę́ę́'. Shimá nihits'ą́ą́' ádingo shibízhí t'óó náshidiiłtį́į́ dóó bił nikidiishkai. Shibízhí bich'ooní, shizhé'é 'ash'ínée bi'diisyį. Shizhé'é 'ádin silį́į́'go shibízhí yik'ee kadeeyá. Hastą́ą́ nááhai yę́ę́dą́ą́' shibízhí 'ádin silį́į́'. Éí 'áádóó t'óó nikidiiyáago níléí Dziłíjiinjį' íiyáá dóó 'aadi nitsilí dóó binaabaahii bił nikidiishkai. *I don't know. Maybe because I was pretty to her. My paternal aunt who named me had*

444

only daughters. When my mother died, my paternal aunt took me in and I became a part of her family. My paternal aunt's husband, the man who adopted me, was killed. When my father died, my paternal aunt became sick. My paternal aunt left us six years ago. After that, I just started walking to different places and went to Black Mesa and that is where I joined your younger brother and his warriors.

Dééd Yázhí had to admit Kiizhóní was truly beautiful to look upon and he was devoted to her and her little one and her little sons and their maternal grandfather. She wondered if her brother planned for the young man to fall in love with her. She was happy the young man was with them. She felt safe in his presence. She felt safe when he was with her little family.

****

Dééd Yázhí and Kiizhóní were assigned to an area that was near the bank of the Pecos River. Dééd Yázhí loved listening to the sound of the water flowing nearby. In listening to the water, she felt free. On their first night, she asked Kiizhóní to accompany her and her little one to the bank of the river because she wanted to greet the water.

"Tó nílínígíí bich'į' shíni'. Tó k'é bidideeshniił, áko nihaa jooba' doo," *I want to go to the river. I want to greet the river so it will be kind to us,"* she quietly said. Being mindful of the picket forts, Kiizhóní responded,

"Ha'íí'ąągo 'índa 'ákǫǫ diit'ash. K'ad éí doo hoot'įį da," *Let's go when the sun comes up. It is too dark to see.*

"Dooda, t'ahdoo da'iighááshdą́ą́' tó k'é bidideeshniił nisin," *No, I want to greet the water before everyone goes to sleep,* she insisted.

445

"Tį'ínee', *Let's go then,* Kiizhóní said as he reluctantly agreed to accompany her to the bank of the river. Finding the safest path to take, he took her hand, and led Dééd Yázhí to the water's edge. Taking her little one in his arms, Kiizhóní silently and patiently stood by as he listened to Dééd Yázhí greet the water and express gratitude toward it for watching over them.

"K'ad ląą, tóhígíí nihaa 'áhályą́ą dooleeł. Biniiłt'aa 'anídaniichéeh dooleeł. Nihik'iha̱ła' doo. Binahjį' da, shí dóó shiyázhí shimá dóó shizhé'é bił ná'ahiidiiltsééł," *Now, the water will take care of us. We can run to it for safety. It will cheer us up. Possibly, through it, my little one and I may see my mother and my father again,* she said as she turned away from the water and allowed the beautiful young Naabeehó man to take her hand to lead her up the bank of the river.

The sound of the running water soothed Dééd Yázhí and caused much of the apprehension she felt about becoming a prisoner of war to fade. As Kiizhóní led her, he told her they did not have to carry water very far; neither did they have to rely on their enemy soldiers to provide them with the water that was yellowed from storage.

The Naabeehó people noticed that when it rained, the water in the river would become very bitter. Dééd Yázhí and Kiizhóní noticed their water jugs would become lined with a white substance that would turn to powder when it dried. The white powder was very bitter. Later, the Naabeehó men learned the white powder was alkali. Recent rains far to the northwest of the reservation loosened alkali deposits that washed into the river, causing the water to become bitter, which led to the Naabeehó people experiencing severe stomach pains. On the days when it rained in the northwest region, Dééd Yázhí worried about the well-being of her little one as well as that of her sons and the old man. She knew the water would be bitter for a few days before it became clear and drinkable again.

Walking to the river one morning, Dééd Yázhí heard the sounds of the soldiers who lived in the nearby picket forts as they laughed and talked loudly. She closed her ears to the sounds of the soldiers. She also heard the soft voices of Naabeehó women consoling their crying children. She knew the children were crying because they were hungry. She heard the sound of Naabeehó men singing songs in their effort to comfort themselves so they could speak encouraging words and words of strength to their families.

On their daily walks to the river, Kiizhóní looked for large pieces of driftwood that had floated down the river and had become wedged in the boulders that lined the riverbank. He took the driftwood back to their camp where he dried the wood, then used the wood to make a triangular-shaped little hooghan *hogan* for Dééd Yázhí and her little one and her little boys. Kiizhóní and the old man preferred to sleep out under the stars where they could forget they were prisoners of war as they watched the beautiful constellations march across the night sky.

Dééd Yázhí had many worries. One of her daily worries was the absence of her younger brother who had not contacted them since they were forced onto the reservation. She wondered if her younger brother had tried to contact them. She further worried for his safety and wondered if he had been taken prisoner on the mountain trail. To ease her worried mind, Kiizhóní reminded her that her younger brother was a well-trained warrior who had been taught to live off of the land.

Another daily worry Dééd Yázhí had was the well-being of her mother and her father. She wondered if they were still in the safety of Dziłíjiin *Black Mesa*. She refused to think they were being held at Fort Sumner as prisoners of war. Her mother was a kind woman who never hurt anyone, so she did not deserve to be held here, she reminded herself. Dééd Yázhí could still hear the screams of her younger sister as she was carried away by the enemy. Dééd Yázhí hoped a kind enemy had rescued her younger sister. She wondered if her little adopted sons had any relatives who were also being held as prisoners at the reservation.

Kiizhóní provided a daily supply of food by gathering edible flowers whose petals were safe to eat, digging up roots of edible plants, and catching locusts and killing prairie dogs and other small animals the Naabeehó people were allowed to eat. He even found a beehive nestled in driftwood that had become wedged in the high bank of the river. After smoking out the bees by slowly burning rotten driftwood, Kiizhóní collected honey for Dééd Yázhí to enjoy.

To keep the camping area free of flies, mosquitos, and gnats that carried harmful diseases, Kiizhóní collected horse dung and mixed it with twigs and leaves and left them to dry. Once dry, the dung was slowly burned during the day and night. As the pungent smoke lazily curled around the camp of each Naabeehó family, it kept the area free of irritating dangerous insects.

Kiizhóní took it upon himself to gather all the children in their camping area and ordered each child to deposit dead intruders from the night before to be buried in a hole. He also kept the men busy cleaning the entire camping area to make it free of sand that had been saturated with urine and feces from the night before. In addition, he kept the children busy throughout the day, asking them to hunt for items that could be used for protection, with which he taught the children how to protect themselves and their mothers and younger siblings. At night, the area had to be burned to clear out the red ants, scorpions, centipedes, and spiders that angrily infested the camp every night.

Every three days, sadness and fear crept over the people who were camped near Dééd Yázhí and her little family. Dééd Yázhí felt great anxiety knowing Naabeehó women were left unprotected from the soldiers and the elements. The Naabeehó men were required to walk for an entire day to the parade grounds at the fort to be counted and to receive their rations. The men would spend the night at the fort, then come back to their women and children the next evening. Dééd Yázhí never slept on the nights when Kiizhóní was away with the men whose families were camped nearby.

****

Evil soldiers took advantage of the women and girls when the Naabeehó men were absent from their camps. To protect themselves and their children, Dééd Yázhí and the women used flat sticks to carry the day's excrement to a designated line they had drawn in the sand earlier in the day. A wide, long path of excrement protected the women and their vulnerable daughters from the mean nasty soldiers. In doing this, the women found the harmful insects and reptiles did not cross such a line either. The women covered their noses and laughed each time a breeze brought the foul smell into their camp. The next morning, the excrement was buried deep in the ground.

To further present themselves as undesirable women, the women and girls covered their hair with mud then plastered their hair with plant leaves and twigs. The women and girls laughed at one another as one looked even scarier than the next. In the morning, the women watched as their means of protection was washed away by a steady flow of clean water.

To protect their women and their daughters from a stubborn soldier who was determined to have his way with one of the women or girls, Naabeehó men took sharp yucca needles and dipped the sharp ends in rattlesnake venom and left the needles for the young boys to use if they needed to in order to protect their mother or their sisters.

Deep holes were dug in the ground at intervals on both sides of the battle line that was drawn to deter the soldiers from coming closer to the Naabeehó women and girls. An uprooted plant was placed in the hole to conceal the deep hole. The women knew the entire area had been cleared of all vegetation so when a plant was seen, the women knew the plant was concealing a deep hole. It was the hope of the women that a nasty soldier would step into the hole and sprain his ankle, causing the soldier to lose interest in the women and girls.

The Naabeehó women who camped near Dééd Yázhí noticed she had calmness about her. Few of her people knew of her ordeal as a captive of the enemy soldiers. Dééd Yázhí would not allow herself to be afraid of the soldiers. She knew she had fought with them and looked them in the eye and had survived. Just in case, she kept a steady supply of pebbles for her slingshot. When a stray insect entered her little makeshift home, she used the insect as her target and perfected her aim and ability to flatten and kill a harmful insect. Practicing her aim on an insect for the protection of herself and her little family helped her suppress humane thoughts for the enemy.

Before the early morning sun fully exposed the valley on the days the men were at the fort, the Naabeehó women and young boys busied themselves by clearing any evidence of their means of deterring their enemy from coming closer. The holes were filled in, plants were left, and the line of excrement was scooped up and placed in a deep hole. When the soldiers came to inspect the area, the puzzled looks on the soldiers' faces told the Naabeehó women their line of defense was not suspected.

One night, a couple of young soldiers had the urge to subdue a Navajo woman for their enjoyment. The Naabeehó women heard the soldiers' footsteps from afar. The lantern the soldiers carried also announced their approach. As the soldiers came closer, they discussed their intentions with one another. The women saw the light from the lantern sway then they heard a heavy thud followed by loud cursing. One of the soldiers yelled,

"What did I fall in? It stinks like those sick savages that live near the fort! Aww..."

The women held their breath. The soldiers retreated, still cussing. The women relaxed and allowed themselves to breathe. Quiet laughter could be heard as the women expressed their relief.

Dééd Yázhí was thankful to the Creator that her little one was a boy. She also thanked the Creator for giving her seven additional little boys. She felt she had fewer worries.

Young Naabeehó girls were never left alone. The women made it a practice to surround themselves and their daughters with their sons when they retired for the night. Dééd Yázhí was kept safe throughout the dangerous nights by eight little warriors who slept snuggled close by her side.

****

Kiizhóní and the men usually returned with rations of one-pound pieces of meat that had already begun to rot. Tucked into the rations were usually round coffee beans and yellowed flour. The flour was dotted with little dark bugs that had infested large bags of flour, which were stored in the commissary at the fort. Many hungry Naabeehó people willingly left the bugs embedded in the flour believing the bugs were adding nutrients to the bread they made. The first time Dééd Yázhí felt the flour, she noticed it felt greasy, which repulsed her. She was used to the dry, free-flowing feel of newly ground corn.

****

Late one night when all sounds of life had quieted and the area had been burned to clear out all harmful insects, Dééd Yázhí and her little one and her sons settled down in their little makeshift home. She was just about to drop off to sleep when Kiizhóní crawled in. Careful not to wake the sleeping little ones, he told Dééd Yázhí he heard the sounds of a lone coyote near the river.

Dééd Yázhí's heart was extremely hopeful with the report. Their supply of jerky had run out and their supply of berries had long run out. Fresh water that at times was bitter, edible plants, and small game was all her family was subsisting upon.

She heard Kiizhóní's quiet steps leave their camping area. When the soft pale light of dawn was nudging the darkness and pushing it toward the western skies, Dééd Yázhí heard someone walking with a heavy step. Fear gripped her heart. She grabbed her little one and held him tight as she waited for the person to enter their makeshift home. In the distance, she could hear soldiers coughing and making angry noises.

A person was standing just outside her home. She grabbed her slingshot and placed a round pebble in it and held it taut in front of her. With a brave, loud voice, she demanded,

"Ha'át'íí lá? Háísh ánít'į? Da'awosh yee'! Ha'át'íísh haniná?" *What is it? Who is it? People are sleeping! What do you want?*

The answer was in a voice she did not recognize. It was the voice of a man. She became afraid. She wondered where Kiizhóní was. She wondered if he was still near the riverbank. She held her breath to listen for the actions of the person outside. She wondered if it was a soldier who strayed from one of the picket forts in search of a woman.

She heard the man's voice again. Someone was whispering,

"Dédii. Dédii. Shí 'ásht'į, nitsilí, nikéé' góne' naagháhígíí. *Dédii. Dédii. It is me, your younger brother who is just younger than you.*

Dééd Yázhí could not believe her ears! No one outside of her family knew her nickname, and the person called her by her nickname. Very few people knew the full name of her younger brother because his name was sacred, so she asked him to tell her his full name.

"Nízhi' ná 'ályaaígíí bee shił hólne'." *Tell me the name that was made for you.*

"Nahat'á Yinaabaah dabijinínígíí 'éí shí 'ásht'į." *I am the one they call One Who Goes to War Around Plans.*

"Nimá dóó nizhé'é shą' haa wolyé?" *What are the names of your mother and your father?*

Dééd Yázhí whispered the name of her mother Nínááníbaa' and her father Hashké Yił Naabaah as the voice spoke their names. She began to wail.

"Háshinee', shitsilí. Da' t'áásh aaníí ni 'ánít'į? Háláane'ęę', shitsilí," *Dear one, my younger brother. Is it really you? Dear one, my younger brother,* she cried as she covered her mouth so as to quiet her uncontrollable wailing.

Her little one stirred. She wanted to jump up and hug her younger brother, the only close relative she had heard from in several years, but she did not want to wake the little ones who were sleeping soundly near her. They had gone to sleep hungry, and she knew they would wake up and begin crying because their little bodies craved food.

Her brother respectfully waited outside until she came crawling out of her little hooghan *hogan*. Into the arms of her younger brother she fell. Although the light was pale, Dééd Yázhí was finally able to see her younger brother in full view. When he visited her at the little shed at Fort Canby, she only heard his voice and saw his image through the little hole in the wall as he walked away from the shed after their visit. Their tears mixed as they hugged and cried and hugged and cried several times again.

"Háadishą' nanináá nít'ę́ę́'?" *Where were you?* she asked. "Aadę́ę́' nihidi'noolkałgo t'óó níháne'. Ahéhee', shitsilí, nihik'idíní'įį'go binahjį' t'áadoo nihitah dahoniigai da. Honíyói

454

lá, shitsilí. Háshinee' dó' íinidzaa. Nida' bik'idíní'įį'go tó baa
náníłch'ął nít'ę́ę́'. Ahéhee'gi 'ánihiinilaa." *When we were being*
chased here, I heard about you. Thank you, my younger brother.
We did not get sick because you were watching over us. You are
a hard worker, my younger brother. You are dear to me for doing
that. You watched over your nephew by bringing him little jugs
of water. We are very grateful for what you did for us.

Dééd Yázhí crawled back into her little home and brought
out her sleepy little one. Speaking to her little one she said,

"Díí dinééh nidá'í nilį́, shiyázhí. Nidá'í k'é bidiní. Binahjį'
nikáa'jį' hazlį́į́', shiyázhí." *This young man is your maternal uncle,*
my little one. Greet your maternal uncle. Because of him, your
life was spared, my little one.

Her younger brother reached out his arms and she placed
her son in her brother's arms. With tears flowing from his eyes,
her brother met her son, and greeted his little nephew saying,

"Yá'át'ééh, shida', she'awéé'. Doo lá dó' naadzólníi da,
shida'. Nimá bich'ą́ą́h nanibaahgo binahjį' nimá yisdáált'á.
Naabaahii yázhí sínílį́į́', she'awéé'. Doo nimá baa yíníłt'áágóó
shį́į́ 'éí nimá doo kǫ́ǫ́ hólǫ́ǫ da doo nít'ę́ę́'. Nimá nihe'anaa'í
yisnááh ádabiilaa. 'Azhą́ shį́į́ nihe'anaa'í bá shínílchíin nidi,
shida' nidishnii dooleeł. Háshinee', she'awéé'. Tó 'Aheedlíinii
nílį́ dóó Ma'iideeshgiizhnii 'éí danicheii. 'Éí beego Naabeehó
be'awéé' nílį́. Nihe'anaa'í yóó'adanishchį. Nik'i dahineezhchą́ą́'.
Yówéé 'ádazhdoonííł! T'áá hazhó'ó nimá Naabeehó dine'é nilį́igo
nik'ijidlíigo dóó naa 'áhályą́ą́go dóó 'ayóó'ánó'níigo t'áadoo
nik'inííchą́ą́' da." *Greetings, my nephew, my baby. You are very*
handsome, my nephew. You are a warrior who has protected
your mother and because of it your mother has found safety.

You have become a little warrior, my baby. If you had not come
running into your mother's life, your mother probably would not
be alive. Your mother was kidnapped by our enemy. Although
you are born for the enemy, I will call you my nephew. Dear one,
my baby. You are of the Water Flows Together People, and the
Coyote Pass People are your maternal grandfathers. In that way,
you are a child of the Navajo people. Our enemy abandoned you
before your birth. They abandoned their responsibilities of caring
for you by running away. Who would do such a thing! It was
your mother who is Navajo, and she was the one who blessed
you and took care of you and loved you without abandoning
you. Tears flooded Dééd Yázhí's eyes as she listened to her
younger brother greet her son.

Looking toward the eastern sky, her brother shook hands
with his little nephew and said in a loving gentle voice,

"Yá'át'ééh, shida' yázhí." *Hello, my little nephew.*

Dééd Yázhí looked into her little one's face. She was so
proud and pleased that her little one peacefully listened to his
maternal uncle greet him so eloquently. Dééd Yázhí was brought
back to the present by the feel of someone's breath on her hair.
She turned around to find Kiizhóní standing behind her. She felt
safe in the presence of two men who loved her. One loved her
as a relative and the other loved her as a woman. Dééd Yázhí
turned to her brother and said,

"Ahéhee', shitsilí, díí dinééh niháíníł'a'. Nizhónígo nihaa
'áhályáągo kǫ́ǫ́ hoolzhish. Ts'ídá t'áadoo nihik'inííchąą' da.
Bíighahí bik'ee ti'dahwii'níihgo nidi bí binahjį' nihitah dahółdzilgo
nihikáa'jį' dahazlį́į́'. Dinééh yá'át'éehii nilį́ lá. Shiyáázh t'áá
bí biye' nilį́ nahalingo shá yik'idéez'į́į'. Ashiiké yázhí tsosts'id

456

yilt'éego bąąh ádahasdjįdgo shit'áahjį' adahineezhcháą'. Éí nidi, t'áá bí ba'áłchíní danilį nahalingo yaa 'áhályą́ągo kojį' nihe'anaa'í ch'ídanihineeskaad. Nihicheii sání nidi nihá yaa 'áhályą́ągo łą́ yiską́. 'Aadę́ę́' yoołjiłgo nihicheii t'áadoo be'iina' bii' haalyáa da. T'áá 'ákónéehee niháíníł'a'. Nihá 'ahéhee' bididíiniił.

Thank you, my younger brother, for sending this young man to us. He has taken good care of us up to this point. He never abandoned us. Even though we suffered from so many things, we were able to draw strength from him and in that way we survived. He is a good young man. He took care of my son as if he were his own child. Seven little boys lost their relatives and they came under my care. Even them, he treated them as if they were his own children, as we were being chased here. He even took care of our maternal grandfather for many days. Our maternal grandfather did not lose his life because he carried our grandfather on his back as we walked here. It is good that you sent him to us. Thank him for us.

After a thoughtful pause, Dééd Yázhí's brother turned to his friend Kiizhóní and said,

"Shádí yaa nahasne'ígíí t'áá'aaníígóó 'ání. Niniiłt'aa shida' dóó shádí bikáa'jį' hazlį́į́'. T'áá 'awołíbee nich'į' baa 'ahééh nisin. Bił háíjéé' dóó shimá dóó shizhé'é 'ałdó' t'áá 'ákódeinízin." *What my older sister said is true. Because of you, my nephew and my older sister's lives have been spared. I am extremely thankful to you for that. My siblings and my mother and my father feel the same way.*

The young Naabeehó man was smiling. He knew he would have done his job of protecting Dééd Yázhí and her little one as best as he could, but it pained him that he was the only one who knew why he was so dedicated to her and her little one. He loved her and her little one and all her adopted sons.

Dééd Yázhí's younger brother remembered he had brought a large pack of food, water, and medicinal herbs. Dééd Yázhí opened the large pack to find large fat pieces of 'ałk'íniilgizh *jerky* made of venison. She broke a little piece off and placed it on her tongue and let the delicious taste of the meat hug her tongue as it coaxed her taste buds to saturate her mouth with the nourishing piece of meat. She also found large bundles of ch'il ahwéhé *wild tea* hidden in the pack. She put her hands over her eyes when she spotted several ears of blue corn. She reverently ran her fingers over several kernels of corn, which were snuggled against the long cob. The pack also held a pottery bowl full of red chili peppers and another held yellow corn kernels. Another bowl offered juniper berries, another bowl was bursting with beautiful plump berries, and still another had yucca roots stuffed in it.

Dééd Yázhí started wailing again, as she said,

"Nihimá dóó nihizhé'é nizhónígo nihiyaahooł'a'," *Our mother and our father raised us well.*

"Aoo', t'áá'aníí nizhónígo nihiyaahooł'a'," *Yes, that is true, we were raised well,* her younger brother agreed thoughtfully.

"Shí dóó shiyázhí t'áá sáhí ch'íniit'áázh hanii nisin nít'ę́ę́'. Nihik'ííníyáádóó nizhónígo nihaa 'áhólyą́ągo hahoolzhiizh," *I thought me and my baby had ended up all alone. Once you found us, you took good care of us,* Dééd Yázhí continued.

"Nihizhé'é nihich'į' anáshííł'a', nádí dóó nida' nihá baa 'áhólyą́ą́ doo, shidííniidgo biniinaa 'aadę́ę́' nihidi'noolkałgo nihik'i dínísh'į́į' nít'ę́ę́'," *Our father sent me back to you, telling me to take care of you and my nephew, and that is why when you were forced to walk here, I watched over you,* her brother answered.

"Nihimá dóó nihizhé'é bił ná'ahiistsą́ą́go shíká 'ííníłwodígíí yiniih dooleeł. Ayóo jiiníba', shitsilí. T'áadoo nihik'iníínícháą' da," *When I see our mother and our father again, they will hear of how much you helped me. You are very kind, my younger brother. You never abandoned us,* she said, as she let her younger brother know how touched and grateful she was by his help.

Dééd Yázhí asked her younger brother what his plans were. He told her he would remain hidden in order to provide food and water for her and her children.

The people in their camping area were up and walking around. Dééd Yázhí became worried when some men kept looking in their direction. Kiizhóní went to meet the men while Dééd Yázhí's brother climbed into her makeshift home for a day's rest. Late that night, under the protection of complete darkness, Dééd Yázhí's younger brother left the little family to return to his hiding spot. He decided to remain an invisible provider because Dééd Yázhí and her baby needed fresh water and fresh meat so he pledged to keep the provisions coming regularly.

Dééd Yázhí became reacquainted with what she had been missing for several years, the closeness of relatives. During the long walk, Dééd Yázhí felt an intense sense of loneliness, mostly because she did not want to expose the lineage of her little one. To heal and raise her spirits she turned to her language.

She vowed to use her language to encourage others. She was determined not to allow herself to become entrenched in sorrow like many of her Naabeehó people.

Dééd Yázhí and Kiizhóní realized the Naabeehó man the soldiers chose as their leader had become preoccupied with their predicament as prisoners of war. Their leader no longer had words of encouragement for his people nor did he try to look for ways to make their life better by speaking to the soldiers on behalf of his people.

Although Dééd Yázhí was a prisoner of the soldiers, she was thankful for her freedom. Her freedom lay in seeing the many little fires with which her people warmed themselves at night. She was free to hear her neighbors speaking Naabeehó. Although meager in portions, she felt freedom in eating the food her younger brother provided which was food she enjoyed as a child. She felt freedom in watching the stars march across the night sky. Dééd Yázhí felt freedom at the touch of her little one and her seven little sons and the gentle old man. She also felt freedom when Kiizhóní breathed on her hair when he stood close by her side to let her know she was not alone.

Each new dawn brought new hope to Dééd Yázhí. She heard prayers being voiced to the Creator as her Naabeehó people's hopeful prayers drifted across the valley below, over the hills, and into the ears of the Creator. Dééd Yázhí prayed for the safety of her sister, the safety of her mother and her father, and the safety of her younger brothers. She also prayed for the safety of her son, her adopted sons, her new maternal grandfather as well as the safety of beautiful Kiizhóní.

After her prayers, Dééd Yázhí would hold her little one close
as she listened to the tearful prayers of the distraught Naabeehó
mothers who were suffering along with their children. She
wished she could feed her people who were suffering, but
she knew the Creator would hear the prayers of her people.
Dééd Yázhí thanked the Creator for providing for her, her little
one, her sons and her grandfather through her brave younger
brother and Kiizhóní.

Chapter Twenty-three
Meeting at the Parade Grounds

When the Naabeehó people were first settled on the forty-square-mile Navajo Indian reservation, they were reminded they had been forced to walk there because they had raided settlements near Dinétah. The sun did its best to bless the Naabeehó people, but people loathed each rise of the sun, because they were suffering. One month blended into the next, soon the beginning of each month went unnoticed. Seasons came and seasons went without notice. The years began to pile on top of one another. There were no events with which the people wanted to associate.

There was nothing to look forward to except the sunset and the night when the cries of the people were subdued. It was at night that the Naabeehó mothers and fathers were able to rest, rest from looking into the faces of their children, whose faces were contorted due to the pain the little ones were feeling. The people filled their stomachs with remembrances of the taste of mutton and filled their children's stomachs with promises of a full meal of atoo' *mutton stew* and jizésí *thin flat bread cooked over hot coals.*

Pain was what the people could count on. Pain from the loss of a loved one, pain from an empty stomach, pain from loneliness, pain from the bitter water the people were forced to drink, pain from watching their loved ones suffer from the horrid conditions of the reservation, and pain from not knowing when the suffering would end. Uncertainty was the greatest pain.

The soldiers found it was easy to lure and take advantage of girls and women with starving relatives by offering promises of food or clean water to drink. The girls and young women who thought they were helping their families followed the soldiers only to get raped by one or two or more soldiers. The girls and young women came back to their camps with no life in their eyes.

The women who did not become pregnant and who survived the rape went back to their husbands without suspecting they had caught any number of deadly diseases, but syphilis was the disease that by far plagued any girl or young woman who had been raped by a soldier or soldiers. Young women who were comforted by their husbands passed the deadly disease to their Naabeehó man who became infected by the disease. Although it was the filthy soldiers who infected the Naabeehó young women and girls, Naabeehó women were blamed for the outbreak in syphilis.

****

For many months, Dééd Yázhí watched over the girls and young women by smearing mud and leaves onto the faces and hair of the young girls and women. Dééd Yázhí and her family lived near three picket forts, leading to the frequent visits of

463

the soldiers. She took special care to make sure she was covered with mud as well. The soldiers came close to the young women and young girls but they would leave, cursing and whipping at the people when they found many of the girls and women were "very dirty."

Kiizhóní told his men to protect their wives and their daughters and to hide them when they knew the soldiers were coming. It was getting difficult to do so because the soldiers were coming around more often. The people held their breath when they heard the horses' hooves in the distance, then coming closer.

****

One day an interpreter came to tell Kiizhóní and his leader and his people that certain Naabeehó leaders and their people were to gather at the parade grounds on a specified day. He further announced that men, women, and children were to appear at the parade grounds so they could be counted. The people were immediately filled with fear. The Naabeehó men became afraid for their wives and their children because the soldiers were always angry. The elders begged their leader not to allow for the children to be counted. The elders claimed that every time the people were counted, their numbers were reduced by death, so they pleaded with their leader to go alone, but the message of the soldiers spoke louder. All the Naabeehó people were ordered to walk to the parade grounds.

On the specified day, Dééd Yázhí and her children and Kiizhóní and their people started walking eastward when the sun was still tucked in its resting place during the night. Dééd Yázhí carried her little one and covered him with her thin rug blanket. As a toddler, her little one was getting heavy. The people walked throughout the day. They did not arrive at the parade grounds until the sun met the western horizon. Kiizhóní and his leader and the men were used to walking to the parade grounds every three days, but the women and children were not used to walking that far in one day. It had been nearly two and a half years since the time Dééd Yázhí and her group of Naabeehó women and children had been forced to walk so far.

With fear in their hearts, the Naabeehó men, women and children walked past the stone buildings their Naabeehó men helped build. The women looked upon the buildings in wonderment. They shuddered at the size of the buildings. The women and children were used to seeing the soldiers who came to inspect and count them on a weekly basis but they were not prepared to see the many soldiers who encircled the parade grounds. Each soldier held a long rifle pointed directly at the Naabeehó people.

Dééd Yázhí's young adopted sons began to cry. They tried hiding behind their mother's rug dress, but there were too many of them to remain hidden behind her dress. Dééd Yázhí watched children running after their mothers as they tried to hide, but their mothers who were walking fast exposed the hiding children. She wondered if she was walking too fast for her sons. She slowed down to protect her little ones. She pulled her rug blanket close around her to protect her little one from being seen by anyone.

Dééd Yázhí looked around. Several Naabeehó leaders were with the people who were under their leadership. Many of the Naabeehó people appeared to be very sick. The sick people could not stand up straight. They stood bent over from the waist. Dééd Yázhí looked at her own group of people who were under Kiizhóní and the main leaders' protection, they looked sad. Many were not well, but they looked healthier than other Naabeehó people.

Dééd Yázhí looked around and noticed women who belonged to other leaders' groups. The women were wearing the type of clothing she had been forced to wear at Fort Canby. Embarrassment washed over her face. The Naabeehó women's clothing was made of thin fabric decorated with what looked like little flower designs. Many women were not wearing rug dresses. Those wearing the clothes of the enemy wore a flimsy top in the shape of a blouse made of deerskin and a flouncy skirt. Both articles of clothing fit loosely, just like the one Dééd Yázhí wore when she lived in the little shed. Upon closer inspection, she noticed the women's skirts were loosely gathered at their waists and the skirts were similar to the one she wore when she worked at the laundry house. Dééd Yázhí immediately felt the shame these women must have been feeling. Her heart felt sad for the Naabeehó women.

Dééd Yázhí had never seen another Naabeehó woman wearing the clothing of the enemy. She remembered how she was worried the Creator would not recognize her in a stranger's clothes. She asked herself if the Creator would recognize these women as Naabeehó women. Dééd Yázhí could only stare.

She was even more embarrassed that she too had been forced to wear the clothing of the enemy when she was held captive. She was deep in her thoughts when she heard Kiizhóní ask,

"Sáaniísh doo bi'éé' biyaa 'ííyol da?" *Does the wind not blow under their dresses?*

"Hóla," *I don't know,* was the only answer Dééd Yázhí could give. "Yáadilá 'óolyé. T'áá hó dahabiil 'éé' yę́ę shą'?" *What about their own rug dresses?* Dééd Yázhí asked in judgment of the women who did not seem to care whether or not the Creator recognized them as Naabeehó. As soon as she voiced the question, she became ashamed of her judgment of her people. The Naabeehó women were just trying to survive.

Dééd Yázhí's shame was increased when she heard Kiizhóní say,

"Akót'éego háádazhdiit'ą̨ hgo biniinaa ch'ééh sodazhdilzin. T'óó yéego hach'į' nidahwii'ná. Nihi'í'óol'ą̨ įł t'óó bits'ą̨ ją į' joonééł. Hatíhílą̨ ne'ę́ę'. *Their prayers are spoken in vain because they dress like that. They just really suffer. They are moving away from our culture. What a sad thing.*

Dééd Yázhí preferred her heavy rug dress that kept her warm during the cold weather and kept her cool and safe from the many harmful insects throughout the hot summers. While still staring at the thin material the Naabeehó women were wearing, Dééd Yázhí watched as a slight breeze gently began to play with the thin skirts and pressed the hem of the skirts against the Naabeehó women's thin ankles while their tattered and torn moccasins peeked out from under the thin material.

"Da' doósh biníkáníłk'aaz da?" *Does the cold air travel through the material?* asked Kiizhóní.

Dééd Yázhí answered, saying,

"Hóla. Dabibiil éé' shį́į 'ałtso bik'i nidahaazt'óodgo biniinaa 'akót'éego ééh daaskai." *I don't know. Their rug dresses probably*

467

became so tattered they had to dress in those clothes. Dééd Yázhí knew the answer. She was too embarrassed to let Kiizhóní know she also had worn that type of clothing herself at one time. Survival is what it is called, she thought to herself as she shuddered at her memory.

"Nibiil ééʼ biiʼ sínítįįgo shił nizhóní, shiyázhí," *I like it when you wear your rug dress, my little one,* Kiizhóní said to Dééd Yázhí as hé looked her up and down with a trace of want in his eyes.

Dééd Yázhí pretended she did not hear Kiizhóní call her his little one. It was the same word her father spoke, to claim her mother. Although she was looking at such sorrowful people, Dééd Yázhí felt warm inside. The warmth began in her heart and radiated to the rest of her body.

Dééd Yázhí needed to regain control over her mind.

"Wónáasii' la' nihe'anaa'í háádadiit'įįhígi 'át'éego nihidine'é háádadiit'įįh," Doo lá dó' dooda da," *Now our people have started dressing like our enemies. How terrible,* she said sadly, knowing she was secretly judging herself. "Nizhónígo hanii nihe'anaa'í háádadiit'įįh." *Our enemies do not dress nicely,"* she added as her anger grew with the soldiers who forced her to wear the clothes of the enemy. Dééd Yázhí was becoming agitated with her people. She wanted her people to fight! Fight to be Naabeehó! She believed she would have fought if she had someone to encourage her in her own language to remain Naabeehó.

Dééd Yázhí's attention was interrupted when she heard a baby crying pitifully. The baby's young mother was wearing a thin blouse and a thin flouncy skirt just like the Naabeehó women they were discussing earlier. The young woman easily lifted her thin blouse in an attempt to breastfeed her little one. The baby grabbed its mother's breast with its skinny little hands, exposing its mother's flat breast that hung down. Dééd Yázhí gasped when she saw a nipple that was swollen and raw slide into the baby's mouth. It was obvious that both the mother and the child were in pain. The young mother was in pain from her little one sucking on a nipple that could not produce milk because the mother was malnourished, and the pain the baby felt was due to starvation. The mother started to cry and soon her little one began to howl as well. Dééd Yázhí knew it was because the Naabeehó people did not have adequate water to drink. The young woman was dehydrated and so was her little one. The little baby arched its back and cried right along with its mother.

Dééd Yázhí pulled her rug blanket around her and held her little one tighter than usual. She wondered who the young woman's leader was. He should be the one taking care of the women and children. Dééd Yázhí wanted to help the young woman but the soldiers were pushing the women toward the far side of the large parade grounds.

The interpreter ordered the men to move to the opposite side of the parade grounds. In a quick action, the men were separated from the women and children. Dééd Yázhí saw Kiizhóní standing with Naabeehó leaders she had never seen or met. She carefully studied each leader's face, looking for her father's handsome features.

Instead of wearing woven rug blankets, the Naabeehó leaders wore blankets that were gray in color and very thin, ones similar to the blankets the soldiers gave Dééd Yázhí after they crossed the big river. Dééd Yázhí looked at Kiizhóní. He had the appearance of a leader with the striped rug blanket draped over one shoulder. Dééd Yázhí knew he proudly wore the blanket she offered him when they arrived at Fort Sumner. It was her rug blanket that he carried over many miles. She gave it to him, believing he had earned it.

****

After the women and children had been counted, Dééd Yázhí was preoccupied with the thin young woman and her undernourished baby, she did not hear the interpreter tell the women and children the soldiers wanted them to stand in a group near their leader. The women were anxious and afraid because they knew the light from the late afternoon sun was their only hope of finding their leader and their men. They desperately wanted to be near their men to feel safe. Commotion ensued. The large crowd of Naabeehó women and children searching for their leaders' colorful leadership stick were running and bumping into one another, trying to get to the opposite side of the wide parade grounds.

The soldiers nervously glanced at the location of the late afternoon sun. An annoyed group of young soldiers decided to rush the women and children to avoid greater confusion when the sun went down and darkness set in. A soldier holding a long rifle recklessly pushed past Dééd Yázhí and when he did, the end of his rifle became hooked on her tattered rug blanket. Not wanting to expose her little one, Dééd Yázhí frantically begged,

"Áłtsé! Áłtsé!" *Wait! Wait!*

The irritated soldier looked at her and yanked his rifle to free it, pulling the rug blanket off of Dééd Yázhí and exposing her precious little one. To her horror, Dééd Yázhí heard many Naabeehó women gasp. As she pulled her little one close to her, she saw many unfamiliar women rush toward her, glaring in disbelief at her little one. She heard a mean woman yell,

"Yáadishą' eidí. Ha'át'íísh biniiyé nihe'anaa'í be'awéé' dah nííł'įįł!" *Why are you hiding our enemy's baby?* The mean woman quickly reached for Dééd Yázhí's baby to pull him out of her arms, while another woman pulled on the mean woman's arms to keep her from the baby so she would not hurt him.

With frenzied women crowding around her, Dééd Yázhí became separated from her adopted sons in all the confusion. Desperately hanging onto her screaming little one, Dééd Yázhí frantically searched for her little boys, afraid the women would trample on her young sons. The mean woman took advantage of her distraction and reached in and grasped her little one by his arms again, nearly pulling his little arms out of their sockets. Silently, Dééd Yázhí fought to take her little one out of the mean woman's grip. A woman who lived near Dééd Yázhí reached in and tried pulling the baby out of the mean woman's arms, screaming,

"Bidíchxííd! Bidíchxííd nidishní!" *Let him go! I said, let him go!"*

In all the confusion, Dééd Yázhí's sons struggled to be rejoined with their mother and their baby brother. They fought their way through and found Dééd Yázhí, then tried protecting her and their baby brother with their bodies but their baby brother was suspended between their mother and two women.

471

The mean woman yelled at the Naabeehó women demanding they join her in taking the enemy's child away from its mother, but the women who lived near Dééd Yázhí yelled back at her in their attempts to protect their young leader's little family.

"Ei 'awéé' nihinaant'áaniishchíín biye' íił'ínígíí nilį́!" *That baby is the stepson of our young leader who is in training!* a women screamed.

The soldiers fired shots into the air to stop the commotion. Dééd Yázhí's little one was finally released by the mean woman. He was crying hysterically. Weakened by the confrontation, Dééd Yázhí fell to the ground and sat huddled on the ground with all of her sons surrounding her. Her young sons sheltered their mother and their baby brother with their bodies.

More soldiers came running out to the parade grounds with rifles drawn, ready to fire into the crowd. The anxious, worried Naabeehó men were held back by soldiers who had their rifles aimed, ready to shoot. From the screams he heard, Kiizhóní sensed the commotion surrounded Dééd Yázhí's son who was born for a white soldier. Kiizhóní felt so helpless!

All of a sudden, there was an even larger number of soldiers who came running out of the large buildings. The Naabeehó women gasped and retreated when they saw the large number of soldiers converging on the parade grounds.

Crying, Dééd Yázhí cradled her son and held onto him with all her strength. In an instant, several Naabeehó women demonstrated their hatred for the white soldiers by rushing in with the mean woman, pulling Dééd Yázhí's little one out of the safety of his mother's arms.

The soldiers fired more shots into the air, but the mean Naabeehó woman would not release her hold on the little toddler with light skin. A soldier rushed in and pushed the mean woman to the ground but she kept her hold on Dééd Yázhí's little one. A brave young woman reached in to pull the baby out of the angry woman's grip, instead, she fell on top of the woman, desperately using all her strength to hold the mean woman down.

A pesky breeze picked up the mean woman's flouncy skirt and playfully pulled it up around her knees. A young woman tried throwing her body on top of the mean woman to keep her skirt from blowing any higher, but young soldiers who were laughing pulled the young woman away. The mean woman finally released her hold on Dééd Yázhí's little one when she grabbed for her skirt to push it back down below her knees.

Dééd Yázhí's bawling little one was finally handed back to his mother. Dééd Yázhí was crying uncontrollably as she tightly held her little one to her bosom. Her little one wailed at the top of his lungs, causing more commotion. Dééd Yázhí tried pulling her rug blanket up around her to hide her little one from all the onlookers, but a soldier standing nearby deliberately planted his heavy boot on her tattered rug blanket.

Many Naabeehó women gathered around Dééd Yázhí to comfort her, but when they saw her little one up close, they gasped and slowly moved away from her. The brave young woman shielded Dééd Yázhí's little one with her body and began consoling the baby. The brave young woman snapped at the Naabeehó women, saying,

"Díí yee' asdzání niha'áłchíní bąąh ádahasdjjdígíí yaa
joozba'go 'áłchíní néidiinil dóó t'áá bí ba'áłchíní danilíjgo 'áyiilaa.
T'áadoo nihits'ą́ą' atídaoł'íní! Ahaa dajiiniiba'go nizhóní dooleeł.
Díí yee' t'áá'íídą́ą' nihe'anaa'í hóló̧. Naabeehó dine'é hanii
nihe'anaa'í danilį́. Díí 'awéé yázhí hanii nihe'anaa'í nilį́. Ha'át'íísh
biniiyé 'ak'ee'diniih nihii' daahééł?" *This young woman took our
children who lost their parents and made them her own children.
Don't mistreat her! We need to be kind to one another. We
already have an enemy. The Navajo people are not your enemy.
This little baby is not your enemy. Why do you have so much
hatred inside you?* Looking directly at the mean woman, she
raised her voice and said,

"Nihe'anaa'í bi'éé' biih yíníyá, 'éí shįį biniinaa nihe'anaa'í
nahalingo 'ak'ee'diniih nii' hééł. Ayóó 'ánit'éé dó', níyol k'asídą́ą'
ni'éé' neidiiyį́! T'óó la' naa yáhóósįjd, shimá." *You are wearing
the clothes of the enemy, that is probably the reason you have
become so full of hate, just like our enemy. You thought you
were someone great, but the wind almost took your clothes off
of you! You have been shamed, my mother.*

Still shaking, Dééd Yázhí kept her head down while in
desperation she whispered comforting words to her terrified
little one who was still crying. She tried pulling her rug blanket
loose, but the soldier would not lift his heavy boot off of her
blanket. Dééd Yázhí wanted to cover her little one to protect him
from her angry people.

A soldier with the voice of authority yelled at the young
soldiers who quickly stood at attention. Two young soldiers were
holding the mean woman to keep her from attacking another
person. The soldier with the voice of authority was an officer,

an older man who used a cane to walk due to a pronounced limp. The officer wore a black patch over his right eye. In his hand, he held a pistol. When the officer stepped forward, the young soldiers saluted the officer and then stood at attention, waiting for instructions. The officer barked,

"What caused the confusion?" A young soldier said,

"That dirty little half-breed there, sir."

"What half-breed?" the officer inquired.

"There, sir," the soldiers said in unison as they pointed at Dééd Yázhí and her little one. Still crying and holding her little one tight, Dééd Yázhí turned herself away from the soldiers to hide her little one. She heard the young Naabeehó 'ashkii *Navajo boy* gasp loudly.

In a gentle controlled voice, the officer asked,

"Is the baby all right?" Without waiting for an answer, he asked, "How is the mother doing?"

One young soldier said under his breath,

"What do you care about these savages? They hate us and we hate them!"

The officer yelled at the young soldiers to remind them they were under orders. Quickly, they stood at attention, looking forward.

The officer walked to where the mean woman was being held. He asked for an interpreter to ask the old mean woman if she was hurt. In the same breath, he asked for the interpreter to inquire of how the young mother and her child were doing. Only Dééd Yázhí's soft sobs and the cries of her little one could be heard.

The impatient officer broke the silence by demanding that an interpreter come to help with communication. A young Mexican interpreter took his time crossing the parade grounds, then listened as the officer told him the questions he wanted answered. Lazily, the interpreter asked Dééd Yázhí,

"Ne'awéé'ísh yá'át'ééh?" *Is your baby doing all right?* After a long silence, Dééd Yázhí quietly said,

"Naabeehó 'asdzą́ą́ ła' she'awéé' shighai yííteehgo ch'ééh áát'įįd. Shibeeldléí 'éí shighadeiłtsóós." *A Navajo woman tried to take my baby away from me. They are taking away my rug blanket.*

The interpreter told the officer what Dééd Yázhí said, then pointed to the rug blanket the soldier was standing on.

The officer used his cane to poke at the young soldier's foot to get him to step off of the tattered rug blanket. With great difficulty, the officer leaned over and picked up the loose end of Dééd Yázhí's rug blanket, then lifted it to place it back around her when he looked into the face of Dééd Yázhí to see if she was all right.

Dééd Yázhí cringed with embarrassment when she heard her oldest adopted son scream with excitement,

"Folton! Folton!" yelled the young Naabeehó 'ashkii *Navajo boy.*

The officer looked for the young voice and smiled when he recognized the young boy who called him by name. The officer reached a hand out to the young boy to greet him, but Dééd Yázhí grabbed the young boy and yanked him behind her, immediately regretting the way she handled her well-behaved adopted son.

The officer leaned over to look into Dééd Yázhí's face. A smile wrinkled his face.

"My Sunflower?" the officer asked, forgetting he was surrounded by his soldiers. "Sunflower! Sunflower! My dear Sunflower, is it you?" the officer shouted as he stepped closer to look into Dééd Yázhí's eyes.

Recognition slowly spread over the officer's face. Forgetting he was also standing in the midst of hundreds of Naabeehó people, the officer loudly and excitedly spoke.

"It's me, your husband! I have come back to look for you! I am no longer fighting in the South. The war is over. I got hurt in the war but I finished my assignment. I have come a long way to find you! Whose baby are you holding? Did you get the letters I sent you?" the tall, gray-haired one asked with great excitement in his voice, all the while overlooking the language barrier that existed between him and his beautiful Sunflower.

A look of fear and embarrassment settled on Dééd Yázhí's face. She did not know what the old soldier was saying but she recognized his voice. Confused, the tall, gray-haired one lifted his hat off of his head and ran his fingers through his hair. Dééd Yázhí caught a glimpse of his hair. It was no longer gray, it had turned white and was thinning. Deeply embarrassed, Dééd Yázhí turned away from him and pulled the rug blanket around her to hide their little one.

The Naabeehó women and the soldiers stared at the officer who had forgotten where and who he was. The women did not know why the old soldier was happily raising his voice, but they could see he was very excited. They had never seen any of the soldiers who came to their camp act this way. They thought the officer was excited to see a little white baby.

"Are all these children yours? Where is …?" the tall gray-haired one said looking around.

Dééd Yázhí heard the subdued gasps the Naabeehó women breathed when the officer reached behind Dééd Yázhí and took hold of the young Naabeehó 'ashkii, but she was not worried. She knew the tall, gray-haired one would not hurt her oldest son. The tall gray-haired one turned to the young Naabeehó 'ashkii *Navajo boy* and pulled him aside by placing his hands on the young boy's shoulders, and said in a gentle voice,

"Son, ask Sunflower if she remembers me?"

The officer finally remembered where he was. Excitement left his face. He stepped back and told the interpreter to tell the Naabeehó women they had to rejoin their leader and stand near their leader to be counted because they were to be given blankets, rations of fresh water from Fort Union, and for the women, yards of colored calico fabric.

The tall, gray-haired one stepped back and blended in with the soldiers while the Naabeehó women who lived near Dééd Yázhí slowly gathered near to show their support for the woman who belonged to their leader, Kiizhóní, who was in training. Reaching out, they helped her up and placed her rug blanket securely around her shoulders.

Shots were fired in the air to get the attention of the Naabeehó people.

"Danihinaat'áanii bíighah daohsjih, nihijiní," *Stand near your leader, you are told,* the interpreter said in a loud bold voice.

Dééd Yázhí was left confused. She wanted to look back to search for the tall, gray-haired one. She desperately wanted to look at his lips, the lips that softly kissed her skin the nights before he left. She wanted to look into his eyes to search for the

478

kindness she saw when she looked into the eyes of the enemy. She also wanted to look at the tall, gray-haired one's hands to see the hands that touched her, the hands that awakened the wanting deep within her. She wanted to touch the arms that held her so tenderly before he disappeared for many months and years. Her thoughts came to a screeching halt with the word "disappeared."

Her thoughts stumbled as she chided herself by talking to herself under her blanket,

"T'óó yee' doo hwééhoozin da. T'áá 'óolyéego nihik'izhníícháá'. Biyázhí, be'awéé' yik'iníícháá'. Awéé' bíká nahwiidláhéédą́ą́' nidi shiyaa 'azhníícháá'. Jó shí da shits'íís bee haa 'áhosisyąąd." *He did not just disappear, he abandoned us. He abandoned his little one, his baby. Even when we were making love, he hid underneath me. I had to shield him with my own body.*

As she pondered upon love with the gray-haired one for a few minutes longer, Dééd Yázhí's mind stumbled on an idea. "What would my father say? Would he, a great War Leader, accept as a son-in-law a man who badly limped and who is blind? Worse yet, would he accept a member of the enemy as his son-in-law?"

To rid her mind of thoughts, Dééd Yázhí stopped in her tracks, stomped her feet, and shook her head and her body. Her sons stopped and mimicked her body movements. She watched in amazement, then a slow, wide-spreading smile covered her face. She loved her little ones. Dééd Yázhí looked back to get one more quick glimpse of the tall, gray-haired one, the one she held dear in her dreams and in her thoughts.

She shook her head again to suppress the thoughts her mind was posing. She quickly joined the Naabeehó women who were searching for the leadership stick Kiizhoní was holding, and then slowly moved toward their leader.

Still shaking, Dééd Yázhí led her young adopted sons to where Kiizhóní was standing. Her sons followed her as they held up her rug blanket. Dééd Yázhí saw Kiizhóní bravely and proudly holding the leadership stick. The bright mustard-colored material that was attached to the stick fluttered in the wind.

Embarrassed and scared Dééd Yázhí collapsed into Kiizhóní's arms. Kiizhóní gathered her and her little one into his arms and held them tight. Her adopted sons stood close by, ready to comfort their mother. Kiizhóní smiled at the young boys who were choking on their sobs. He reached out and wiped the tear stains off of their brave faces then drew them into the fold of his arm.

Kiizhóní asked Dééd Yázhí,

"T'áadoósh hait'éego da 'atídaniilaa da?" *Did they hurt you in any way?*

"T'óó yee' shaa yáhóósįįd. She'awéé' bizhé'é bił ná'ahiistsą́, 'áko nidi t'áadoo biye' k'é yidííniid da." *I am so humiliated. I saw my baby's father again, but he didn't greet his son,* Dééd Yázhí wailed as she leaned against Kiizhóní.

Immediately, Dééd Yázhí became embarrassed that she only thought of herself and the pleasure the thoughts of love with the tall, gray-haired one brought her. Kiizhóní interrupted her thoughts when he said,

"Jó doo Naabeehó nilį́į da, 'éí biniinaa t'áadoo niyázhí k'é yínéístį́į da. Nihe'anaa'í nilį́. 'Ei nihe'anaa'í k'é doo bił daniłį́ da. Kojí niyázhí bik'éí t'óó'ahayói. Bínaaiké 'ayóó'ádabó'ní.

Bimá sání hóló. Bicheii hóló. Bidá'í yił k'é 'ahidoo'niid. Shí nidi, t'áá shí shiye', she'awéé' nilįįgo baa nitséskees. T'áadoo baa níni'í, shiyázhí. T'áá shįį hait'éego da niyázhí k'é yididooniiłgo da 'át'é." *He is not Navajo, that is why he did not greet your son. He is our enemy. Our enemies do not respect kinship. Over here, your little one has many relatives. His older brothers love him very much. He has a maternal grandmother. He has a maternal grandfather. He greeted his maternal uncle. Even me, I think of him as my own son. I think of him as my baby. Don't grieve over it, my little one. He may greet your little one sometime in the future.*

Dééd Yázhí leaned into Kiizhóní's arms. She was yearning to have a loved one speak such encouraging words to her. Dééd Yázhí allowed her mind to soak in his gentle, kind words.

Kiizhóní loosened his grip on Dééd Yázhí and looked her and her little one over to see if they were safe and unharmed. The people under Kiizhóní and his leader's leadership encircled Dééd Yázhí and her children. The people spoke gentle, encouraging words to Dééd Yázhí and her sons. Dééd Yázhí could not hear what her people were saying because her ears were still ringing, but she knew her young sons understood their people.

In the dim light of the setting sun, the Naabeehó men were counted and then given their rations. Jugs filled with fresh water that were very heavy had been added to the rations, surprising the people. The women were given yards of bright colored fabric. The women were embarrassed and surprised at receiving the fabric. Many women gave the fabric to their children to carry. The people were counted according the number of items handed out to them.

Throughout the night, the people walked following the soldiers who rode horses as they held their lanterns high in the air. Dééd Yázhí was relieved that she had to concentrate on where she placed her steps instead of thinking about the dramatic events of the day. Walking in the night was slow. She listened intently for the sound of the rushing waters to signal they were near their camping area. Her little one was very heavy, but Dééd Yázhí insisted she carry her little one while Kiizhóní carried her adopted sons, three little boys at a time, stopping only to set them down as he picked up three other boys. Dééd Yázhí and her people arrived at their camping area when the sun had fully risen in the sky to illuminate the wide valley they had walked through to get back to their camp. Smoke from small, lazy fires cast a shadow on the Naabeehó people.

That night, Dééd Yázhí was tired but she could not sleep. Everyone was quiet and the only signs of life were the little flickering fires across the valley and the lights that shone forth from the picket forts. Dééd Yázhí sat watching the sunrise. She thought of the tall, gray-haired one. She shuddered. Every time her mind revisited the meeting with the tall, gray-haired one at the parade grounds, Dééd Yázhí felt as if it were another person who had loved him and not her.

The man who left her that day long ago at Fort Canby, after making gentle love to her, was not the same man she saw at the parade grounds. Although his voice was the same, the man she saw at the parade grounds did not have the same body as the man she slept near as their skin touched.

He is much, much older now, she thought as she reached up to touch her face to feel the smoothness of her skin. She thought of the cane he had to use to walk from place to place. Dééd Yázhí remembered the tall, gray-haired one had a slight limp when she loved him, but she could not believe how heavily he leaned on his cane to walk. Her mind then drifted to the way the tall, gray-haired one had so much difficulty bending over to pick up her rug blanket. She remembered the eyes that she was so afraid to look into when she loved him. Dééd Yázhí shut her eyes tight to shut out the fact that the tall, gray-haired one wore a black patch over his eye. She wondered about the need for the patch over his right eye. I saw only one eye that has the same color as the deep turquoise eyes of the fat horned toad, she thought. She then thought of his hair that was once gray but had turned white. He must have seen extreme hardship for his hair to turn white, she thought as compassion stirred in her heart.

Dééd Yázhí told herself that if it was not for his voice and the gentle way he handed her rug blanket back to her, she would not have recognized him. She wanted to hear him sensuously pleading for satisfaction as their bodies moved as one. Hot, hurting tears began to flow out of her eyes and mingled with her hair sending the faint scent of yucca into the air. She knew the tall gray-haired one loved the scent of yucca root on her hair.

Dééd Yázhí hurt for what the tall, gray-haired one had become. She thought of the way he spoke kindly to her people and how he scolded his own young warriors. Hot tears danced in her eyes before they made a straight path down her face to rest on her rug dress. Dééd Yázhí could feel the heat that still made her cheeks glow. Although embarrassed by the tall, gray-haired one, she knew she still loved the memory of him because she had nurtured his memory when she needed to feel or see kindness in such brutal places.

Dééd Yázhí's mind accused the tall, gray-haired one as being the enemy. She started to cry when she remembered once again that her little one was not claimed by his father. She wished the tall, gray-haired one would have greeted their little one in the same way her own father greeted her and her siblings when each of them were born. Resentfully, she whispered,

"Ch'osh nidi biyázhí k'é yiłniih. Naaldlooshii 'ałdó' dabiyázhí k'é deiłní. Hó shą? Haye' doo ts'íí 'át'éégóó ti'hoo'ní yénásdzá. 'Éí nidi t'áadoo hoł íljid da. Yáadilá 'ájít'éé dó'." *Even bugs greet their little ones. Animals also greet their little ones. What about him? His son was surrounded by extreme suffering. Even that, did not mean anything to him. What a disgusting one he is.* Confused thoughts marched relentlessly through Dééd Yázhí's mind.

As if to torture her, her mind played the dramatic scene over and over again. She remembered the sounds of her little one crying; the sounds of her little adopted sons crying out of fear that she and their baby brother would be hurt; the sounds of the mean women yelling hateful words at her little one; the sound of her own body crying, afraid her little one would be taken away from her and hurt by her own people; the sounds of the mean soldiers yelling at her and her people; the sound of the tall, gray-haired one excitedly screaming the name he gave her long ago when their bodies touched; the sound of the tall, gray-haired one speaking to her in an excited voice. Still, this was only one day out of the many days her little one had

484

lived through. Tired from thinking, Dééd Yázhí returned to her makeshift home and allowed herself to finally fall asleep, hoping she would not dream about the events of the day.

Two days after Dééd Yázhí and her little family returned from the dramatic day at the parade grounds, the soldiers stationed at the picket forts started coming around more often than usual. They barked at the Naabeehó people telling them to clean their areas, whereas, cleanliness never seemed to have made a difference to them before. The people wondered what brought about the change in the soldiers' orders.

Dééd Yázhí spoke the words many of her people had thought when she said,

"Dahanáá' hanii doo bee da'joo'įį da! Nihinaagóó t'áá'ákwííjį hasht'eh dahóníilzin! *Can't they see with their eyes! Every day we keep our surrounding areas clean.*

The Naabeehó people were given a shovel, barrels, and boxes of white powder to sprinkle all over the ground. The people thought of the white crust that appeared on the bank of the eastern side of the river. Through the interpreter, the people learned the white powder was a disinfectant. The people were told to scoop up the urine and fecal waste and place it in the barrel to be dumped in a designated area which was Kiizhóní's daily expectation of his people. Dééd Yázhí and her people pretended to be busy with the activity of cleaning their camping sites.

When the soldiers came to Kiizhóní and his leader's area, the soldiers looked around, kicked at the people's rug blankets with their dirty boots and told the people to keep their camping areas clean. Although Kiizhóní and his leader lost many elders and infants while they were being held as prisoners of war, many more would have perished if Kiizhóní had not insisted that his people keep their areas clean of human waste.

Soon, the soldiers began asking many questions by way of an interpreter who was constantly in tow. They made it a practice to inspect each little makeshift lean-to the Naabeehó people called home. Dééd Yázhí kept her little one hidden out of the fear that the soldiers might be so bold as to take her little one away from her. The tall, gray-haired one knew of her little one, a thought that terrorized Dééd Yázhí all through the nights and days that followed their meeting.

When the soldiers insisted on counting the women, children, and babies more often, the Naabeehó mothers began to cry. They knew each time the men, women, or children were counted, many deaths of the Naabeehó people followed.

Little did Dééd Yázhí and her people know that it was the tall, gray-haired one whose orders the soldiers were following. They were told to look for the young Naabeehó woman with a toddler whose skin was white. The soldiers looked but did not see the child because Dééd Yázhí kept her little one hidden.

Chapter Twenty-four
Relative in the Water!

Naabeehó women who lived in another settlement and who lived in nearby camps recognized Dééd Yázhí as the woman who caused so much confusion at the parade grounds. Soon, the women blamed her for the change in the soldiers' protocol. The mean Naabeehó woman was among them.

When Kiizhóní was preparing to leave to go to the parade grounds to receive his rations and to be counted, he told the old man to stay behind. The old man was showing signs of fatigue. Kiizhóní worried the old man did not have the stamina to walk for a length of time, so he asked him to stay at the camp and watch over Dééd Yázhí and her little ones.

"Nihidine'é doo choohoo'į́įgóó 'awéé yázhí bimá yik'ee dadeeznih. Nihe'anaa'í bá 'ajishchínígíí biniinaa dahojoosłáá'. T'óó shił baa hojoobá'íyee'. Asdzání 'ayóo jooba'ii nilínígíí nilį́į nidi nihidine'é 'éí doo dayoo'į́į da. 'Ashiiké yázhí bąąh ádahasdįįdígíí dah yidii'eezh, sha'áłchíní yiłníigo. T'áá kǫ́ǫ́ sínídáago shá bich'ą́ą́h hoshíníkée dooleeł, shicheii. Haashílá nihits'ą́ą́' atídayólééh lágo." *Our people have come to resent the*

487

little one's mother. It is because she bore a child for an enemy, that is why they hate her. I feel so much compassion for her. She is a very kind woman but our people do not see that. She took in orphans and called them her children. Stay here and scold anyone who will hurt her, my maternal grandfather. Don't let anyone hurt her in any way.

A smile broke over the old man's face. He was happy not to have to walk two days just to be given bad food, although he had plans for the greasy flour they were given. He responded, saying,

"Aoo', aoo', aoo', shicheii, shitsóí nihá baa 'áháshyą́ą́ doo. Shooh, ak'áán haa da wólééh lágo. 'Ak'ánígíí shí dóó shicheii yázhí danilínígíí chonídeiil'įįh. Ei 'akánígíí náltłohgo doo chohoo'įįgóó nitł'iz yileeh. 'Éí bee 'adiltł'įhí dóó bee 'adiltąshí bá tsé 'áwózí nahalingo nímazgo dóó nitł'izgo 'ánídeiil'įįh. Bee 'adiltł'įhí dóó bee 'adiltąshí biih nídeii'niłgo bee nida'iiltązh łeh. Ayóo shicheii yázhí yídaneedlį. 'Ákót'éego naabaahii yázhí 'ídlįįgi yídahooł'aah. Bee 'adiltł'įhí dóó bee 'adiltąshí dóó 'ak'áán shįį́ bee hamá bich'ą́ą́h nidajibaah dooleeł." *Yes, yes, yes, my grandson, I will take care of my granddaughter for all of us. Don't do anything with the flour. Those who are my grandsons and I use the flour. When the flour gets wet, it becomes extremely hard. We use it to make what look like little round, hard rocks for our slingshots and we shoot those. My grandsons really enjoy that. In that way, they are learning how to become warriors. They will most likely use the slingshots and the flour to protect their mother. They will fight to protect their mother.*

Kiizhóní laughed, knowing he would be leaving Dééd Yázhí and her little one in good hands. He knew the old man was teaching the little boys, but he had not suspected what the little boys were learning.

That evening, Dééd Yázhí asked the old man to sleep lightly that night so she could rest throughout the night. The old man agreed and lit a small fire after he moved his bedding closer to his adopted family whom he had promised to protect. Morning came slowly and the day's activity of cleaning the area was started.

As a distraction, Dééd Yázhí decided to take her children to the river. Her brother had not come to visit in several days. They had run low on water so she asked her two oldest sons to carry their jugs while she carried her little one in her rug blanket. She asked her younger sons to make sure they picked up more pebbles than usual. The boys understood why they needed extra protection. Dééd Yázhí smiled to herself when she remembered the old man teaching her young sons to use a slingshot effectively.

On the bank of the river, Dééd Yázhí was glad to see several women at the river's edge also filling their water jugs. She placed her little one in the lap of his older brother, asking all her sons to watch over their baby brother while she scooped water into the jugs with her hands. After each scoop, she glanced back at her children to ensure their safety. Just when she reached down to scoop more water into her jug, she heard her little one scream followed by the screams of her young sons.

Dééd Yázhí was horrified by the scene before her. She dropped her half-filled jug of water into the river and ran up the narrow bank to her children. The mean Naabeehó woman had her little one suspended in the air as the woman rushed to the fast flowing river.

"Díí yee' nihe'anaa'í ti'danihiyoołníhígíí be'awéé' nilį́!" *This is a baby who belongs to our enemy who tortures us!* the mean woman screamed.

The unthinkable happened! Slipping on the muddy bank, Dééd Yázhí could not get to her little one fast enough to stop the mean Naabeehó woman from throwing her screaming little one into the cold, turbid waters of the river.

Screaming, Dééd Yázhí dove into the water to catch her little one. She could see him on the surface of the water, then he would disappear. She kept her head above water so she could scream as loud as she could to get someone's attention. Her little one was being carried along by the current toward the eastern side of the river. He would drift up against debris that was lodged among fallen branches then the churning waters would carry him off again, carrying him farther away from his mother, who frantically fought the debris that kept pulling her down.

Dééd Yázhí was horrified. Her little one was not making any noise as he drifted along. His little body bobbed up, then disappeared, and then came to the surface again. Dééd Yázhí was terrified and felt helpless. All she could think to say was,

"Shimá, kodi! Shizhé'é kodi! Shíká'ahi'nołchééh, t'ááshǫǫdi! Kodi! *My mother, over here! My father, over here! Please help me! Over here!*"

The waters were pushing her, blinding her, and pulling her down with the weight of her thick rug dress. She vowed not to give up even when she could not see her little one's body. For only a second, before she was rushed further down the river, Dééd Yázhí saw some Naabeehó people standing on the water's edge. She began screaming even more, crying,

490

"She'awéé'! Shiyázhí! She'awéé'! She'awéé'! Shiyázhí! She'awéé'!" *My baby! My little one! My baby! My baby! My little one! My baby!* over and over again as water kept filling her mouth.

When she could no longer cry out, Dééd Yázhí felt herself becoming weak. She was spinning in the current of the river. She could not believe her rug dress and her moccasins were aiding the waters to pull her farther away from her little one. Her hair was heavy with debris.

In a helpless and weakened state, Dééd Yázhí appealed to the fast flowing water as her baby drifted farther away. Incoherently she pleaded,

"Tó 'Aheedlíinii niidlį́. Nihaa 'ádahołyą́, t'ááshǫǫdí!" *We are of the Water Flows Together People. Take care of us, please!*

****

Kiizhóní did not trust the old soldier who recognized Dééd Yázhí and who did not greet his son. Impatiently, he stood in line to be counted and to receive his ration. As soon as a young soldier took his number of identification that was stamped on his token, Kiizhóní told his leader he was returning to their camp to make sure his family was doing fine. He was grateful the land was flat as he sped along. He kept his eye on their sloping hill where they were camped. As he ran, he prayed, asking the Creator to protect his family. When he reached the two picket forts just before his camp, Kiizhóní knew something had happened. He saw soldiers running up a hill that led to the river. His first thought was that Dééd Yázhí's younger brother had been discovered, but sadly that was not the case.

He entered his camp as people were screaming at him, saying Dééd Yázhí's baby had been thrown into the river and Dééd Yázhí had jumped into the river after her little one.

"Háádą́ą́' áhóót'įįd? *When did it happen?* Kiizhóní yelled, sick with anguish.

"Ániídíyee'," *A little while ago,* was the answer.

"Niha'áłchíní dóó nihicheii nihá baa 'ádahołyą́," *Take care of our children and take care of our maternal grandfather,* Kiizhóní yelled as he sped toward the river. At the river he saw Dééd Yázhí's sons crying, pointing down the river. He looked and saw Dééd Yázhí floating far down the river. Without thinking, he jumped into the river, yelling,

"Nihicheii bich'į' nídóhkááh. Ałhaa 'ádahołyą́ą́ dóó nihicheii baa 'ádahołyą́. Nihimá dóó nihitsilí yázhí bił nídeeshkah." *Go back to our maternal grandfather. Take care of one another and take care of our maternal grandfather. I will come back with your mother and your baby brother.*

Kiizhóní knew it was dangerous when he jumped into the waters that were closest to the swift-running current. He was carried along so fast, his eyes could not focus on the river bank. Everything was a blur as he sped by. The current kept pulling him down, but he fought to swim back to the surface. Each time he surfaced, he looked for Dééd Yázhí.

Far down the river his body raced, carried by the fast-flowing current. Kiizhóní was thankful and afraid of the current. For a second, he saw people whizzing by on the bank of the river. They were pointing down the river. It was too late. Kiizhóní saw logs and debris rushing toward him. He raised his head and with all his strength turned his body and felt his body slam into the logs. He did not expect to survive. His last thought was a prayer.

"ShiTaa', nihíká'anilyeed." *My Spiritual Father, help us.*

****

Dééd Yázhí hurt all over her body. She could hear people talking. They were speaking their words as if they were in a rush. She could not feel the cold, fast running water against her body anymore. She felt like she was being carried farther away from the riverbank. She wanted to scream, She'awéé' shą'? *Where is my baby?* but she could not form the words in her mouth, only in her mind. She desperately wanted to ask, Háadi shą' ásht'į? *Where am I?* but she could not form those words either.

Dééd Yázhí felt light. There was no weight pulling her down. She tried to move her feet, but they would not move. She wanted to scream. The only sensation she felt was warmth. She wondered if she was back in her cradleboard. Permitting herself to believe so, she fell asleep and slept for a long time.

When Dééd Yázhí woke up, she could hear the fast words spoken again. She listened. Somewhere in the far distance Dééd Yázhí could hear her mother talking in a soft voice. She tried to move but something heavy was holding her down.

"Shi-má," she heard herself weakly say.

Slowly the weight was being lifted away from her body. Dééd Yázhí tried shaking her head, but it was held down too. She tried opening her eyes but her eyelashes would not move. In a panic, she screamed with all her might,

"Shimá!" *My Mother.*

The things pushing her down were moving away. All of a sudden, a bright light came streaming into her eyes. She looked around and saw several women leaning over her. They were looking at her with such interest. They were wearing bright-colored clothes similar to the ones the Naabeehó women wore at the parade grounds. Using all her strength to lift her head, she looked at her body, she was dressed in the clothes she wore as a prisoner at Fort Canby!

"Háadishą́ ásht'į?" *Where am I?* she asked in a panic, but no one answered. They just stared. The people standing over her looked just like her own Naabeehó people, but their language was spoken so fast, as if they were in a hurry.

All of a sudden, Dééd Yázhí remembered her little one and started sobbing.

"She'awéé' shits'ą́ą́' taah dayiishxango t'óó bikéé' taah yishwod. Shiyázhí shą'? She'awéé' shą'?" *They threw my baby into the river, which is why I jumped into the water to go after him. Where is my little one? Where is my baby?*

Dééd Yázhí lifted her hands to her breast. They were full. She began sobbing pain-filled sobs again. Her head was throbbing with pain. She put her hand up to her head and felt her hair. Her hair was filled with twigs, sand, leaves, and small pieces of wood. The women who had been cleaning her hair pointed to a small pile of what seemed to be trash. Entwined in the trash were strands of her hair, long and tangled.

Dééd Yázhí began to shiver. The women rushed to her side and lay beside her, on top of her, and at her feet and her head. She realized why she could not move earlier. She felt she would never warm up without her biil éé' *rug dress* and her kélchí *moccasins.* A soft piece of fabric was placed over her face to warm her face and to keep out the light so she could rest. Dééd Yázhí closed her eyes, thinking about herself being in a cradleboard. The thought brought her mind rest, but she yearned for her little one.

Throughout the day and the night, Dééd Yázhí mourned the loss of her little one, her son. During the night, she could hear the voice of her mother comforting her in gentle words that brought warmth to her. When she was not asleep, Dééd Yázhí was crying for her little one. Her sobs would nearly choke her when she thought of her little one being thrown into the water by the mean Naabeehó woman.

"Shiyázhí, Shiyázhí, Shiyázhí," *My little one, My little one, My little one,* was all Dééd Yázhí could say in between such hurtful sobs as she mourned the loss of her son.

Dééd Yázhí thought she was strong. She had survived being kidnapped and being held captive, she had survived the loss of her mother and her father, she had survived the loss of her sister and her younger brothers, and she had survived losing the love of a man she learned to love only to find him again on the side of the enemy. Dééd Yázhí told herself she was strong, but the loss of her own child she was finding nearly impossible to bear. She could not believe her body could hold so many tears. Dééd Yázhí thought, even my breasts are crying, they are releasing milk in anticipation of my little one but his distant relatives, the turbid waters, have claimed him.

Dééd Yázhí did not know how long it had been since she jumped into the river because she was kept in a cocoon. Her face was covered with a soft piece of material to keep her from distinguishing the day from the night. She knew she felt stronger because she was ashamed of the thin clothes she was wearing. She remembered back to when she was held prisoner at Fort Canby, when her captors forced her to wear thin clothes. It was the thin clothes that concealed her large belly that announced she was carrying a child. She remembered how humiliated she was in wearing the clothes, and now she felt the shame once again.

In her dream one morning, Dééd Yázhí heard the voice of her mother once again speaking soft gentle words. Her mother was talking to someone. Dééd Yázhí listened intently. She also heard the sound of a child as it choked on soft sobs.

Her mind began spinning when she heard her mother say, "Ních'aad, shiyázhí. T'áadoo nichaaí. Nik'éí 'ádin nahalingo nichah. Ních'aad. T'áadoo nichaaí, shiyázhí. T'óó naa hojoobá'ígo nichah." *Don't cry, my little one. Don't cry. You are crying as if you do not have any relatives. Don't cry. Don't cry, my little one. You are so pitiful when you cry.*

Dééd Yázhí started crying because she knew her mother was speaking to her. Out of grief, shame, and weakness, Dééd Yázhí fell asleep again.

Why isn't my mother coming close to me? she wondered as tears made a continuous path out of her eyes and disappeared into the piece of fabric that covered her face. A woman lifted the soft thick cloth from Dééd Yázhí's face. From her reclining position, Dééd Yázhí looked around for her mother. Confused, she softly said,

"Shimá ..." *My Mother...*

A woman who looked just like her mother was kneeling over her and asked,

"Ha'át'íí lá?" Haash yinílyé?" *What is it? What is your name?*
Confused that the woman who looked like her mother could not
recognize her, Dééd Yázhí feebly asked,

"Shimá shą'?" *Where is my mother?* She looked into her
mother's face and explained,

"T'áadoo tsíhodeeskézí she'awéé' bikéé' táyi' dah yiishte'.
She'awéé', shiyázhí baa nitsídiiskosgo t'óó baa 'atínídinishdleeh.
Ts'ídá t'áá'awołíbee shijéí neezgai." *Without thinking, I jumped
into the water after my baby. When I think of my baby, my little
one, I just begin to cry. My heart is in extreme pain.* As Dééd
Yázhí spoke, she hugged her chest in pain.

The woman leaned over her and began speaking, but Dééd
Yázhí could not fully understand the woman. She wanted the
woman to slow the speed of her speech. Crying and hoping
someone would understand her, she said,

"Shiyázhí, she'awéé' nihe'anaa'í ła' yáshchíín. Shiyázhí bitsį'
łigai dóó bitsii' łitsóóhíyee'." *My little one, my baby is born for
one of our enemy. My little one's skin is white and his hair is light
brown.*

The woman leaning over her spun around and spoke some
words that tumbled out of her mouth. An older woman got up
and walked away from the group. The women keeping Dééd
Yázhí warm began to stir. They stared at Dééd Yázhí, then looked
away as their attention was directed toward another direction.

Dééd Yázhí wondered why her mother did not recognize
her. She looked into the young woman's eyes hoping she
could communicate with the woman in the same way she
communicated with the tall, gray-haired one. Her thoughts were

497

interrupted when she saw a slender man carrying a large bundle in his arms as he walked toward them. Dééd Yázhí could hear a little one crying and sobbing softly.

The little one was mumbling,

"Má, má, má," in the midst of desperate little cries. The young man gave the bundle to the woman who looked like Dééd Yázhí's mother. Dééd Yázhí heard her mother speaking softly again to the little one the same words she thought she heard her mother saying,

"Ních'aad, shiyázhí. T'áadoo nichaaí. Nik'éí 'ádin nahalingo nichah. Ních'aad. T'áadoo nichaaí, shiyázhí. T'óó naa hojoobá'ígo nichah. Nimá níkánootááł." *Don't cry, my little one. Don't cry. You are crying as if you do not have any relatives. Don't cry. Don't cry, my little one. You are so pitiful when you cry. Your mother is looking for you.*

The little baby began to cry such sad sobs when Dééd Yázhí's mother stopped talking.

The women helped Dééd Yázhí sit up, but Dééd Yázhí pushed herself back down. She felt faint and helpless. She could hear the little cries of "Má, má, má" softly ringing in her ears.

Dééd Yázhí wondered why her head hurt so much. The skin on her face felt as if it had been badly burned by the sun. Fighting the pain and dizziness, Dééd Yázhí lifted her head, then her shoulders. Her mother helped her sit up.

Dééd Yázhí pulled the covers off of the little one's face and looked into the face of the little one. The little one's face was bruised so badly and the baby's eyes were swollen shut from crying. The little one was shaking uncontrollably. There was no telling what color the little one's hair was because of all the mud

498

and debris that clung to its head. Hoping and praying it was her little one, tears of love began pouring down her face. Dééd Yázhí softly said to the little one,

"Shiyázhí? Shiyázhí?" *My little one? My little one?* At the sound of her voice, the little one began to whimper hoarsely, saying,

"Má, má, má."

Dééd Yázhí never thought she would look upon a baby where it's own mother could not recognize him because of his badly lacerated and bruised face. All she could do was cry and ask in a soft voice,

"Shiyázhí? Shiyázhí? Niísh ánít'į́?" *My little one? My little one? Is that you?*

At the sound of her softened voice, the little one tried to open his badly swollen eyes and screamed out a loud cry that was so pitiful. The cry broke Dééd Yázhí's heart. The little one turned away from her but when she spoke, the little one turned toward her and listened, then began crying inconsolably.

Dééd Yázhí was gently pulling the mud and debris to free the little one's hair when the baby screamed in pain. She saw light brown locks of hair peeking out. Dééd Yázhí heard herself shrieking,

"Shiyázhí! Shiyázhí! Háshinee', shiyázhí!" *My little one? My little one? My dear, my little one.* Her little one answered by weakly saying,

"Má, má, má." Her little one was choking on his sobs and shaking uncontrollably. He tried in his limited toddler language to tell Dééd Yázhí about his experience in the rushing water amid pitiful sobs.

The women all hugged one another and began to cry. They had all taken part in saving the little baby's life and caring for him. Although the white soldiers at Fort Sumner had mistreated the women, they had compassion for the little white baby at the request of the young Navajo woman who was married to one of their Mescalero men.

Dééd Yázhí noticed her little one was suffering from dehydration. His lips were dry and his throat was dry from crying the entire time he was separated from her. When she offered her little one her breast, her little one slowly emptied both of her breasts and fell asleep in her arms.

A few of the women busied themselves by gently removing dirt and debris from the little one's hair and washing his little bruised body. Amazingly, the little one slept through the cleaning while Dééd Yázhí held him the entire time. While the women were cleaning the little one, Dééd Yázhí's mother insisted she be the one to bathe Dééd Yázhí and clean her hair. Dééd Yázhí was so grateful for all the attention. Her body hurt but her mother had a gentle touch as she cleaned her wounds.

After resting, Dééd Yázhí wanted to ask the young woman with the gentle touch, "Haash yinílyé?" *What is your name?* Instead, Dééd Yázhí was so surprised when the young woman asked her,

"Haash yinílyé?" *What is your name?*

Without answering, Dééd Yázhí turned around, surprised the young woman could speak her language. The two women just sat and stared at one another. Finally, Dééd Yázhí timidly asked,

"Haash yinílyé?" *What is your name?*

"Shí Dzáníbaa' yinishyé," *My name is Little Young Woman Warrior,* her mother answered in a sweet soft voice. It was too much for Dééd Yázhí' to take in! She was confused! Although her face hurt, she closed her eyes real tight to focus her mind on the present.

"Nishą', haash yinílyé?" *What about you, what is your name?* her mother asked again.

"Shimá, shí 'éí Dééd Yázhí dashijiní ..." *My mother, they call me Dééd Yázhí ...*

She looked into the face of her mother and noticed signs of recognition beginning to crawl across her mother's face.

"Shimá, ni yee' Nínáánibaa' yinílyé. Shideezhí yee' éiyá Dzáníbaa' wolyé," *My mother, your name is actually Nínáánibaa'. It is my younger sister who is called Dzáníbaa',* Dééd Yázhí said as she corrected her mother.

The young woman lifted her arms in the air, screamed a high pitched howl, and called out at the top of her lungs,

"Dédii! ShiDédii! Da' niísh ánít'į̃? Háshinee', shiDédii! Háadishą' naninάά nít'ę̃ę̃', shiDédii? *Dédii, my Dédii! Is it you? My dear one, my Dédii. Where were you, my Dédii?*

Dééd Yázhí could not believe her ears or her eyes. Her beautiful younger sister had grown and looked just like their beautiful mother. No sound came out of her mouth. Her open mouth gave a clue of her total surprise. She slumped back and stared at her younger sister. The scenarios she had conjured up in her mind regarding the disappearance of her younger sister were slowly disappearing from her mind, making her feel lightheaded. Finally, Dééd Yázhí found her voice and hoarsely asked,

501

"Da' niísh ánít'į, shideezhí yázhí? *Is it you, my baby sister?* She screamed as she weakly lifted her arms to hug her younger sister back.

Dééd Yázhí screamed out in pain as she shrieked,

"Háshinee', Záanii, shideezhí. Ha'át'ííshą' haniná kodi? *My dear Zonnie, my younger sister, what are you doing here?*

"Nihimá dóó nihizhé'é shą'?" *Where are our mother and our father?* Dzáníbaa' screamed. "Bił nanikaiísh?" *Are you with them?* she quietly asked.

Dééd Yázhí cried,

"Nidaga', yisnááh ánihi'diilyaa yę́ę́dą́ą́', íídą́ą́', nihimá t'áá yiiłtsą́ą́ nít'ę́ę́'! *No, the day we were kidnapped, that day is when I last saw our mother.*

The two sisters sobbed and cried as their tears mingled on the blanket wrapped around Dééd Yázhí's little one below them. Each sister identified the parent they favored the most while trying to hold back tears. Dzáníbaa' and Dééd Yázhí hugged, cried, screamed, hugged again and cried again. Dééd Yázhí did not mind the pain that limited her movements as she moaned,

"Ayá! 'Ayóo!" *Ow! Ouch!*

Dzáníbaa' grabbed her older sister and hugged her so hard they both shook. No one, other than her husband, had called her Záanii since she and her sister were separated that terrible day. Dééd Yázhí later learned from her sister that she was married to the man who rescued her little one. She also learned he was a member of the Naashgálí dine'é *Mescalero people*, as were all the women who helped rescue and care for Dééd Yázhí and her little one. Sobbing Dééd Yázhí told her younger sister about her baby who was thrown into the rushing waters.

Dééd Yázhí was told by her younger sister that most of the Naashgálí dine'é had been forced to walk to Fort Sumner from the south, but after several months, most of the Naashgálí people stole away to their old lands in the south. Dééd Yázhí found the few Naashgalí dine'é who remained behind to be kind people. Dzáníbaa' sadly told her sister the Naashgálí dine'é were accused of stealing and raiding just before their homes and tipis were burned by soldiers and were forced to walk to Fort Sumner.

Dééd Yázhí shook her head in sadness as she told her younger sister that she and her little children were also accused, along with all the Naabeehó people, of stealing and raiding from nearby settlements, and that was why they had been forced to walk to the dreadful place the soldiers called Fort Sumner.

The two sisters sat holding hands as they shook their heads in sadness because the two sisters knew in their hearts they and their people were innocent, free from any guilt. Dééd Yázhí and her younger sister knew their father and their brothers would never do anything to be declared thieves.

Dééd Yázhí also knew Kiizhóní was not a thief but was a man who was respectful, kind, and good just like her father. Dzáníbaa' also knew her young Naashgálí man was not a thief. He was kind, gentle, and respectful as well. They knew it was the white 'anaa'í *enemy* who were the thieves.

Dééd Yázhí was relieved when the morose subject was interrupted when a little boy, a toddler was brought forth who was introduced as Dzáníbaa's son. Dééd Yázhí saw another side of the Naashgálí man who was married to her younger sister, when she became a witness to the kind way the young man treated her sister and their baby. She saw love passing between the couple.

Dééd Yázhí looked away in sadness. She could feel a distant yearning in her heart. She yearned to feel an uninterrupted love of her own. Her tears of joy and love for her sister mingled with her tears of having missed out on love. Love found her twice, but Dééd Yázhí had to admit the men who were the source of love were taken from her both times. She silently vowed she would never allow herself to feel the love of a man again.

Dééd Yázhí screamed! She forgot to let her sister know their brother Nahat'á Yinaabaah *One Who Goes to War at Night* was living near Fort Sumner and he was supplying her family with meat, fresh berries, silky blue-corn flour, and fresh sweet water. In sadness, she told her younger sister they had not seen her younger brother in many days.

Dééd Yázhí told her sister of the seven little boys she adopted and who depended upon her. She also told of the gentle old man whose words of encouragement helped them survive desperate times. For a minute Dééd Yázhí wondered whether she should hold back on telling her sister about the beautiful Naabeehó man named Kiizhóní. She decided she wanted her younger sister to know about the young man who provided sustenance, guidance, strength and love for her family when he took her and her children under his care. The description of the young man matched the man Dzáníbaa' would want for her older sister.

Dééd Yázhí was reluctant to tell her younger sister about the tall, gray-haired one and becoming a prisoner at

Fort Canby, but after reminding herself of the fact that her younger sister must have suspected the father of her baby was a member of their anaa'í *enemy,* Dééd Yázhí told of how her heart remained a captured heart.

Each sister told the other about what happened from the time they were forcefully separated. Tears, anger, and remorse poured out of each sister as they listened to each other's story. Their stories led them back to the amazement they felt at finding each other again. The two sisters could not believe they had been kept as prisoners of war at Fort Sumner for over two years. They mourned the years that denied them of the love of their mother and their father as well as their brothers and each other.

They voiced their deep gratitude to the river for their reunion. They even took time to briefly acknowledge the mean Naabeehó woman whose horrid action sent Dééd Yázhí downstream to save her little one.

Stopping all conversation, Dzáníbaa' realized the young man they rescued from the river could be Kiizhóní. She asked her husband how the young man they rescued was doing. Dzáníbaa' also asked if the young man had recovered from the wounds he suffered when his body slammed into the trap of logs and debris.

Dzáníbaa's husband got up to check on Kiizhóní. The Naashgálí *Mescalero* man helped a badly bruised Kiizhóní walk to where Dééd Yázhí and her younger sister Dzáníbaa' sat visiting.

Weakened but happy, Kiizhóní fell into the arms of Dééd Yázhí. This was the first public expression of what their hearts had felt for many months. Although his face hurt, Kiizhóní could not help but leave kisses all over Dééd Yázhí's sweet, bruised face. Dééd Yázhí winced when he reached up and caressed her hair. Holding her close, Kiizhóní told her what happened after he jumped in the water to try to save her and her little one. Dééd Yázhí could feel his tears drop into her hair. Kiizhóní took the time to lift her little one, kissing him gently several times on his face, saying,

"Honíyói lá. Naabaahii yázhí síníłįį'. Tó bii' nisíníbaa'. Nikáa'jį hazłį'ígíí 'ayóó át'éego baa ahééh nisin, nimá dó' ayóo yaa ahééh nízin. Honíyói lá. *You are resilient. You have become a little warrior. You went to war in the water. I am thankful you survived, your mother is also very thankful. You are strong.* Dééd Yázhí smiled at Kiizhóní's words as she placed her hand in his strong hand.

Dzáníbaa' told Kiizhóní and her sister they placed the large branch and poles in the water to catch small game that fell into the water. She told her sister and Kiizhóní the young group of Naashgálí women laughed and teased at Kiizhóní "being a good catch". The young women playfully flirted with Kiizhóní. Dééd Yázhí was thankful for the trap because she and her little one also got caught up in its snare.

Dzáníbaa' loved caring for her older sister and she felt a great sense of accomplishment in having had a part in healing her sister and her little one and Kiizhóní. Healing was a lengthy process for Dééd Yázhí.

As Dééd Yázhí and her younger sister visited, two men sat back and admired the two women. Dééd Yázhí realized this was the first time she was able to be with Kiizhóní without so many distractions, but they both admitted to each other they missed their young sons and the old man and they worried about them.

Dééd Yázhí promised herself that when she felt stronger, she would walk to the river's edge to thank the swift flowing water for sparing the life of her little one and the life of Kiizhóní as well as her own.

One night, she asked Kiizhóní to walk with her to the steep bank of the river. As they sat on the bank of the river, Dééd Yázhí and Kiizhóní prayed to their Creator, thanking Him for reuniting them and for taking care of their little one. Dééd Yázhí also thanked the Creator for the old mean woman. It was the actions of the old mean woman that reunited me with my younger sister, she painfully thought.

She also prayed for her little adopted sons. After her thoughtful prayer, she said,

"Sha'áłchíní, 'ashiiké yázhí, 'ayóo bídahasááh dóó bídin nishłį́. Haa da shą' daat'į́ t'óó nisin łeh. Bił nída'ahiistsą́ągo 'índa doo shich'į' anáhóót'i' da doo. K'ad éí t'óó yéego bich'į' shíni' íí'á. Nihicheii dó'. Háida shą' baa 'ádahalyą́. *My children, the little boys, I miss them and I long for their presence. I wonder how they are doing. When I see them again, I will not have any problems. Now I am very worried about them. Our maternal grandfather too. Who is taking care of them?*

Kiizhóní reassured Dééd Yázhí, saying,

"Diyin na'áłchíní yaa 'áhályą́. Nitsilí dó' ashiiké yázhí t'óó bił baa hojoobá'í yee'. Éí 'ashiiké yázhí dóó nihicheii yaa 'áhályą́. Kojí dó' nideezhí bił ná'ahiiniłtsá. 'Éí baa hózhǫ́. Shá 'ashja'iilaago nitsilí hadínéeshtaał. *The Creator is taking care of your children.*

Your younger brother also feels much sympathy for the little boys. He will take care of them and our maternal grandfather too. Over here, you have been reunited with your younger sister. That is joyful. I will go look for your younger brother the first chance I get.

Kiizhóní was always touched by Dééd Yázhí's love for her people. He held her and her little one tightly in his arms as he said,

"Ayóó'anihíínísh'ní, shiyázhí nohłíinii." *I love both of you, my little ones.* Dééd Yázhí smiled and her heart smiled too as she said,

"Shí shįį 'ałdó' ayóó'áníínísh'ní. Nizhónígo nihaa 'áhólyą." *I probably love you too very much. You take such good care of us.*

Kiizhóní was elated by Dééd Yázhí's announcement of a probable love for him. He hugged her tightly and reluctantly released his tight hold on her when her little one screamed from the pain he felt from his bruises as he was being crushed by the two people who loved him so much.

Dééd Yázhí walked to the water's edge and said,

"Shí Tó 'Aheedlíinii dine'é nishłį. Ma'ii Deeshgiizhnii dine'é bá shíshchíín. Táchii'nii dine'é 'éí dashicheii nááná Tó Dích'íi'nii dine'é dashinálí. 'Ákót'éego 'asdzání nishłį. Shideezhí bił ná'ahiistsánígíí 'ayóo baa shił hózhǫ́ǫ́ dóó baa 'ahééh nisin."
I am of the Water Flows Together People. I am born for the Coyote Pass People. The Red Running Into the Water People are my maternal grandfathers, and the Bitter Water People are my paternal grandfathers. In that way, I am a Navajo woman. I am very happy about seeing my younger sister again, and I am very thankful for that.

Chapter Twenty-five
Fast Flowing Waters Sing A Beautiful Song

Nothing could part Dééd Yázhí and her younger sister, Dzáníbaa'. Dééd Yázhí enjoyed being with her sister but was afraid to allow herself to fully enjoy the presence of her sister because she was afraid her dear Dzáníbaa' would be taken away again.

When her younger sister did or said something to make her laugh, Dééd Yázhí felt as if some of the laughter stayed within her body. Her laughter would not come all the way to the surface. Instead it stayed in her throat and became a hard lump. The lump kept Dééd Yázhí from fully enjoying her life with Kiizhóní and her little one, as well as Dzáníbaa' and her husband and their beautiful son.

Dééd Yázhí told Dzáníbaa' she had heard about the Naashgálí dine'é *the Mescalero Apache people* through stories their Naabeehó people told about the people who lived across the river. She reported she had never seen a Naashgálí dine'é or anyone on the west side of the river. Dééd Yázhí related the words of the old man when he told her never to go to the river alone, saying,

"Yíiyá. 'Ei Naashgálí dine'é ła' ayóo danihijoołá, jiní. 'Ayóo tsé yee da'diłniih, jiní. Niyázhí tsé yee nídeididoołniił. Díkwíniilt'éego tó nílínígóó 'ałnánéiikahgo t'éí yá'át'ééh. Niidlą́'ígó 'éí t'áá nihich'į' daastxi' dooleeł." *Scary. The Mescalero Apache people do not like us, it is said. It is said they can really throw rocks. They might hit your little one with a rock. It is better if there are several of us who go to the river. When there are many of us, they will be more careful and subdued.*

Dééd Yázhí said she used to wonder why the Naashgálí dine'é were hostile when they could have all the good water they wanted, whereas her people suffered from stomach pains whenever they drank the water that left a white crust on their side of the river. Dééd Yázhí wondered if a person who drank the water that left a white crust on the river bank also had a white crust on their bid *stomach.*

Dzáníbaa' told Dééd Yázhí she always wanted to cross the river to be with her Naabeehó people who were settled on the opposite side of the Pecos River. Dzáníbaa' snickered when she told Dééd Yázhí she heard reports that the Naabeehó women were very hostile toward the Naashgálí men and would throw rocks at them if any of the Naashgálí men made attempts to swim in the river. Many brave Naashgálí men tried swimming in the river but they were chased out of the river by the angry Naabeehó women who threw large rocks at them. Dzáníbaa' reported to her older sister that the Naashgálí dine'é *Mescalero people* claimed the angry Naabeehó women were just as angry as the strong currents that would attempt to pull them into the swift, swirling water.

Dééd Yázhí hugged her younger sister when she expressed in perfect Navajo what the Naabeehó women would most likely be saying as Dzáníbaa' said,

"Ei Naashgálí hastói Naabeehó 'asdzání yidáahjj' daniljj̢go yiniinaa taah nídaalwo'. Tó nílínígíí tsé'naa nida'doołk̢ǫ̢łii' asdzání nihits'ą́ą́' dah deididoolóós'. Hatíhíláa ne'ęę'. Asdzání danilínígíí baa 'ádahołyą́." *Those Mescalero men want our young women and that is why they get into the water. They will swim across the river and lead our young women off. What a dreadful thing. Take care of the young women.*

In telling her younger sister stories, Dééd Yázhí remembered when she visited the river on days when the river rose and flowed angrily by. She always found it interesting that the ground on the eastern slopes of the river was covered with an uneven crusty coating of white, whereas the western slopes of the river were of a natural color. Dééd Yázhí also remembered how the water from the river usually carried an increased bitter taste after rains flushed water through the normally lazy, flowing river and wondered if it was the white crust that made the water bitter. Dééd Yázhí said she liked to measure how high the river ran by the line of white crust it left on the riverbank. Her people found out later that the water running from the eastern washes and ditches was bitter because the ground on that side of the river contained much alkali.

Dééd Yázhí told of how she always suspected the water running on the western side of the river was sweet because she rarely saw the white crust hugging the bank of the river. She remembered back to a time when she witnessed the fertility of the soil on the western side of the river as well. During the spring and summer seasons, the Naabeehó people noticed how the blades of grass on the western bank were taller, thicker, and deeper in color, whereas the grass on the eastern bank was stunted in its growth and had a pale green color, and wilted before turning yellow. Living among the Naashgálí people on the western side of the river gave Dééd Yázhí the chance to taste the water coming from the wash. It was as she expected. The water was sweet.

Dzáníbaa' hugged Dééd Yázhí tight and told her not to stop telling her stories. With tears running down her face, Dzáníbaa' told of how lonely she was for the words of her mother and father and her siblings as well as the words of her Naabeehó people. She thanked Dééd Yázhí for reminding her they belonged to three water clans of the Naabeehó people, therefore water was not an element that was to be feared.

Dééd Yázhí told her younger sister she never felt intimidated by the angry waters of the river. She just listened to it as it rushed by. She found the water to be kind to her. Dééd Yázhí urged her younger sister to join her to visit the flowing water for the purpose of greeting it. One day while sitting on the bank of the river with her younger sister, Dééd Yázhí told her sister of the many nights she lay awake in her little makeshift home Kiizhóní made for her. She said,

"Sha'áłchíní' ałtso da'iiłhoshgo dóó doo 'íits'a'ígóó tó nílínígíí t'óó yíísínísts'ą́ą' łeh ne'. Tó t'áá bí nízinjį' nílį yiits'a'go binahjį' doo 'atah 'ąą̨héeshjéé' nishłį da nisingo 'áshósin łeh ne'. Tó nílínígíí 'ákót'éego shaa jooba' nisin łeh ne'." *When my children all go to sleep and all was quiet, I would listen to the water running in the river. The water was free to run wherever it wanted to flow and because of that, it made me free, free from my status as a prisoner of war. In that way, the water was kind to me.*

Dééd Yázhí further told her younger sister

"Naashgálí dine'é ha'níigo t'óó baa hodiists'a' łeh ne'. Haa da shą' danoolnin nisin łeh. Ła' kóníghánídę́ę́' yiiłtsą́ągo da shą' haa deeshnííł nisin łeh ne'. Saad, Naashgálí, t'óó shił nizhónígo diits'a' łeh ne'. Nááná ła' diné'é 'ayóo dabidziilígíí 'ádaolyé nisin łeh nít'ę́ę́'. Ła' yiiłtsą́ągo da shą' ha'át'íí bidideeshniił nisin łeh nít'ę́ę́'." *I would just hear about the Mescalero Apache people. I used to wonder about their appearance. I always wondered what I would do if I saw one up close. I liked the name Naashgálí. It sounded like it represented a really strong people. I wondered what I would say if I ever saw one of the Mescalero people.*

Dzáníbaa' laughed at her sister's recollections. Thoughtfully, Dééd Yázhí added,

"Naashgálí dine'é 'ayóo dajooba'íígíí 'ádaolyéé lá. Yisdádaninizdzį́įz dóó naa dajoozba'. Shí dó' ayóó 'át'éego shaa dajoozba'. She'awéé' dóó Kiizhóní 'ałdó' yaa dajoozba'. Nihidine'é t'óó 'ádaaníí nít'ę́ę́' lá." *The Mescalero people are people who are really kind. They rescued you and showed you kindness. They also were very kind to me. They also showed kindness toward my little one and Kiizhóní. Our people were not telling the truth.*

****

Dééd Yázhí knew some of her people were hostile just like the soldiers who held her people as prisoners of war. One day when she and her little one and Kiizhóní were visiting the water that flowed quiet and slow, they saw Naabeehó men and children throwing rocks at them as the children yelled angry words at them, thinking they were of the Naashgálí people.

Dééd Yázhí was sad the men did not discourage the children from yelling mean words. She was sad her Naabeehó people were permitting their children to become angry just like the soldiers.

Dééd Yázhí surprised herself when her thoughts drifted to the soldiers. She had not thought of a soldier in many days. She had not even seen one in many days. She thought of her son's father but she did not see him as an angry, hateful soldier, instead she thought of him as the kind man who saved her life. The tall, gray-haired one was the one who gave her their little one, and it was her little one who gave her a reason to survive the most difficult of situations.

Upon returning to the camp of her younger sister, Dééd Yázhí asked Dzáníbaa' where the rest of her husband's people had gone. Dzáníbaa' told her when the Naabeehó people were forced to walk to Fort Sumner, the Naashgálí dine'é *Mescalero people* left because they were told the Naabeehó people were very warlike. Many of the Naashgálí dine'é left after a year of being held as prisoners of war during which time, the men helped build many of the buildings at the fort.

To demonstrate her husband's love for her and their child, Dzaníbaa' told Dééd Yázhí,

"Shí 'éí t'áá kóó shidine'é bíséłdáa dooleeł díiniid. She'awéé' bizhé'é 'ałdó' t'áá kóó niiltee'. Azhą shį́į́ bidine'é yóó 'anídahineest'įį' nidi, bí 'éí doo háajigo da nihits'ą́ąjį' shíni' da shidíiniid. T'áá kwe'é nihaa 'áháshyą́ągo nihíséłdáa

514

doo shidíiniid. Hastiin yá'át'éehii baa shi'deeltį́į́ lá nisin łeh. Ayóó'óósh'níí dóó bí 'ałdó' ayóó'áshó'ní. Nihiyázhí ayóó'áyó'ní 'ałdó'. Nihaa 'áhályą́ągo t'ahdoo dichin yéego biih niidéeh da. Hastiin yá'át'éehii nilį́. *I decided to stay here beside my people.*
My baby's father also decided to stay. Even though his people
escaped, he told me he did not want to go to another place. "I
will stay here beside you and take care of you and our little one,"
is what he told me. I think I was given to a good man. I love him
very much and he loves me very much. He also loves his son very
much. Under his care, we have not really fallen into hunger. He is
a good man.

Déed Yázhí responded by saying,

"Nihizhé'é 'éí 'ei hastiin t'áadoo nihik'inííchá'íígíí bił nilį́į
dooleeł. Nizhónígo nihaa 'áhályáníígíí 'ałdó' bił nilį́į dooleeł.
'Aóó', t'áá'aaníí, hastiin yá'át'éehii baa ni'deeltį́į́ lá, shideezhí.
Ná baa shił hózhǫ́. Shí dó' éí baa 'ahééh nisin. Nizhónígo' baa
'áhólyą́ą dooleeł, shideezhí."

Our father will respect that man because he never left you
alone to fend for yourself. He will also respect the fact that he
takes good care of both of you. Yes, my younger sister, you have
been given to a good man. I am happy for you. I am thankful of
that as well. Take good care of him, my younger sister.

The two sisters hugged and held one another tight,
knowing their closeness would begin to melt the hurt they had
experienced at the hand of their enemies.

****

Although Déed Yázhí was happy and thankful for being with
her younger sister, she still felt a deep sadness as she stood on
the bank of the river and looked into the fast-flowing waters.

515

She wondered when she would see her father and her mother and her younger brothers. She wondered when she would be able to introduce her son to the tall, gray-haired one. She wondered when she would be reunited with her seven little adopted sons and the old man. She missed them all so much.

Dééd Yázhí shook her head as the thoughts began to solidify in her mind.

"Yáadilá 'ánísht'éé dó'. Shideezhí yee' bił ná'ahiistsą́ą́ dóó k'ad ba'ałk'ee nahísíitą́. Eí baa 'ahééh jinízin dooleeł, yáadilá, *What in the world am I? I have been reunited with my sister and now we are staying with her. I could easily be thankful for that,* she said as she chided her thoughts.

At night, Dééd Yázhí loved to walk to the river's edge and look across the river to see the many tiny fires that flickered proving her people were still being held as prisoners of war. She knew her people did not have firewood, so they made sure the coals never completely died out and became cold. They burned whatever they could find.

Thinking back, Dééd Yázhí thought of the time when it was very cold and the soldiers at the picket forts gave the Naabeehó women shoes for their cold, blistered feet. The shoes the soldiers gave the women were boots, very narrow boots with high heels. The shoes the Naabeehó people needed were mocassins. Dééd Yázhí remembered the old women wheezing as they tried so hard to push their feet into the narrow boots. The high-heeled boots were useless to the Naabeehó women.

The Naabeehó men disassembled the boots and used the leather tops of the boots to fashion crude moccasins for the women. The foot of the boot was, in some cases, used for dipping water out of the river for drinking. Some people were so desperately cold they used the foot part of the boot as fuel for their fire so they could keep warm during one or two long, cold nights. Looking across the river, Dééd Yázhí wondered what fueled her peoples' fires.

****

The sound of the flowing water still drew Dééd Yázhí close to it, especially at night. The nights were peaceful with the constellations flickering to announce their placement in the sky, which let the Naabeehó people know the season that was upon them. Dééd Yázhí remembered some years when the seasons did not change. It remained warm for many months and when the cold winds blew in, it remained cold for many months. Many of her people were focused upon their plight rather than concentrating upon the environment that made attempts to announce the season that was upon them and the cultural activities that should be taking place.

Dééd Yázhí looked up at the constellations that looked down upon her and winked, announcing it was early fall. She thought of the many days Kiizhóní led the Naabeehó men out to the cleared fields in the spring season to plant the corn kernels the soldiers gave them. The kernels were pale and were not of any distinct color like her father's corn kernels which were vibrant colors of white, yellow, blue, red, and sometimes a mixture of colors. Like the years before, the crops failed. The long irrigation ditches Kiizhóní and his men helped dig were useless because the ditches were lined with the white crust that steals life out of everything it covers. The corn stalks grew a few inches, wilted and turned yellow, then turned inward toward the ground to die.

To keep the fall season alive within her, Dééd Yázhí sang the corn-grinding song her mother taught her when she was a little girl.

"Ajik'áago, díí nihiyiin bee nizh'di'a'go doo ch'ééh adidáah da. Shá bíighah ajik'áago nidi bízhneel'ą́ą́go áhooł'įįh." *When you grind corn, sing our corn-grinding song so you will not get tired. It enables you to grind corn all day long.* Although there was no corn to grind, Dééd Yázhí sang the song and moved her arms as if she was grinding corn.

Dééd Yázhí was thankful to the night sky. It was kind in bringing her mother's words back to her. The night sky also kept her mother's teaching close to her ears. She looked up into the sky and whispered,

"Ahéhee'." *Thank you.*

****

Sitting on the riverbank holding her little one tightly in her arms and sitting near Kiizhóní settled Dééd Yázhí's heart. She missed her father and her mother and her younger brothers. She greatly missed her brave little sons and her maternal grandfather.

Kiizhóní promised Dééd Yázhí he would return to their camp to gather their sons, but he was not strong enough. He still had many bruises and scars that were forming on his smooth skin which were testimony of the trauma he suffered from slamming into the branch in the river, so Dééd Yázhí did not allow him to leave to return to her children. Kiizhóní also wanted to inform her younger brother that she and her little one had survived and had been rescued by his younger sister, Dzáníbaa', and her husband's people. Kiizhóní reassured Dééd Yázhí her children were being cared for. Still, Dééd Yázhí prayed for the full recovery of Kiizhóní and she prayed often for the safety of her children.

The water gave her the peace she needed to bear the loss of her children and her maternal grandfather. On the nights when she could not sleep, she woke Kiizhóní and together with her little one, they quietly stole away to listen for the sounds of their people from across the river. The water kept Dééd Yázhí strong.

****

When the weather changed dramatically from being relatively peaceful to where the winds blew blinding sand across the valley, Kiizhóní decided it was safe to return to their camp under the protection of the winds. He made plans to leave during the night and to travel only at night. Knowing of his plans, Dzáníbaa's husband created a small portable brush arbor that was surprisingly light in weight. Kiizhóní was advised the soldiers would not be as suspicious if they saw the brush arbor thinking it was a Naashgálí *Mescalero* who was sleeping in it.

Sleeping during the day and traveling at night, Kiizhóní walked upstream along the river bank to find the camp he and Dééd Yázhí occupied before the unfortunate incident. After walking many nights, Kiizhóní saw parts of the landscape that were familiar even though he was looking at the landscape from the opposite side of the river.

Under the disguise of the brush arbor, Kiizhóní watched for his people. He saw them obtain water from the river's edge, but the sand blown by the wind kept him from seeing his people clearly. One morning, when the wind had subsided,

519

Kiizhóní saw some children and their mothers standing near the river. One boy saw him, picked up some rocks and threw them at him. Disgusted, Kiizhóní yelled at the boy saying,

"T'áadoo nááná ła' tsé bee nániłne'í. T'áá ni nidine'é da ła' tsé bee nídidíílniił. Naabaahii hanii 'ákót'éego 'ídahooł'aah łeh. Łł ahojooba' yee' bił íhoo'aah. Háíshą' ninaat'áanii nilį. Doo hashkał dah yíyéłígíí ninaatáanii bee bił hodoonih. *Don't hit anyone with rocks. You might hit one of your own people with a rock. A warrior does not learn in that way. They learn from the standpoint of kindness. Who is your leader? Your leader will be told about the unruly behavior you are displaying.*

Kiizhóní knew if he started to swim across the river, the young boy would tell others and they would join him in throwing rocks. Disgusted and discouraged and not wanting to call attention to himself, Kiizhóní decided to camp overnight and call to Dééd Yázhí's younger brother again.

After several calls throughout two nights without a response, Kiizhóní decided to return to Dééd Yázhí and her little one. Although they were under the protection of the Naashgálí dine'é, he did not feel Dééd Yázhí and her little one were completely safe.

Tired and worn out from walking and fighting the wind and the sandstorm, Kiizhóní slipped into the brush shelter that was made for Dééd Yázhí and her little one. Knowing she and her little one were safe, Kiizhóní lay quietly waiting for morning when Dééd Yázhí would wake up and find him sleeping next to her little one.

Dééd Yázhí stirred. Kiizhóní held his breath and quietly said,

"Shí 'ásht'į. Nihaa nánísdzá." *It's me. I have come back to you.*

"Shitsilíísh bił ahiiniltsá? Sha'áłchíní shą'? Nihicheii shą'?"
Did you see my younger brother? What about my children?
What about our maternal grandfather? Dééd Yázhí asked with
great emotion in her voice.

Kiizhóní's heart was breaking for his Dééd Yázhí but he could
not give her any news to alleviate her emotional pain as he
responded,

"Ádin ga'. Tł'ée'go, da'awoshgo t'éiyá yishwoł nít'ę́ę́'. Jı̨́ı̨go 'éí
niyé chaha'oh shá 'áyiilaa yę́ę́ bii' hanínáshyı̨h nít'ę́ę́'. Tó nílínígíí
t'éí yishdlą́ą́go bikiin ahééníshwod. Nihe'anaa'í binaabaahii tó
nílínígíí yibą́ą́hgi dabighan dóó t'áá 'áádóó nihidine'é hadeisííd.
T'óó'ahayói hada'asííd lágo bik'íníyá. Nihidine'é 'éí yéego
bich'į' nidahwii'náá lágo bik'íníghal. T'áá 'ákwe'é nitsilí biba'
naasháago díkwíí jį́ shı̨́ı̨́ 'azlį́į́', áko nidi t'áadoo 'ákwe'é nádzáa
da. Shá 'ashja'iilaago 'ákǫ́ǫ́ nídeeshdááł, na'áłchíní dóó nihicheii
hanáádínéeshtaał." *Nothing. I traveled, running only at night.*
During the day, I rested under the portable brush arbor your
brother-in-law made for me. I survived going and coming back
by drinking the river water. Our enemy's warriors (soldiers) are
watching our people from the bank of the river. I found there
are many who are watching our people. I saw that our people
are really suffering. I waited for your younger brother there for
several days but he never came back. When it is convenient
for me, I will go back again to look for your children and our
maternal grandfather.

Dééd Yázhí stirred. Kiizhóní heard her softly praying. He
knew her heart was breaking. He reached out to her and
whispered,

"Na'áłchíní bił nída'ahiidííltséełgo 'át'é. Hágo." *You will see*
your children again. Come here.

521

Dééd Yázhí, desperately needing comfort, wanted to move closer to Kiizhóní but instead, she said,

"She'awéé' bizhé'é hólǫ́." *My baby has a father.*

"Aoo', shił bééhózin," *Yes, I know,* Kiizhóní quietly answered.

Dééd Yázhí stirred again, picked up her little one then moved closer to Kiizhóní and made his arm her pillow. Kiizhóní was happy to hold Dééd Yázhí until the white light of dawn announced the approaching morning. He caught the scent of her hair that was newly washed with yucca soap. The scent was very sensuous. He kissed Dééd Yázhí's hair and breathed in deeply then looked up. Through the openings of their brush arbor, he saw stars flickering to let him know the Creator knew their children were all right.

"Ahéhee', shiTaa', niha'áłchíní nihá baa 'áhólyą́. 'Ahéhee', yá'át'éehgo kwe'é nánísdzá. Ahéhee', shiDééd Yázhí dóó biyázhí shá baa 'áhólyą́ą́ nít'ę́ę́'. Dééd Yázhí bideezhí hastiin yił iiná 'ííł'ínígíí dóó bidine'é nihá bik'ijídlíi le'. Ahéhee', shiTaa'. *Thank you, my Spiritual Father, for taking care of our children. Thank you that I came back safely. Thank you for taking care of my Dééd Yázhí and her little one for me. Bless Dééd Yázhí's younger sister's husband and his people. Thank you, my Spiritual Father.*

With those words, Kiizhóní fell asleep to get much-needed rest.

****

One night Dééd Yázhí could not sleep. Loneliness was getting the best of her. Dééd Yázhí and her younger sister's reunion increased her loneliness. She wanted to see her father's face and his smile. She wanted to see her mother and hear her mother's voice. She wanted her father and her mother to greet her little one. She wanted her younger sister to be reunited with her mother and father as well. Dééd Yázhí also wanted her mother and her father to meet Dzáníbaa's son and her husband.

Dééd Yázhí's thoughts stopped when she asked herself, "How could I tell my mother and my father about my baby's father?" She thought back to the day at the parade grounds when the tall gray-haired one saw her and saw their little one she was holding. He did not greet his son.

Dééd Yázhí admitted to herself that whenever she heard her sister's sweet laughter, she felt a deep sense of guilt. She wanted their mother to know her sister was alive. She wanted their mother to hear her sister's laughter because their mother was her sister's favorite parent, while Dééd Yázhí's favorite parent was her father.

To console herself, Dééd Yázhí decided to walk to the river's edge in the darkness. Even though the river nearly claimed their lives, she was still drawn to it. Slowly she picked her way through the darkness.

Even though it was night and her people were resting, Dééd Yázhí wanted to find a safe place where she could hear her people talking, praying, singing, crying, and possibly laughing. To remain close to her little sons, she especially wanted to hear the sound of children talking, laughing, and crying.

Sitting on the bank of the river, she looked up to see the night sky she loved. It reinforced her sense of freedom. She thought, the night is when sounds are carried through the air more easily.

Dééd Yázhí saw small, flickering fires of her people. There were not many fires. She wondered what her people were burning with which to warm themselves and to cook the rancid meat for themselves and their family.

Dééd Yázhí looked up the river to look for small flickering fires in a futile attempt to hear the voices of her adopted sons. Kiizhóní promised her he would go up the river to look for her children and the old man once again, but they both knew getting her sons and the old man across the river was impossible.

Dééd Yázhí listened to the water splashing against the rocks. All of a sudden she heard a loud plop in the water. Afraid it was a soldier who heard her, she jumped up and silently ran back to her sister's camp and fell into her bedding beside her little one. She missed her own bedding. Feeling the need for safety and comfort, Dééd Yázhí sang a song as she lay snug in her bedding. She wanted to feel the rug blanket her mother made for her. Her own rug blanket brought her mother closer to her. Her adopted sons loved sleeping on her rug blanket, which also kept her and her little one warm at night.

Dééd Yázhí was cautious. She did not want to go to the river for a while. She felt someone had possibly seen her or heard her sitting on the bank of the river humming. She decided to stay away from the river until the person or animal no longer suspected her to be on the riverbank again.

****

As long as Dééd Yázhí was going to sit on the bank of the river, especially at night, Kiizhóní did not want to travel up the river again to look for Dééd Yázhí's adopted sons. He also wanted to look for Dééd Yázhí's brother. It had not rained in many days so Kiizhóní was hoping for a shallow area of the river to cross over to the other side. He worried about the picket forts though. He knew the soldiers watched over the Naabeehó people during the day and throughout the night. Getting seven children and an old man across the river would be difficult, but for Dééd Yázhí's sake, he was willing to try.

Dééd Yázhí promised Kiizhóní she would not to go to the river alone or at night. Although apprehensive, Kiizhóní took the brush arbor Dzáníbaa's husband made for him, and left at night to walk up the river.

Walking at night, Kiizhóní could see the lights from the kerosene lanterns shining above the picket forts. He could hear the soldiers talking loudly to one another. He looked past the picket forts and saw small fires flickering. He knew the Naabeehó people were using all they could find to build their fires.

Kiizhóní knew the people were not warm, they were only using the fires for light and for cooking the small pieces of meat they were given in the rations. He could smell the faint scent of pitch. The Naabeehó people used the pitch they obtained on the mountain trail as medicine but the people also used the pitch to burn the insects off every evening, and then they used the pitch to keep a small fire going, far into the night.

Kiizhóní slept under his portable brush arbor. It protected him from the weather elements and the watchful eye of the soldiers but it did not protect him from insects, so he slept lightly each night.

Reaching the place that was across the river from their camping site, Kiizhóní observed the activity of his people from afar. At night he listened for the low coyote howl that signaled Dééd Yázhí's younger brother's presence, but the night went by without a sound. As a result, Kiizhóní was getting very tired because he was not getting much sleep.

After several days of hiding and watching, Kiizhóní did not get a glimpse of the children or the old man. The soldiers were keeping an even more watchful eye over the Naabeehó people, so Kiizhóní did not make an attempt to cross the river, although the river was not running very deep. During the day, Naabeehó children stood near the river gathering rocks to send them sailing in Kiizhóní's direction. He decided to camp so he could call for Dééd Yázhí's younger brother.

Coyote call. No answer.

A louder coyote call. No answer.

A sad, drawn out coyote call. No answer.

Sad about disappointing Dééd Yázhí again, Kiizhóní left to return back to Dééd Yázhí and her little one.

****

Back at Dzáníbaa's camping area, Kiizhóní sadly told Dééd Yázhí about his unproductive return to their camp up the river. Dééd Yázhí could not wait until nightfall to go to the river. She knew the river would help heal her of the loneliness she felt for the people she loved.

As soon as darkness covered the entire valley, Dééd Yázhí quietly crept to the riverbank, the place that allowed her to unload her troubles. Sitting down on a jutting rock, a slight breeze blew through her hair that was slowly peeling each worry off of her shoulders. Dééd Yázhí began to hum the little song her father sang to her when she was little. With tears pouring down her face, she softly hummed and watched the little fires flickering across the river. Every once in a while she could see a Naabeehó person walking, and when she saw a person walking around Dééd Yázhí desperately wanted to scream out to the person to hear a greeting coming back to her. The picket forts not only interrupted the serene scene far away across the river but they also interrupted the safety she felt on the opposite side of the river.

Dééd Yázhí heard a faint painful rendition, an echo of the song she was quietly humming. She turned her head to keep the breeze from whistling in her ear as it blew past her ear. Once again, she faintly heard the song but she could not hear the entire song. The song stopped. She reverently scolded the breeze, telling it not to tease her.

"T'áadoo shich'į' nahoyíłnání! T'áadoo kǫ́ǫ́ naanídííldisí. Doo yee' chohoo'į́ígóó ti'hooshnííh. Shijéí neezgai. Shimá dóó shizhé'é ts'ídá doodagóó bíhásááh. Shitsilíké 'ałdó' t'áá'awołíbee bíhásááh. Sha'áłchíní 'ałdó' bídahasááh dóó bich'į' shíni' íí'á. Háida shą baa 'ádahalyą́ nisin łeh t'áá 'ákwííjį́. Nihicheii dó', t'áá daats'í nihidine'é baa dajooba' dóó baa 'ádahalyą́ nisingo bik'ee ti'hooshnííh. *Don't cause me trouble! Don't be twirling around here! I am suffering in an extreme way. My heart hurts. I miss my mother and my father so deeply. I also really miss my younger brothers. I miss my children and worry about them too. Every day I wonder who is taking care of them. I wonder if our people are kind to our maternal grandfather and taking care of him too. That is what tortures me.*

527

Dééd Yázhí stopped scolding the wind and turned her attention to listening to the sounds from across the river. She sat holding her heart as she thought of all the people for whom she was lonely.

She had been lonely for the tall, gray-haired one, but he never acknowledged their little one. Now, she was lonely for his memory, which was fading fast from her mind. Tears began to slide out of her eyes at the thought of how her little one had to struggle to survive the long walk while she hid him from his own people. It was one of his own people who tried to kill him! she sadly thought.

"Shiyázhí nizhónígo baa' áháyą," *My little one is well cared for,* she breathed. Her little one was with her younger sister. Dzáníbaa' had convinced her to leave her son in case a soldier found her. Dééd Yázhí had reluctantly agreed.

Dééd Yázhí shook her head to chase her thoughts away. All of a sudden, she heard the faint sound of someone singing again. She turned her head to see where the sound was coming from. Looking toward the picket forts, she whispered,

"Doo daats'í deidiits'a' da?" *Maybe they do not hear it?* The soldiers in the picket forts did not seem to be concerned about the singing.

She listened once again. She held her hand over her heart. In between the splashing of the water and the breeze, she heard someone singing again. She decided to walk farther down river to see if the singing would get louder there. The rocky bank was difficult to walk on. Dééd Yázhí looked up to see where the moon was. Clouds were covering the moon. She wondered if she should wait until the moon came back out before she walked farther. She could not feel the breeze that was bothering her earlier. She decided to continue walking, thinking the darkness would hide her from the sharp eyes and ears of the soldiers.

Dééd Yázhí found an area where she could sit and listen for the singing. She listened but there was no sound. All she could hear was the lapping of the water on the rocks below. She shivered. There was not even the sound of the soldiers talking in the picket forts.

Just when Dééd Yázhí decided she could not stay away from her little one any longer, she stopped because she heard a distant song. A man was singing. It sounded as if his heart was breaking. Dééd Yázhí shivered once again. It was cold. She leaned forward to listen and the song began again. The song was coming from the waters that were flowing slowly by.

No, she thought.

The man was singing the song her father used to sing to her and her younger sister. Dééd Yázhí could not believe her ears! Afraid to believe what she was hearing, she covered her ears. Overcome by a sense of deep sadness and longing, she started sobbing.

"Ge'!" *Listen!* she said. She closed her eyes to heighten her sense of hearing. Her shoulders shook uncontrollably. She could not hear the song being sung all the way through. The breeze was picking up a word here and there and dropping it beside her ears. She would not allow her mind to think it was truly her father singing the song. It's the song all Naabeehó fathers sing to their daughters, she thought as she tried to calm herself down.

Desperate to hear the entire song, Dééd Yázhí decided to move down the river a little ways. In the darkness, she carefully picked her way along the bank of the river. The song ended. Dééd Yázhí was desperate. She wanted the song to continue. Her heart was breaking.

"Shizhé'é ..." *My father* ... she whispered as hot lonely tears poured down her face. She had to hear more of the voice, hoping it would bring the sound of her father's voice close to her ears and comfort her hurting heart.

Dééd Yázhí sat down on a flat rock. Feeling the need to explain to the environment her reason for being there, she softly said,

"Háíshįį shizhé'é biyiin yee ni'di'a'. T'óó yídéests'įįł nisin." *Someone is singing my father's song. I just want to hear it.* She peered across the river for any sign of the person who was singing.

She had to steady herself on a rock to keep from falling into the river. It was no mistake, the beautiful song was being sung again. The one singing was experiencing deep pain. Dééd Yázhí could feel the pain. She grabbed at her heart and listened as she heard the song. Without thinking, she began to sing along with the person singing the song. The man stopped singing. Dééd Yázhí continued singing. She wanted the person across the river to hear her.

Dééd Yázhí listened. Her heart was beating not only in her chest but also in her arms, in her hands, in her head, in her ears, in her eyes, and in her shoulders. The person began singing loudly. Dééd Yázhí looked around her to see if someone was watching. The one singing sounded a lot like her father. The rise and fall of his voice sounded much like that of her father.

All of a sudden, she thought she heard her name being sung. Then she heard her younger sister's name being sung. Dééd Yázhí could not speak. Shaking, she began singing her father's song. Her voice trailed off so she could listen for a response. She heard the voice of a man in great pain bellow out,

"ShiDédii shą'? ShiDzáníbaa' shą'?" *Where is my Dedii? Where is my Dzáníbaa'?* She heard her father's tortured voice choking on the names of his daughters. In response, Dééd Yázhí hoarsely cried out,

"Shizhé'é! Shizhé'é! Shizhé'é! Shizhé'é! Shizhé'é! Shizhé'é! Shizhé'é!" *My father! My father! My father! My father! My father! My father! My father!* In between her words, Dééd Yázhí heard her father asking,

"Háísh ánít'į́?" *Who are you?*

Still keeping her voice down, Dééd Yázhí shouted,

"Shí 'At'ééd Yázhí Naazbaa' yinishyé, shizhé'é! Shí 'éí 'ásht'į́! *My name is Little Girl Warrior Who Came Home, my father. That's me!*

Dééd Yázhí heard the man say,

"Háshinee', she'awéé'." *Dear one, my baby.*

Dééd Yázhí could not control herself. She looked up into the sky. It was still very dark. She jumped up and started running back to her sister's camp. Falling and tripping, she tried making her way back in the dark. It was of no use. Dééd Yázhí could not see where she was. Her heart was beating so loudly she could not think. She kept looking across the river to see if she recognized any landmark but nothing seemed familiar.

While running, Dééd Yázhí stepped in a mud-soaked area and slipped, then began tumbling and sliding down toward the river. She could not believe this was happening! The beginning of a scream escaped her lips before Dééd Yázhí could bite into her lip to keep herself from screaming. She frantically and desperately grabbed for roots to keep herself from falling but she slid even farther down, bringing the roots down with her.

Dééd Yázhí reached for large boulders to break her fall, but they too began sliding down right after her. Finally, her body slumped down on the wet ground among many weeds that were irritating her scratched skin.

The sound of roots breaking, rocks sliding down, and weeds being crushed loudly echoed along the river. Dééd Yázhí shut her eyes real tight and held her breath, hoping she had fallen upon a safe spot.

To her horror, she heard the sound of horses' hooves riding along the top of the riverbank. Dééd Yázhí decided to stay in the weeds until the soldiers passed by. The soldiers rode back and forth several times. She decided to wait until the faint light of dawn appeared to climb back up the slippery bank. Exhausted, she fell asleep hanging onto a thick, exposed root.

Dééd Yázhí woke to find herself completely covered with mud. Not far from where she sat precariously held up by weeds, Dééd Yázhí watched as soldiers appeared above the river. She heard them talking and urinating into the river. Just when she would start to move to give her muscles a rest, more soldiers appeared, who also urinated into the river. The faint sound of a bugle's cry brought the urinating to a stop.

In the faint light of dawn, Dééd Yázhí looked around her. She was sitting on a narrow ledge and below her were more weeds lining the riverbank below. Above her, she could see a cleared area where she slid down the embankment. Many loose rocks sat precariously above her, ready to slide down with the slightest movement.

Soldiers lowered buckets down on ropes to obtain water from the same river they urinated into. Dééd Yázhí shuddered and shivered. She was cold from the wet mud that covered her thin blouse and skirt and her exposed skin. The weeds pasted to her body by the mud created a camouflage that partially hid her body. The weeds that stuck out from her body caused her to look like one giant weed. She could not move.

Dééd Yázhí knew her little one was crying. Her breasts were full and leaking. She could not believe she was so close to her father, and now she was so far. She shuddered when she thought of the soldiers discovering her on the opposite side of the river. Looking down at her legs and her thin blouse and skirt, she was relieved she was the same color as the mud that lined the riverbank, so she decided to stay hidden by the mud and the weeds that surrounded her.

The sun seemed to resist being pulled across the sky toward the western horizon. When the sun was finally setting, Dééd Yázhí started searching for a way to climb back to the top of the embankment. The dim light of dusk hid her from her enemies as she climbed her way back up the bank. She pulled out rocks to create holes where she could place her mocassined feet as she slowly climbed the steep embankment.

At the top, Dééd Yázhí looked up to find the moon big and round just above the eastern horizon. In the pale light of dusk, she ran along the riverbank softly singing the song her father sang to her. She could not wait to tell her younger sister their father was alive and was also a prisoner of war at the fort.

She kept looking for the one picket fort that had the brightest light. In searching for it, she saw a figure coming toward her. In her fright, Dééd Yázhí fell to the ground, hoping the person did not see her. Soon, there were two figures walking silently. Her ears were ringing.

Someone said in a low-pitched voice,

"Dédii."

Dééd Yázhí's heartbeat was louder than the person's voice. Once again, the person said,

"Dédii." Dééd Yázhí knew it was not Kiizhóní because he hardly ever called her by that name so she stayed on the ground. One of the figures standing above her asked,

"Haísh ánít'į? *Who are you?*

Dééd Yázhí remained quiet. The figure said,

"Díí yee' asdzání ła' Dééd Yázhí wolyéego haniitá." *We are looking for a young woman named Little Girl.*

As more words were spoken, Dééd Yázhí recognized the voice of Kiizhóní. In a weak voice, Dééd Yázhí responded, saying,

"Shí 'éí 'ásht'į." *That is me.*

This is the second time I have said that, she thought. Dééd Yázhí's thoughts began to overwhelm her. First it was her father she responded to and now it was Kiizhóní. Still puzzled, curiosity got the best of her when she asked,

"Háíshą' áłtsé shíízhi'?" *Who called my name first?*

"Niyé níízhi'." *Your brother-in-law called your name.*

Dééd Yázhí knew immediately why her brother-in-law called her Dédii. That is what her younger sister and her family called her.

With Kiizhóní's help, Dééd Yázhí got up and explained her muddy appearance in the pale light of the moon, after which she told Kiizhóní about hearing her father singing and calling to her. She asked the two men to take her to her sister right away so she could tell her sister about their father. Dééd Yázhí found it difficult to walk. Without permission, Kiizhóní picked her up and carried her back to her sister's camp.

Upon seeing her older sister covered completely in mud, Dzánibaa' began to laugh hysterically, then cried tears of relief, then spit out bouts of scolding followed by letting Dééd Yázhí know she had caused much worry to everyone.

Dééd Yázhí told her sister and Kiizhóní about her visit to the water that had lured her far down the river. Dzánibaa' could not get enough of the reciting of the events of the previous night when Dééd Yázhí heard her father singing, and Dééd Yázhí wanted to retell her experience so as not to forget each incident, no matter how insignificant. In between each repetition of the story, the two sisters cried as they held one another.

For two days, the two young families waited for the clouds to obscure the bright light of the moon. The two sisters carried their babies while the men carried their bedding and a sparse package of food containing a few pieces of roots and berries and a jug of water. The landscape was dark. Only lights from the picket forts and flickers from small fires could be seen dotting the landscape across the river. Light from the picket forts seemed to be less bright as the four people walked along.

Dééd Yázhí wished she had paid more attention to the number of picket forts she passed when she was returning from hearing her father singing. The safety of her little one and Kiizhóní and her sister's family were dependent upon her recollection of the place where she greeted her father. As they silently walked, Dééd Yázhí prayed, asking the Creator to lead her to the spot where she spoke to her father.

Dééd Yázhí told the truth when her younger sister asked her, "Ts'ídá háadishą' nihizhé'é ni'di'a'go sidíníts'ą́ą́'?" *Exactly where did you hear our father singing?*

Dééd Yázhí answered with a weak,

"Ch'ééh hádínísh'įį'." *I am trying to find it.*

Kiizhóní offered to lead the two families down the river. Dééd Yázhí asked to stop several times so they could listen for their father's voice singing. Only the talking of the soldiers and the crying of Naabeehó babies and children could be heard as the group walked slowly and quietly along.

All of a sudden, everyone stopped at the same time to listen to the faint sound of a song. The two sisters heard the melody of the song they used to hear as little girls. Dééd Yázhí wished she could pick up her younger sister and fly to their father. Trying hard to control her emotions, Dééd Yázhí began singing the song she heard her father singing. Her younger sister started crying and in between sobs joined in singing the song. The two sisters were singing, stopping every once in a while to listen for their father's little song.

Eight sets of eyes peered through the darkness to see where the song was coming from. The silence forced them to continue walking. Kiizhóní offered to carry Dééd Yázhí's little one and held Dééd Yázhí's hand as he led the others along the river. The young Naashgálí *Mescalero* man carried their supplies and his baby. Dzáníbaa' carried the jug of water. Dééd Yázhí still sore from the fall, followed Kiizhóní as he carried their bedding and her little one.

The group stopped to listen. The singing from across the river was getting louder. No longer were the two sisters hearing only a melody but actual words as well. The group continued walking as they were guided by the song. At times excitement was taking over their sense of remaining obscure, causing Dééd Yázhí and her sister to stumble in the dark. The sound of the running water was the constant guide for the young men while the sound of their father's voice was pulling the young sisters along as they were blinded by their tears as they followed Kiizhóní. Dééd Yázhí and Dzáníbaa' held on to each other as they sang and cried and sang and cried.

Dééd Yázhí stopped in her tracks. The others quietly questioned her action. Dééd Yázhí was torn. She was walking toward her father but walking farther away from their younger brother and her seven adopted children and their maternal grandfather.

Kiizhóní reassured her by saying,

"Nihizhé'é bił ná'ahoołtsą́ągo, nihe'ashiiké dóó nihicheii bíká deesháałii' áádę́ę́' nídeesh'ish. Nitsilí 'ałdó' hadínéeshtaał."

When you two see your father again, I will go and get our sons and our maternal grandfather and I will bring them back. I will also go look for your younger brother.

Dééd Yázhí's worried heart was calmed a little. She appreciated the way Kiizhóní claimed her sons as his own. Kiizhóní stopped. They had been walking among thin cottonwood trees that lined the river bank. The sound of the sisters' father's singing was coming directly from across the river.

Dééd Yázhí and Dzáníbaa' sang louder. Up to this point, they had sung softly. Now their lungs were bursting with excitement as they boldly sang their father's little song. The group stopped and listened for the full sound of their father's song.

They heard the sound of a man's voice asking,

"Dédii, niísh ánít'į? *Dédii, is that you?*

Still afraid to believe her ears, Dééd Yázhí answered, yelling cautiously, so as to not alert the soldiers,

"Aoo', shizhé'é. Shideezhí Dzáníbaa' dó' kǫǫ sizį." *Yes, my father. My younger sister, Dzáníbaa', is standing here too.*

The answer from across the river was one Dééd Yázhí and Dzáníbaa' had been waiting to hear for years! But, they heard an unfamiliar sound, that of their father sobbing loudly. Although the water in the river attempted to carry their father's voice downstream, the two sisters heard the distinct sound of their father's voice bursting forth saying,

"Yá'át'ééh, sha'áłchíní! Háshinee', háshinee', sha'áłchíní. Ayóó'ánihíínísh'ní! Doo ts'íí 'át'éégóó nihídin séłįį' nít'ę́ę'!" *Greetings, my children. Dear ones, dear ones, my children. I love you. I have been desperately missing you!*

They all heard the beginning of a scream. Dééd Yázhí watched as Dzáníbaa' placed her hand over her mouth to stifle her scream. Dééd Yázhí knew her sister had been waiting many painful months and years to hear her father or her mother claim her as their beloved child. In the dim moonlight, Dééd Yázhí watched tears of love pour down her sister's face as her Naashgálí husband wrapped his free arm around Dzáníbaa's waist to hold her as she slowly dropped to the ground. The Naashgálí man hovered over Dzáníbaa'.

Dééd Yázhí fell near her sister as their sobs shook their bodies. She then turned toward Kiizhóní and her little one and threw her arms up in the air. Kiizhóní dropped their bedding and grabbed Dééd Yázhí in his free arm to hold her close. Dééd Yázhí lifted her face and without realizing it, Kiizhóní lowered his face to kiss her on the lips.

"Ummmmm," was all Dééd Yázhí could say as she kissed his soft, trembling lips. More kisses followed before Dééd Yázhí and Kiizhóní regained their senses.

Dzáníbaa' cried out to ask,

"Shizhé'é, shimá shą'? Shimá shą'? *My father, where is my mother? Where is my mother?*

Unexpectedly the two sisters heard their father say,

"Nihilahkéí 'ałdó' kǫ́ǫ́ siké!" *Your brothers are also right here!*

Kiizhóní grabbed Dééd Yázhí and hugged her close as their lips found one another's again. Kiizhóní had been worried about Dééd Yázhí's younger brother. He placed his hands over his mouth and made the sound of a lonely coyote howl. He waited. Once again, he made the sound of a coyote howl to catch the attention of Dééd Yázhí's younger brother. He listened. Dééd Yázhí listened. Her little one listened. They all heard, but wondered what would happen next.

A beautiful sound reached their ears. The flowing water in the river could not hold back the call of the coyote as it came sailing back across the waters. Dééd Yázhí was not just hearing things. Her younger brothers were safe with their father. She looked up toward the black sky and whispered,

"Ahéhee', shiTaa'." *Thank you, my Spiritual Father.*

Immediately, Dééd Yázhí felt her posture improve. Several of her worries had been alleviated, however, they had not heard of their mother yet. The two sisters were wondering what their father was hiding from them. They could not wait to get across the river to fall into the arms of their father and ask about their mother.

Dééd Yázhí called her father again, but she did not hear him speak. She only heard the grown-up voices of her younger brothers, but she could not understand what they were saying because the wind picked up their words and carried them into the dark sky above them and scattered them.

Kiizhóní searched for a narrow place to get Dééd Yázhí and her sister and their babies across the river so they could be reunited with their father and their brothers. He stepped into the river and found it very cold. He worried about the little ones.

The group heard the brothers of Dééd Yázhí and Dzáníbaa' excitedly calling from across the river. Clouds had separated to allow a ray of moonlight to drop on the reuniting family. Peering across the river, Dééd Yázhí could see several people stepping into the water. Her heart beat faster. She could not tell if it was her father stepping into the water or if it was her brothers, or if it was soldiers. Dééd Yázhí became afraid when she saw several men enter into the water one by one.

Afraid the soldiers had heard them and had come to capture them, Dééd Yázhí covered her mouth as she leaned heavily against Kiizhóní. She could hear the figures asking one another to lock arms as they made a strong chain of warriors. They were speaking her language.

Another voice was heard as it came closer and asked,

"Shádí, shideezhí, nihíísh óht'į́?" *My older sister, my younger sister, is it the two of you?*

With tears in their voices, the two sisters answered in unison,

"Aoo', shilah, nihí 'íit'į," *Yes, my brother, it is us.*

Brother and sisters embraced one another, crushing their bodies against one another. Nahat'á Yinaabaah *One Who Goes To War With Plans* picked up Dzáníbaa' his younger sister and held her close. He had not seen his younger sister since he saw his sisters being kidnapped that one sad day, a long time ago. He released his younger sister and pointed to their brother, Tł'ée'go Naabaah *One Who Goes to War at Night,* who stood patiently waiting to greet his sisters.

Tears mingled as the four siblings hugged and cried with one another, but the chattering teeth of the young warriors in the water reminded the siblings they had to quickly begin to cross the cold river. Déed Yázhí was led to the first young warrior whose neck she held onto as he held her up. She moved from one strong warrior to another, as they leaned down so she could hug their neck as she moved closer to her father who stood on the bank of the river with his arms outstretched. She could feel the warriors rocking back and forth as the current lifted them up and down as well as sideways. Déed Yázhí crossed the river without her feet ever touching the bottom of the river. She worried about her little one crossing the river even though they decided Kiizhóní and the young Naashgálí man would carry the babies across.

Déed Yázhí felt her feet touch the bottom of the river. She saw a large figure waiting for her. She knew it was her father waiting for her. Sobs were already escaping the big man's body. Déed Yázhí reached toward the large figure and heard a loud sob escape the strong man's body. He had difficulty whispering,

"ShiDédii, háshinee', shiDédii! Shiyázhí! *My Dedii. My dear one, my Dedii! My little one!*

A loud sob exited Dééd Yázhí's body that ended in a loud high scream as she tried to say,

"Shizhé'é! Shizhé'é! Shizhé'é! T'áadoo hanii náániideestséeł da nisin nít'ę́ę́'. Shizhé'é!" *My father! My father! My father! I thought I would never see you again, my father!* That was all Dééd Yázhí could say. Her breath had been taken by the cold hovering above the water when she crossed the river.

Father and daughter looked toward the river as they watched Dzáníbaa' being led out of the water by a strong, young warrior whose arm was still locked with the arm of the warrior beside him. Dééd Yázhí released her hold on her father as he lunged forward to catch his youngest child, who was about to fall back into the water.

Dzáníbaa' nearly collapsed onto the river bank, out of her father's reach, when she said,

"Shizhé'é, háadi shą' nanináá nít'ę́ę́'? Ch'ééh háninádésht'įįh nít'ę́ę́'. Shizhé'é, háshinee', shizhé'é." *My father, where were you? I tried looking for you. My father, dear one, my father.*

Catching Dzáníbaa', father and daughter fell onto the river bank. Dééd Yázhí cried as she watched her sister reunite with their father. She refused to feel a sense of relief until Kiizhóní and the Naashgálí man had crossed with their little ones.

Dééd Yázhí's father gently set Dzáníbaa' down on the river bank and went to lead Kiizhóní out of the water. Dééd Yázhí could hear Kiizhóní's teeth chattering. She also heard the collective sound of the warriors' teeth chattering as they bravely stood in the water helping their leader's children safely cross. She felt bad, she knew from experience just how strong the river current was and how cold the water was.

Kiizhóní crossed and the little one on his back was untied. Dééd Yázhí could not find the scream that threatened to crash into the air around her. Her baby was all wet and his body was limp. Her father calmly said,

"Díí 'awéé' doo náhididziih da." *This baby is not breathing.*

Dééd Yázhí saw her father breathing into her little one's mouth. She held her breath as she whispered,

"Shiyázhí, hanichxééh, t'áá shǫǫdí, shiyázhí." *My little one, cry, please, my little one.*

Dééd Yázhí heard her father breathe a soft breath into her little one's lungs once again. Instead of air crashing around her, the air was crushed by her little one's loud cry near his maternal grandfather's ear. Quickly, Dééd Yázhí was handed her little one as her father turned to help his young Naashgálí son-in-law step safely onto the river bank. Her father took his little grandson the young Naashgálí man carried on his back.

Dééd Yázhí's father turned to help his sons cross the river with their sister's few belongings. Once Dééd Yázhí's brothers were safe, Kiizhóní went to help the strong, young warriors to come across and stayed until all the men were safely back on the bank of the river.

Carrying his little grandsons, Dééd Yázhí's father led the water-soaked group to his camp as his daughters were carried by their brothers. At the camp, Dééd Yázhí and her younger sister were presented by their father to their mother, Nínáánibaa'. Dééd Yázhí and her younger sister and their mother all fell to the ground in one crying heap as they desperately tried to get even closer to one another. Their bodies shook from the many years they had been deprived of one another's presence. Dééd Yázhí and Dzáníbaa's father collapsed with them and the four bodies cried in unison as the sisters listened to their mother's raw, high-pitched scream that exited from her body releasing the pain she carried for many years.

Before long, the crying heap of bodies was surrounded by their brothers, and later, the people who loved Dééd Yázhí's mother and father. Dééd Yázhí could feel warmth from the love the people felt for her mother and her father and their children.

As if jerked by a chain, Dééd Yázhí's mother, Nínáánibaa', lifted herself away from the crying heap and asked for the sacred bag she carried. Out of the bag, Nínáánibaa' pulled two beautiful rug dresses she wove before she left the protective folds of Dziłíjiin *Black Mesa.* With women surrounding them, the two sisters pulled off their blouses and skirts made of thin material and slid into their new rug dresses.

The scent of the sheep who gave their wool brought many memories to Dééd Yázhí. She felt her body involuntarily respond to the scent by taking a deep breath that began a cleansing of her soul and her body and her mind.

With their father's people as witnesses, Dééd Yázhí watched as her mother left the crying group to welcome the little warriors who had just joined her family. Everyone held their breath as her mother was handed Dééd Yázhí's little one.

Nínáánibaa' lovingly spoke to the little one and said in a velvet voice,

"Yá'át'ééh, shitsói. Nimá sání nishłį́. Tó 'Aheedlíinii yázhí nílį́. Naabaahii yázhí nílį́. Nimá bich'ą́ą́h nisíníbaa'. Ahéhee'. Ayóó'áníínish'ní, shitsói. Háshinee'..." *Greetings, my grandson. I am your maternal grandmother. You are a little member of the Water Flows Together people. You are a little warrior. You went to war on behalf of your mother. Thank you. I love you, my grandson. Dear one...*

Dééd Yázhí noticed her crying, shaking little one had stopped to look into his maternal grandmother's eyes and listened. Dééd Yázhí felt sobs slowly exiting her own body. She had waited many months to hear her mother greet her little one. She closed her eyes out of reverence as her mother's words were being spoken. Her mother then gently handed her grandson to Hashké Yił Naabaah, the child's grandfather. Nínáániíbaa' turned to Dzáníbaa's little one and greeted him with the same loving greeting she spoke to Dééd Yázhí's little one. Dééd Yázhí watched and listened as her sister wailed softly as she listened to the heartfelt greeting her child was receiving.

Dééd Yázhí hugged Dzáníbaa' and quietly whispered,

"Niha'áłchíní bik'éí t'óó'ahayói. T'áá 'ákónéehee bich'ą́ą́h nisiibaa'. Ahéhee', shideezhí, ninahjį' she'awéé' bikáa'jį' hazlį́į́'." *Our children have many relatives. It is rewarding that we went into warfare on behalf of our children. Thank you. Because of you, my little one's life was spared.*

The two sisters held one another and cried as their father prepared to voice his ceremonial greeting of his little grandsons. Hashké Yił Naabaah gently picked up Dééd Yázhí's shivering little one in his left arm and began to greet his little warrior by saying,

"Yá'át'ééh, shicheii yázhí. Tó 'Aheedlíinii dine'é binaabaahii yázhí nílį. Bił da'ahijigáanii dine'é bá shínílchíín ..." *Greetings, my little grandson. You are a little warrior for the Water Flows Together people. You are born for the ones who are fought against (the soldiers)...*

Dééd Yázhí heard people gasp, but her father proudly held her little one in his left arm as he continued greeting her son, saying,

"Ma'ii Deeshgiizhnii dine'é 'éí danicheii 'áádóó bił da'ahijigáanii dine'é 'éí daninálí. 'Azhą shį́į́ nihe'anaa'í ła' bá shínílchíin nidi shí k'é nidíiniid, áko k'ad dóó kodóó shicheii yázhí nidishnii dooleeł. Shiyázhí 'ałdó' nidishníí dooleeł. Nicheii nishłį. K'ad t'áadoo nichaaí, nik'éítah néínídzá. Níhásááh nít'éé'. Ayóó'áníínísh'ní, shicheii yázhí. Háshinee'." *The Coyote Pass people are your maternal grandfathers and the soldiers are your paternal grandfathers. Although you are born for one of our enemies, I have greeted you through kinship, so now and from now on, I will call you my little grandson. I will also call you my little one. Now don't cry, you have returned to your relatives. I have missed you. I love you, my little grandson. Dear one.*

Dééd Yázhí watched as her father gently handed her son to Kiizhóní and hugged them tightly. Her father then turned to his youngest daughter and gently picked up Dzáníbaa's little one in his left arm and began a greeting that was similar to the way he greeted his first grandson. Once again, she heard her people gasp when they heard the young toddler's father was a member of the Naashgálí *Mescalero people.* Her father proudly completed his moving ceremonial greeting.

Once she heard her father and her mother greet her son and her nephew, Dééd Yázhí felt a peace descend upon her that

546

she had not felt in several years. She felt her body sigh heavily which caused her entire body to shudder as if it was releasing the deep hurt and hardship she had endured for years. She was home. Although she was not back in Dziłíjiin *Black Mesa,* she was with her family again and among her own relatives.

Dééd Yázhí was touched by the actions of her Naabeehó people who were under her father's leadership. The people returned to their scanty campsites and came back with little gifts for their leader's grandsons.

Dééd Yázhí made a promise to herself that she would share this beautiful evening with her son when he grew older. She asked Kiizhóní to help her preserve the memories of the night so they could both tell him of his people's bravery in rescuing him.

As the light of day peeked over the eastern horizon, Dééd Yázhí and her younger sister placed their heads in their mother's lap and told their mother and their father and their brothers of the horrible events that led up to their being chased to Fort Sumner and the events that led to the meeting of the two sisters.

The women cooked a meager breakfast of fresh meat and warm goat's milk. The tears of Dééd Yázhí dripped onto her mother's open hand to be kept safe. Dééd Yázhí declared she was truly home among her people, her Naabeehó people.

Dééd Yázhí whispered,

"Shimá." *My mother.* Her mother lovingly looked into her daughters' eyes and said,

"Shiyázhí, ołhosh. Shaa nánoo'áázh. Nihiyázhí bich'ą́ą́h nisoobaa'. Nihité'ázíní binii'gi nánoo'áázh. Ayóó'ánihíínísh'ní, shiyázhí. Hanáołyííh." *My little ones, go to sleep. You have come* back to me. *You went to war on behalf of our little ones. You are back among your relatives. I love you, my little ones. Rest.*

Nínááníbaa' turned to Kiizhóní and said,

"Ahéhee', shiyázhí dóó shitsóí bich'ą́ą́h nisíníbaa'go kodi nizhónígo shaa nát'áázh. *Thank you, went to war on behalf of my little one and my grandson and because of what you did, they have come back to me.* She also thanked her oldest son for providing for Dééd Yázhí and her little one. Dééd Yázhí heard her mother talking to her Naashgálí son-in-law.

****

From behind her people, Dééd Yázhí heard sobs people were having difficulty controlling. Kiizhóní held out his hand to Dééd Yázhí. He gently lifted her to her feet and said,

"Shooh" *Look.*

Dééd Yázhí looked in the direction Kiizhóní was pointing. Her father's people parted. Seven little boys and an old man came tumbling out from behind the people. Dééd Yázhí slumped against her father and Kiizhóní as seven little boys came running to her, bumping into her, nearly knocking her over. The little boys whimpered in unison,

"Shimá..." *My mother...*

Elated, all Dééd Yázhí could say through her tears was,

"Háádę́ę́'shą'? Háshinee', sha'áłchíní! Háshinee', shicheii! *From where? Dear ones, my children! Dear one, my maternal grandfather!*

Still holding her, Kiizhóní whispered in her ear,

"Nilahkéí dóó nizhé'é binaabaahii nihe'ashiiké yázhí dóó nihicheii kodi nídeizh'eezhii' kodi yaa 'ádahalyą́ą́ nít'ę́ę́' lá,". *Your brothers and your father's warriors brought our little boys and our maternal grandfather back here and cared for them.*

548

All Dééd Yázhí could think of was how her brother and her sister and Kiizhóní helped her and her children survive such hopeless and desperate times. The tall gray-haired one was there as well in the beginning.

Exhausted, she breathed,

"Ahéhee', shiTaa'. Ahéhee'..." *Thank you, my Spiritual Father. Thank you...*

I was never alone, she thought, before she drifted off to sleep with her head resting on her mother's soft lap.

Her father was singing the song he used to sing to his daughters when they were little.

Acknowledgments

Shimá dóó Shizhé'é *My Mother and My Father*

I thank the Lord for placing me in the home of my mother and father. It was with generosity they shared historical events of the Navajo people. My father always encouraged me to search for the truth regarding my people. He also made sure I learned about the Navajo culture, which placed me in an advantageous position in that I have taught Navajo history classes and now I present this novel which is based upon Navajo history and the Navajo culture.

While still living at home, I accompanied my parents when they traveled throughout the Navajo Reservation to preach at camp meetings, Sunday services, week-long vacation Bible school events, and visits to churches. Our travels took hours and with no radio in our pick-up truck, my parents shared stories and historical events that were embedded in each place we visited. Many of these stories you will see on the pages of this novel.

Shimá Sání *My Maternal Grandmother*

My maternal grandmother, who was blind, came to visit us once a year. Her visits lasted a month or more. During the times when my grandmother was visiting, my chore after school was not to wash dishes or sweep the floor, instead, my "chore" was to keep my grandmother company so she would not get lonely when my mother was at work. It was during these quiet times that my grandmother would ask me to sit near her so she could tell me stories about when she was a little girl. I was showered with a rich historical rendition of the Navajo Long Walk based upon her first hand accounts and those of her relatives. "Ánísts'íísí yééd̨ą́ą' Hwéeldidéé' atah náníshtł'á..." When I was little, I along with others walked back from Fort Sumner...

Sha'áłchíní *My Children*

I thank the Lord for my four children. Although my children never met their maternal grandfather, and my two youngest children never met both maternal grandparents, it is through the stories presented in this novel that my children have met their maternal grandparents as well as their maternal great grandmother.

Shité'áziní *My Relatives*

Although the subject of the Long Walk was a painful memory, I had the special privilege of having relatives who were generous in sharing information with me. I was always excited to find a historical document that reiterated the telling of historical events by my relatives.

My cousins Marilyn Nez and Jane Horseson, my aunt Rose Claw, and my sister by clan Maxine Kescoli are the ones who helped shape the stories or who filled in the blanks.

At a time when Navajo elders refused to discuss the Navajo Long Walk, Clarence Blackrock, Sr. began telling me stories about the return of the Navajo people from Fort Sumner. No matter how difficult the stories were, he looked into my eyes and said, "T'óó nahojoobá'íyee' ła' ałyoí ch'ééh bínidabídíłkidgo. Nizhé'é yéę' ei bína'ídíłkidígíí 'ayóo bił bééhózin nít'ę́ę́', éí biniinaa k'ad nił hodeeshnih. T'áá nił hashne'ígi 'át'éego baa náhodíilnih, shideezhí." I have sympathy for you. In vain you ask different ones for information. Your father knew all the things you are asking about, that is why I am going to tell you now. Tell the story in the same way I am telling you, my younger sister.

Helen Yazzie, my paternal uncle's widow, shared stories with me saying, "Ha'áłchíní hólǫ'ǫgo nákéé náháne' bee bił hojilne'go 'ál'į'. Éí hane'ígíí yinahjį' ak'idadiitįįh łeh." When you have children you tell them about their history. It is that history that helps them understand.

To the many Navajo elders who just happened to talk about an incident regarding the Long Walk of their people.

Salina Bookshelf Publishing, Inc.

I have been so blessed to have worked with many extremely dedicated individuals who put forth so much effort into taking a manuscript and bringing it to fruition as a novel. Mr. Eric Lockard (Owner of Salina Bookshelf, Inc. and Publisher), and Mr. Corey Begay (Art Director) were patient, very kind, very helpful, highly supportive, caring, and nurturing throughout this whole process.

I sincerely appreciate the integrity and respect with which the team at Salina Bookshelf Publishing, Inc. handled my story and the story of Navajo elders.

Eric Lockard

Knowing that Salina Bookshelf Publishing, Inc. is predominantly a publisher of children's literature, I presented the manuscript to Eric Lockard and asked him to help me find a publisher for my novel.

To my surprise and elation, Eric accepted my manuscript for publishing. In doing so, Eric has increased his level of contribution he has made to the Navajo people in helping to maintain and preserve their history. The Navajo people have found Eric to be a loyal ally, he has helped them maintain and preserve their language, their culture, and their history through the books he has published.

Corey Begay

Corey spent endless hours formatting the manuscript to place it into the form of a novel. He was meticulous in his formatting and worked tediously to produce a product that brings honor to Navajo elders.

Bił Ałhééʼdahoniszínígíí My Acquaintances

Upon our first meeting at Fort Sumner State Monument NM., Mr. Scott Smith, a park ranger, treated my children and I like royalty. He took time out of his busy day to show us various points of interest and answered my many, many questions with ease. During our many returns to the Fort Sumner State Monument for the purpose of research, Scott never failed to drop whatever he was doing and spent hours with us. I came to know Scott as a prolific and thorough researcher; I always felt safe with his responses regarding the Long Walk and the status of the Navajo people as prisoners of war.

Ford Burkhart

It was an honor to have such a distinguished person in the field of editing to agree to copy-edit my manuscript. Mr. Burkhart's kind and encouraging comments gave me the confidence to present the painful history of my people to the public. I deeply appreciate the value Mr. Burkhart placed upon maintaining the voice of my Navajo elders.

Navajo Youth

I wrote this novel for several reasons. First, it is to share with Navajo youth the truth about their history as told by their Navajo elders; second, it is to inform Navajo youth about the strength of their ancestors and their Navajo people; third, it is to present the painful history of the Navajo people from an unusual viewpoint—that of a love story; fourth, it is to inform Navajo youth about the strength of love in terms of survival of an individual, a family, and of a people; and finally, it is to instill within Navajo youth and Navajos of all ages pride for their people, knowing they come from strong lineage.

Navajo Women

Navajo women exemplify elegance, grace, and strength. It is because of Navajo women that I decided to write a historical romance novel. After all, it was the strength of Navajo women that helped our ancestors survive such desperate and destitute times during their status as prisoners of war at Fort Sumner.

Map

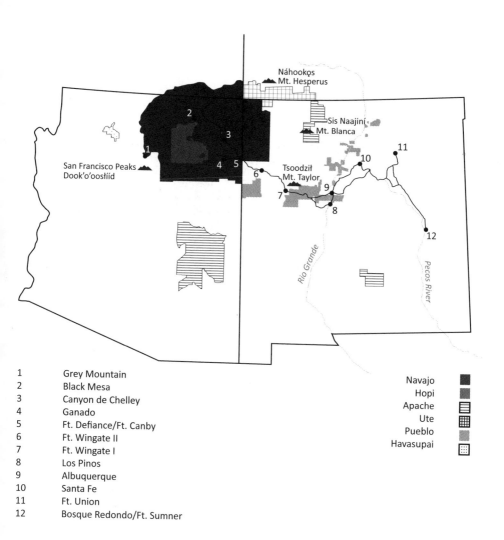

1	Grey Mountain		
2	Black Mesa		
3	Canyon de Chelley		
4	Ganado		
5	Ft. Defiance/Ft. Canby		
6	Ft. Wingate II		
7	Ft. Wingate I		
8	Los Pinos		
9	Albuquerque		
10	Santa Fe		
11	Ft. Union		
12	Bosque Redondo/Ft. Sumner		

Navajo
Hopi
Apache
Ute
Pueblo
Havasupai

Dééd Yázhí *Little Girl Warrior Who Came Home* carefully and silently led her younger sister closer to the edge of the river. They listened for the singing of the song their father sang to them when they were children. Stopping once again to listen, only the sounds of the river water lapping against the river bank could be heard. The two sisters held their breath and held one another as they walked and listened.

"Ge'," *Listen*, Dééd Yázhí said when she heard the song faintly coming across the water. In unison, the two sisters began to softly sing in answer to their father's song. Dééd Yázhí wished she could see as she peered through the black night.

Out of the black night, the sisters heard a voice say,

"Yá'át'ééh, sha'álchíní. Da' nihíísh óht'į? *Hello, my children. Is it the two of you? Dédii? Dzáníbaa'?*" Being careful so as not to alert the solders, the two sisters answered by cautiously calling back,

"'Aoo', nihizhé'é, nihí 'íit'į." *Yes, our father, it is us.* The two sisters began to shake when they heard their father's words explode across the water as he said,

EVANGELINE PARSONS YAZZIE

HER ENEMY, HER LOVE